Soul Trap

by Janet M. Woods

RoseDog Books

PITTSBURGH, PENNSYLVANIA 15238

RoseDog Books
585 Alpha Drive
Pittsburgh, PA 15238
Visit our website at *www.rosedogbookstore.com*

ISBN: 978-1-4809-7198-1
eISBN: 978-1-4809-7175-2

Soul Trap

Friday, 31st May 1985

I don't want to go. **I – DO – NOT – WANT – TO – GO!** I'm writing this to keep me occupied until my transport arrives – *and* because I need to moan. I don't want to worry Mary any more – it's not fair on her. She's had more than enough to cope with these last few weeks, what with the shock of me getting myself all smashed up, and the hospital visits and everything. As far as *she's* concerned, it's all settled and decided – I'm going to be a good lad and go and vegetate at Derek's, and that's that. I've put up all my best arguments against it, and had them all shot down in flames, and I just haven't the heart – or the strength! – to argue any more.

The hell of it is, of course, that from all practical points of view she's right – Derek's right, Pauline's right, Jenny's right, the whole family's right! I'm the one who's being illogical.

But I can't help it – I still feel aggrieved and hard-done-by. When Hayward came by on Rounds and confirmed that I can go home at last, it sounded wonderful. Hospitals are fine, just as long as *I'm* wearing the white coat; but I'm not so keen when it comes to Consumer Testing! (Show me a doctor who *is*!) The trouble is, I *can't* go home – I've got to go to Derek's. I want my *own* bed, for Pete's sake! Is that *really* too much to ask? I *know* the bed at Pat and Derek's will be a darned sight more comfortable than these awful stiff hospital sheets and rubber-covered pillows and mattresses, but there is *nothing* quite the same as your *own* bed – now is there? OK – I have to admit the stairs would be a problem. And if I had my bed brought downstairs – and it *would* be a little crowded! – there's still the bathroom to consider. So – with Derek's place being so ideal, and with Derek and Pat so willing to have me – what can I possibly say?

It all sounds so feeble and petty when you put it into words. People just don't understand. Almost everyone seems to share this idyllic picture of 'Life in the Country' – but I'm a *City* Boy! I *like* the town! I never did have any yen for Rusticity. (*Is* there such a word? I must look it up when I have access to a dictionary. *If* I can remember!) OK – so Derek's place isn't exactly the Back-of-Beyond – I mean, it's not much more than thirty miles from home! But it *is* all surrounded by fields and trees and hedgerows and 'Beautiful Views', and all the other (to *me*!) rather unappealing things you find in Rural Midlands England – and I feel stifled with boredom already. Me – I like PEO-PLE! Well – come on – why else would anyone in their right mind (?) elect to become a psychiatrist?!

Funny – I still can't equate it with our Derek! A son of mine, actually buying a place like that and going to live in the country? Ah, what Love can do! I mean, *he's* a City Boy, too – born and bred. And I will never forget all the fuss when he was, what – 15? 16? – and he suddenly lost all interest in horses and went crazy about motorbikes instead. The things he said *then* about 'mud and muck' (to put it more politely than *he* did!) would have hardly led one to expect him to wind up at Manor Farm House, Gorsey Hallowell, Nowheresville! And poor old Bob had to be sold – we couldn't just keep him standing around there doing nothing, now could we? And while I was never *keen* on horses and all things equestrian, by that time I had got rather attached to Bob and Penny. It's different, somehow, when they belong to your kids – they become Part of the Family. And poor Jenny, of course, was still mad-keen on horses, and we didn't want her riding alone. It was hairraising enough when the two of them were out on horses together, but how could we be happy about a 15-year-old girl jauntering around those lanes all by herself? And you can't *make* a lad go riding just to take care of his twin sister, now can you? (Ah, the Joys of Parenthood! And now, just History and Yesterday's Problems!) Rugger-practice and motorbikes – that's all Derek was interested in, in those days – before he progressed to fast cars and girlfriends, of course!

4

Strange, looking back, how we used to worry about him, and how angry that worry used to make me. Mary somehow managed to take it in her stride – but then, that's my Mary! The way he used to spend money like water – *our* money, usually, or that's the way it used to wind up! – and seemed to do any damn' thing but *work*, all through college. The cars he wrote off! That awful Julia he got himself in such a state about, and nearly flunked his Finals because of it! No wonder my hair is grey.

And now – here he is, 35 next month. How on earth did *that* happen? He's got a lovely wife, and – come on, George! – no-one could ask for a better daughter-in-law than Pat. He's got three wonderful children, he's doing really well in his career, and he's a Man of Property, to boot! Who could possibly have foreseen it?

Although I *still* don't really understand what he wanted to go and buy *that* great place for. I mean, he's an architect, not a farmer! I *know* he's doing very nicely out of renting the land to Thompson down the road, who is glad of the extra grazing. And I know they did need somewhere a *little* larger than the flat, when Child Number Two decided to put in an appearance. And when you've got kids, a bit of garden never comes amiss. But did they have to go to quite such *extremes*?! And I know Pat has always lived in the country; but I honestly thought *that* place would be a little isolated, even for her. Her parents' bungalow is in the middle of a village, after all, not stuck a couple of miles outside one, with the nearest neighbours at least half-a-mile away. And even then it's only the Thompsons – no-one she can really relate to. They were darned lucky to find a sensible, down-to-earth woman like Mabel to give her a hand with that great barn of a place – *and* to keep her company while Derek's at work. But it's all more expense, isn't it? Still - if it suits *them* – none of *my* business, I suppose. (Keep your nose out, Dad – don't be such a bossy, interfering old so-and-so!)

They're *still* stuck with that albatross of a cottage next door, that nobody wants to live in. I did warn Derek – but did he listen to the Silly Old Fossil? No, of course not! "It's an investment, Dad," he said. "We'll do it up and make a killing renting it out. They'll be queued up wanting to live there – you'll see!"

So we all mucked-in and lent a hand – Mary, Jenny and I. Pat was expecting Kyle at the time – that's right – and we didn't want her overdoing.

5

And a nice job we made of it, if I do say so myself. And there it stands, in all its glory – empty. Well – furnished, but *sans* occupants. Oh, no shortage of prospective tenants – Derek was right about that! They come. But they don't stay. They just get nicely settled in and everything seems fine. Then they hear the local gossip about the place being haunted, and you don't see them for dust! Crazy. But people are *very* suggestible. If it were the house itself, that would be a little easier to understand – that *is* at least 300 years old, and in a house of that age there must have been any number of Deaths and Disasters which could conceivably give rise to that kind of silly story. But the *cottage*?! That was build only about sixty years ago, and there is no record of anyone ever having died there. Derek checked it out when all this nonsense began getting beyond a joke, and even the old man who lived there last, and who had occupied the place for any number of years, died several miles away in hospital.

It doesn't even *look* spooky. It's not particularly rustic or quaint – just plain, ordinary, sort-of-square and a little ugly, built prosaically in red brick. It's not surrounded by dark trees, or standing all alone – it's only a few yards back off the road and right next-door to the farmhouse, obviously built for farm-labourers in the days when the place was still a working farm.

It was that first family who moved in that started all the trouble. What was their name, now? Magee, I think. *Mrs.* Magee sowed the seeds of this ridiculous story, and it not only took root, but is self-propagating. Every lot of tenants who hear it and hurriedly move out only add to the credibility. Magee himself seemed a decent-enough, down-to-earth chap – it wasn't *his* fault. But fancy being married to a hysterical woman who could make her husband give up his job because she sees spooks – or some such rubbish! – in a perfectly normal house! Damn, it makes me realize how grateful I ought to be for my practical, sensible Mary! (I am, I am!) I mean, how many hours did *we* spend in the place, for Pete's sake? We cleaned, renovated and redecorated the whole house, and not a hint of anything out of the ordinary! I know the dogs used to fuss a lot, and didn't want to be in there, but I still maintain that was just boredom and lack of attention – we were all too otherwise-occupied to keep fussing them! And I know that Pat used to say the place "gave her the creeps" – but that was only because it was so dirty and unkempt-looking – enough to give *anyone* the creeps! I'd be surprised if the place had had a window washed, the "lawns" (!) mowed, or a new coat of paint in twenty years! But at least Pat had more sense than to start seeing spooks! Some bright wallpaper, and some nice white gloss instead of all that awful brown varnish, soon cheered the place up considerably. It **had** to be better than that hovel the Magees were in before. I don't suppose old Thompson had spent a penny on it in living memory! It was about time it was condemned as 'Unfit for Human Habitation'. Me, I wouldn't put **animals** in it – always assuming I had any to **put**, which - thank the Lord! – I haven't. Whereas Derek spent quite a bit, not only on decorating, but modernising the whole place – putting in proper heating, updating the plumbing, and even installing a fitted-kitchen and new bathroom suite. And at least the cottage has a good damp-course and a slate roof – not thatch! So you'd have thought the silly woman would have been only too happy – it was only just down the lane from their old home, so no further for her husband to walk to work, and actually closer to the village with the school and the shops and the bus-route on the main road. Plus a lot of mod-cons. she hadn't got at the other place. But – no. *She* decides the place is haunted and she can't live there a moment longer – drags the whole family back to Co. Mayo, or wherever – which, I cannot help suspecting, may have been the object of the whole exercise in the first place! But, of course, the story got around, and has left poor Derek with a Bit of a Problem. Thank *you*, Mrs. Magee!

The new chap, who works for Thompson now, tried it for a couple of weeks, then moved into lodgings in the village, even though it's a lot further for him to get to work, and it must be quite a pull up that hill on a bike. Started off happy as Larry, saying how convenient it was, how comfortable – he'd even begun to plant his own vegetables in the back garden. (I've just had a thought, here – could it possibly be that he was actually *too* close to the farm, and thus available any time Thompson chose to call on him? Possible, I suppose. I know *I* wouldn't care to be at Thompson's beck-and-call – he's a surly old cuss, and possibly not the most reasonable of men!) Or perhaps it really was that he – the hand, that is! – heard the gossip and got the wind up.

Anyway – however that may be – it seems to have formed a pattern. People come, settle in and then – gone! Oh – except for the three ladies, of course! Two spinsters and a widow – I believe they were sisters. They came to see the place, but hadn't got more than a couple of feet inside the door before they started screaming! Takes some crediting, doesn't it, in this day

7

and age – and in Wildest Warwickshire, of all places?! Do people seriously believe in such twaddle, or does it just liven up a rather mundane existence? Either way, it's a pain!

Still, I didn't set out to bemoan Derek's problems, but my own! Although really, I suppose, it would be more sensible, and certainly more constructive, to try to make myself feel a little more amenable to the inevitable. I'm *going* to Derek's, and that's that – so I might as well *try* to enjoy it. OK, let's look at it rationally:

Point 1:I'm damn' lucky to be alive. That silly young idiot in the big hurry to overtake me on a blind corner could easily have killed me. He *did* kill himself, *and* the poor chap in the Mini coming the other way. OK – he injured me worse than I've ever been injured in all my sixty-nine years, and I'm feeling *very* sorry for myself! But I *am* alive – *and* on the mend – and they're kicking me out of hospital at last. They say I've got to take it easy for a while – 'peace and quiet, no stress, plenty of rest, gentle exercise' – oh well! I suppose the quickest way to get back to full fitness – *and* to work! (*I* still haven't given up hope of that, no matter what *anyone* says!) – is to do as I'm told. *With* a good grace, if possible!

Point 2:I'm darned lucky to have a son and daughter-in-law who are willing to take me in while I convalesce – not all parents are so fortunate. And I do enjoy going to Derek's for Sunday visits – even the occasional weekend. I get on so well with Derek these days, now he's grown up – he's a son *any* father would be proud of, and darned good company. And I'm very fond of Pat. I'm also pretty sure she will manage to look after me really well without driving me to distraction by fussing intolerably. And she's a very good cook, which will be much appreciated by both my taste-buds and my stomach, after all these weeks of hospital food! I pray I may *never* have to look at a corned-beef sandwich again! (And even *that* was preferable to being fed through a tube!)

And I love the kids. At 7, Kurt is starting to get really interesting – wanting to know, and learn, and understand all sorts of things. It boosts my ego to play 'Grandpa, the Fount of All Wisdom'! I can get away with it for the moment, but who knows for how much longer? Make the best of it, George!

At 5, little Kirstie is still the same sweetheart she has always been – as shy and timid as a young deer, as fresh and pretty as a rosebud drenched in dew.

She loves to sit on Grampy's knee and let him read her fairy-stories – almost as much as Grampy enjoys it himself!

And Kyle, at the advanced age of two years old, is a wriggling, squealing little bundle of mischief – never still, always noisy, always filthy – a universal delight. So, OK – it may not be HOME, but it certainly has to be THE NEXT BEST THING!

Point 3:How many times have I complained recently about being too busy and snowed-under with work to get round to doing all the things I want to do? Well, this should certainly knock *that* excuse on the head! WORK is OUT for a while. (What's the betting I won't be able to remember what all those things were, now I've got the time to do them?!) I shall just have to try to occupy myself in a useful and/or interesting way, even if there isn't much going on. Surely I've got *that* much initiative? Even if my head (not to mention the rest of me!) took a Really Good Bashing, it *is* still attached.

Point 4:As I mentioned before, until I can climb stairs safely, No. 43 is *not* the most suitable place for me. It will be *much* easier to manage at Manor Farm House. There *is* plenty of room (with a vengeance!) and that downstairs bathroom clinches it.

So – right! I think I've talked myself into a more positive attitude at least! It really may not be so bad. Mary will be there at weekends, and once the schools break up, she and Jenny and Elizabeth can all come and stay for the duration. I will *not* resent Mary having to stay to look after Elizabeth while Jenny's at work – poor Jenny can't be breadwinner *and* full-time mother, both at once, although I know, these days, women are *supposed* to be able to. She is doing her best. She took quite a drop in salary when she changed her job, but the hours that an Educational Psychologist works are a lot less anti-social than those of a doctor! But even so, she is still very glad of Grandma to lend a hand, and I honestly can't deny that Mary is in her element. I enjoy helping out myself, under normal circumstances, and I'm really glad they came to live with us after the marriage broke up. I love having them around. If I'm absolutely honest, even though I get on so well with all three of my kids, Jenny has always been the one I've related to most deeply. We think alike, Jenny and I – or so I like to imagine! I can't remember ever having a cross word with Pauline – or a moment's worry! – but she is far more like Mary than like me. She not only *looks* like her mother, but has the same calm practicality – the perfect Homemaker, the natural, contented Earthmother. And I've already gone on at length about Derek! He may be my only begotten son, but if he takes after anybody in the family, it certainly isn't *me*! But Jenny? I cannot deny that there has always been a certain special Something between us – a little extra bond that comes from genuine understanding. She has Mary's dark hair and dark eyes, of course, just like the other two. And, on the surface, she shares that Madonna-like serenity that Mary and Pauline possess so very strongly. But underneath there is *something* of me. As well as something that is totally Herself – some secret Jenny I feel I can never truly touch or understand. She's so deep, so complex, my Jenny. And, God, so lonely! I *wish* she could find the right man!

The very last thing we would have wished for her – or expected! – was a broken marriage. I will *never* understand David Morris! (And never forgive him, either!) Some people just don't seem to know when they're well-off. But it's done, and we can't change it, and I can't really deny that I enjoy having Jenny back at home. And Elizabeth is such a *good* kid – just like her mother at the same age. A little more outgoing and mischievous, maybe – not *quite* so earnest! – but very intelligent for not-quite-five, a real joy, and never a moment's trouble.

I am a darned lucky man! Three kids all grown-up and doing very well for themselves, and five wonderful grandchildren – not a bad apple in the bunch! All healthy, intelligent, and *very* beautiful. Oh, I know Pauline's having fun with our Paula right now, but what can you honestly expect from a young lady of 16 who looks like *she* does? Of course her mind is on other things than sitting at a desk! Of course the young men take notice – heck, *I* would have done, myself, as a young man! Yes, OK, it is a bit of a worry – but I think I would be *more* worried if she were a real Plain Jane, with *no* boyfriends, and her nose always stuck in a book! She's a good kid, and as sensible as you can expect at that age. I honestly don't think she's going to get into any *real* trouble – she's not stupid. And, while academic qualifications are good to have, they aren't the End of the World! So *what* if she gets B grades instead of the A's we know she is capable of? Will it really be a Major Disaster? And – who knows? – she *might* just take after her Uncle Derek, who nearly drove *his* parents to desperation because he never put his nose in a book outside school, and never did his homework, or any kind of revision.

And he still managed nearly all A's! There *are* people who can do it although, not being one of them, I will never know how. It's not fair . . . but then, when is Life *ever* fair?

Ah! I do believe they are coming for me at last! And about time, too!

Sunday, 2nd June

I have to admit it hasn't been a bad weekend – in fact, it's been lovely having so many of my family around en masse, after being restricted by hospital visiting rules. But Mary, Jenny and Elizabeth left to go home about an hour ago, and I am feeling totally bereft and miserable already! God, it was so good, being able to sleep with my own wife again, after all those weeks apart! What indescribable comfort, just to hold her in my arm (the good one!) and breathe in the warm, sweet smell of her! To me, at least, she is even more beautiful in her sixties than in her twenties – maturity suits her. She must be, absolutely without exception, the most beautiful woman I have ever met – both inside and out. And it's all *real*, all natural – she looks just as good when she first wakes up in the morning as when she's all dressed up to go out. God, I am a lucky man! But – I *miss* her! I can't help it – I resent every minute I have to spend away from her. And now I won't see her again 'til Friday evening! How am I going to get through the week? And all the other long weeks to follow? It's *six* whole weeks before the schools break up on 12th July! And she's going to be stuck in town, and I'm incarcerated here!

Would you just listen to me?! Talk about melodramatic! Anyone would think I was on a par with the Count of Monte Christo, for Pete's sake, not staying in great comfort with my son and his family! I have *got* to stop feeling sorry for myself – there are countless millions of people worse off. I've just got to content myself somehow – but I am *not* looking forward to it. Still – writing down my woes – *and* my blessings – does seem to help a little, and it does help to pass some time. So maybe I'll try keeping a sort of diary of what happens while I'm here – if anything does! - see if I can stave off the self-pity – not even let it get started. Surely I can find some way of keeping myself occupied, without overdoing things? It would be much worse if it

11

were late autumn, or even January or February. Right now, everything is looking at its best, with all the new leaves, and the gardens full of flowers.

Actually, I was quite surprised when we arrived on Friday to see how tidy and well-kept the place looked – better than I've ever seen it. It's such a big place to keep up, it takes a lot of work – and with Derek in full-time employment, he naturally can't manage it all by himself. And good help can be hard to come by! I said, "Good Lord – looks like old Harry's been putting his back into it!"

The poor old fella must be at least fifteen years older than I am, and *I* certainly wouldn't want to try to keep on top of a place *this* size, especially one that had been let go to rack-and-ruin as badly as this. So really, he does pretty well, considering, even if the results aren't always *quite* what one would wish!

But Derek flashed Mary a surreptitious look (does he think I'm blind, or just stupid?) and said carefully, "Don't you remember, Dad? I *did* tell you . . . Harry's packed it in. Says his sciatica's too bad. But he did recommend someone else, thank goodness, and I can't help feeling we got the best of the bargain – it really did need someone slightly younger! Old Dan's doing a nice job, wouldn't you say?"

I would indeed! But . . . I simply can *not* remember Derek mentioning any such thing before! And it doesn't matter what *anyone* says, *or* how they try to gloss it over – it scares me - and humiliates me. Makes me feel like an old man. And I'm not ready for that yet! What did that bash on the head *do* to me? How much *more* have I forgotten? Just how illogical and unreasonable *am* I being? Makes you wonder, doesn't it? And just how can I manage to be cool, calm and objective about my *own* mental state?!

Calm down, George – no good panicking! What's done is done. (My God, *how* original and philosophical!) But true, nonetheless, even if trite. I *am* getting better. I remember *most* things now – I think! I still can't recall all the phone-numbers I always knew by heart – I didn't even have to *think* to bring them to mind, just *dialled*! Now I even have to look it up when I want to phone *Mary*! My own home phone-number – gone – wipe-out! And – fairly naturally, I suppose, I am more emotional and more easily overwrought than usual. But I *am* getting better – I've just got to give it time. Being impatient isn't going to help. I've just got to do as I'm told, for once – rest, try to take things easy, and *not* get all-in-a-state! That's what convalescence is all about. How many times have I explained all that to *other* people? Strange how hard it is to take your own good advice!

OK – I am going to get a good night's sleep, then tomorrow I am going to wallow in decadence and try to learn "How to be Lazy in Comfort"! Goodnight.

Tuesday, 4th June

God, I feel *such* a fool! What a good start to all my resolutions! Everybody was very sympathetic, of course, and very kind to the Invalid - obviously putting it down to "the poor old chap not being quite himself yet". And, somehow, that made it fifty times worse! And when it was all over, *they* all saw the funny side of it. Wish *I* could.

Yesterday *began* OK. Derek brought me a cup of tea first thing before he went to work, then Pat brought me breakfast in bed. I stayed put – and out of the way – until she'd taken the kids to school. Then I got up in a leisurely fashion – I only need a *little* help now – and she set an easy chair out on the lawn for me, because the sun hadn't got round to the patio yet. There was a cool little breeze, but the bushes gave me some shelter, and the fresh air was very welcome. I tried to get into a book, but I still find it awfully hard to concentrate, and reading still seems to give me a headache, so I was glad when Kyle came out to play on the grass with a box of toys. I found his antics much more entertaining than my book, and the time up to lunch passed enjoyably enough. Boy, he's a little rascal! Wonder if *I* ever had that much joie-de-vivre, even at his age? Hard to imagine!

We had a nice light lunch, then Pat went off with Kyle to a mother-and-toddler group down in the village – she says it does her good to have a gossip with the other mums, and Kyle likes playing with the other kids. Pat said – rather wistfully, I imagine! – that it might help to take some of the sting out of him! She assured me that Mabel would be there in case I needed anything, and – oh yes, Dan might be around, he usually comes on a Monday – and I needn't disturb myself if the phone rang, I must just try to have a nap - was I sure I would be all right . . . ?! Mabel and I managed to persuade her that we really could cope without her, and finally got the two of them on their way. I did *start* to take a nap, but just as I was dropping off, the phone rang. I couldn't help overhearing Mabel's half of the conversation – I had duly been moved up on to the patio by now, following the sun – and the kitchen door was open. She was saying, "I'm sorry, Dad, but I can't come just now . . . no, listen . . . yes, I'll be down later on, when Mrs. Hanson gets back . . . no, I can't, not while she's away, I'm taking care of the poor old gentleman . . . yes, the doctor, Dad, *you* know, the one that had that terrible accident . . . no, he's not to be left . . ."

'Poor old gentleman' indeed! She must be at *least* my age, herself, if not a couple of years older! No – hang on! – she's Old Harry's daughter, isn't she? I was forgetting that. And I don't suppose he sired her when he was only about 13! So she probably isn't *quite* as old as me. But she *looks* older. (I hope!)

Anyway, be that as it may, I really am not at my last prayers yet, and it annoyed me to have anyone doubting that I was fit to be left alone. So I went inside and interrupted the conversation, and assured Mavis that I would be perfectly all right if she wanted to pop down and visit her father for a little while – I was going to take a nap, and could manage very-nicely-thank-you. She wasn't at all happy about it, but her father was evidently 'in one of his do's' about something, and her loyalties were divided. We both won. Harry got his visit from his daughter, and I got left alone for the first time since the accident. It felt quite strange when she finally departed, after an awful lot of fidgeting about whether I wanted a cup of tea, should she take the phone off the hook so it wouldn't wake me up, and so on and so forth. Nice woman. Very kind. But it was good to get rid of her for a while.

So – revelling in the unaccustomed independence – *no*-one to worry about me, or tell me what I *ought* to be doing! – I settled down again. I was in that hazy borderland between waking and sleeping, and things were beginning to blur a little round the edges, when I suddenly became aware of a movement in the yard, and roused a little to check it out. I saw a middle-aged man, wearing none-too-clean work-clothes, a cap and heavy boots, and carrying an axe across his shoulder. I remembered what Pat had said – obviously, this must be the paragon, Old Dan. I called, "Hello, there!" and the chap stopped in mid-stride, looked in my direction, then nodded his head and touched the brim of his cap. I couldn't see his face very well, and he didn't speak – but he did acknowledge my greeting. Then he turned and carried on

14

with whatever he was doing. He headed past the barn and down into the meadow, where I lost sight of him.

Well, it was a drowsy sort of afternoon, with the bees buzzing in the flowers and the faint hum of some sort of farm-machinery in the distance. I had nothing to do, and all the time in the world to do it in. And none of the clatter and chatter and general comings-and-goings of a hospital ward to contend with. Heaven! So it did ***not*** take me long to drift away again on a Sea of Dreams . . .

Suddenly, I jerked awake – wide awake. Something had penetrated through the layers of sleep to wherever my mind was wandering – something I ought to notice. But what? I sat quite still, trying to work it out. Then I caught a movement out of the corner of my eye, and carefully turned my head to investigate. My heart gave a lurch – walking away from me, towards the barn, was a man – a youngish man. Well, to be accurate, he wasn't a ***youth,*** but a mature chap, maybe in his mid-thirties – tall, thin and dark-haired. He stopped outside the barn, and turned to face the house, eyeing the upstairs windows in what struck me as a very furtive way. Who was he? And what was he up to?

I looked all around, and strained my ears to listen, but there was no sign of Old Dan, and I couldn't pick up even the faintest thud of his axe. Maybe he had gone on down to the woods right at the bottom of the meadow. And it was obvious from the stillness that Mavis hadn't returned. I was suddenly very aware of the total isolation of this place. And I was suddenly very afraid. I couldn't help thinking of all the awful things you hear on the News or read in the papers. And I have had my fill of making the headlines, thank you very much! And I was suddenly sure what had awakened me – the chap had been standing looking down at me! He had obviously decided I was either fast asleep, or not worth bothering about, or both. But it gave me an awful, creepy feeling to think he had been so close – ***how*** close? – and had been watching me while I was unaware. I was both very angry and very scared. What if he . . . ? And what could I do about it, anyway? I was all alone, nearly twice his age, and not exactly at my all-time best. (Not, if I am honest, that I would have stood much chance in a physical altercation against a chap like that, even ***before*** the accident! He must have been about six-foot tall and, whilst not heavily-built, he looked wiry and agile and well-muscled.)

Suddenly I remembered the dogs . . . where were they? I know neither of them is exactly what you could call a 'guard-dog' – Judy is about the silliest, softest, sloppiest black labrador I ever did see and, in the way of most basset hounds, Droopy is exactly that. But you'd think they could at least summon up the energy – or the courage! – to put up some sort of a show, and bark at a prowler! But I couldn't see a sign of either of them, and could only conclude that they were either off for a stroll in the woods – maybe keeping Dan company – or had decided that Discretion was the better – or safer! – part of Valour, and were playing Least in Sight.

So – it was just me and the prowler. And I have never felt so frail and helpless – impotent! – since I was a kid. The stranger stopped his surveillance of the upstairs windows, and turned and opened the barn door. That may *sound* easy enough. It isn't. That barn is in a state of dilapidation – one could almost say dereliction – and the doors hang at rather crazy angles. The chap flinched at the noise the hinges made, and flashed a wary glance over his shoulder in my direction. Fortunately, I had taken the precaution of observing him through half-closed eyes, slumped back in my chair as before, and from that distance he must have thought I was still asleep. Satisfied of that, he disappeared into the barn, to reappear a few moments later carrying a ladder. (Well – what was I *meant* to think?!)

He hoisted it carefully and, with one eye on me, walked stealthily across the yard, out of my sight behind the corner of the house. After a few moments of indecision, I decided I couldn't just sit there like a dummy, so I humped out of the chair as quietly as possible, crept to the corner and peered cautiously round, holding my breath. The ladder was propped up against the side wall of the house, right under the landing window! Then the man appeared out of one of the outhouses, carrying some tools. I dodged back hurriedly out of sight – I had already seen enough. I had to *do* something. I risked another quick peep, just to be certain where he was, but he was already halfway up the ladder. So I headed as fast as I could, and as nearly on tiptoe as I could manage, to the kitchen door and made a beeline for the telephone, praying the chap hadn't somehow cut or disconnected the line. But when I picked it up there was the reassuring buzz of the dialling-tone – PHEW! I considered for a second – should I ring 999? But Derek keeps a list of Useful Numbers beside his phone, and I decided to try the local police station.

A voice at the other end introduced itself as Constable Moffatt, and I tried to be calm and coherent as I explained that I was at Manor Farm House, Banebrook Lane, alone with a burglar. He asked if I was *sure*!! But when I told him I could actually hear the chap attacking the window-frame, he did agree to get there on the double – 'just in case' – e.t.a. about five minutes. At a time like that, five minutes seems like an eternity. I was in an agony of impotence. My instinct said I ought to go out there, tell the chap the police were on their way, and prevent any more damage to Derek's property. But I couldn't help feeling, with the more rational part of me, that it just might be more important to avoid any more damage to Derek's dad! I did not much relish the thought of having my head bashed again, and the chap *was* armed with a hammer and chisel!

In the end, I settled for keeping a surreptitious eye on him from the corner, and a very inept housebreaker he seemed – not to mention full of nerve, standing up there in broad daylight, in full view of the road. But maybe being blatant is the best way – if a car *did* happen to pass by, the occupants probably wouldn't suspect a thing!

At last I heard an engine – faint, but getting closer – and before long a police car swept importantly into the driveway. The chap up the ladder was certainly a cool customer. He turned his head to see who it was, then began to climb unhurriedly down to the ground – obviously intending to bluff his way out of it. Two policemen and I all converged on him – they from one side, I from the other. But he didn't try to make a break for it; just said, "Hi, Fred, Bill – you got trouble?" in an incongruous and totally-unexpected American accent! The sergeant didn't answer him direct, but looked at me with an unfathomable expression and said, "Sergeant Grimshaw, Sir – and Constable Moffatt. Would you be the gentleman who called us just now?"

I said, "I am indeed, Sergeant – Dr. George Hanson. My son, Derek Hanson, owns this property."

The burglar looked at me curiously, frowning a little, then said, "You called the cops, Sir? How come?"

The sergeant raised his eyes to heaven and said, in a mock-patient tone, "Seems some chap was up a ladder, trying to break in. You see any suspicious characters hanging about?"

17

The young constable coughed behind his hand, in an ineffectual attempt to hide a grin. To my mind, this was *not* the very best way to handle the situation! The American looked a little confused, and said, "The only guy up a ladder here was me, but . . . aw, come on! You can not be serious! You thought I . . . ? Oh heck! Look, Sir – I wasn't trying to break in, I . . . "

"No, of *course* not!" I snorted. "Perish the thought! *Anyone* can see that you were cleaning the windows! Window-cleaners always tiptoe around with a hammer and chisel, trying not to make any noise, and looking furtive!"

His face stiffened at that, and he said through tight lips, "I was trying not to waken you – I didn't do a very good job seemingly! I wasn't *cleaning* the windows – not today, at any rate. But Mr. Hanson did ask me to fix the sill, where we found a little patch of rot. He didn't want it getting any worse, and wind up having to replace the whole frame. I'm real sorry if I scared you, but he did say he had told you about me. I would have introduced myself, but you looked fast asleep, and I didn't see the need to disturb you. Bad decision, yeah? Sorry, Fred!"

Fred raised his eyes to heaven again, and sighed. "OK, Dan," he said, "no real harm done."

Dan?! Oh, thanks, Derek! "*Old* Dan", indeed! How was *I* supposed to know? Naturally I thought it had the same connotation as "Old Harry" – nobody told *me* that "Old Dan" is only about half Harry's age!

I felt *such* a fool! The police accepted my apology with shrugs and more sighs, and Dan (bless him!) was at pains to explain to them that I wasn't well . . . oh, ta everso! I did *not* need *him* to defend me! They said, "Don't worry about it!" and "Better safe than sorry!" and trite words to that effect, piled back into their car and headed back to the village, leaving me feeling thoroughly patronised. Dan asked if I was sure I was OK, and was there anything he could do for me, but I wasn't feeling particularly gracious just then and was a little off-hand, if I'm honest about it. He shrugged, and went back up his ladder to get on with his interrupted repairs. *I* went back to the patio to feel foolish and sulk, and pretend to be asleep when Mabel and Pat and the kids got home. *I* had no intention of bringing the subject up, but the police saw Mabel on their way back to the village and hinted that she should get back – pronto! And she felt moved to confess to Pat and, naturally, Pat told Derek, who hooted and thought it a great joke. Idiot! He in turn told Mary,

18

so now everybody knows. And – OK, I *know* it's childish, *but* – I *hate* being laughed at!

What would Derek have said if it *had* been a burglar and I *hadn't* called the police, eh? That's what *I'd* like to know! That would have been a different story, wouldn't it? He's have been laughing on the other side of his face *then*! OK – I know it's not really Derek I'm so sore at – it's just that I feel such a *fool*. It's easy enough to be wise with hindsight, isn't it? I mean, when Derek pointed out that the back-door was standing wide open, and the chap only had to walk in, never mind all that palaver with ladders and hammers and windows . . . well, yes, it's obvious *now*! But, at the *time* . . . ? I keep trying to excuse myself on the grounds that I had just been woken from a deep sleep, and couldn't expect to be thinking clearly; but, somehow, it doesn't make me feel a whole lot better. What if the same thing had happened *before* the accident? Would I have handled it the same *then*? I have an awful suspicion that the answer has to be 'no'. I can almost swear I would have been a lot more confident, for a start – let the chap know I was awake, and asked a few questions before calling the police. And I am *sure* I would have taken that open back-door into account! I mean – he had to walk right *past* it to come and look at me sleeping, and again on his way back!

Mary was sweet to me on the phone, trying to smooth my ruffled feathers and soothe my wounded pride. Said it was a very *sensible* thing to do, and she was proud of how I had handled it! But it's no good – I still feel a Proper Charlie. It was that other chap – the one with the axe – who confused the issue. He looked *far* more like my idea of 'an odd-job man'! The *real* Dan is not what I expected at all, at all! The funny thing is – no-one seems to recognise the other man. And no-one can explain what he might have been doing in Derek's yard and waltzing off down Derek's meadow, bold as brass, and without so much as a by-your-leave! In fact, nobody seemed to want to hear about *that* bit at all! Odd. When I mentioned it to Derek, he got quite shirty – said, "Look, Dad – you admit you were half-asleep. What if it was really a little *more* than half? You were expecting Dan to show up, right? So you dreamed it. Simple. Just forget it, Dad – no harm done!" Oh, he smiled. But there was a note of – what? – impatience?– in his voice. He obviously didn't want to discuss it any more, and metaphorically slammed the door in my face.

Pat and Mabel gave each other funny looks, and tried to stay off the subject. But I could feel their embarrassment. They obviously didn't know quite what to make of it – 'Is the poor old codger going permanently ga-ga? Is this only the beginning of what we've got to look forward to? Or is it, God willing, just a temporary aberration?' Oh yeah.

It was so vivid – so real. I can still see that man in detail, in my mind's eye: the way the sun hit him, the shadow of his cap masking his face, the texture of his rough work-clothes, the way the light glinted on the blade of the axe he was carrying. I suppose it could ***possibly*** have been a dream. But I have never before had a dream that I didn't immediately recognise *as* a dream when I woke up! Oh, I know it happens! But – I'm only 69, for crying out loud! I am ***not old yet***! Anyway – ranting and railing is not going to change it. So let's see if we can come up with a rational explanation . . .

I may, of course, actually have seen a real person, no matter what Derek says! The fact that nobody seems to ***know*** the chap is ***not*** totally conclusive! It could have been someone who works on a neighbouring farm, taking a shortcut across Derek's land. Maybe I just didn't describe him very adequately? Or maybe he is just relatively new in these parts, and hence not immediately recognisable? There could be all sorts of explanations, other than that Dad is going loopy and having hallucinations! I know people in a community of this size take pride in thinking they know everybody (not to mention Everybody's Business!) – but do they ***really***?

Thursday, 6 June – some ungodly hour a.m.!

At that point, the kids got home from school, so I decided to pack it up. My hand was about falling off, anyway! Then yesterday I had to go for physio. at the hospital (groan!) so I never got round to putting pen to paper. But I woke up about an hour ago, and I'm blowed if I can go back to sleep again! I'm sick of tossing and turning, so I might as well try to occupy my mind. Here we go again!

Actually, you know, this diary lark probably isn't such a bad idea. 'Thinking on paper' makes me look at things more thoroughly and more clearly than I might otherwise. And with a regular record, I may be able to keep better track of any progress – improvements in my condition may be slow, and hard to appreciate in the short-term. This may help me to recognise them, and not get too depressed. And it does give me some sort of occupation at times like this – which, if I try hard enough, I just may be able to kid myself is '*Useful* Occupation'!

I did start out again by trying to read, but with no more success than before. I determinedly stuck it out for a whole page, then realised I was only going through the motions – I hadn't taken in a single word. The letters were dancing in front of my eyes, and it was all I could do simply to focus, never mind make any sense of the words. Writing is much easier, funnily enough, particularly where I can just waffle on like this, and not have to worry about any sort of literary merit! The stress of yesterday, the journey to and from the hospital, and the effort of the physio., gave me a nagging headache, and although it is finally beginning to wear off, I feel out-of-sorts and shaky. And I don't want anybody to notice – they'd only fuss. I'm **OK**. I *will be* OK, at any rate. I'm determined I will get back to normal, skull-fracture or no. The actual brain-damage was minimal, and I must have more than enough spare brain-cells hanging around doing nothing to compensate for those that were wiped out in the crash. They'll just have to stop free-loading and earn their keep for a change! It takes time, that's all.

And, as well as the purely physical side, there is, after all, the psychological and emotional angle to consider. It shakes you up, that sort of trauma! You *know* all about road accidents, and how they don't *always* happen to Other People. But I still did not, seriously, expect it to happen to *me*! Oh yes - I've always tried to take sensible precautions – I've always had my car serviced regularly by reliable mechanics; I have always made sure that my tyres were in good nick and at the right pressures; when my eyesight began to be just a little less perfect than it used to be, I got properly-corrective spectacles, and I always wore them when driving. I have always observed the Rules of the Road – *and* made a proper Will, so Mary and/or the kids would be provided for "just in case" – but none of that Preventive Magic was strong enough in the end to save me from the young idiot who wrote off my carefully-maintained car, that I polished so lovingly every Sunday morning, and very nearly wrote me off along with it! He certainly wrote off The Way Things Were!

Ever since that awful moment of realisation of what was going to happen – through the agonised grinding and crunching of metal, tearing of flesh and crushing of frail bone . . . the jumbled half-awareness of unimaginable pain, sirens, spinning lights, urgent voices, pitiless rain . . . the incomprehensible depths of oblivion . . . the rolling red-and-black vortex that whirled me, terrified, back to consciousness, and the torture of awakening . . . on through the endless frustrating days of helplessness, indignity and loss of self determination – I have been in a Different World. Gone is the confident, seemingly-secure, well-organised, comfortable, predictable world I strove so hard to achieve – that I planned for in my youth, built over the years with painstaking care, and had latterly grown accustomed-to. I suppose, in effect, I had become complacent. Maybe even a little smug. I am so used to telling *other* people how best to handle their emotional crises. Now it is time to see if I can handle my own!

I feel almost like Alice – Through the Looking Glass. Things seem to be reversed, turned upside-down. *I* am supposed to be the *doctor*, not the patient! I am supposed to be the one with the *answers* – in theory, anyway! I have also become rather used to being the Responsible, Competent, Omniscient, Omnipotent Adult – first with my own children, now with my grandchildren. I've been Father, Provider, Protector, Adviser, Comforter, Family Law-Enforcer. Now suddenly my 'kids' are looking after *me*! Now they are saying, "Behave yourself, Dad!" and "Don't worry, Dad – we've got it all in hand!"

Yesterday evening my granddaughter – my little Kirstie, all of five years old – sat beside my bed and read *me* a bedtime story! And how's *that* for standing the world on its head!

Oh, yes – I know they all *mean* well. They're trying to help me. They want me to get well. But it does require a lot of adjustment! I still find it hard to accept. And I can't help just a niggle of fear, of self-doubt – will I *ever* be quite the man I was? Or will I have to be 'realistic' and accept a new role?

> *"The old order changeth, yielding place to new,*
> *And God fulfils Himself in many ways*
> *Lest one good custom should corrupt the world."*

Tennyson's 'Morte d'Arthur'. It always gave me vague shivers, but I never related to it so deeply before. I know things have to change. We have to take our turn, then move along to make room for the next generation. The mighty oak-tree crashes, and the waiting seedlings race towards the light. It is natural. It is right. But I just wasn't ready for it *yet*!

Before all this, I felt so strong, still vigorous, still in my prime – and I really didn't *look* too bad for my age, even if I do say so myself! I have always kept myself pretty fit and alert, without going through all the song-and-dance about it that is so fashionable nowadays. Now, each morning when I shave, I wonder who is that old man in the mirror: ("Good morning, Old Man – and how are you today? Where did *you* come from? Are you – can you really be – ME?")

I don't *feel* that old. And come on – let's be positive! 69 really *isn't* all that old! And I come from a line of great longevity – my father, after all, is a very hale and hearty 95! My mother is a sprightly 91, with all her faculties intact, and both my grandfathers saw 90 in good shape. I am a mere stripling beside them!

I have just had a Nasty Accident, that's all – what can I expect? But I am still here, and I *am* going to recover. Fully. I am *not* finished yet. And I will not let a silly incident like that on Monday upset me unduly, whatever the explanation! I am being well cared for – best of food, best of everything. I've got nothing to really worry about – so I shall sit back, lap it up, and be treated like a king! I am going to Bounce Right Back!

Right – that's better! It never hurts to hit your problems head-on, analyse them rationally and truthfully, and admit to what you're really afraid of.Let's just accept that I am not at my all-time best right now, but I am going to be just fine! Of course I'm all shook up; of course I'm not feeling 100% – it wouldn't be reasonable to expect it. But I am alive, and out of hospital, and I'm on the road to recovery. And the birds are just beginning to sing outside, greeting the dawn. I think I can probably manage to settle down now for another couple of hours, until Derek brings my tea – so this positive note seems a very good point at which to stop!

Still Thursday – later

Well, I did drop off, and I had quite a refreshing nap, so I don't feel too bad at all – my head hardly aches now. It's mid-morning, and Pat and Kyle have just left to go to the shops. Mavis would, I am convinced, normally have gone with them, but they are obviously not prepared to risk a repeat of Monday's shenanigans, and have discovered plenty for Mavis to do in the kitchen. My God! There I go again! I didn't even realise I was doing it, until Kurt pointed it out, saying "Grandpa – why do you keep getting Mabel's name wrong? Why do you call her Mavis now? Is it because you hurt your head? Does that make you get people's names wrong?"

I immediately resolved that I would make sure I got it right from then on, but – I have just **written** it – **twice**! (Did anyone spot the Deliberate Mistake? Oh yeah!)

Still – let's not get side-tracked again. There was something I meant to make a note of earlier on this morning, and then I got maudlin and bogged down with introspection. Now, what was it? Ah, yes – I know! A little incident that took place yesterday morning that I've been meaning to take a closer look at:

Pat drove me in to the hospital, and there is no way you can keep young Kyle hanging around for that length of time, so we left him with Ma . . . yes, Mabel! And while we were on that that nice straight stretch of road where Pat wasn't having to concentrate too hard on her driving, she suddenly said, "Dad – that man, you said you saw – the one you thought was Dan . . . " She seemed at a loss how to proceed, so I gently prompted, " What about him?"

I can't quite think of a word to describe the look on her face as she said hesitantly, "Well . . . it's just that . . . you won't mention him to the kids, will you?"

Now that struck me as decidedly odd! I mean – why on earth should I? Conversely – why on earth **shouldn't** I? I said, "No, all right, love – if you'd rather I didn't. But may I ask why?"

She looked as if she wished she were anywhere else, but tried to sound nonchalant, saying, "Well, it's just . . . you know how nervous Kirstie is of strangers! I don't want her upset again, thinking about a strange man wandering around our yard."

I said, "Upset **again**? I didn't know you'd had any sort of upset with her!"

And she said hurriedly, "Oh, it was nothing really! With you feeling so poorly, we didn't want to worry you with it. It was just that silly fuss about the cottage – I mean, **we** know it's ridiculous, but the kids at school, of course, came up with all sorts of lurid stories, and scared **our** kids half to death! They were starting to . . . well, it's only natural they should start to imagine things, isn't it? It's enough to give *me* the creeps, never mind kids of that age! Only you know how it annoys Derek – he's got no patience with such rubbish! And it *has* all settled down now – but if they hear *you* thought you saw a man with an axe, it's bound to start it up all over again, so . . . "

The poor girl looked really miserable – I think she wished she'd never raised the subject. I started to try to find out exactly what she meant by that last bit, but we had got into the town and the traffic by then, so I let her put all her mind to her driving – I am not totally confident in cars yet! And when we got to the hospital, of course, I got diverted by my 'physical jerks'!

But the roads were fairly quiet again on the way home, so I seized the opportunity and said, "Pat – when you say I *thought* I saw a man with an axe, exactly what are you implying, love? Are you suggesting I was dreaming – which is Derek's pet theory! – or that I may have been knocked so sideways by my injuries that I was hallucinating and imagined the whole thing? Or could you be saying that what I interpreted as a man, the children might think was a ghost? Or what? I need to understand just what we're talking about here."

For a few minutes, she didn't reply. But we were approaching a lay-by, and she pulled the car off the road and stopped. She just sat there for a while, looking bleak – most unusual for our Pat; it takes a lot to upset her. They she drew a deep breath and said, "Dad – I wish I *knew* exactly what I mean – but I don't! I need to talk about it – but Derek won't. We have always been able to discuss *everything* – except this silly set up with the cottage – it just makes him so *angry!* And I do understand why! He doesn't believe in ghosts – well, neither do I really! But I always hated that cottage! And I'm not sure why! I love Manor Farm – but I *hate* the cottage. And now it's beginning to ruin our lives, spoil our dreams and threaten our hard work. It's making my husband bad-tempered, and it's terrifying my children. And I don't know what to do about it, Dad! I'm frightened – but I don't know what of! I can't stop people from gossiping and concocting silly stories! And I shouldn't be worrying *you* with it! I wouldn't have, only . . . "

I said, "Don't be silly, love! I appreciate your concern, but I can assure you it's not necessary! Now, come on – tell me! All of it! I want to know everything – especially about this man with the axe!"

She gave me a searching look, then smiled and shook her head. "Same old Dad!" she said. "Obviously it would take a lot more than a skull- fracture to quench *your* curiosity! OK. There isn't really much to tell – and I don't know why I'm letting it worry me. I'm sure there's a perfectly rational explanation. You see, we don't really know what the McHugh children may have said . . . "

I couldn't place the name. "McHugh children?" I queried.

"Yes, Dad," she said. "You know – the first family who came to live in the cottage?"

"Ah! Of course!" I said sagely. "Yes, I remember!"

(I could have sworn it was Magee!)

"Well, you know what it's like," Pat continued, "those kinds of stories never seem to lose in the telling! And of course the village children pounced on it straight away! And they got *our* kids quite frightened, with all sorts of blood-curdling nonsense! Even Kurt! We've done our best to explain that it *is* just stories – and the kids have tried to be very sensible, really. But when inexplicable things happen . . . "

"Go on," I said.

"Well," she said, "several times they've seen a strange man – an old man with an axe. In the yard – behind the chicken-coop – down in the woods – and Kirstie *swears* she saw the same man one day looking out of one of the upstairs windows in the cottage! She was so sure that Derek dashed straight over there – and found it had been locked up as usual. He went all over the house, but there was no sign of anybody, and nothing had been disturbed. We put it down to maybe a reflection on the glass, and an over-active imagi-nation! We were sure she was telling the *truth* – she really *believed* she saw a man. But she couldn't have – there was no-one there. And on a couple of oc-casions, she and Kurt have both seen him at the same time. But *we* can never find him – or any sign of him. No prints from those heavy boots they say he wears – nothing! They also say they've seen a couple of strange children – a boy about Kurt's age, and an older girl. Well, in a village, this size, they know every child in the area! And we couldn't find anyone who had young relations to stay. These kids don't go to the village school – and no one seems to know who they could possibly be. And, believe me – strangers don't usually stay a mystery for very long around here! So we don't know what to make of it, at all. We can only suppose that all the horror stories are making the kids unsettled, and genuinely frightened that they are living next door to a 'haunted house'. Not funny! But it has all died down over these last few weeks, and we were hoping . . . then *you* go and see a man who matches the description the kids gave us! And I was afraid that if you casually happened to mention him, it might start the whole thing up all over again!"

I said "Listen, Pat – I do see the problem! And I will be careful what I say! But – I can tell you quite categorically that no-one has ever mentioned this man in *my* hearing, so I don't think he's been passed on to my imagination as it were. Now, *I* don't believe in ghosts, any more than Derek does, and until you seemed to suggest it, I had never considered the possibility. If it's any reassurance – I would swear to it that the chap I saw was as real as you or me. There was nothing in the least sinister or insubstantial about him – he was a perfectly ordinary, very solid farm-labourer, whose name could easily have been Dan, as I assumed! I was not in the least afraid – it was broad daylight, bright sunshine – and when I called to him, he turned and touched his cap to me. Maybe he does sometimes take a shortcut across your meadow – and maybe he knows he shouldn't! That could account for why you and Derek have never seen him – he makes darned sure he stays out of your way! I would say you could easily be right about the reflection in the window – Kirstie wouldn't be the first to be fooled by that sort of thing! A trick of the light looks like a face; and it's not hard to see why she would imagine it was the face of this man – he's obviously been very much on her mind! She *is* only five – and with all the hoo-ha that seems to have been going on, it's no wonder she's frightened! As for the 'strange kids', love – come on, maybe the local grape-vine actually slipped up for once! It's not beyond the bounds of possibility, you know! Or maybe they weren't *staying* here – maybe they were out for a picnic, and wandered off while their parents were having a siesta! There could be any number of answers to *that* riddle – and none of them in any way sinister or spooky! What *I* think is that it's a pity you haven't got a decent guard dog, to stop all-and-sundry using your place as a right of way!"

She had to laugh! "I know!", she said, "Our two are hopeless, aren't they? Dan says they're neither use nor ornament! But the trouble is, Dad – I'm not happy at the thought of having a potentially-dangerous animal anywhere near our kids! We do *not* need *that* kind of tragedy – and it happens all too often, doesn't it? With Judy and Droopy, you may be in severe danger of being *licked* to death, but that's about it! Although – I must admit I don't like the idea of this chap wandering around with an axe! And I just can't think who he can possibly be! I can't think of *anyone* around here who fits the description, and – honestly, Dad – our meadow isn't a shortcut to anywhere! It only leads down to the woods, and the Banebrook in the hollow – and that's all fenced off, because of the kids – it was one of the first things we did when we moved in. There's no way through – so where can he be going?"

I said, " I'll tell you what – I'll be hanging around for a bit. I'll keep my eyes open, and if I see him again – I'll *ask* him! OK? Now, I'm hungry – let's go home!"

So we did. And Pat did seem a little happier for having got all that off her chest. Looking at it again, though – what exactly are we to make of it? Well – several points come to mind:

1. I cannot help feeling a little relieved – and vindicated! I am *not* the only one to have seen this man – there are two other independent witnesses. The odds against my 'dreaming' or imagining a person who matched exactly the description the children gave must be astronomical! He is a real person, and I *did* see him, exactly as I thought!

2. It's about time Derek got some sensible tenants who would treat all this nonsense with the contempt it deserves! The place standing empty is only going to fuel the gossip. It may be great fun for the locals, but it is all going too far. There is no excuse for scaring innocent kids, and I'd very much like to give the scaremongers a piece of my mind!

3. I must have a little talk with our Derek when I can find the right moment! It's no good him getting on his high horse and just refusing to talk about it! I recall that always was his way of handling his problems, but this is not simply going to fade away just because he doesn't like it. These things are better discussed, and it's not *Pat's* fault – no point in blaming her. I think she's been pretty level-headed, all things considered!

I am not at all happy with Derek's security arrangements. Its crazy that just *anyone* should be able to stroll in, any time they feel like it! Surely, there must be some way to make the place a little more inaccessible? Not *all* the weirdos in the world make their way to the inner-cities, no matter how much he might like to think so!

… slight interruption there! I heard the sound of chopping wood close by, so I just wondered…but it's only Dan. Again. Darned chap seems to practically live here – must be costing Derek a fortune! He didn't see me, so I didn't speak. I don't know what it is about him, but – I dunno! – I just don't trust him! I must make some casual enquiries – I mean, who the hell *is* he? And what is he doing here? He seems totally incongruous in an 'English Village'! He's not even a camera-clicking tourist, but doing odd jobs! *Very* odd! And there's something funny about his looks too – now, what is it? I know! It's his eyes! I was too flustered the other day to notice consciously, but it's coming back to me now – they're blue! And with that very dark – almost blue-black – hair you would expect them to be brown. "Irish-eyes" – isn't that what they call them? Probably got some Irish blood in his ancestry somewhere – not too unusual for Americans. And he's too thin. Gaunt. Yes, that's a very good word. Our Derek's not overweight, by any stretch of the imagination, but *this* chap . . . ! They must be about the same height, I should say, but Derek could give this fella twenty pounds, maybe more! All in all, he strikes me as a *very* rum customer! He seems intelligent enough – so why hasn't he got a *proper* job? What's a young chap like him doing, taking on all the heavy work that other people don't want to do for themselves? Is he married? Where does he live? How long has he been in England? And how much does Derek actually know about him? I hope he checked out his references thoroughly! Knowing Derek, I doubt it! He is far too trusting. I have to admit Dan is doing a nice job, and certainly putting his back into it – he was attacking that wood just now as if it had done him a personal injury! But – something's not right! I wish I could put my finger on it. I shall have to keep my eyes and ears open – and maybe ask a few carefully-worded questions. Mavis might be the best candidate – if I can't get *her* talking, I'll eat my hat! The real problem will be most likely be getting her stopped!

Nosy old so and so, aren't you George? You bet your buttons I am!

Friday, 7th June – the wee, sma' hours again!

Exactly as I thought! Derek hasn't got the foggiest notion about Dan's background – took him on Old Harry's recommendation, pure and simple! And when I asked how Old Harry knew him so well – do you know what his answer was? "Dad how should *I* know? He's only an odd-job man, for crying out loud! Why all the big fuss?" !!!

Sometimes I despair! The chap runs tame all over the property, at all hours of the day and night, quite often when nobody's home – but nobody seems to feel the need to know the first thing about him! Derek doesn't even know where he lives! Can you believe that? Yes, knowing Derek, I can! – although I must admit I did hope he'd get a little more sense as he grew up! Seems my optimism was unjustified!

And now I've put his back up – he thinks I'm interfering! So he **wouldn't** tell me any more, even if he could! He says I'm bored and cooking up a little excitement for myself! Oh – **and** that I'm feeling a fool about what happened on Monday, so of course I'm blaming Dan for it! Codswallop! I am **not** that childish! It was a simple misunderstanding. And if you **will** tiptoe around looking that furtive, what can you expect? It's just that, at my age, and after so many years in my profession, I have learned not merely to take people at face value – or at their **own** valuation!

It is safer by far to be too suspicious than too trusting – and anyone with nothing to hide shouldn't mind. If this fella *is* perfectly legit., he should understand. I'll see if I can find a good opportunity to sound Mabel out today – she's a little more curious than Derek! And maybe a friendly chat with Dan himself – see what story *he* tells?

Right – I think a little more sleep is in order. And Mary will be here this evening, thank the Lord! The week *has* passed – somehow! So we can look forward to a better couple of days – **and** nights! – over the weekend .

Later . . .

Well, this gets "curiouser and curiouser"! I managed to collar Mabel this morning, while she was hanging out the washing. I had to lead into it a little circumspectly – began by asking after her father's sciatica! Now, Mabel is the kind who never objects to discussing matters medical – or to having a little moan about how demanding her father is becoming. She gave me the perfect opening when she said, " . . . but I can't help being glad he's given up trying to keep *this* place at last, Dr. Hanson! It was far too much for him, silly old soul! It needed a younger man."

I said, "Absolutely! Lucky for Derek that your father knew Dan! Is he a relation of any kind?"

"Of *ours*?" she exclaimed. "No - never in this world! Why, whatever could have given you that idea?"

"Oh," I said innocently, "nothing specific. It was just that Derek said your father gave him a recommendation, and he seems an unlikely sort of person for your father to know. I thought he might be a descendant of an aunt or uncle of yours who had emigrated to America, come looking for his roots, the way Americans do . . . "

"Oh, bless you, no!" she cried. "Nothing like that! As for a recommendation – I wouldn't quite put it *that* way – Dad doesn't know him from Adam! He was just leaning on his gate one afternoon, the way he does – smoking that smelly old pipe of his, I shouldn't wonder! – when this young man comes up the lane with a big pack on his back, and naturally Dad passed the time of day with him. They got talking, like, and he asks Dad if he wants any jobs done around the place. Well, of course, Dad does all his own bits – he can still potter enough to cope with his own place – so he said no, he didn't. So this Dan asks him if he might know anyone who did – so naturally Dad told him about Mr. Hanson, and showed him how to get here. And Mr. Hanson took him on right away – as did quite a few others, when the word got round! But – not meaning any disrespect, like – and not denying he does seem a real good worker – *I'd* like to know a bit more about him, first, myself! He could have been anybody, turning up out of the blue like that – and you do you hear so many dreadful things! Maybe, living in the city, you'd be more used to strangers, but . . . "

"Oh, I agree with you!" I assured her quickly. "You can't be too careful! Still, if he's been around for – let's see, would long it be now . . .?"

"Beginning of April, he come!" she supplied, nodding her head decisively. "All those weeks – and still nobody knows anything about him! Not as I can make out, anyway, and it being none of my business, I suppose you'd say! He's *close*, he is – oh, pleasant enough! – but he doesn't give much away. If you'd credit it . . ."

She was well into the subject by now, and all I had to do to keep her in full

31

spate was to raise my eyebrows enquiringly, nod or shake my head at appropriate intervals, and make the right sort of encouraging tongue-clicks, etc. She's a voluble soul, is our Mavis – nothing reticent about *her*! To cut a very long story short, what I discovered was:

a. Nobody knows Dan's other name! When asked, he smiles and says disarmingly, "Just call me Dan." And people seem willing to leave it at that! "Oh, all right, Dan . . . " !!!

b. Nobody seems to be sure exactly where he's living! Now, this is ridiculous – in a place where Everyone is supposed to know Everything about Everybody Else's Business? Give me strength!

c. The foregoing remain possible because *if* he ever receives any mail, it doesn't come to the village! The postman has never delivered a letter to him, and no mail has ever been left at the Post Office "to be called for"! So – either he doesn't *get* any mail (!?) or he's fixed up a mailing-address in Warwick or somewhere, out of the immediate area. Now – *why?*!

d. Mavis explains it all – not quite to her own satisfaction! – by deciding that he is "one of them hitch-hikers", taking a cheap way round Europe. I might have been inclined to agree if he were younger – but isn't he a little *old* for that? It's possible, I suppose – but he's not your average college-student!

e. Nobody knows how long he is planning to stay – but his 'regulars' hope it will be for a long time to come! His energy and reliability have made him *very* popular, and his rates are reputed to be 'very reasonable'. Well, no doubt they *are* – I don't suppose the Inland Revenue is taking a cut - not to mention V.A.T.! And what about visas and work-permits and all *that* sort of thing? Looks very like a case of Three Wise Monkeys Syndrome, to me! The people in these parts know when they're on to a good thing, and they have no intention of rocking the boat. Let Officialdom take care of itself – why ask questions when you may not like the answers? What you don't know lies easy on your conscience!

At that point, the subject of all the speculation put in an appearance, and Mabel rather guiltily remembered she had work of her own to do, and departed – leaving me with plenty to mull over. I would have strolled across and tried my luck with Mr. Mystery Man himself, but he's up on the roof of one of the outhouses, replacing some broken tiles – not the best place for a Casual

Chat! So my curiosity will have to wait – for ***now***!

I think I've got time for a short toddle down the lane before lunch. "Gentle Exercise", here I come!

Monday, 10th June – 2.30 a.m.

This is getting to be a habit! When Mary's here, I'm fine. I can sleep straight through. Or if I do happen to wake, I can stay relaxed in her warmth, and soon drift off again. But when the other side of the bed is empty, I simply cannot settle, no matter how tired I am. Once I'm awake, I'm awake, and that's that. It's probably best not to fight it - I'll just occupy myself for a while.

We had a wonderful weekend – apart from one 'little' incident. The weather has been glorious – blue skies and sunshine, with just a few fluffy and unthreatening white clouds sailing along in the little breeze that has kept the temperatures really comfortable – England at its best! And that was particularly nice, because we all trooped off to the Village Fete on Saturday, and conditions couldn't have been more ideal. The bunting waved cheerfully, the local brass-band played military music, the turf was dry and springy underfoot, and it was very reassuringly exactly what a village fete ***ought*** to be. I didn't much appreciate having to be pushed around in the wheelchair, of course, but I have to admit I couldn't possibly have coped otherwise, so I tried to accept it with a good grace. There were all sorts of stalls and games, a gymkhana, a fancy-dress parade and all the usual competitions. Mary won 1st prize for her fruit-cake – hardly surprisingly! Pat won a 2nd in the flower-arranging, and Droopy won the 'Floppiest Dog' award! The Village-and-Surrounding-Area were out in full force, all being very friendly and sociable – even my 'friends' from the Police stopped for a solicitous word, asking if I was 'feeling better' – but Mary soon jollied me over it! The local vicar, the Rev. Oliver Fifield was very attentive – hoped he would see me in church on Sunday morning! When I told him I am not a religious man, he took it in good part, and recommended a visit to the church some other time – it evidently has some interesting features – and assured me that I will be welcomed by his good lady and himself if ever I feel like a cup of tea and a chat. Seems a nice sort of chap, and he couldn't really say any fairer than that, could he? I might just take him up on it.

I was also introduced to a very nice young lady who runs a mobile library, and she has promised to make sure she includes us on her round this coming week, and brings some books on the history of the locality – she actually has one in which Manor Farm House gets a mention! It would be interesting to know a little more about the place where I'm staying, so I shall look forward to that.

Jenny bought herself a leather handbag from the handicraft stall, which – along with several other items, we learned – had been both hand-made and donated by Dan, proceeds to the New Church Hall Fund. Jenny was delighted with it, and I must admit the workmanship is very good. It's evidently what he does 'in his spare time', meaning when it's too dark or too wet for his usual occupations!

I kept catching sight of 'the man himself' all through the afternoon – he was here, there and everywhere, helping with this, that and just-about-everything, to the manner born! He appears to have quite a way with elderly ladies – well, perhaps not *just* the elderly ones, come to think of it! I suppose he could be thought, objectively, to posses a certain haggard charm! Anyway, he seems *very* much at home.

It was a very satisfactory – if tiring – day, and we all went home very much in charity with the world. And most of yesterday was very pleasant, too – Pauline, Roger and Paula joined the family party – and we really are becoming quite a tribe when we get together! We don't get the privilege of young Paula's company quite so much as we used to – there really isn't much here to occupy a girl of her age, and she tends to be busy with her own affairs. Yesterday, she seemed fairly content to sunbathe – or "work on her tan", as she put it! – although she did seem to have a weather-eye out, waiting for some-thing or some*one*. Derek laughingly informed me she was hoping that Dan might put in an appearance – ye gods! But he managed to make my day by staying away for once, so if it *was* him she was waiting for, she was disap-pointed. I am just very thankful that she lives at a safe distance – out of *his* way, at least! He must be . . . oooh, well over *double* her age! That sort of in-volvement we can do very nicely *without*, thank you very much! Trust Derek to think it funny!

The only sour note came just before tea-time, when the women were all in the kitchen, and Derek, Roger and I were lounging on the patio. The kids had been playing in the meadow – sometimes out of sight, but not out of earshot – and the dogs were with them. Suddenly we heard the dogs start barking – not the excited yapping of play, but a nasty, *snarling* sort of bark, cut short by a sudden yelp of pain. Derek was already on his feet and running when we heard the children screaming, and he was halfway to the gate before they came into sight, racing towards the house in panic.

Droopy was with them, lolloping along as fast as his little bowed legs would carry him, and he didn't even break stride when he reached Derek, but just kept racing towards the house, scooted through the open kitchen-door, nearly knocking Mary flying, and disappeared. By this time, Roger had caught up to Derek, and Pat had put her head out of the door to see what on earth was going on. She saw the kids clinging to Derek, and off she hared too, with Jenny in hot pursuit. Utter chaos!

The women brought the children back to the house, all of them in tears – and it was some time before we could make any sense out of the hysteria. Derek and Roger had gone together into the meadow, and came back a few moments later, with Derek carrying the limp form of Judy in his arms.

The story we *finally* pieced together was this – the children were all having a race down the field, and Kirstie had stopped to tie Kyle's shoe-lace, while Kurt and Elizabeth kept running. Suddenly, Kirstie heard Judy growl, and looked up to see the old man with the axe, standing looking down at them. Judy flew at him, barking, but before she reached him, he swung his axe at her and knocked her flying! Kurt and Elizabeth turned around at the noise, but all they saw was Judy leaping in the air, then falling over. They saw no sign of any man, and Kirstie swears that he simply 'disappeared'! But Judy wasn't moving, and they thought she was dead – so, naturally, they ran to the house for adult help.

The dog wasn't dead – but she was certainly unconscious! We decided she had probably had a stroke after racing around in the heat, and phoned immediately for the vet. He lives only about a mile or so away, and – luckily! – was willing to come straight away. He was there within about ten minutes, by which time the dog was coming round, but still very groggy. He examined her thoroughly, and couldn't find any specific problem – all her limbs seemed to be working, she can see and hear, and she wasn't running a temperature. In fact, the vet. seemed to be saying her temperature was very *low*! Strange!

He was obviously puzzled, but wanted to get back to watching the cricket, so didn't muck about for *too* long.

Judy recovered progressively all evening, and ate her dinner with *almost* her accustomed gusto. We, also, eventually got our tea, even if it was darned late, and nobody had much appetite for it even then – even Droopy, who had finally been remembered, located, and physically dragged out from under Kurt's bed! He did pick up a little when he found that Judy was all in one piece, and on the mend. But when Derek tried to put them out into the garden before bedtime, they broke away from him, and both huddled in a corner, trembling! He had to put their leads on and accompany them, and even then they weren't keen!

The worst problem, though, was poor little Kirstie. The child was absolutely hysterical, but even when we got her comforted and calmed-down a little, we could not budge her from her story. We pointed out that if there *had* been a man in the middle of that open meadow, as she said, there was no way he could have departed without Kurt and Elizabeth seeing him. And if the dog had actually been attacked with an axe, there would have been *blood*, and the animal had absolutely no visible injuries. But it made no difference – she was adamant. And terrified. And, fairly understandably, *her* insistence terrified the rest of the kids. Little Kyle swore *he* had seen the 'bad man' too – but a two-year-old is *not* the most reliable witness! Kurt was badly shaken – for a start, he is very attached to both those dogs – and very worried for his sister. And poor little Elizabeth didn't know quite what to make of it! She kept trying to make helpful – and really very logical! – suggestions, which did *not* go down too well with Derek! *Her* theory was that if the man was a 'really truly ghost', then his disappearing-act would be not only possible, but pretty much to be *expected* – and that a 'ghost axe' would not necessarily draw blood! (Where *do* they get these ideas from?) Anyway, logical or not, it was not very helpful just at the time! We were trying to convince Kirstie that she had *not* come into contact with the Supernatural, not make out a good case for it! I'm pretty sure we never did make much impression, actually, but the chaos did eventually subside, and a rather-subdued normality began to reassert itself.

Mary, Jenny and Elizabeth left about eight o'clock – it was already past Elizabeth's bedtime - but Pauline stayed to help Pat get the kids bathed and into bed. When they had disappeared upstairs, Paula said, "Grandpa – *could* it have been a ghost?"

Derek nearly hit the roof! "God dammit!" he roared, "don't anybody *ever* say that word in my hearing again! I am sick and tired of such nonsense! Did you see the *state* that kid was in? Can you wonder at it, with everybody filling her head with such a load of . . . "

"Well, don't yell at *me*!" Paula flung back at him – she can usually give as good as she gets! "*I* didn't do anything – I only *asked*!"

Derek controlled himself with an effort. "Sorry, kidder," he said. "I didn't mean to take it out on *you*. But you can see what we're up against, can't you? And I have *had* it with all this carry-on! We just get it all nicely settled down, and then your *grandfather* has to go and set it all off again. . . "

"Now, hang on there a minute!" I cut in. "Just what am *I* meant to have done? Pat asked me not to mention that chap I saw, and I have been very careful not to! Give me credit for a bit more sense than *that*, Derek, if you don't mind! Since when have I been known to go around frightening children?!"

That pulled him up short! He rubbed his hands over his face, sighed deeply, and said, "OK, Dad – point taken! I'm sorry – OK? It's just that this is getting very unfunny! Any suggestions? Anyone? And Dad – don't you *dare* suggest we should sell up and move into town!"

"As a matter of fact," I said, "I think that, at this point, that would be the worst thing you could do. You know my views on this place – we won't go through all *that* again! But we don't want the children to think you're running away – that would look as if there were something to be afraid *of*. You jolly-well ought to know my views on 'ghosts', too, by now – but I *do* think your security's abysmal! If you could do something to tighten it up, you might be able to stop ordinary mortals traipsing around all over your property – and *don't* try to tell me they don't, or how could *I* have seen the same chap the kids have been seeing? Then they might feel safer, and not so prone to imagine things! Secondly, I think you ought to go all-out to get somebody *living* in that cottage, to knock all the silly stories on the head. Surely there must be *someone* with enough sense to ignore the gossip? Even if you didn't gain financially, it'd be worth it. While it's standing empty, you're asking for trouble. Now – here's a thought, for what it's worth – what about young

Dan? He practically lives here anyway – and he seems like a fairly level-headed chap, not likely to start jumping at shadows . . . "

"Sounds like a good plan," agreed Roger.

"Nice one, Grandpa!" seconded Paula, rather more enthusiastically than I could really like.

"Mmmm . . . " said Derek. "I did offer it to him once, but he said he couldn't afford it – even when I knocked the price down. But – you're right, Dad – the money's not the first consideration. Just someone living there would help, wouldn't it? And the kids think the world of Dan. OK – I'll ask him."

Pat and Pauline came back down at that, and Pat seemed very relieved when Derek explained the plan to her. He has also promised to get a security firm to come and look over the place, and see what suggestions they can come up with. So Pauline and family were able to leave on a more positive note, and Derek, Pat and I were able to go to bed feeling we had at least got things in hand.

It seems to have been a fairly peaceful night, thank Goodness – the kids appear to have slept through, with no nightmares. At least, I haven't heard any disturbances upstairs as, I must admit, I rather expected. I can hear Derek and Pat moving around now – their alarm-clock went off a few minutes ago. So – here beginneth another day. And another week.

Later . . .

Kirstie was a bit pale and heavy-eyed this morning, but seemed quite eager to go to school – she probably feels *safer* there, poor kid! Kurt was a bit pre-occupied, and quieter than usual; and even young Kyle seemed a little sub-dued. Pat was putting on a pretty good show of 'normality', but it was a bit brittle – a little like a rime of thin ice on a pond. And I think kids soon sense it when grown-ups are upset.

I wish I could make out exactly what happened to the dog! She seems fine this morning. A little fussy, perhaps, and both of them are sticking close – to the house, and to each other! But they both appear to have got their appetites back. But – what on earth *caused* it? Some kind of a fit? I want to think it was just racing around in the heat – but then you'd expect her temperature to have been raised – and it wasn't. Would it have had time to come down before the vet. arrived? Possibly. *I* dunno – I'm not a vet. But surely animal physiology can't be all *that* different!

Never mind. She recovered pretty quickly, that's the main thing. Kids get so attached to animals – they'd have been awfully upset. I remember how devastated *I* was when old Chester was killed, when I was – what – 10? Still – that's life, I'm afraid. And you can't shield them from it, no matter how much you might like to.

This other stuff is unhealthy, though. *That's* what we've got to put a stop to. I think that was quite a good idea of mine, about Dan . . . I can't pretend to be exactly fond of the chap, but surely *he* isn't going to be put off by a lot of silly stories! And if we can stop *them*, maybe we can put an end to this rigmarole once and for all.

It's a bit like bindweed, really – once it gets a hold it is *very* tenacious, and spreads everywhere! When Pat had gone off to take the kids to school, and I had moved into the garden, Mavis came out with the washing and said – very hesitantly, and quite unlike her usual hearty self – "Dr. Hanson, Sir – could I . . . well . . . could I have a word, like?"

I assured her I would be only too glad, but it was harder than usual to get her started. Eventually, she blurted out, "Well, see, Sir – I heard what happened yesterday, and – I wouldn't want to poke my nose in where it's not wanted, but – well, I'm worried! I don't know what I ought to do – see, Mr. and Mrs. Hanson won't hear of it – but it's on my mind something awful. I wouldn't want to upset the kiddies – but, you being a gentleman, like – would you be so kind to look at this, Sir . . . ?"

(Sometimes I wonder which *century* she is living in! I did ask her to call me 'George', but she got quite upset – "Oh, I couldn't do that, Sir – why, it wouldn't be fitting!" !!! Oh well!)

She groped in her apron-pocket, and fished out a black-and-white photograph. I took it, and – ah-*ha*! A farm-labourer, in heavy boots and a cap – the very same man I had seen, but carrying a scythe this time, instead of an axe! He was even touching the brim of his cap, in the very same way as when he greeted me, and the background showed what certainly looked like Derek's yard and part of the outhouses!

I nodded in satisfaction, and said, "This is the man all right, Mabel! So you *do* know him! Why the secrecy? And where did you get the photograph?"

She went white, and backed away half a step, her hand to her mouth. "Oh, Sir!" she whispered, "Do you mean to say as **this** is the man you saw?"

"Indeed it is!" I affirmed, "I'd know him anywhere! Now, come on – who **is** he?"

For a while she protested that she would 'rather not say', but when I insisted it was her duty to tell me everything she knew, and help clear this matter up, she reluctantly gave in. "All right, Sir," she said, "seeing as you insist – but don't go telling Mr. Hanson! I've already been as good as called a trouble-maker over it, when I mentioned it before, not meaning any harm, as I hope you'll believe! And I'm not used to having my word doubted! I would have left then, like my Albert wanted me to – 'Mabel,' says he, 'we're not so pushed for money as you should have to stand being insulted!' – and no more we are! But, there – Mrs. Hanson swore as she'd be lost without me, and I hadn't the heart to abandon her, the poor lamb! So I overlooked it. But it's been on my mind something awful – and maybe **you**'ll know what to do about it, being a doctor and all. **This**, Sir – " she tapped the photograph, "is old Tom Hillyer, as used to work here for old Mr. Jeffries when the place was still a farm. Lived in that very cottage for better than forty year, he did!"

"Ah!" I said. "And where does he live now?"

"That's just it, Sir!" she hissed. "He doesn't! What I mean to say, Sir, is – he died – oh, about, let's see – maybe eight year past – over in St. Catherine's Nursing Home, where they sent him because there was no-one to take care of him – Mrs. Jeffries being too old, and him having no family living."

"Where did you get the photograph, Mavis?" I asked.

"In the attic, Sir," she confided conspiratorially. "The Jeffries didn't clear it when they left – there's all sorts of old stuff up there! We'll have to get round to having a turn-out one of these fine days, but – bless us! – we've got all we can do as a general rule, keeping a big place like this! Anyway, when Mr. and Mrs. Hanson asked me if I could bring to mind anyone like the kiddies were describing, he sort of popped into my head right away. 'Why, that sounds like Tom Hillyer!' says I. 'Only it couldn't be, because he's dead!' Fair snapped my head off, Mr. Hanson did!"

(Yes – I can imagine!)

"He shouldn't have been sharp with you, Mavis," I soothed. "It was a perfectly innocent remark. So – you went looking, and you found this photograph? And this is definitely Tom Hillyer?"

"Oh, *yes*, Sir!" she exclaimed. "Him, and no other! Of course – he was younger there than when I last remember him – but it's him all right."

"Very well," I said. "Now – think carefully, Mavis – was he a local man, do you know? Was he born in these parts?"

"Oh, now . . . " she frowned. "*That* I couldn't rightly be sure of. I *think* so. Dad might remember, I suppose . . . is it important?"

"It could be," I said. "What I'm wondering, Mavis, is – did he maybe have a brother? Or a son? Someone who might bear a strong superficial resemblance to him? Because if the man in this photo died eight years ago, then it couldn't have been Tom Hillyer I saw, could it? But the likeness is uncanny – I could have *sworn* . . . but if he had family close by . . .?"

"Well, Sir . . . " she said doubtfully, "I never heard of any family, and I do know there was no family he could go to when he was ailing. And there were precious few attended the funeral. And seeing old Tom was around 80 when he died, any brother would have to be quite a bit younger, from what I can make out! Now, he *did* have a son – *and* a daughter – but they were killed in London during the war. Only about 6, the little boy was, and the girl was about 10 or 11. They had gone with Mrs. Hillyer down to London, so she could take care of a sick aunt, or some such – then, in one of the bad raids, the house they were staying in took a direct hit, or so we heard. They never did come back – killed outright, the whole family! Terrible thing, it was. And old Tom Hillyer, he lived on here, all alone, until the day they took him to the hospital just afore he died. So I suppose you have to make allowances, don't you? A surlier, meaner-tempered man never lived! But it was enough to make him bitter, wasn't it, Sir?"

God, what an awful thought! To lose your wife and your children in one go, like that! Brrrr!

"It was indeed, Mabel," I agreed, suppressing a shudder. "It's a sad world! Look – do you think your father would be in if I were to call? I've been meaning to pop down and have a chat . . . "

"Oh, Sir!" she cried, "Now that would be nice! He'd enjoy that, would Dad. He misses the company you know, now he doesn't get about so much.

But don't you go trying to walk all that way, now will you? You just wait 'til after lunch and Mrs. Hanson can drop you off, and then collect you when she fetches the kiddies from school. I *do* feel better for having talked to you, Sir – you *will* sort it out, Sir, won't you?"

I'm glad *someone* has faith in me!

"Well, I'm no Sherlock Holmes," I admitted, "but I'll certainly do my best!"

Which seemed to satisfy her: she was singing, 'I'll take you home again, Kathleen' as she belatedly began hanging the washing on the line – and she has a surprisingly lovely singing-voice!

But *what* a pretty little tangle, eh? I keep looking at this photograph of Tom Hillyer, and I could almost swear . . . but that's ridiculous! The man is *dead*. However, I did see someone who looks almighty like him – or, rather, someone who looks a lot like he did when this photo was taken, maybe 30 years ago! I wonder . . . what about an *illegitimate* son? Now, there's a thought! Yes, I must definitely pay a visit to Old Harry, get him reminiscing about Old Times – and Old Scandals! This might be a scandal that Mavis was too young to have known about – or to remember. But her Dad might well remember it. I'll track this chap down if it's the last thing I do! At least it's been a welcome diversion from my own woes – and really, you know, I don't feel too bad at all! I think I'm beginning to 'get my head together' at last, and feel a little more like my old self.

And – it may be petty, but – wouldn't it be satisfying if I *could* crack this little mystery, eh? Show young Derek his old man isn't completely over the hill *yet*! Hercule Poirot, move over!

Tuesday, 11th June, 3 a.m.

I am more and more glad that I started putting my thoughts down on paper. It started out as Sheer Desperation born of Tedium, but I am beginning to suspect it just may have a more practical application. This little set-up is developing in very interesting ways, and it's not a bad idea to have a record of *exactly* what happened, and when. Even under normal circumstances, it can be difficult to keep all the little details clear in your memory – they do tend to become blurred, and it is impossible to swear, "It happened in this way, and no other." I actually woke up about an hour ago, but before picking up my pen, I reached for my 'diary' and I have been reading through the events since I left hospital. Seeing the whole sequence in black-and-white, step-by-step, I am even more aware that we do have some sort of 'Mystery' here. I am also aware that any real solution of the mystery may well be an anticlimax – after all, this is Real Life, not Fiction! But I cannot deny that I am enjoying the opportunity to flex my mental muscles in rather unaccustomed ways, and that it would give me great satisfaction to be able to de-bunk this whole thing and come up with 'The Answer' and a perfectly rational explanation. I do not deny that I am bored. But I *do* deny that I am 'cooking up' this problem be-cause of it! After all – the kids had started seeing this man-with-the-axe, *and* got the wind up pretty badly, long before *I* had any part in it! On the other hand – having had the Mystery put right in front of me, where I cannot help but see it – I shall *not* turn up my nose at the mental exercise! Derek's attitude has put me on my mettle! Not to mention the fact that this state of affairs cannot be allowed to continue unchallenged. *Someone* has to try to sort it out and put it right. OK – I *may* be being what Mary calls 'Patriarchal' – but I will *not* sit back and twiddle my thumbs while my grandchildren are being upset! The longer I spend here, the more aware I become of the unhealthy undercurrents. This nonsense has to be *stopped*, once and for all! It is no good Derek simply laying down the law, and telling them, "There are no such things as ghosts!" We have to be able to give them an alternative explanation of their fears – because their *fears*, at least, are very real! Denying them is not enough.

So – I found it helpful to have a record of how I found out about the problem, and how I got involved in it in the first place. I am very glad I wrote down about my encounter with the man-with-the-axe *before* I knew any of the background. When I first described him, I had no idea there *was* any mys-tery. So *that*, at least, was an objective sighting. And it certainly reassures me that I had not simply been 'infected' by some sort of hysteria! I *saw* the chap for myself *before* I heard about him from anyone else. So at least *I* can be sure of my facts – even if it may not convince too many others! And setting my thoughts down on paper does help me both to organise and analyse them. It is also, quite simply, useful occupation! (I rather enjoy talking to myself!) So – let's get back to it, and bring the record up to date . . .

When Pat got home, I told her I fancied a chat with Old Harry. She glanced round to be sure Mabel was out of earshot, then said, "Rather you than me! He's enough to talk your ear off! All those reminiscences of his – they're endless! And once he gets started, you can't stop him. He can tell you every little thing that's happened in these parts for the last 80 years, at least! Or *claims* he can, anyway!"

I didn't bother to try to explain that was exactly what I wanted!

So she drove me down there right after lunch, and Old Harry was quite flatteringly pleased to see me. His cottage is becoming something of an anachronism, with the linoleum on the floor, the wood-burning range, and the pots of geraniums on the window-sills. As the 'old folks' die – or move into retirement homes – so the places where they used to live are torn down or modernised, and that distinctive flavour of 'Days Gone By' is lost for ever. Inevitable. But it still makes me feel just a little sentimental – even if *I* wouldn't want to live in a place like that if you paid me! I like my creature-comforts far too well, I'm afraid!

But it does bring back memories of childhood visits to great-uncles-and-aunts – men who wore flat caps on weekdays and bowlers on Sundays, their white walrus-moustaches stained yellow from the Woodbines or Players Navy-Cut they seemed to smoke interminably. Of paraffin-lamps suspended above white-scrubbed kitchen tables. Of women in print-dresses, who smelt faintly of lavender, pouring *very* weak tea into fine bone-china cups decorated with flowers. Of rooms with uneven stone floors, and tiny latticed windows over-grown with creepers – so dark you had to stand on tip-toe to try to make out the big old pictures in heavy frames, depicting sentimental subjects like the Souls of Good Children being wafted to Heaven in the arms of white-robed angels with long, golden curls and enormous feathery wings; or patient dogs waiting in vain beside chairs that would never again be occupied by their dead masters. Days long gone. But briefly evoked by cottages such as Harry's.

He regaled me with very weak tea, too – in a flowery china cup! And his long-dead wife smiled shyly from several faded photographs – in each one of which she is wearing a print-dress! I could almost smell the lavender! Brrrrr!

I quite enjoyed my visit, even if it was a bit of a wash-out from the point of view of providing me with the information I *wanted*! Harry remembers Tom Hillyer well – and he agrees with his daughter about the chap's charming disposition. But *he* can go back further, and maintains that the tragedy was *not* the reason for Hillyer's ill-nature. According to Harry, Hillyer *was* born locally, but he was an only child, his mother having died shortly after his birth. His father, James, never remarried, but was also a surly, bad-tempered man, who had very little to do with anybody. *He* died in about 1930, with no other relations in the area but his son, daughter-in-law and two grandchildren.

Tom Hillyer had married a woman called Emily Plackett, who was 'in service', working for Mrs. Jeffries at Manor Farm. When Tom also got a job on the farm, I suppose Proximity was probably enough, and they got married shortly after, and moved into the cottage. They had a daughter, Anne, and about five years later, a son called Arthur. Tom Hillyer appears to have followed in his father's footsteps, 'keeping himself to himself' and never really making any friends – he was not even forthcoming when well tanked-up on ale at the Banebridge Arms. Alcohol only made him more surly and taciturn than usual.

His wife was a 'timid rabbit of a woman', according to Harry – 'terrified of her own shadow' – or, more likely, terrified of her husband! But there weren't the same support facilities in those days, and she probably never even considered doing anything but suffering in silence. The locals were evidently very surprised when she was actually 'allowed' to go to London to nurse some distant relative – *and* to take the children with her! The popular explanation was that she may have had 'expectations' from said relative, and Hillyer didn't want to risk upsetting the apple-cart! So – at a time when many people were fleeing London for the relative safety of the countryside, Emily Hillyer and her two children headed for London. And they never came back. Tom Hillyer lived alone at Manor Farm Cottage up to the last week of his life, still as sweet and charming as ever.

It is not absolutely conclusive, of course, but there was never any scandal about Tom or his father having an 'affair' with another woman. And Old Harry had obviously never heard of anyone in the vicinity who resembled Hillyer in looks. It doesn't mean that no such person exists, but I am forced to concede that it does make it unlikely that such a man is actually living locally and wandering around the neighbourhood in broad daylight. The sort of striking physical resemblance between the man I saw and the photograph of Tom Hillyer would surely not go unremarked! Unless, of course, the discrepancy in *time* could account for it? If Tom Hillyer looked like that thirty or forty years ago, he could have changed a lot in the intervening years. People who knew him well then may be dead or housebound, or have impaired vision, by now! And younger people may not remember. Although – hang on! *That's* not valid, is it? *Mavis* remembers him well enough – she recognised the children's description positively enough to go and look out that old photograph! "That sounds like Tom Hillyer!" she said, straight away – and got a rollicking from Derek for her pains! So surely she would pick up the resemblance to a living, local man? Mavis may not be highly educated, and her intelligence may not be Brain-of-Britain standard, but she is by no means stupid – *or* visually-impaired! Like her father, she's nobody's fool! *He* may be over 80, but he's a sharp old cuss. I *thought* I was being fairly subtle – channelling him into telling me what I wanted to know by seemingly-casual questions – Ha! He knew what I was up to, all along! It would obviously take a smarter man than *me* to run rings round Old Harry!

But – I also got the feeling that he has a soft spot for Derek & Family – especially the children. I think he *wanted* to help – he was not being deliberately obstructive. It's annoying that the-facts-as-he-knows-them don't seem to fit my theories, but – 'facts is facts'! Not *his* fault! I suppose it *was* too simple. And yet – I am convinced there must *be* a perfectly simple explanation – if only we could see it. It's like a crossword-clue that nearly drives you demented – once you know the answer, you think. "Of course! Why couldn't I see that before?" Obvious once you know. So we shall just have to keep worrying at it, shan't we? And, in the meantime, take all the practical steps we can to keep the problem under control. A bit of decent security could go a long way! Derek has been far too lax and trusting. I'm almost beginning to feel it's a good thing I came here, after all – although not for the reasons originally stated!

And we must get somebody living in that damn' cottage! No sign of dear Dan yesterday, so that's still up in the air. But no doubt he'll be around before too long! God – *what* a slap-happy arrangement! No-one seems to keep a check on him at all! I tried to find out how Derek can tell how much to pay the fella – I mean, if it's by the *hour*, does anyone keep count how many hours he actually works?! It doesn't look much like it to *me*! But it's no good trying to help Derek – he does not appreciated my 'interference'! He started off by saying "Oh, come on, Dad – you only have to look at the place! You can *see* what he's done!" But when I pointed out that that was very vague, he just got stroppy and refused to discuss the matter any further. Typical. I am beginning to remember why I was so relieved when he did decide to marry Pat and get a home of his own. We get on much better when we are not living under the same roof, my son and I! He always did do awful things to my blood-pressure! I *know* he's a 'grown man' now – I *know* he's 'doing very nicely for himself' - but sometimes I can't help feeling it's more luck than judgement, and that one of these fine days he's going to come unstuck! Oh, shut up, George! He never did listen to the 'Silly Old Fossil', and I *don't* suppose he's going to start now!

At least he's not drifting like young Dan – I suppose that's something. I would guess they can't be far off the same age, but – I would not care to see a son of mine in that condition! That young man worries me. There is something badly wrong somewhere. Something incongruous – something that doesn't quite fit. But what is it, exactly? I can not put my finger on it. What I'd like to know is – why *here*? What brought him to Gorsey Hallowell, of all places in the world? I almost want to ask, 'Who – or what – is he *hiding* from?' He just appears one day – out of the blue – walks in with a pack on his back – and *stays*? No-one knows who he is. No-one knows where he's from – I mean, the 'United States' covers a fairly large area! It doesn't exactly pin it down much, does it?! No-one knows why he came here, or why he is staying, or how long for, or anything! Not even his surname, for Pity's sake! And yet they all seem to accept him as if he were part of the furniture! I *know* good handymen are hard to come by, but this is ridiculous! And I tell you something – *if* I can ever manage to corner him, he will find that not everybody is quite so gullible and easily put-off! 'Conventional good manners' are all very well, but . . . !

The trouble is, of course, that it is – officially – none of *my* business! Derek should have insisted on details before he took him on – *and* checked up on the answers! But – who knows? If I can just get the fella talking – 'friendly interest', no more, from a 'garrulous old man' – I might just be able to make some sense of it all. It may be all perfectly innocent and above-board, of course. And if so – if he hasn't got anything to hide – he shouldn't mind, should he?

And if I am going to be in any sort of shape for 'sleuthing', I had better see if I can tuck in another nap before it's time to get up!

Later . . .

Dan did turn up this morning, but I didn't get chance to speak to him – **again**! Pat was planning to go into the village to get her hair done – she's quite friendly with the local hairdresser, who has a son about the same age as Kyle. So the two lads play together, while the women do-the-doings. Anyway, it was a lovely day, and Pat suggested I might like to go with them and take a short stroll around the church and the churchyard – there are some interesting old headstones – and although I've been threatening to go ever since Derek and Pat moved here, I have never actually got through the church gate. There are a couple of 'memorial' benches in the churchyard, and the coffee-shop is only just across the road, if I fancied a little rest-and-refreshment, so I took her up on the offer. I'm glad I did. I particularly enjoyed the sense of freedom and independence it gave me. I was in no rush – which made a nice change. All my life seems to have been one long hurry – except when it suddenly ground to a shuddering halt! But now I am feeling well enough to enjoy things again, and this seems like a pleasant oasis – perhaps I am beginning to get the hang of this 'convalescence' lark, after all! That sort of gentle stimulation felt very good. I have always been interested in old buildings – in a vague sort of way, admittedly! – and graveyards seem to hold a morbid sort of facination for most people. Somehow, there is something very peaceful about the **long** dead. And it is interesting to follow the fortunes of local families, as depicted on their memorials.

St. Mary's Church is quite small, and was evidently built in the 12th century. I'm afraid the finer points of architectural interest were lost on me – I'm a little vague about such things. But I enjoyed the atmosphere, and the list of vicars, dating right back to the consecration of the church. There are some interesting carvings, and some stained-glass which – not being of an artistic disposition – *I* like, although Derek dismisses it as 'worst of Vulgar Victorian'! All *I* know is that I always find stained-glass pretty – I love the jewel-quality when the light comes through it, never mind all this finicky, hi-falutin' talk about 'artistic merit', etc. Load of rubbish! And, although I am anything *but* 'religious', I cannot help being strongly aware of the 'atmosphere' of churches, particularly such *old* ones.

Outside in the sun again, I got into conversation with an old chap called Sid Bushey – Bushey being one of the names you can trace via the headstones for quite a few generations. He was pottering around with a barrow, a rake and a bass-broom, but at the speed he was moving, it was fairly obvious that there was no way he could keep the place in such good shape all by himself. But – guess who helps him? Oh, yes! Right first time!

"You can't often get young-uns to put their *backs* into it," complained Sid, "but that there Dan – you can't see un for dust!"

Another convert! This is all very laudable, I'm sure. 'An honest day's work . . . ' and all that. Why doesn't it quite convince *me*? Have I just got a nasty suspicious mind? Probably. But I won't be swelling the ranks of Dan's Fan Club *just* yet!

Anyway, it was a nice way to spend a morning – very relaxing, with a lark singing somewhere out of sight high overhead, and the crickets chirping elusively in the short dry grass. I hadn't even got as far as thinking about retiring to the coffee-shop when Pat and Kyle came looking for me, but I was certainly ready for lunch when we got home.

Dan didn't come back this afternoon, so I wrote a bit and napped a bit. And now it's dinner-time and Derek's just come home, so I think I'll pack up and go and try *not* to argue with him!

Wednesday, 12th June

I had another Physio. appointment today. Again, Pat was kind enough to take me, which saves hours, and an awful lot of aggravation, waiting for an ambulance. Wonder how long it will be before I'm fit to drive again? Or even emotionally *ready* . . . at the moment, even *thinking* about it gives me cold chills! But it is early days yet – no point in worrying about it at this stage. But – oh, for a return to independence! I must just keep reminding myself how very lucky I really am. Pat is not only a careful and competent driver, but a very pleasant companion, and doesn't seem to resent at all the amount of time she is devoting to me. I mean – waiting around hospitals is no *fun*, and she has plenty of her own work to keep her busy, what with cleaning that big house and looking after three kids.

I didn't *enjoy* my 'physical jerks', but I tried to oblige everybody by doing as I was told, and I came away with another appointment for next week. Definitely above and beyond the call of duty! It has left me feeling drained and out-of-sorts again, but I managed to do justice to my lunch, and it is a really lovely afternoon to sit outside in the shade. I really appreciate the fresh air and the peace-and-quiet at times like this – perhaps my family were right about my coming here, after all. I just miss Mary!

When I first sat down, I had every intention of trying to think through in an orderly fashion all the information I have gathered from Mabel and her father, and see whether it helped in any way to explain what has been going on here. But I have to confess that my thoughts quickly dissolved into dreams, and I awoke with a jerk when the kids got home from school, having just reached a brilliant conclusion which solved the whole mystery. Unfortunately, I cannot remember what it was, and I am convinced it would be utter nonsense even if I could. Oh well! Mind you – things do seem to have settled down a little, so let's hope we can retain the status quo. Fingers crossed!

After dinner I couldn't seem to stand the television, so I came back out into the garden again where it is cool and quiet. The dusk is just starting to make it difficult for me to see to write, so I will pack up for today and sit back and watch the bats swooping after insects in the twilight. Derek just turned the lamp on in the lounge, throwing a pool of golden light across the lawn, and I was lucky enough to be able to watch a hedgehog trundling past, intent on its own business.

Darkness is really taking hold now, and I suppose I had better go inside before I begin to get chilled – the heat soon fades when the sun disappears. And I would rather like to make the decision *myself*, before Derek or Pat comes out giving me instructions! I think I am ready for a milky drink and bed, in any case.

Thursday, 13th June

I had a really good night last night. I did wake up about 2.30, but I had a drink of water and was quite glad to lie down again. Before I knew it, I had drifted off again, and slept right through until Derek's alarm clock woke me – his and Pat's bedroom is right above this room. At least we don't seem to have problems with the kids during the night, which is a great blessing. It certainly helps if everybody can get a decent night's sleep.

It is another lovely day, and we have just had lunch. I am back out in the garden, and I must admit I am beginning to appreciate this place more and more. It would appear that Dan cut the lawns yesterday, while I was away at the hospital. I just wish I could be sure whether that was out of pure consideration, so that the noise of the mower wouldn't disturb me, or whether he preferred to avoid giving me the chance to collar him! Of course, I suppose it *could* be that it was just that the lawns needed a cut and it had nothing to do with *me* at all! However that may be, the place looks really neat and tidy, and the flower beds are a riot of colour. Derek and Pat have opted for the 'cottage-garden' look, which is very appropriate in a place like this, and not too labour-intensive.

This morning, the young lady with the mobile library kept her promise. Her name is Christine, and a bright, intelligent and sociable girl she is, too. I found it so difficult to actually climb into the van that she very kindly selected some books on local history, which is the subject I was most interested in, and carried them out for me to examine. I chose a couple which look as if they should fill the bill, and she sat and chatted while Pat made us all a cup of coffee. So that made a pleasant interlude, even if I'm not sure how I'm going to cope with actually ploughing through the reading-matter. So far, I have only glanced at a few pictures, and read a few chapter-headings. Perhaps it would be a good idea to limit myself to a little at a time, see how we do. It's not exactly a matter of life and death, is it? Only for my own interest. And I *think* Christine said I could keep them for four weeks, so there's no rush.

51

Later . . .

I had to stop at that point because the Vicar, Oliver Fifield – who evidently likes to be known by his local nickname of 'Jolly Olly'! – called by to see how I was doing, and stayed for at least an hour. He is actually so open-minded and non-dogmatic that I really enjoyed our conversation, and didn't feel in the least inhibited by our differences of opinion. He noticed my library books and suggested that, as I seemed interested in local history, I might like an introduction to a local historian – a man called Christopher Wainwright, who lives in the village and is the curator of a small museum in Roddenhill, a slightly-larger village nearby. It seems he is an archaeologist – officially retired, but still getting involved in projects which take his fancy – and has dug up quite a lot of interesting artefacts in the surrounding area. Olly assured me I will find him a very entertaining and informative companion, and has promised to ask him to call when he has some spare time. I didn't like to pour cold water on such a kind offer, although I would usually prefer to make my own arrangements, with people of my own choosing. Still – let's not be negative. This Wainwright just *could* be all Olly cracked him up to be – we shall simply have to wait and see. *If* he turns up at all, that is! I think I've just got time for a refreshing nap, now, before the kids get home from school.

Later still – just gone midnight, actually!

Oh, how I wish I had decided against that nap! And *what* was that I was saying about things 'settling down'? I think that was what you could definitely call 'speaking too soon' and 'tempting Fate'! I am still feeling so totally *un*-settled, that there is absolutely no way I am going to drop off to sleep, so I may as well see if setting things down on paper may help me to clarify my thinking, and try to work out what actually *happened*. OK – let's try for a clear, rational, no-nonsense report – even if 'clear' and 'rational' are not exactly how I feel!

I must have dropped off almost as soon as I closed my eyes. I have absolutely no idea how long I had been sleeping, but suddenly I was aware of being cold. ***Really*** cold. I suppose I imagined that the sun had gone in, because, as I mentioned before, it was a really warm and pleasant afternoon. And I was assailed by the most awful feeling of ***dread*** I have ever experienced. The only thing that ever came close was when we were enjoying a family outing to the park, when Derek and Jenny were only about three years old. We had taken some bread to feed the ducks, but there were a whole flock of geese and some swans as well, and one of the swans took exception, and frightened Jenny half to death. Mary and I were so busy extricating Jenny from this mob of birds that we momentarily took our eyes off Derek - a ***very*** unwise thing to do! Suddenly I *felt* he was missing, and was quite relieved when I turned to look for him and saw him scampering merrily away from us at full speed across the grass. The relief was because (a) he was still in sight, and hadn't been abducted, or anything dreadful like that, and (b) it was a large sweep of grass, so he was in no danger from traffic. I set off in pursuit, but soon realised that my relief was premature – the most enormous dog I have ever seen was galloping towards us. It seemed about the size of a donkey, and somehow I could tell that this huge animal and my little son were on an exact collision course. I was yelling at the top of my voice for Derek to stop and come back, but he never ***did*** listen to me, then ***or*** now. The owner of the dog was also shouting at the top of ***her*** voice, but with about as much success. In fact, I think we both did more harm than good, because as both these projectiles were hurtling towards one another, they were looking over their shoulders, giving huge grins to their pursuers, and hence could not see one another. The inevitability of the collision was ***awful***. It was almost as if the world went into slow-motion, and I could see with great clarity exactly what was going to happen, but was totally powerless to stop it. As I vainly tried to close the gap, the two met – at quite considerable speed – and both went flying in a jumble of arms and legs. ***I*** was still running, in that awful state where it feels as if you are trying to run through water. Before I could reach them, both Derek and the dog resurrected themselves, and to my horror my sweet little, big-eyed three-year-old swung back his arm and clouted the dog – which was taller than he was – hard, across the nose! My imagination of what those enormous jaws could do to young flesh cannot be described! "***Bad doggy!***" yells my innocent little son, sticking out his chin belligerently, totally unfazed by the size of his opponent, "***Bad, bad doggy!***" And he raised his arm to thump the dog

53

again! Incredibly, the poor animal plonked its rear end on the grass, hung its head and sat there looking dazed and very chastened! I *almost* felt sorry for it! The dog's owner and I both arrived at the same moment, and each grabbed for our respective charges. "You stupid woman!" I bawled, furious with relief, "Why don't you keep that great brute under control?!"

"Why don't you keep your *child* under control?!" she screamed back – with some justification, as I have since had to admit!

Anyway – neither protagonist was really hurt, in anything but their dignity, and we dragged them away in different directions, with Derek still screaming for me to let him down so he could 'smack the bad doggy *again*'!

But I digress. I think I am actually putting off trying to accept what happened this afternoon, but that is not going to make it go away, so stop playing games, George, and get on with it! What I was trying to explain was that awful feeling of utter *dread*. But as my senses began to revive, the dread became tinged with anger – I was suddenly sure that that blasted Dan was standing looking down at me again. I glared at where I expected his face to be, and . . . nothing! But then my eyes were drawn, almost involuntarily, to a spot much lower down, and I found myself gazing directly into the tear-filled eyes of a little boy. His face was grubby and streaked where he had wiped away the tears from his cheeks, and his snub little nose was running. I had never seen this child in my life before, and I was so surprised it took me a moment to react. We just stared at one another in silence. I was just starting to say, "Hello, young fella – what seems to be the matter?" when the child started to *fade*, right in front of my eyes. One moment he appeared as solid as I am, but within a few seconds I could see the lawn and the hedge right *through* him. Then he was gone. And suddenly, so was that awful, marrow-chilling cold – the sun was shining as brightly as ever, and the breeze that lightly ruffled the foliage was *warm*. At the same time, I realised that, during the encounter, there had been total silence. Now, I could hear a blackbird singing in the lilac bush, and the buzzing of a bumblebee in the snapdragons. It was a little like the sensation when your ears 'pop', with altitude, or from a nasty cold in the head.

I can only imagine the look of total startlement on my own face. I have never, in all my life, had any experience even vaguely like that. I felt almost *paralysed* – as if I had forgotten how to *function* normally. I have no idea

54

how long I sat immobile, with my thoughts in complete turmoil. I *must* have been dreaming. And yet I was convinced, deep down in the core of me, that I had not. Suddenly I almost panicked – I did not want to be *alone*. I almost fell, in my haste to get out of the chair, but I managed to regain my balance and staggered in a rather uncoordinated way into the kitchen. The sight of Mabel, humming as she stood ironing one of Kirstie's dresses, was so normal and reassuring that I could have hugged her! She looked up, and immediately became concerned. "Oh, Sir!" she cried, "Why, whatever is the matter? You *do* look bad!"

I managed to sound reasonably normal, I think, as I assured her that I was *fine* and had just come in looking for a cup of tea! She immediately switched off the iron, kind motherly soul that she is, and bustled around putting the kettle on, while I sat down at the kitchen table and tried to stop my hands from shaking. It is really difficult for me to admit this, but I wanted to *cry*! I can hardly remember the last time I cried but, sitting at that table, I had to really *fight* the tears. Luckily, I won the battle – Mavis was quite worried enough, without me starting to bawl like a baby! And a cup of hot, sweet tea was just the thing to help me regain control and soothe my jangled nerves. Mavis had a cup of tea herself, but drank it in sips while she carried on with the ironing – for which I was grateful, as it stopped her from observing me too closely. And by the time Pat and the kids got home, I was able to give a fair imitation of being my normal self. Nobody seemed to notice anything, anyway, and I managed to get through the evening in good order. Pat did just happen to remark that I looked tired, but I made the excuse that it had been a busy day, what with the visits from Christine and 'Jolly Olly', and that seemed to satisfy her. Derek was in a really cheerful mood, and once the kids were in bed we spent the evening on the patio with tall glasses of cool lager and light conversation. Nice - much better than the telly. And the shock has been gradually receding. But, even though I really *am* tired, my brain just will not switch off.

What on *earth* really happened? I keep veering from one explanation to another. And yet – can I really *doubt* that I 'saw a ghost' - whatever *that* may mean? I don't *believe* in ghosts – but maybe they don't have to wait for my belief! I find that when I really get right down to it, my knowledge of the subject is actually very sketchy. I have never studied it in any serious detail. I do recognise the 'drop in temperature' phenomenon, and I know that if any-one else were trying to convince me of that experience, I would trot out a lot of facile nonsense about 'fulfilment of expectations', etc.! But this was *my* ex-perience, not someone else's. And, somehow, all those glib excuses simply wont *wash*. We don't have to go as far as 'wandering spirits of the dead' – 'psychic echoes' maybe? – but *something* happened that was beyond the previous bounds of my experience! I am going to have to do some serious studying to find out exactly what. I may have to rethink my whole philosophy – I have an awful suspicion that I have been arrogantly blind in my certainty that the whole subject could be simply dismissed as delusion, imagination or fraud. I suppose I could *conceivably* have been imagining things or suffering a delusion – but there was absolutely no possibility of fraud! At least I can exclude *that*.

I am still feeling jumpy – although I'm not quite sure *why*. Maybe it *is* simply 'fear of the Unknown' – I mean, that 'child' certainly didn't hurt - or even threaten – me, in any way. And yet I have never been so frightened in my life. I wish I could talk it over with someone, but I can't quite decide *whom*. It needs to be someone I can *trust*. I do *not* want to worry Mary with it – and I don't want to frighten Pat. And I cannot believe I would get a whole lot of sympathy from Derek! Perhaps I just have to talk to *myself* for now. And the advice I am going to give myself is to stop chasing it round my head, turn off the light, settle down and GET SOME SLEEP! I can always appraise it again tomorrow, in the 'cold light of day', and try to come up with a *strat-egy* for dealing with whatever is going on here.

Thanks, George – that's good advice, and I'm going to take it. Sweet dreams, Old Son – goodnight.

Friday, 14th June

Today, Jenny and Derek are 35 years old. It hardly seems possible – my youngest children are halfway to their 'three-score years and ten'! We're hav-ing our usual 'Birthday Bash' tomorrow, and I can only hope the weather de-cides to improve before then! Since I came here, we have had the most glorious spell of almost-unbroken June sunshine, but that all changed about three-o'clock this morning, with a really spectacular thunderstorm, which passed almost directly overhead. The lightning was some of the most impressive I have ever witnessed, and for a while the peals of thunder seemed almost incessant. The rain was almost a physical assault for about twenty minutes, then eased off into a sullen downpour which seems to have set in for the duration – there will be no sitting out in the garden today, that's for sure! And even though this is a big house, with so many people coming tomorrow it is bound to be crowded, and it would be much more pleasant if we could hold the party outside as usual. We have been incredibly fortunate these last few years, since Pat and Derek bought this place. Still – maybe it'll have cleared up by tomorrow, with a bit of luck. The noise of the storm couldn't help but wake the children – it sounded more like an artillery bombardment! – but Derek and Pat soon managed to get them settled down again once the thunder moved away.

I phoned Jenny before she left for work, just to wish her many happy returns, **and** to try to cheer myself up. Hearing her voice did help, and I also had a quick word with Mary, and a 'Hi, Grandpa – love you!' from Elizabeth. You'd have a job to find a better tonic.

I am currently ensconced in the front room, with the reading-lamp on – the heavy clouds are making the room so dark that I could hardly see to read or write. Even so, it is depressing. Such a long run of beautiful weather has obviously spoiled me, and I am feeling very out-of-sorts, with a nasty nagging headache. I suppose that **could** have a lot to do with the disturbed night, not to mention the events of yesterday afternoon. And what are we to make of all that, pray, in the cold almost-light of day? I have been re-reading my notes of last night, but already the doubts are creeping in. I was practically convinced that I had had some sort of 'supernatural' – or at least 'paranormal' – experience, but now I am fighting a sickening feeling that maybe what I experienced was actually subjective: in other words – a delusion. And I confess I do not relish **that** idea at all. Could it be delayed reaction to the trauma? And if so – do I tell Hayward about it? I have a very strong disinclination to mention it to **any**body! I mean – if I **were** to give Hayward chapter and verse of all this rigmarole – and I admit I do **not** fancy the job! – what is he going to **do** about it, pray? Apart from sending for the straight-jacket and the men in the white coats, that is! **I**, if anyone, ought to be aware that the neuropsychiatry of traumatic brain injury is still in its infancy. And, today, I am also very much aware that my own contribution to the field is over. Done. Finis. I know, deep down, that I will never be going back to work. The amnesia is much less of a problem now – but my reasoning and cognitive abilities are unreliable. And by the time they recover completely – if they ever do – I am going to be too old to start again. Science is moving on, but I have been forced into a backwater, and I don't think I am going to be able to push myself back into the main flow. I don't somehow think that miracles are on the agenda. And I am feeling more than a little sorry for myself. If I believed in 'karma' I would believe I had been *very* wicked in a past life! But I have to learn to deal with reality some-how, not only for my own sake, but for the sakes of all my nearest-and-dearest.

It will be good to see Mum and Dad tomorrow – I haven't seen them since I came out of hospital. They don't get about as much, now Dad has packed in the driving, but Jenny is going to call and pick them up on her way tomorrow, and Mary is going to pick up *her* parents and Great-aunt Flora. I wonder how many 35-year-olds actually have all four grandparents not only alive, but in remarkably good health? Not too many, I would imagine! Not to mention a great-aunt of 93 – reportedly just as sharp as ever! I haven't seen Flora for quite some time, but Mary assures me she hasn't changed much, which is a great relief. I don't want to even imagine what a gap that generation will leave when they *do* go – our birthday and Christmas get-togethers will never be the same again! But I must try to remember that we are lucky that we have had the pleasure of their company for longer than many people can enjoy their relations. Actually, of course, many people can't stand the sight of their relations to start with! I was fortunate to be blessed not only with won-derful parents, but with very acceptable parents-in-law. And Mary's Aunt Flora can only be seen as a bonus – she is a very unusual woman! She has a sharp tongue, an acerbic turn of phrase, and she has never suffered fools gladly – but she is kind-hearted under the prickly exterior, has a razor-sharp intelli-gence, and had the guts to battle her way into her chosen career of Medicine, when many girls were being cowed into submission and parentally-acceptable marriages. I never did meet her parents – they were quite elderly before they had children, evidently, and were dead before I started courting their grand-daughter – but maybe I should give them *some* of the credit - for not standing in her way, even if they didn't actively *support* her decision. And qualifying in Medicine isn't exactly easy, even today, never mind when the whole profession was totally male-dominated, and a woman's place was 'in the home'. Flora doesn't seem to have regretted a minute of it, however, even though she never did marry; she seems quite contented living with her brother and sister-in-law, now she is too frail to cope alone. I suppose she is lucky that Dennis – and more especially Kathleen! – seem to love having her. Anyway – I shall enjoy having their company again. Before the accident, we always visited one set of parents on one Friday night, and the other set on the next Friday. I wonder if we shall ever get back into the same sort of routine, or whether that is finished for good? I suppose – to coin a phrase – only Time will tell.

As for the other problem – do we opt for Damage to the Little Grey Cells, or Visiting Spirits from The Other Side? I'm not even totally sure which I would prefer! The 'experience' was so subjectively 'real' that I am finding it difficult to believe that it may have been 'all in the mind', even though I have always been firmly convinced that

At that point the phone rang. Pat answered it, but popped her head round the door to say it was a Chris Wainwright, asking if I would speak to him. I wasn't at all sorry to be interrupted from my maudlin meandering on, so I picked up the extension with alacrity. I rather liked the sound of the chap, and assured him there was no need for him to apologise for disturbing me. He said that 'Jolly Olly' had suggested he would enjoy a visit with me, and was I, by any chance, free this afternoon? I was only too relieved for a respite from all this ridiculous introspection and self-pity, so I assured him I would be pleased to see him, and he promised to turn up around two o'clock. Pat seemed more than happy with the arrangement, and has gone off to whip up a batch of scones because, she predicts, there will be a *lot* of talking, and talking is hungry work! She's a lovely girl. What a shame Jenny's marriage didn't turn out as favourably as Derek's! And who would have predicted it would have been that way round? If anybody had ever asked *me* for a prediction, I would have put money on Jenny's judgement rather than Derek's, any day! And it wasn't just Jenny's judgement, was it? *I* was convinced David would make her an ideal husband, and so was Mary. The only dissenting voice, funnily enough, was Derek's! He *always* called David 'a creep' and a few other choice appellations which I would prefer not to commit to paper! Whether that was wisdom on Derek's part, or simply coincidence, we shall never know.

Later – 7 p.m.

Well, Pat was certainly right about the talking – we hardly paused for breath! And we were *very* glad of the scones! I can't remember when I last related to a stranger in that way, but I feel strongly that I have just made a friend for life. When Chris walked through the door, I saw a tall, rangy man with wiry iron-grey hair, and a weather-beaten, craggy sort of face. And the rapport was instantaneous, even though we come from such different disciplines. I only hope he enjoyed the afternoon as much as I did – even though I can hardly doubt it. He certainly seemed very much at home, and very enthusiastic about every topic we touched on – which were pretty wide-ranging! He and Pat knew each other by sight, although they had never been 'formally introduced', and he has evidently met Derek briefly, in passing. He is just about the same age as I am, and married to a wife of whom he seems unreservedly fond – he says they were childhood sweethearts who could now give Derby and Joan a run for their money! Nice. His wife's name is Helen, and she sounds like a lovely person, with interests very similar to Mary's – she, also, is a non-stop knitter, an enthusiastic needlewoman, and a wonderful cook. She is also an amateur water-colour artist, and quite involved in Chris's work in the museum. Chris says they saw us at the Village Fete, and would have liked to come over and introduce themselves, but were afraid we might think them too pushy! I told him I wished they had, and we made tentative arrangements for the four of us to get together at his house on Sunday afternoon, so the women can get to know each other as well. I'm looking forward to it. What with the party tomorrow, it's going to be a busy weekend, and should keep me from getting depressed again, whatever the weather. Actually, the forecast is good for tomorrow, so we're keeping our fingers crossed that the meteorologists have got it right for once.

Right – it sounds as if Derek and Pat have finished tucking the children up in bed, so I think I'll go and be sociable for a little while, then try for an early night so I can hopefully be in good form for the weekend. Mary and Jenny aren't coming until lunchtime tomorrow, because of collecting assorted 'ancestors', but I was so encouraged by my meeting with Chris that I feel more positive than I have for quite some time, and I don't resent Mary not being here nearly as much as I had dreaded. I have, after all, got plenty to look forward to.

Monday, 17th June

Well, that was *quite* a weekend – I certainly can't complain about boredom, whatever else! And I think writing a report of it is going to keep me out of mischief for quite a while. Let's see if I can keep it chronological and coherent . . .

The first incident was a phone-call from Mary, about ten o'clock on Saturday morning. She said, "Now, George – I thought I better ring and warn you, because I don't want you going off the deep end and upsetting Jenny – she's quite upset enough already! I didn't want to tell you before, because I know you of old, but – David insisted on taking Elizabeth this weekend, even though he knows perfectly well, of course, that it is Jenny's birthday celebration. Before you go into orbit – he *is* bringing her to the party; but that means that we have to have him and Wanda there as well. And I want both you and Derek to *behave yourselves* – or else! It's not what any of us would *choose*, but it's what we're stuck with, so let's try to make it as easy as we can for Jenny *and* poor little Elizabeth. I want you to promise me, George, that you will be on your *very best behaviour*. Do I have your word?"

What could I possibly say? But I was – and am! – *furious* with David Morris! Oh, we know he 'has his rights' – he reminds us of them often enough - *when* it suits him! He's ignored his daughter for months, as far as I'm aware, but he has to have her for the weekend of her mother's birthday! There is absolutely no doubt - he does it deliberately, to cause as much grief as possible. But I did take Mary's point about not upsetting Jenny any more – though I can't quite see why I should be supposed to need a *lecture* about it! *Derek* might be suspected of being liable to cause a fracas in the middle of a party and in front of all our guests, but I hardly think that *I* needed instruction in the matter. I hope my *manners*, if nothing else, would have been quite sufficient to prevent me from committing any such solecisms! Especially with David's parents present – Charles and Elspeth already feel quite badly enough about the whole situation, without that! They are such a *nice* couple, and some of our oldest friends – you would have to go a long way to find two more satisfactory people. How they came to have a son like David must be one of the Great Mysteries of the Universe! *I* wouldn't want to upset them for the world. David can do an impressive job of that all on his own, without any help from *me*!

When I passed the news on to *my* son, I *swear* there was smoke coming out of his ears! I had better not even *try* to report his comments. Luckily, Pat found plenty of jobs to keep him busy, and finally managed to extort a Promise of Good Behaviour from him. Personally, I think it was unnecessary – he is actually very careful of Jenny's feelings, and whilst, of course, he was very angry on her behalf, he knew as well as the rest of us that having a go at David would do more harm than good. But it had already managed to pour a dollop of cold water on our parade, even though the *weather* had decided to relent. It was cloudy and a little doubtful-looking first thing, but as the morning progressed the cloud broke up, and by lunchtime the sun was back in all its splendour. So we were able to set everything up outside with easy minds – even if I, personally, didn't actually do more than sit and watch the rest of them fetching and carrying.

Jenny arrived first, with Mum and Dad. They sat down with me on the garden hammocks, while Jenny gave me a quick kiss then went off to help Pat with the food and drinks. Mum and Dad are actually looking very well – Dad seems to have completely recovered from that nasty bronchial infection he suffered for most of the winter, and looks as though he has put back the weight he lost. Mum was her usual controlled self – she took out her knitting as soon as she sat down, and sat peggling away while still managing to keep a sharp eye on everything that was going on. She gave me quite a catechism about my own state of health, but seemed reasonably satisfied that I really am on the mend. It wasn't long before Mary arrived with Dennis, Kathleen and Flora in tow, so we were quite a group of 'oldsters', even if Mary and I are not of the same generation as the other five. Derek came bearing a huge tray of cups of tea for us all and, after greeting all his illustrious forebears, proceeded to put me on the spot by saying, "Mum – will you please keep an eye on the Old Fossil? We've invited Dan – you know, the chap who does all the work around the place? 'Dan, Dan, the Handyman', right? Only Dad's got a real down on him, and I had an awful job persuading Dan that he really would be welcome. If Dad goes and upsets him, I am **not** going to be very happy! Just ride herd on him for me – all right?"

Oh, thank you, Son of Mine! Off he waltzed, leaving my assorted relatives looking at me accusingly!

"George!" said Mary reproachfully, "What on earth can you possibly have against that young man? I mean – look what a difference he's made to this place! I wouldn't have thought anybody could have knocked it into shape in the time!"

I would have done better **not** to try to explain. Every word I said only made it worse - nobody understood in the slightest. Mum finally clinched the matter by fixing me with a piercing stare over the top of her spectacles and saying sternly, "George – how many times have I told you about these **pets** you take? It really is time you stopped acting like a pompous, disapproving old man! You always did **chunter**, even when you were only about six years old! I hoped you would have grown out of it by now!"

Is there an answer to a speech like that?!!! If there is, **I** have never been able to come up with it! I decided that silence was most definitely the wisest form of valour, and ignominiously withdrew from the fray. Call me craven if you will, but I know when I am overmatched. And I will only be 70 next birthday!

Fortunately, by then the other guests were arriving, and took my family's minds off me. There were some canvas chairs by the hammocks, so Charles and Elspeth joined our merry band – most of the others were a generation or two younger, with quite a few pre-teen children, so things soon became fairly lively and quite noisy. It's at times like that that it's an advantage to have no near neighbours! Dan arrived, looking very clean and 'smart-but-casual' in navy slacks and a pale-blue short-sleeved shirt, to be greeted ecstatically by the children, most of whom he seemed to know by name. Derek fielded him and brought him over to introduce him to our group – giving **me** warning looks! Dan looked a little embarrassed – perhaps he was overwhelmed by the sheer weight of numbers and the blatant curiosity of all these 'old folk'! He said, "Sir!" and "Ma'am" as Derek made the introductions. His manners are charming, if strangely dated! Derek insisted on pulling him up a chair, then shooting off to get him a drink, leaving Dan surrounded by a horde of children, all wanting his attention. Derek soon shooed them away when he got back, and Dan said with a rueful grin, "Heck – I feel some like that Pied Piper guy!" – which went down very well with the Oldsters! They all fell for the charm immediately, and Mum kept shooting me *very* strange glances!

It must have been about four o'clock when David and Wanda finally arrived with Elizabeth, who went racing over to give Jenny a big hug. Jenny was in the middle of a game with a group of other little girls, but Elizabeth evidently cried, "There's my Dan!" and launched herself at him like a guided missile! He is certainly popular, although quite *why* is still a mystery to *me*. All our young lady wanted was to cling round his neck, chattering excitedly – and I think we were all amused by his discomfiture. He seemed to feel that she ought to be paying her respects to her Revered Forebears, and was doing his best to make her notice us. Elizabeth, of course, who feels she can see us old fuddy-duddies any day of the week and twice on Sundays, twiddled her fingers carelessly in our direction and carried on noticing *him*! Then Kirstie arrived. She and Elizabeth always have had a little cousinly rivalry going, and she had no intention of letting Elizabeth have it all her own way. Before you know it, she's sitting on one of his knees, and Elizabeth has claimed the other, and both are competing for his undivided attention. Under those circumstances, it was quite funny – although Dan obviously wasn't totally happy about it, probably unsure of our reaction. Up until then, it was all quite entertaining. Then David wandered over 'to say hello'. I think most of us did speak, albeit not exactly overenthusiastically, although I could swear Flora actually said "Hmmmmph!" quite loudly. I only hope Charles and Elspeth didn't hear her, even though they would probably understand if they did! None of us made any move to introduce him to Dan, so David took it upon himself. Dan obviously felt at somewhat of a disadvantage, wearing not only David's daughter but Kirstie as well. He managed to shake hands with David somehow, and David only pulled up a chair next to him and sat with us, apparently completely at ease, even though the atmosphere had suddenly turned decidedly chilly. He then went into his well-practised 'needling routine', with that awful smug smile on his face. On the surface it was all perfectly 'friendly'– David Morris has a real talent for making innocuous-sounding remarks, which are actually insulting and offensive as hell. Dan was obviously in no doubt that he was being 'got at', but managed to answer pleasantly, trying to avoid a scene and – not knowing David – probably hoping that if he didn't bite,

David would get bored and give it up. Fat chance! Mary, Mum and Elspeth did their valiant best to come up with various topics of conversation, but David in that mood takes some stopping. I can't remember now exactly how it came up, or exactly how he phrased it, but David suddenly came out with some snide remark about Dan's 'obvious liking for little girls'! Oh – my – God. There was absolutely no mistaking his implication, and that was obviously one step too far – no way was Dan simply going to let *that* one go. But none of us was sure just what he might *do* about it. *We* had all simply frozen in horror. I feel now I should have done *something*, but – at the time – I had simply no idea what. Dan went rigid, then stood up and handed the little girls over to Mary. "Go to your Grandma, sweethearts," he said quietly, turning his back full on David. Then, looking around our motionless little group, he said, "It has been fierce privilege for me to meet you-all. Will you please excuse me, I have to leave now." And he turned and walked away. Elizabeth tried to follow him, but Mary held her back saying, "You stay with me, love."

"Oh no, *Nanny!*" sneered David (He knows how much she hates being called 'Nanny'!) "She's coming with me. Come on, Lizzie – we're leaving now."

Elizabeth, quite naturally, did not want to go. They hadn't been there more than ten or fifteen minutes! So David grabbed the poor kid by the arm and began to drag her away, screaming. We all tried to persuade him to change his mind – Elspeth wound up in tears herself, and Charles got very angry, but none of it did the slightest bit of good. Jenny – who had evidently been in the kitchen doing some first-aid on little Olivia's grazed knee – heard Elizabeth screaming, and came running over to see what was going on. *She* knew better than to bother arguing with him, but did her best to comfort Elizabeth, cuddling her and saying quietly, "Go with Daddy, sweetheart. I'll see you tomorrow evening. Run along now . . . "

When Elizabeth still resisted, David picked her up and carried her bodily away, collecting Wanda – who was chatting pleasantly to some of Pat's friends – as he passed. She didn't look too pleased herself, but has probably learned that arguing with David in that mood is pointless. I *never* expected to say this about the woman who blatantly had an affair with Jenny's husband almost throughout their marriage, but – I *almost* felt sorry for her! We could still hear poor little Elizabeth screaming as they drove away.

65

Luckily, Derek had been otherwise occupied, and didn't get in on the act until after David had left, so we *didn't* have to send for an ambulance, and Derek is *not* facing a charge of G.B.H. He was pretty livid, but when he saw Jenny's strained face he managed to control his anger and worked hard to revive the party spirit. Everybody did their best, but it was forced and brittle, and I think people departed earlier than they otherwise would have done. It has left a very bad taste, and a mood of depression. What can we *do* about it? David *does* have legal rights of 'access', whether he deserves them or not. Biologically he *is* the child's father. But he is one darned nasty piece of work, and on *this* issue I can sympathise with Derek's yearning for slaughter. But it wouldn't solve anything, would it? It would only put Derek in the wrong. And Jenny swears David only takes it out on *Elizabeth* if anybody crosses him. She is convinced that he has no real desire to spend time with his daughter at all, but takes her simply to spite Jenny and the rest of us; and I am sure she is right. I feel a real fool for encouraging Jenny to marry him, but I was certain that he would make her an ideal husband. He is good-looking, intelligent, witty, and doing really well in his profession; and having known his family so well for so long, we had absolutely no reason to suppose he was so different from the rest of them. He made a very good job of disguising the fact until after the wedding! Although – knowing him as I know him now, I can't help wondering what on earth made him want to marry somebody like Jenny. If *Wanda* is what he really wants in a woman, you would have a job to find a *less* likely candidate than our Jenny!

I must admit, though, that the restraint that *Dan* showed has put him up several notches in *my* estimation. That was a really awkward situation, and I can't see how else he could have ended it. Once David starts that routine, none of us have ever found the way to make him stop. But Dan didn't dignify that remark with any attempt at an answer, but simply left quietly; and we all felt that he walked away with all the honours. There was absolutely no excuse for David to be so blatantly offensive – he had only just *met* Dan. I cannot help feeling there were two reasons for it – firstly, he wanted, purely and simply, to spoil the party for all of us; and secondly, Elizabeth obviously thinks the world of Dan.

When Derek had finally got over his rage enough to realise that Dan was missing, he initially wanted to blame *me*! Luckily, there were plenty of witnesses to vouch for my complete innocence, and Derek was not too reluctant to have another grievance against David, so I did get an apology – which I graciously accepted! Although, even now, I can't help feeling rather guilty that I didn't manage to defuse that situation before it blew up in such a nasty way. I'm still not sure just what I could have done to prevent it, but I knew David Morris meant trouble, and I *should* have been able to able to step in *somehow* and spike his guns. Instead, I sat there like a ninny and let him have it all his own way. I feel *pathetic*!

Dan actually phoned about nine on Saturday evening – to *apologise*! He told Pat, who answered the phone, that he was 'real sorry for spoiling our party – he *knew* he shouldn't have come'!! Pat assured him that it was in *no* way his fault, and none of us would dream of blaming *him*, but he replied that he knew David was 'gunning for him' and should have 'up and left' before it got to that stage – 'in front of all of them elderly ladies, an' all!' He obviously doesn't know *our* 'elderly ladies' very well, does he?! It would take an *awful* lot more than that to shock Mum or Kathleen, and as for Flora . . . ! *Her* verdict was that, while she was naturally very sorry for Jenny and Elizabeth, it was the most 'enlivening' display she had witnessed for ages! I think she really enjoyed every minute of it, the wicked old bird! But – long may she reign, eh? It'd take more than David Morris to faze *her*!

Jenny looked pale, but managed a nice job of disguising just how upset she was. She went back to organising the children's games, then later did more than her share of clearing up. We all wanted her to sit down and put her feet up, but she insisted that she was 'fine' and quite capable of driving Mum and Dad home as previously arranged. They agreed, but suggested that she pack a few things and stay with them overnight, which we all thought was a good idea. I wasn't at all happy to think of her driving back through those dark lanes all on her own, late at night. So she took an overnight bag, and off they went, while Derek drove Dennis, Kathleen and Flora home.

So Saturday turned out to be *quite* a day! Actually, apart from that one contretemps, everything went very well. The weather was kind, and I did enjoy seeing so many of the people whose company I have missed recently. Pauline and Roger were there – both as quiet and unobtrusive as ever, but Paula had other fish to fry, and didn't honour us with her presence. I can understand it. There would have been no-one else there anywhere near her own age. I suppose we are going to have to get used to it – she is bound to be branching out on her own from now on.

I was absolutely shattered by bedtime, and not at all sorry to turn in. But Mary was with me, and somehow her presence always makes almost anything all right. She insisted that any 'post mortem' on the party could wait until the next day, and I dropped off in no time and slept like a log.

Later – 1.45 p.m.

Well – writing up Saturday occupied the whole morning! Now we have just had lunch, and I can settle down again to record Sunday – *if* I can stay awake long enough, that is!

I think we were all feeling a little 'après party', and Derek was still fuming about David all through breakfast. Then Mary said quietly, "Derek – I never thought you took after your father much in anything, but I have to admit you are beginning to *chunter* in just the same way! Do give it a rest, dear!" ***That*** shut him up in a hurry, although I'm not quite sure just where everybody gets the idea that *I* carry on like that! But it's one of these family fallacies that will not seem to fade away, no matter what the evidence to the contrary. I suppose I'm stuck with it. I wonder, though – *is* there actually such a word? I'm jolly well going to go and see if Pat and Derek have got a dictionary in the house!

They have – and, just as I suspected, there is ***no*** listing for 'chunter'! The nearest is 'chunder' which, it appears, is Australian or New Zealand slang, meaning 'to vomit'! Charming! While I was at it, I remembered to look up 'rusticity', and that *is* a proper word. I feel ridiculously smug, and somehow vindicated – although I'm not quite sure why! It doesn't really *change* anything, does it?

I asked Derek whether he had spoken to Dan about moving into the cottage, and he said, "Didn't have chance! I was hoping to talk to him later, when things had settled down a bit, but he'd left by then. Still – no doubt he'll be round before too long – if that ***** Morris hasn't put him off us for good, that is . . . OK, OK, Mum! I'm not going to say another word!"

Chris Wainwright phoned, as agreed, about eleven o'clock, and Mary was quite happy to go along with our proposed visit. He offered to come and pick us up, but Mary insisted she was quite capable of driving, so he gave us directions to his cottage and we promised we would be with them just after two, and stay for tea.

Jenny got back in plenty of time for lunch, still doing a nice job of camouflaging her feelings. She and Derek may be twins, but they are different in almost every way. I suppose it wouldn't help much if she did let off steam like Derek does, but sometimes I wish she wouldn't control herself *quite* so rigidly. She helped Pat with the washing-up after lunch, but then declared that, as she and Mary both had their own cars, she was going to head on home and get a few jobs done before Elizabeth was due back about 6.30. She left at the same time as Mary and I were heading off to the Wainwrights, and managed to smile very convincingly as she hugged and kissed me goodbye. How I *wish* I had some answers to offer her! But it's beyond my control, I'm afraid, so I tried to put it out of my mind and concentrate on being sociable.

Chris and Helen live on the far side of the village. Theirs is the last house before the open countryside begins, and is several hundred yards from its nearest neighbour on the village side. It is a delightful house, built of mellow Cotswold stone, with a well-kept thatched roof and lattice-paned windows. It goes by the charming name of "Chatterbrook Cottage", and somehow looks as though it belongs in exactly that location. The gardens are nicely screened by flowering shrubs, and filled with an absolute riot of hollyhocks, lupins and delphiniums. Chris was standing at the gate to greet us, and Helen came out when he called to tell her we had arrived. She is a delicately-built five-foot-nothing – tiny beside her tall husband – and so dainty she reminded me of a Dresden shepherdess. Her hair is the most beautiful silver, cut fairly short in loose curls, which I would imagine are natural. She was simply dressed in a sleeveless summer frock, the blue of which accentuated the blue of her eyes. Fortunately, her disposition seems to be as beautiful as her appearance – she has a quiet, grave charm, and she talks willingly and intelligently without in any way trying to dominate the conversation – and she is obviously as devoted to her husband as he is to her. They really are a lovely couple, and Mary is as delighted with them as I am.

They offered us a cup of tea or a cold drink, but we had not long finished lunch, so went for a tour of their property instead. The inside of the cottage is just as meticulously kept as the outside, slightly dim after the bright sunshine outside, but glowing with rich colours and glinting with the odd gleam of brass or pewter. It is actually quite a large property. The downstairs comprises a big lounge, a 'den' which Chris uses as an office and study, a room devoted to Helen's needlework, a modern conservatory which has been cleverly blended in to match the character of the place, a dining-room and a huge old kitchen, not to mention a downstairs cloakroom and the hall, filled with the somnolent ticking of a grandfather-clock. We didn't go upstairs, but it obviously covers the same area, except for the conservatory.

We then went outside to relax on the patio, which has the most wonderful view, as the land behind the cottage dips away into a valley, then rises in tree-clad ridges to the skyline. The garden is quite large, and Helen has a row of beehives at the bottom, so the whole place is a-hum with the drone of insect wings. We also discovered the reason for the name of the cottage – there is a little brook with a stony bed, which flows from over the road, across the garden, and away down the slope into the valley. Helen told us that the place was originally called "Stanbeck", meaning a stony stream in a valley, but the noise of the water chattering over the stones was so cheerful and friendly that she began to call it 'the Chatterbrook', and swears that the sound helped to keep her from feeling too lonely when Chris was away on his long trips. Finally, they changed the name of the cottage accordingly. I like it.

"Speaking of names," said Mary, "do you – as locals – know why the village is called **Gorsey** Hallowell? I know the 'Hallowell' part is for the 'holy well' – which we **must** get round to visiting one of these days, George! – but this whole area seems almost totally devoid of gorse-bushes! Maybe it has some other derivation?"

"Actually," said Helen, leaning forward eagerly, "we've been doing quite a lot of research, recently, into the local place names. And they are really **very** interesting. 'Gorsey' evidently has nothing whatever to do with gorse-bushes – it is really a corruption of 'De Coursey'. A family called 'De Coursey' came here in early Norman times, and laid claim to the land on which the holy well stands. Over the years, the name 'De Coursey's Holy Well' has turned into 'Gorsey Hallowell'. Have you ever been into our little church, Mary? There are a couple of De Coursey graves in there, with elaborate monuments. The De Courseys actually paid for the building of the church. There was an old wooden Saxon building on the site before that, but it was replaced by the stone church back in 1177, I think it was."

I had noticed the graves, and read the inscriptions, but I had not for a moment connected 'De Coursey' with the name of the village!

"That *is* interesting!" cried Mary. "I hadn't really appreciated what an *old* village this must be. Is it in the Doomsday Book?"

Chris assured her that it was, and went on to tell us that he is convinced that there has been human occupation on the site for thousands of years, well back into prehistory. It seems that whilst it is not generally accepted by the archaeological experts, *he* is sure that the holy well has actually been a sacred place since the days when Stonehenge was being built! They both seemed a little embarrassed when they went on to confess that the site of the Holy Well is somewhat run-down these days, and is the main haunt of the local yobs, who are not likely to win many prizes for 'Keeping Britain Tidy'! It evidently is no longer worth visiting, which seems an awful shame.

Anyway, that aside, we were both so fascinated by Chris's revelations that Helen suggested that we might like to take a drive over to Roddenhill and have a look at some of the exhibits in the Museum. Chris was a little embarrassed – said he was sure we didn't want to spend our Sunday afternoon that way. But when Mary assured him that *we* would thoroughly enjoy it but would quite understand if *he* didn't want to spend his weekend at the place, he soon changed his tune and became quite enthusiastic. He has a large four-wheel-drive vehicle, so we all piled aboard – I in the front with Chris and the two women in the back – and off we went.

Roddenhill is quite a large village – quite a bit bigger than Gorsey Hallowell. The Museum fronts on to a cobbled square around a village green, with a pond and some ducks in the middle. It is an old building, with floorboards that are anything but level, and I really had to watch my step. I was glad of Mary holding tightly on to my arm! Chris apologised, and explained that money is tight – the Parish Council is funding the Museum project, in the hope that it may help to attract tourists. Personally, I think it may be just a little off the beaten track, and will have a job to compete with nearby Stratford and the well-known attractions of the Cotswolds, but I suppose we shouldn't be negative. It was absolutely fascinating anyway, and any tourists who *do* find their accidental way there are in for a treat. Chris is doing a wonderful job, although I can't help suspecting that Helen's artistic skills lie behind the success of the dioramas. They are trying to follow the history of the area, right from the very earliest times to the present day flora and fauna and geographical features, with historical events and folklore adding human interest. Chris declares there is still an awful lot to do, and still an awful lot of research in the pipeline, but I have a feeling he would be very much at a loose end if that were *not* the case – he is obviously having the time of his life! Mary enjoyed the tour just as much as I did, and we are both keen to go again – there was so much to see, it was difficult to take it all in and digest it in one visit.

We learned on the way home that Chris actually spent most of his working life excavating a Mayan site in the jungles of Central America! He said, "What an idiot I was! I was born and brought up in this village, you know, but when I was young I couldn't wait to get away! If Helen hadn't loved the place so much, I probably never would have come back here – it always seemed deadly dull, and I craved the exotic. So poor old Helen had the slog of bringing the kids up more or less by herself all those years, while I messed around trying to make sense of an alien culture. Then, all of a sudden, about twelve years ago, I began to wonder what on earth I was doing, when my own home was right on top of an even older site – although I didn't realise then just *how* old! The history of my own native land was a closed book to me, and I still have a lot to learn about Saxon, Romano-British, Celtic and pre-Celtic history. So I came back, and my only regret now is that it took me so long to acquire a bit of sense! There's more than enough here to keep me occupied for as long as I can carry on, and at least we can spend a bit of time together, at last."

Mary enquired about their children, and almost wound up regretting she had asked! It seems they had a son and a daughter – Alan and Melissa. Alan would have been about a year older than Derek and Jenny. He trained as a pilot in the R.A.F., but just after he got his 'wings', his plane crashed on take-off and he was killed instantly. What can you say? Melissa is 32, and married with two small daughters, but she and her husband are marine biologists, and they are living in Australia where they are studying the Great Barrier Reef! Helen and Chris went out to visit three years ago, but haven't seen them since. So it's a good job they have got an absorbing interest to keep them occupied, isn't it?

Helen fed us a lovely tea, and we sat companionably on the patio until we really had to make a reluctant move. Mary had to drop me at Manor Farm, then still had the journey home, so we didn't stay too late, even though none of us were in a hurry for the visit to end. It was a really pleasant afternoon, and I feel sure we have begun some lasting friendships. Mary and Helen have arranged to phone each other during the week, and Chris has promised to call for me on Thursday, and take me to see some of the interesting places in the locality – weather permitting. I am very much looking forward to it.

Now my poor hand is almost falling off from all this writing, and I am going to call it a day.

Tuesday, 18th June

Well, yesterday was a really quiet day – all I did was make notes about our exciting weekend. I had a good rest, and though I still feel just a little lethargic I am looking forward eagerly to going out with Chris tomorrow. I'm keeping my fingers crossed about the weather – today there is quite a lot of cloud, interspersed with bright sunshine, and quite a sharp little breeze. Pat has put my chair in a sheltered nook, with strict instructions to come inside if I feel in the least chilled, but I'm warm enough at the moment. I feel somehow *stifled* inside, these days, and I prefer to be out in the fresh air.

I did so much writing yesterday that I didn't get round to mentioning that when Mary phoned to report that she had arrived home safely, I asked her if David had brought Elizabeth back in good shape, and she just said yes, Elizabeth was fast asleep in bed. But that was obviously the 'softened' version for *my* consumption! Pat phoned yesterday evening to see how Jenny and Elizabeth were feeling after all the upset, and I couldn't help overhearing what she told Derek while they were washing-up. Derek's reaction was hardly *quiet*! The arrangement has always been that David brings Elizabeth back by half-past six, so Jenny can get her settled down and into bed in reasonable time, and nothing had been said to the contrary on this occasion. Jenny, as I mentioned, left here early in the afternoon, so was back in plenty of time, but 6.30 came and went, and there was no sign of David's car, and no word from David. Poor Jenny was all on her own, going quietly demented and, quite

73

naturally, imagining the worst. David refuses to have seatbelts fitted in the back of his car, and he has often been heard to boast that consumption of alcohol never affects *his* driving! So Jenny's imagination must have been running riot – I know *mine* would have been! They didn't finally turn up until nearly eight o'clock! By that time, of course, Elizabeth was overtired, and past her normal bedtime, so she was fractious and non-co-operative, and getting her bathed and ready for bed was not easy. And she had school the following morning. She is evidently still really miserable, but refuses to say anything about the weekend or what went on with David, and Jenny is – wisely, I think – not forcing it. But – *what* a damn' set-up, eh?! It's all right for the people who *make* these rulings – *they* don't have to live with the consequences! Jenny did have a word with Amy Russell, her solicitor, a few months ago to see if there was anything that could be done about this drinking-and-driving carry-on. But the police have never stopped David when he has been driving while over the legal limit, and he has, so far, managed to avoid accidents, so it is Jenny's word against his, and nothing can be done *before* the event. If he ever does have an accident because he is intoxicated, and injures or kills Elizabeth, then Jenny can be sure that he will suffer the full penalties under The Law! And Jenny has to hand that innocent little girl over to him, theoretically every other weekend! Luckily, in practice, it doesn't work out quite that often. David pleads 'pressure of work' and 'travelling out of the country' to explain why he doesn't avail himself of the pleasure of his daughter's company more often. Oh – *and*, of course, he is entitled to take her for four weeks in the summer. Jenny wants to make plans to go to the seaside with her friend Karen and her family, but David never will pin things down until the very last minute. Elizabeth is already asking whether they can go with Auntie Karen and Uncle Clive, and poor old Jenny can't give her a straight answer. It would do them both a lot of good – but what does David care? He does it on purpose, I know he does. I mean, even his own *parents* take Jenny's part in this – doesn't say much for him, does it?! Unfortunately, none of us have any bright ideas, or any influence over David Morris, so we shall simply have to await his pleasure.

There has been so much else going on these last few days that I haven't had much chance even to think about my strange experience on Thursday. (*Was* it Thursday? Oh well – whenever!) But, although I now feel a little distanced from it, and the impact has receded a little, it is still there, like a nasty little undercurrent. I keep having this niggling little thought, quite against my will – Thomas Hillyer's son, Arthur, was about the same age as that little boy. And, now I come to think of it, there was something very *dated* about the child. I didn't notice it consciously – but the child's clothing did look more like the sorts of things *I* would have worn at that age than the clothes my grandchildren wear. He was wearing a very grubby shirt – but a button-up-the-front cotton shirt, not a tee-shirt with writing and pictures all over it. He had on – I am almost sure – a pair of grey-flannel shorts, but they were down to his knees, not the short-shorts of today. And I could almost swear his shoes were battered brown leather lace-ups, not trainers or sneakers or whatever-you-call-em, and that his baggy socks needed *garters* – which I haven't seen for years! The socks our kids wear now stay up without such dated contrivances.

I feel almost a traitor to the Cause of Rational Thinking even to *allow* these thoughts; but then I remind myself that I may do more good if I examine the issue thoroughly and try to *prove* to myself that such a thing is impossible. So as soon as I can get her alone, I am going to ask Mabel whether there are any more photographs of the Hillyer family up in the attic. And – just in case there are – I had better make a record of my recollections of the boy's appearance, so I can't doubt whether I am making my own memory fit the facts. Now, let's see – as I believe I said before, he was about five or six years old, and of about average height for a child of that age. He had a roundish face, and rather sandy hair – he had the strange 'bleached' look of people with fair eyebrows and eyelashes. His hair was cut in a 'short-back-and-sides', but with longish 'bangs' hanging over his forehead. It was fine hair, quite straight, and looked as if it could do with a wash. His eyes were a sort of hazel, I think – although, if there *is* a photo of Arthur Hillyer, it will be in black-and-white, not colour! Even so, I'm sure I would recognise the face if I *did* see it – or not, as the case may be!

I think Mabel must have heard me – she came out with the washing just as I was writing that, and when she finished pegging the clothes up on the line, she came over to ask if I would like a cup of tea or coffee. I told her a cup of coffee would go down a treat, and she came back a few moments later with not only the coffee but a plate of biscuits as well! When I asked her about the photograph, she looked worried – as I said before, she is pretty sharp, and she obviously wondered why on earth I would want photographs of a long-dead family of whom I had never met a single member. But she didn't ask – just pursed up her lips and pondered for a few moments.

"Well, Sir," she said at last, "there's a whole stack of albums up there, all full of photos. She was a right one for photos, was Mrs. Jeffries! But I can't rightly say if she had any of the Hillyers, other than that of old Tom, as I gave you before. But – I'll tell you what . . . I'm just off to have a dust around upstairs, and I'll have a quick look in the attic while I'm up there, if you like. If I do find any, maybe I could put them in the top drawer of your bedside cabinet?"

I told her that would be perfect, and thanked her for her trouble. She obviously realised without me telling her that it would be best if nobody else knew about it. But she was still looking worried as she left me. I must admit, I don't much enjoy being sneaky, myself, but at this stage there is no point in involving anyone else. As far as Pat and Derek are concerned, things seem to have quietened down again since the incident with the dog – I still haven't told anyone about my 'sighting' of the boy, *if* that is what it was! And I don't **intend** to, unless it is absolutely unavoidable!

Later – 8 p.m.

I wasn't planning to write any more today – my hand was still a little sore after yesterday's marathon. But something so horrible – so totally incomprehensible – has happened that I simply **have** to try to make some sort of sense of it. Just as we were sitting down to lunch, Pat got a phone call from the school, asking her if she would come and pick up Kirstie, who seemed unwell. Naturally, she dashed off at once, insisting that Mabel and Kyle and I carried on with our lunch. I wasn't too worried – at that sort of age, kids seem to come down with all sorts of minor ailments. It was quite a while before Pat and Kirstie arrived back – Pat had called in at the doctor's surgery on the way home, and – even though it was out of her usual surgery hours – Dr. Beckett very kindly agreed to give Kirstie a check-over, saying it would probably save her getting called out tonight. Sensible woman! Obviously, as a village doctor, she has a rather different attitude from what I'm used to in the city! Anyway – she couldn't find anything drastically wrong: the child's temperature was normal, and her chest was clear, even though her pulse-rate was slightly raised. But Kirstie was very pale, and obviously feeling quite unwell – she was on the verge of tears, and had been unable to eat any of her lunch. She still insisted she wasn't hungry, and all she seemed to want was for Pat to cuddle her tight. Mabel cleared the table and washed up the lunch things, and I took Kyle out into the garden, where I did my best to occupy him with toy cars, soldiers, Lego bricks – anything! But he's a lively little rascal, and has a very short attention span! It was darned hard work, and I was soon exhausted, which made me feel *useless* again. At his age, some children are still taking afternoon-naps, but our young rapscallion has more than enough energy to see him right through to bedtime and some-times beyond. But what can you expect – his father was *just* the same! Any-way, I determinedly struggled on, until Mabel very kindly came out and offered to take him for a trip down the meadow on his toy tractor, which was actually a great relief. I went inside to see how Pat was getting on. Kirstie had finally dropped off to sleep, and Pat was just laying her down on the couch in the living-room. The child was still pale, her forehead was damp with beads of sweat, and she was restless even in her sleep. Pat was just about to ring around her friends, to see if one of them could pick Kurt up from school and keep him until Derek could collect him, but everybody she tried seemed to be out, and none of them answered their phones. I said, "Don't worry, love – I'll be here. If you take Kyle with you as usual, I can look after Kirstie for the little time you'll be away."

She accepted my offer gratefully, and made us a cup of tea. Mabel and Kyle returned from their 'ploughing', then Pat strapped Kyle into his car-seat and gave Mabel a lift down into the village on her way to the school. Almost as soon as they had left, Kirstie woke up. She asked for her mother, but I explained that Pat and Kyle had had to go and fetch Kurt, and she ac-cepted that quite happily, thank Goodness. But she climbed off the sofa, and came and sat on my knee, clinging tightly round my neck, and trem-bling slightly. I asked if she felt sick, and she shook her head. I asked if she had a pain in her tummy, and she didn't seem quite sure about that. So I said, "What *kind* of a pain, sweetheart?" She considered for quite some time, then she whispered, "Not really a *pain*, Grampy – a sort-of *cold* feel-ing. Grampy – I'm *scared*!"

I thought perhaps she was afraid she was really ill, and might have to go to hospital, or something like that. But she shook her head at my reassurances and said, "Not *that* kind of scared, Grampy!"

"*What* kind of scared then, sweetheart?" I asked.

"I mustn't talk about it," she whispered, hiding her face in my shoulder.

"Who says you mustn't?" I asked, quite concerned at this. "If we don't know, we can't do anything about it, can we? *We* won't let anybody hurt you, sweetheart – no matter what anyone says. Now, come on – *who* says you mustn't talk about it?"

"Daddy says there's no such thing," she whispered, with a tear running down her soft little cheek. "He says we mustn't be scared – but I can't *help* it, Grampy! You won't tell him, will you?"

Oh dear.

I *knew* Derek's attitude wasn't helping the children.

"You're still scared of the man with the axe?" I asked gently. "You can talk about it to *me*, lovey. And if Daddy knew you were *this* scared, he would talk to you about it, too. *And* Mummy."

"Aren't *you* frightened, Grampy?" she asked, looking me in the eye for the first time. "I think Mummy is, even if Daddy says there's nothing there. But – there *is*, Grampy. *Truly*, there is. Arthur says so. He wants us to help him, and Annie and his Mummy. Only I don't know *how*. And I'm too scared . . . " She hid her face in my shoulder again, and her thin little shoulders shook beneath my encircling arm. By this time, I knew exactly what she meant about the *cold* inside. I felt almost physically sick myself. But I had to try to get to the bottom of this – if possible before the rest of the family came home.

"Can you tell me about Arthur?" I asked. "Who is he?"

"He's the little boy who lives in the cottage," she whispered, so quietly I had to strain to hear her. "He's so *sad*, Grampy! And *he's* scared too. Grampy – can *you* help him? I told him you're a kind man, and really, really clever. He told me you could see him, not like Mummy and Daddy. *Did* you see him, Grampy?"

What on earth could I *say*? "I did see a little boy," I said carefully, "but I didn't know for sure that it was Arthur. He didn't stay long enough for me to ask him who he was. And he didn't speak to me. Does he talk to you?"

"Uh-huh," she said, nodding, and becoming visibly more relaxed. "He talks to all of us. Only we be just little kids, and we don't know what to do.

Even Kurt. Kurt always knows what to do, but not now. And Kyle is just a baby. But *you* could help him, Grampy – couldn't you, please?"

"I'm not sure, love," I said. "I don't even know just what sort of help Arthur needs. But I could *try*, if it would help you to feel better."

"I *do* feel better," she said, and she certainly looked it. "Shall I tell Arthur to come and talk to you, and tell you all about it?"

I cannot pretend I liked the sound of *that* one little bit! But the child was looking at me so trustingly, I hadn't the heart to let her down. "*If* you see him," I said, reluctantly. "But you are *not* to go looking for him – do you give me your word?"

"I promise, Grampy," she cried, clapping her hands.

"So – it's not *Arthur* you're scared of?" I asked, somewhat perplexed.

"Oh, *no* – not Arthur!" she assured me earnestly. "Arthur's just a poor little boy, even if he is dead. *He* wouldn't hurt us. Nor would Annie, even if she's a big girl. Nor would Arthur's Mummy. But we're all scared of Arthur's Daddy, and the . . . and the . . . " At this broke down in tears again, flinging her arms around my neck.

I just held her tightly for a few minutes, stroking her hair and assuring her it would be all right, and we wouldn't let anyone hurt her. But we needed to finish this, if at all possible, and time was running short. So I had to push a little. "You're scared of Arthur's Daddy – is he the man with the axe?" I asked, just to confirm the point, although I already knew the answer. She kept her face hidden, but nodded several times.

"And what *else*, Kirstie?" I persisted. "You said you were scared of Arthur's Daddy and the – what? Who? I need to *understand*, sweetheart, if you want me to help . . . "

It took a while, but in the end she whispered, so softly that I could hardly hear her, "The . . . the . . . Spider!" She was rigid with terror – and I have to confess I was not very happy myself! I felt as if someone had suddenly poured cold water down the back of my neck. I tried to elicit what she meant by 'the Spider' – somehow, the capital letter came across very strongly, and not for one moment could I manage to believe she meant any ordinary common, garden or house spider! But it was no good.

"I *can't*, Grampy!" she wailed, "*Please* – I can't! *Arthur* will tell you – I'm too *scared*!"

There really seemed no point in upsetting her any more, so I did my best to reassure her that she had been right to confide in me, and that I would do my very best to help Arthur – *if* he would come and tell me what exactly the problem was! She was pathetically grateful, and perked up remarkably quickly – which was a good job, because at that point we heard the others returning. I have never known Kurt to be able to do anything quietly, and he and Kyle together sound more like an attack by a Zulu war-party than two small boys coming home from school. But I was still so all-at-sea that I didn't feel ready to talk about it to anyone else, so I stipulated, "I think this had better be our secret, just for now," to which Kirstie solemnly agreed.

Pat was very relieved to see Kirstie so much recovered. "I'll leave them with you more often, Dad!" she joked, and went to start getting the dinner, leaving me feeling miserably guilty. What on *earth* was I thinking of, talking to the child like that? Derek would have a blue fit if he knew! And yet – what else could I have done? That little girl desperately needed to talk to *somebody*, and she obviously didn't think she would get the help she needed from her parents! *Not* that I am blaming them, mind! In this situation, we're *all* pretty much out of our depth! Derek is only passing on to his children what I instilled so firmly into *him*. Which is what my parents instilled into me – and theirs into them, I shouldn't wonder! Were we all wrong? I felt quite certain of it while I was talking to Kirstie, but now I'm not so sure. But – in that case – why am I so *scared*? Because I am. I am terrified of seeing that child again – although I honestly don't know why. Probably because I have no foundation for understanding what we are dealing with here. And probably because – if Kirstie has anything to do with it! – I shall have *another* child looking at me with trusting eyes, secure in the knowledge that I am a 'kind man and really, really clever', and know *exactly* what to do! What have I been and gone and got myself *into*? How am *I* meant to 'help' the child, for pity's sake?! What sort of 'help' does a dead child *need*? How does Kirstie know his name? How does she know that I saw him? If it really is the 'ghost' of Arthur Hillyer, why is he *here*, not in London where he died? All I have are questions, with not the glimmer of an answer in sight. Maybe things will be better in the morning. I hope.

At least Kirstie seems back to her normal self – she ate her tea, watched some television, then went to bed quite happily, and Pat and Derek are telling themselves complacently that it was 'just a chill' (?) or maybe 'something she ate'! I only hope I never have to disillusion them!

Later still – 11 p.m.

I did ***not*** intend to write any more tonight, but – whilst getting ready for bed, I opened the top drawer of my bedside cabinet to put my glasses away. And there was a photograph. It is one of those school photographs, in a beige cardboard surround, with 'Happy Christmas 1940' inscribed on it in flowing red script. It shows a picture of two children – a little boy and an older girl. On the back is written, in faded ink and careful, old-fashioned handwriting, 'To Mr. and Mrs. Jeffries. With Respectfull Best Wishes from Tom and Emily Hillyer, Anne and Arthur.'

The face of the boy is unmistakable. He matches exactly the description I wrote down earlier today. He is, without the shadow of a doubt, the boy I saw in the garden last week. He is also Arthur Hillyer, who was killed by a bomb in the London Blitz over forty years ago. And all my strongly-held beliefs of a lifetime – my whole world view – my whole philosophy – have been shattered all to flinders.

Wednesday, 19th June – 3 a.m.

It's a while since I've done one of these early morning writing sessions, but I woke up a few minutes ago and my brain is seething with so much overload that I know I am not going to be able to simply drop off to sleep again, even though I am quite tired after yesterday. Jotting down a few notes may help to keep me occupied, if nothing else.

I have just realised – much to my disgust! – that I have got my days muddled up again. It's not ***today*** I'm supposed to be going out with Chris, is it? It's tomorrow. Today I've got another physio. session. Damn and blast. I do ***not*** feel like it. For some reason – wishful thinking, maybe! – I had got it firmly fixed in my head that I was off out with Chris this morning. I could really have done with a complete break from the pressures here, and I'm sure it would have done me much more good than the physio. Still – needs must, eh? I suppose I had better be a good boy and do as I'm told.

Also, I do *not* relish the thought of spending all that time in the car with Pat. I feel ridiculously guilty – as if I have done something really *wrong* – and I don't want to face her. I'm afraid I will find it impossible to act normally, and she will *guess* what went on – but that is crazy. It's about the *last* thing she would guess! And – *what* did I do wrong? How *else* was I meant to handle a situation like that, for Pete's sake? The child *needed* to talk about it, and we are going to *have* to come up with some better explanation – we can't just keep telling her, 'There is no such thing'! It is obviously making things *worse*. *She* believes it. And if she can't turn to her family for help when she is literally terrified, what *is* she supposed to do? OK, we don't understand it. But *something* pretty weird is going on. I find it even *more* difficult to believe that Kirstie and I would have the same 'delusions' – not to mention, if she is to be believed, Kurt and Kyle as well! And how do we explain the photographs?

People all over the world, in all ages from earliest times to the present day, have reported 'ghostly' experiences. I still can't help feeling that an awful lot of it is bunkum, but perhaps there is more than a grain of truth there that I have hitherto been missing. I was never brought up with any religious conviction, and have never felt any need – or wish! – to believe in an 'afterlife'. In fact, I find the thought quite repulsive. I mean – let's suppose, just for argument's sake, that the 'ghosts' of the Hillyer family *are* still hanging around Manor Farm House, for some totally inexplicable reason: they must already have been here for over *forty years*, in the case of Emily and the two children, anyway. In all that time, little Arthur, at least, has got no older – he doesn't appear to have progressed in any way. He doesn't go to school – he hasn't even lost his baby-teeth – or their etheric equivalent, anyway! He will never grow up and learn to drive, or start to go out with girls, or get married, or have children, or any of the things that the passing years usually bring. He seems to be trapped in a timeless limbo. And – from what I saw, and what Kirstie said – he does *not* appear to be happy! He is 'sad' and 'scared'! Does he actually have to spend all Eternity as a child terrified of his own father?! What a prospect! *Why?* It doesn't seem to make any *sense*! But what other explanation will fit all of the facts – even if I limit those to the things I know of my own knowledge? I have racked my brains over and over, and I simply cannot come up with *one* rational explanation. I am, very reluctantly, beginning to feel that maybe I owe Mrs. McHugh an apology! (Or was it McGee? No – I've checked back through my notes, and it was McHugh.)

This is ridiculous. I am trying to stay calm and rational, but sitting here in bed all alone, I am getting indisputably jumpy. I keep expecting little Arthur – or, worse, his father! – to appear out of nowhere. I must somehow try to control my imagination, and approach the problem scientifically. But that is very much easier said than done! And I cannot quite decide why the thought is so terrifying anyw

Oh – my – God.

That was *not* my imagination! The two library books I borrowed were stacked one on top of the other, beside the lamp on my bedside cabinet. They are both hard-covered books. Suddenly, the top one fell on to the floor, and the bottom one flew open, and the pages began to turn. I was nowhere near them – well, certainly not close enough to have bumped them in any way! – and there was no-one else in the room. No *living* person, at least! The pages of the second book turned quite steadily and methodically for a while, as if someone was riffling through, looking for a particular passage. Then it stopped, leaving the book lying open, about halfway through.

I sat rigid in bed for I don't know how long, but nothing else happened. I forgot to mention that just before the first book fell, I suddenly felt cold – I am almost sure I remember seeing my breath smoking in the air. Now it is warm again – a warm June night. My heartbeat has calmed down now, and the hair on my head has stopped crawling, so I think that whoever or whatever it was has now departed. I am still afraid to move, but I am going to have to be strict with myself and try to find out what that was all about. I am going to have to look at that open book. Perhaps there is some sort of explanation there. Could it, conceivably, have been Arthur, trying to answer my questions in a way I didn't expect? Maybe manipulating the books was easier than actually appearing and trying to hold a conversation? Even so, I have always been led to believe that psychokinesis requires an awful lot of psychic energy – and I have never even *heard* of a display like *that*! Oh, this is *crazy*! What on earth am I babbling about?! I am going to put my pad and pen away, and jolly well read that book, starting with the page at which it is lying open!

Later – 4.40 a.m.

Thank Goodness it begins to get light so early at this time of year! Somehow, it is much easier to be rational – or brave? - in daylight. Once the sun started to brighten the window, I got up and opened the curtains. It is a beautiful morning, and the birds are singing all around, and my night-time horrors have been dispelled. (Well, *almost*, anyway!)

I have just read the chapter indicated, but I'm really not much the wiser! It was all about a local legend of how the De Coursey family was driven out of the area during the fourteenth century – by a curse, no less! It seems that there was a lot of resentment in the neighbourhood at the De Courseys claiming the site of the holy well, which was, at that time, a place of pilgrimage. Although the Christian Church had taken over the well some centuries before, they were having difficulty erasing memories of its pagan origins, and had decreed that the 'miracle cures' claimed for the well were more probably diabolical than holy! Now, that sound most improbable to *me*! It's not often the Church will pass up an opportunity like that! But that is what the writer claims, and who am I to dispute it? Evidently, there was still an ancient pagan cult in the vicinity, who called themselves 'The Guardians of the Well', and refused to accept anything to do with Christianity but kept right on worshipping the pagan goddess to whom they claimed the well belonged. And I think the Church was afraid that many of the supplicants who brought 'offerings', whilst nominally Christian, were still hedging their bets and offering up prayers to this old goddess. Anyway – along come the De Courseys and are granted the land by William the Conqueror. They, of course, are good Christians, and make big endowments to the Church – they evidently built several churches in the vicinity, not only at Gorsey Hallowell but at Roddenhill, Saltrap, Lobbesden and Copsford as well. They also built a small monastery near to the well, and the monks exercised much stricter control over the goings-on there. Relations between the De Courseys and the 'Guardians' seem to have been somewhat strained from the beginning – to put it mildly! And the problems got worse rather than better with the succeeding years and generations, until, some time in the thirteen-hundreds, things came to a head. The legend tells that the then lord, Gervase De Coursey, whilst out hunting one day, ravished the beautiful young granddaughter of the Chief Priestess of the 'Guardians'. Said Priestess then cursed the whole of the De Coursey lands with a horrendous curse called 'De Coursey's Bane' or the 'Soul Trap'. This seemed to mean that the soul of anyone who died in that area would be unable to pass on, either to heaven or to hell, but remain incarcerated there for Eternity! Charming. It also stated that anyone who was living in that area at the time of the curse, or any descendant of the De Courseys, would be drawn back, no matter where they actually died, so there was no escaping the curse by running away. After that, the whole area became plagued by 'apparitions and wandering spirits', until in – what was the date now? – fourteen hundred and something, I believe – the Chief Priestess of the 'Guardians' of the time was prevailed upon 'by the earnest entreaties of the local populace' to remove the curse, open the Soul Trap, and allow the enslaved souls to carry on with their interrupted journeys to another plane of existence!

What a load of mumbo-jumbo! And yet – somehow, this garbled, non-sensical story rings bells somewhere at the back of my head. I don't *believe* it. I *can't* believe it. But *something* very strange is going on. And there are some echoes of relevance somewhere.

I want, desperately, to believe that I *imagined* that episode with the books. Or dreamed it. But I simply can't manage it. And the top book was still on the floor this morning. Somehow, there are so many links – even if the threads are tangled along the way – that I really cannot credit that my *brain* is to blame for this whole rotten muddle! But I am having severe credibility problems, and I think I am probably going to have to stop trying so hard to squeeze some sense out of it, and simply leave things to brew for a while in my subconscious. There has to be an answer *some*where!

I am also feeling most uncomfortably 'overlooked'! Can I *really* be seen and heard by invisible beings, of whose presence I am mostly unaware? That is *not* a pleasant thought! And yet – what happened last night seemed in no way *malicious*. Just the opposite, in fact! It would seem that whoever or whatever manipulated the books was trying to be helpful, and to explain, albeit in a clumsy and obscure fashion, what is going on. If only that legend were a little less far-fetched! But I suppose it is just possible that the story has got distorted over the centuries, and any kernel of truth may be unrecognisable by now. I mean – we know that there *is* a very ancient holy well nearby. We know that there *was* a family called De Coursey living in the area after the Norman Conquest. And History tells us that there were *many* conflicts between the Christian Church and pagan religions. The part I find greatest difficulty with is, of course, the 'soul' angle. I have never truly been able to picture a 'soul' clearly, or to believe in the usual definitions by the Church, or by psychic mediums, etc. Perhaps the only way in which I am going to be able to get to grips with this aspect, is to think of a 'soul' as a discrete package of a personal 'life force' – pure 'energy'. Maybe 'energy' is a word with which I will find it easier to cope. No 'Supernatural' overtones!

I can hear Derek and Pat moving now, so I will pack up – I am absolutely gasping for a cup of tea! Not to mention some nice, normal, *human* companionship!

Later – 6.30 p.m.

Well, that did *not* turn out to be the ordinary, rather boring, day I was expecting! I never did get to my physio. appointment, but I think I have more or less stopped shaking now. I feel as if I will never be able to forget the events of today, they seem so indelibly imprinted in my brain, but perhaps I had better make a note of them anyway – just in case! No doubt I never will forget the broad outline, but the details could well fade away, and I cannot help feeling we may need every tiniest clue if we are ever to make sense of this utter lunacy.

However, *one* good thing has come out of it – my 'secret' is a secret no longer, so at least I can stop feeling guilty and so *alone*. I now have *plenty* of company, even though nobody is much wiser about what exactly is going on than *I* am. But I am waffling. If this account is to be of any value, I must try to be as clear and concise as possible. A simple chronological report will no doubt be the best way – *if* I can achieve such a thing out of the chaos!

It was lucky that Derek didn't leave the house at his usual time this morning. He was supposed to be going to inspect a site in Durham, and didn't expect to be back until Friday evening. He decided he might as well let the morning rush-hour traffic clear a little before he started out, but he was all ready to leave when Pat got back from taking the children to school. Dan had just arrived, and made a start on trimming the hedge between the front drive-way of the house and the garden of the cottage, so Derek went over to have a word with him when he carried his suitcase out to his car. They were still talking, very seriously, when Pat and I were leaving for the hospital, so we went over to say hello to one and goodbye to the other. Derek had just given Pat a hug and a kiss, and we were turning to go, when we were suddenly rooted to the spot by the most horrendous *screaming* I have ever heard in my life! It was obviously more than one voice, and it was accompanied by thunderous bangings and crashings, as if someone were frenziedly smashing furniture. For a moment, I think we were all too shocked to think straight, wondering what on *earth* could be going on. Then it became apparent that the noise was coming from *inside the cottage*! Pat blanched and clung to Derek, who quickly transferred her into my arms, saying, "Get her inside, Dad! And *stay* there! Dan – I'm going for the keys!" And off he raced.

I tried to obey his instructions and take Pat inside, but she refused to move. She was obviously terrified, but she had a really stubborn set to her mouth as she said, "*No*, Dad – I'm *staying*! I *have* to!"

I really didn't have the right – or the strength – to force her, so we were both still there when Derek got back. "I've told Mabel to call the police – *and* lock the doors!" he gasped. "You up for going in with me, Dan?"

"Let's go!" said Dan, already on his way.

I think Pat and I both felt the same – I badly did *not* want to go into that cottage; but I also knew I was going to. With one accord, still arm in arm, Pat and I followed after. We caught up with Dan and Derek at the front door – Derek was cursing as he fumbled with the keys, and Dan was peering through the front windows. "Can't *see* anything," he announced. Then he noticed us. "Sir," he said, "Mizz Hanson, Ma'am – best you go back to the house – no telling *what* might go down!"

"Dad – Pat – get *out* of here!" Derek concurred.

"If *you* go in there," stated Pat, in a voice I have never heard her use be-fore, "then *we* are coming too! I will *not* wait out here, wondering – besides, you might need us!"

I am sure all this happened in a lot less than the time it has taken to tell, and all the while, the awful screaming and banging had continued. Suddenly it stopped as abruptly as it had started, and silence rushed in to take its place.

We all looked around at each other, listening intently. No sound at all came from inside the cottage. Finally, Derek made an obvious effort, and tried again to find the right key.

"Wait for the police, Derek," Pat pleaded. "It doesn't sound as if you can help anybody *now* . . . "

"We can't *know* that, Pat," he replied, "and I'd never *forgive* myself if . . . ah! That's the one!" He inserted a key, the front door suddenly swung open and – God, *how* can I describe it? I felt as if a blast of icy wind rushed out, although I know it was *not* icy wind, because it didn't even ruffle my hair. Pat and Derek didn't seem to feel it at all, even though they too were standing directly in front of the door, but Dan seemed affected even worse than I was – he actually staggered, went deathly pale, and seemed to be finding it difficult to breathe. We were all very concerned, but he insisted he was all right, and led the way into the house, with the rest of us bunched close at his heels.

Inside, all was eerily still – the only sounds I could hear were my own heart pounding and Dan's laboured breathing. He took a couple of steps inside, then stopped, gazing in a rather unfocused way up the stairs. "*Don't* shut the door!" he pleaded, in a sort of strangled whisper. "Don't shut . . . it was locked, they couldn't get *out*!"

Derek flashed me a look I simply cannot describe, but said carefully, "Who, Dan? *Who* couldn't get out?"

If I hadn't known for sure that Dan had been stone-cold sober just a few minutes before, I would have sworn that he was *very* intoxicated. He seemed to be finding it difficult simply to stand on the spot, and was weaving uncertainly. He didn't answer Derek's question direct, but pointed up the stairs, saying thickly, "Up there – they came from up there – so feared, so awful *feared*! Only . . . the door was locked, and they couldn't . . . oh, *God*! They ran – they ran this way – down here . . . "

And he began to stagger down the hallway towards the back of the house, with us in *very* unwilling pursuit. He stopped in front of the doorway to the back room. "In here," he croaked, pointing to the doorway. "They went in here . . . this is where it all comes from . . . in here . . . "

It was horrible. It seemed totally unreal, and yet, at the same time, most gut-churningly real. I could see the effort it cost Derek to say, "Stand back, all of you!" as he reached for the doorknob, but before he could reach it, Dan grabbed his arm. "No!" he cried, "don't *touch* it! Can't you see the *blood*?!"

Blood?! *What* blood?! The hallway was a little dim, but the brass knob shone out in the gloom, perfectly unsullied, just as it always had been.

"Blood?" queried Derek, drawing his hand away sharply.

Dan shook his head as if to clear it. "No," he whispered, "it's not there now. But it was. When he came out, after . . . He closed the door, and got blood all over the knob – red and thick and sticky. But no, it's not there *now* . . . "

I don't know for sure about the others, of course, but *my* skin was crawling! But there was absolutely no point in standing there in the hallway – we *had* to look into the room. Even our sceptical Derek was a little windy, and pulled a tissue out of his pocket to wrap around the handle before he touched it. I can remember, even in the midst of all the total incomprehensibility, being amused when he didn't know quite what to do with the tissue after he opened the door. He obviously didn't want to keep it in his hand, but he didn't want to put it back in his pocket either, and he didn't want simply to drop it. What he actually did with it, in the end, I can't remember. I can simply recall the flood of relief I felt when the door opened and we were met by a glory of bright sunshine pouring through the big window. There was no-one there. Nothing in the room was out of place, or damaged in any way. It was simply one of the rooms where I and my family had spent many uneventful hours, stripping wallpaper, painting and decorating and hanging curtains. I felt almost as if I had been in a dark dream and had suddenly awoken to normality – at that time I hadn't thought it through any further.

"Nobody here!" I announced loudly, determined to dispel the urge to whisper, which had possessed us since we entered the house.

"Not in here, anyway!" agreed Derek. "Let's check out the rest of the place!" We turned to leave the room. Then we saw Dan. He hadn't actually entered the room with the rest of us, but was standing – half-crouching, actually – in the doorway. His eyes were glazed and far away, darting from side as if following movements that none of *us* could see. Suddenly, he began to scream, in a shrill, high tone, quite unlike his usual deep, rather gravelly, voice – "*No! No! No! No! No, Daddy, No! Mummy, Mummy, Mummy, Mummy, No, Daddy, No!*" He cringed even further, throwing up his right arm as if to protect his head, his eyes screwed up tight, and still screaming, "**No, Daddy, PLEASE** . . . "

I think it was a good job that Pat **had** accompanied the expedition. While Derek and I were still frozen in shock, Pat darted over to Dan, grabbed his arm, slapped his face, and yelled, "Dan! Dan, come **back**!"

Abruptly, he stopped screaming. His eyes suddenly refocused on the here-and-now, and his mind was obviously back in the same world as the rest of us. For a moment he gazed in a puzzled way into Pat's eyes, then whirled around and fled down the hallway towards the front door, in a shambling, uncoordinated run, totally unlike his usual neat, controlled movements. It took a moment – probably a fraction of a second, actually! – for the rest of us to look at each other in disbelief, then set off after him in a hurry. I think it was a case of 'the devil take the hindmost', although Derek did have the grace to make sure Pat and I were ahead of him before he slammed and locked the door behind us.

Dan was on his knees, about halfway to the garden gate, retching violently. We all rushed over to him, by which time he had lost whatever he had had for breakfast. He looked awful. He skin had an almost greenish tinge, and he was trembling violently. We got him to his feet, and with Pat one side of him and Derek the other, with me to open gates and doors for them, he managed to stagger back to the farmhouse. As we were going in, and Derek was calling, "It's all right, Mabel – it's only us!" we heard sirens, and soon a police car was skidding to a halt in the gravel at the gate.

"Dad – are you OK?" Derek asked me. "I mean – are you up to looking after Dan? I'd better go deal with the police – although what I'm going to **tell** them, God only knows!"

We assured him that we could cope perfectly well, and he left us to it. Mabel rose to the occasion like a seasoned campaigner. She must have been pretty terrified, left all alone in the house to mind Kyle, and with no real notion of what was going on, but she made no fuss and simply set to, putting the kettle on and fetching a blanket to wrap around Dan, who still seemed only semi-conscious. His teeth were chattering, he was shaking violently, and he kept muttering, "I'm **OK** – just cold, so **cold**!"

And he was. His hands felt frozen. And the temperature outside was around 75° Fahrenheit. We sat him down on the sofa in the lounge, in the full sun, and wrapped him in the blanket. I asked Mabel to warm a little milk, and he managed to sip it somehow, even though his hands were still shaking and his teeth were rattling against the rim of the mug. One of the policemen tapped on the door, poked his head round and asked if we needed an ambulance, but Dan vetoed this so vehemently that I didn't insist. In fact, I couldn't quite see what the hospital could do for him – he wasn't injured, and he wasn't sick in the normal sense of the word, and I didn't think he was going to want to try to explain to them what *was* wrong! He kept insisting that he 'fit be better directly', and began to demonstrate this within about five minutes. The shivering gradually subsided, and his colour improved perceptibly, until within about half-an-hour he seemed almost back to normal. None of us wanted to talk – in fact, I had absolutely no idea what to *say*! Dan appeared to be dozing, with his arms wrapped tight around himself, and Pat and I just sat quietly, holding hands for comfort and trying to get over the shock.

It must have been nearly an hour before Derek finally came back in. He sank down in one of the easy chairs, and covered his face with his hands. Pat went and sat on the arm of the chair beside him, and cradled his head in her arms. They sat like that for a couple of minutes, then Derek gave a deep, shuddering sigh and scrubbed his hands violently over his face. "Coffee!" he announced, looking up. "I could use a *brandy*, actually, but if I once got started I'd probably drink the bottle!"

Right on cue, Mabel appeared with a tray of steaming-hot, strong coffee for us all. "Join us, Mabel," invited Pat. "I think we all need to talk about this . . . "

"Thank you, no," said Mabel decidedly. "Somebody better keep an eye on young Kyle, and he doesn't need to hear this – he's going to help me make cakes with cherries on them. Maybe we can talk later." And off she marched.

For a while, we all sipped our coffee in silence, until Pat tentatively asked, "What did the police say, Derek?"

"What *could* they say?" he replied. "I'll give them their due – they *searched* thoroughly. I didn't really know what to tell them, at first. Then I decided that the only sensible thing to do was to tell them the truth, even if it did sound crazy. It could have got awfully complicated if I'd tried concocting some sort of story – even if I'd been thinking straight, which I wasn't! I mean – there was no sign of a break-in or anything, and nobody else has got a key. Well – at first, they looked at me as if I'd just been caught red-handed stealing the Crown Jewels. Then one of them sort of nudged his partner and said, 'Manor Farm, Gorsey Hallowell – right?' I said, 'Right!' And they gave each other a really strange look, and stood there rolling their eyes and nodding like a couple of mandarins! As if that *explained* something! I said, 'I assume our reputation has gone before us?' and they admitted they *had* heard stories! Anyway – like I said – we searched the whole place, and – zilch! It was all back to normal, just like it always is. They had sent for a canine unit, to check around outside – but that dog wasn't having *any* of it! The handler had to practically *lift* it out of the van, and then it just kept whimpering and desperately trying to get back in, with its tail tucked tight between its legs! Dirty great big alsatian – *you* know! – and absolutely terrified! The chap managed to drag it down the lane a bit, and as soon as it got away from the cottage it perked up, jumped over the stile and raced around the field with its tongue hanging out and with that *embarrassed* look dogs get when they feel they've been a proper charlie! Didn't pick up a thing! The only good it did was to my *credibility*. None of those guys had ever seen it act *that* way before – they kept assuring me it was usually totally fearless and ready to tackle anything or anybody. But it wasn't going near our damn' cottage, not for a whole sackful of Scoobie-Snacks! What the poor guys are going to put in their reports, God only knows, but I don't envy them! That reminds me – *I* better report in and let *my* boss know I'm not on my way to Durham!"

He picked up the phone and explained how he had suddenly been over-taken by 'the runs' while on the road, so had quickly made his way home, and hoped to be back on the job by Monday! They promised to tell the Durham end not to expect him, and to cancel his hotel booking. When he put the phone down, he looked around at us, shrugged and said, "Well – what else could I say? I didn't want them to think I've suddenly developed a bad case of Bats in the Belfry – even if I *have*! What about *you*, Dan? Sorry – I should have asked before."

"I fit be fine directly," Dan assured him, "even I can't deny I *am* some shook up right now! Sorry 'bout all a that fuss – I'll clean up the mess before I leave. How's about *you*, Sir?" he asked, looking at me. "You stood up to all that pretty good, seemingly!"

"Aaah, he's a tough old codger," my dear son assured him. "Comes of being fossilised so long! Sorry – family joke!" he explained, as Dan looked puzzled. "You *are* OK, Dad, aren't you? You *look* OK!"

"*Physically*, I feel OK, just – as Dan puts it – 'some shook up'." I affirmed. "As for *psychologically* – I'm not sure I'll ever be OK again! Has *anybody* got any idea what on earth is going *on* here? Although – come to think of it – before you answer that, I'd better call the hospital and make some excuse why *I* didn't turn up!"

Pat very kindly offered to make the call for me, explaining we had had 'unforeseen problems' at the last moment – although she didn't tell 'em exactly what those problems were! They were a bit miffed, I think – I can't blame them not liking missed appointments – but unfortunately not miffed enough to refuse to reschedule for next week. (Worst luck!) Once all *that* was out of the way, we had no more excuse for putting off a discussion of what had happened, but nobody seemed very keen to begin. So I took a deep breath, and said, "I think maybe I had better make a confession . . . " and did my best to explain clearly about my experience with Arthur, and what Kirstie had said. Derek and Pat were both absolutely aghast when they realised what that poor child had been going through. Derek, particularly, was almost overcome by remorse, clutching his head in both hands, and saying in a strangled voice, "God, Pat, I'm *sorry*! I'm so *sorry*! I just had no *idea* – I was trying to *comfort* the kid, not make her afraid to even *tell* me . . . "

"Hush, love, hush – it's all right!" Pat soothed him. "We *know* that – it's my fault as much as yours – *I* didn't understand either! I've known all along there was something wrong, but I didn't know what. I thought it was just *me*, being silly, and I didn't know what to tell the kids anyway! So I just kept telling them there was nothing to be afraid *of*, just a lot of silly *stories* by people who didn't know any better! I thought I was *helping* them – truly I did! But – oh God – what are we going to *do*? What *can* we do?"

I said, "Calm down, both of you. I don't think there is any value in trying to apportion *blame* here – in fact, I don't think any of us *are* to blame. This is something completely outside of our experience, and *I* haven't had a clue how to handle it, either. So let's put all that behind us, and try to do better from now on. OK? Actually, I haven't told you everything yet . . ." And I went on to explain about the incident with the books, and the legend that seemed to have been pointed out to me.

"What happened just now . . . " put in Dan tentatively – he had been merely listening gravely up to this point. "Could he have been *punishing* whoever it was tried to make contact with you, you reckon?"

"Who do you mean by 'he'?" queried Derek, looking puzzled.

"I think Dan means old Tom Hillyer," I said, never doubting for a moment that I was right. "Alias 'the man with the axe'. I suppose that could make some kind of cock-eyed sense. Kirstie seemed to be saying that the whole family are still hanging around, and that they are all afraid of dear old Tom. *They* are trying to get *us* to help them, and *he* is bent on stopping them – and/or us! Is that how you're seeing it, Dan?"

He sat quite still for a few moments, studying his boots. Then he sighed, and nodded his head slowly. "That's about the size of it," he said quietly. "And after what I saw in there, I swear I wouldn't put *anything* past him!"

"Yeah!" said Derek, sitting forward. "What on earth *happened* in there, Dan? I mean – *I* didn't see anything out of the ordinary! I heard those *noises* all right, though, or I'd think you'd all gone bug-house! God, I never want to hear anybody scream like *that* again, as long as I live! What did *you* see?"

"Sumpun *I* never want to *see* again, longest day I live!" replied Dan reluctantly. "But – OK – I guess you-all need to know. Just don't be too surprised if I make tracks for the john in a big hurry – I could just lose that good coffee, *thinking* about it merely. But first – I reckon maybe *I* have a confession to make, also. I came here – not just to this locality, but this property – for a reason. It's a long story, but I'll cut it short as I'm able. I lost my Mom when I was real little, and when I was 15 year old, my Pa married again – a real kind lady called Millie. She was real good to me, and I will be beholden to her with my dying breath. I never was able to spend so much time with her as I would liked – my Pa and I didn't rub along so good, and I run off to get shuck of him. But, couple year ago he died, so I was able to go stay a spell with Millie and her family. She and her two kids – my half-sister and half-brother – had gone to live with Millie's parents. Her Pa has Alzheimers, and I guess you know that can be some hard to cope with. Her Ma is a real spunky little lady, and real kind like her daughter, and they made me real welcome, said I could stay long as I liked. Well, my own life was going through a bad patch right around then, so I was suited real nice – I always wanted to live in a proper family, and not having one all my own, theirs was the next best thing.

But being around the place, I couldn't miss there was something **wrong**, and finally Millie explained it me. Seemingly, her mom was born and raised in this village. She was one of three sisters – Harriet, Millie's mom, was the youngest – she married a Yank and moved Stateside when she was about 23. Millicent, who was the eldest, moved to Scotland when she married. She's a widow now and came back last year to live in Warwick. The middle one was Emily – who married a guy called Tom Hillyer and came to live in that cottage out there. Oh yeah – Emily Plackett was my stepmother's aunt, even they never actually met. Howsomever – the three sisters were real close, even they lived so far apart, and they wrote each other regular, and sent photos of their children, such. Then, suddenly, in late 1940, Emily stopped writing. There was no word from her to either of her sisters and, with a war going on, they got real worried. They had never had no contact with her husband, Tom – he seemed downright unneighbourly – but they wrote him and begged for word of what had come of her. He never replied. So in the end, they wrote to the local vicar – a guy called Fairfax, Olly not being here in them days – asking if he could give them news of their sister. And he wrote back a real kindly letter – they keep it still, and I have read it – telling that there had been a tragedy: Emily and her kids had gone down to London to care for a sick aunt, seemingly, and gotten killed in an air-raid. Well, naturally, her sisters were real upset, but worse, they couldn't work out what he **meant** – they knew their own family history real good, and neither of them could work out who this 'sick aunt' could possibly **be**. They didn't have any kin in London, and they didn't have no surviving aunts, nor cousins, nor anyone they could think of who could fit the bill. Only, being so far away, it was real hard to find out any details for sure. Tom Hillyer was singing dumb, and when they wrote to friends of theirs who still lived local, asking if it could have been an aunt of **Tom's** she had gone to care for, they all swore that Tom didn't have no surviving female kin on either side of his family. So, the wind-up was that they got no joy, and for a lot of years there didn't seem much they could do, 'cept go on with their own lives. But they were never easy in their minds. And then, seemingly – eight or nine year ago, I think it was – Harriet commenced to having nightmares. I think she kept it to herself for a spell, but the dreams kept coming, and it was making her real low, and she was losing weight, and her family commenced to getting real worried. So, finally, she confessed – she kept having this awful dream about her long-dead sister Emily. Seemingly, Emily kept calling to her for help, crying that she and the kids were 'trapped' and couldn't escape, and they were so scared . . . I reckon it must been powerful upsetting for her sister. And she came to have almost a . . . an obsession, yeah? . . . she can't get it off of her mind that she has to help her sister, *some* way. But she's a real frail, elderly lady, and real occupied caring for her husband. Well – like I said – I *owe* 'em. And I wasn't half so busy right then as you might suppose. Also, I had found that – even I go on real good with Heather, my half-sister – my half-brother, Marvin, and me don't jog along together real harmonious, if you take my meaning – not so much as to make living under the same roof a real *joy* for any of us! So I offered to come and see if'n I could find out exactly what had gone down, and if I could trace this mysterious 'aunt' in London, and maybe set Harriet's mind at rest. I went to London first, and I slogged through all the records I could find, but I couldn't come on *any* Emily, Annie and Arthur Hillyer being killed in *any* air-raid, through the whole blamed war. So I came to Warwick, and Harriet's sister Millicent insisted I stay with her – she claims *she* is still real upset by the whole thing, also, and would dearly love to know what happened her sister and her little niece and nephew. So I commenced to checking out local records, and I went through all the births, marriages and deaths in both the Plackett family and the Hillyer family, for generations – and *I* can't find any 'aunt' who could have been in London in 1940. And both Millicent and Harriet swear there was no 'friend of the family' that they *called* 'aunt'. So – dead end there. So I figured the next step was to come here, see if I could take it any further. Only both Millicent and Harriet warned me that folks in these English villages can be real suspicious of strangers, and might not be too awful keen to answer questions. So I'm real sorry if you think I've been here under false pretences, but I figured this 'handyman' kick would take me all round the place, and I could keep my ears pinned back, and maybe pick up the odd bit of information here and there. And I figure I have come up with *some* answers – after today, I *know* that Emily and the kids didn't die in no bombing-raid in London. They died right here, in that cottage. And Tom Hillyer killed them . . . "

Well – I *did* say that there was more to Dan than he was letting on, didn't I? It's nice to be proved right about *something*, even if it really isn't the most important issue! And – OK – I admit I did suspect something a little more – what can I call it? - 'dodgy', maybe?

Anyway – I am going to have to tighten up this account. If I keep reporting verbatim – or as near as I can remember! – I'm going to be here all night! Chris Wainwright phoned a few minutes ago – said he had heard we had had some trouble, are we all all right, and am I still fit enough to go out in the morning? Nice of him – he sounded genuinely concerned, and I assured him we are all still in one piece and I will explain a little more fully tomorrow. *That* should be some fun! Right – back to the story . . .

Derek and Pat reassured Dan that they understood *why* he had handled things that way, and agreed he probably *would* have run into a stone wall if he had simply walked in and started asking questions. But we all still wanted to know exactly what had happened to him in the cottage, and he did his best to explain, even though he would obviously have much preferred *not* to talk about it. He said that when Derek had opened the front-door of the cottage, he had been hit by 'an icy blast – stinking – real *foul*, real evil!' It was so overpowering that he had to fight to hang on to consciousness – he said he felt as if he had been swept partially into another dimension, with transparent images superimposed over the real world, or – as he put it – 'like two *times*, Then and Now, both happening together'! He could see three people – a woman, a girl and a little boy – racing down the staircase in absolute panic. The woman desperately tried to open the front door, but was unable to do so quickly enough, and herded the children into the back room. Dan shuddered as he told us that when Derek opened the door to that room and he went to follow us in, it was as if the consciousness of the little boy actually *swamped* his own, and from there on he experienced the events *as* that little boy. He still seemed to be having some trouble in separating the boy from himself – he kept saying things like "I saw . . . no! No! Not *me* – *him* . . . !" It was quite distressing even to *listen* to, and it obviously upset *him* badly. He claimed that it was a winter's night, and the room was lit only by the dim glow of a dying fire. He said 'Mummy' and 'Annie' – dressed in their night-clothes – rushed over to the big curtains over the french-door, and were desperately trying to get *that* door unlocked, while Arthur – absolutely terrified – cowered in front of the fire. Before 'Mummy' could get the door open, 'Daddy' charged into the room – with an axe! *Oh*, yes! At that point, I began to feel just a little sceptical

– I had a feeling we had to get that axe into it somewhere! Although I am probably being quite unfair, and indulging in a little more wishful thinking. Anyway – it was pretty horrible, and Dan's complexion had turned positively ashen again, as he forced himself to tell us how 'Daddy' proceeded to hack his wife and daughter to pieces. He then turned to the boy, and lifted the axe. The child raised his arm in a futile protective gesture but, before the axe could fall, Dan suddenly became aware of *himself* again, and of Pat yelling his name. He – as he so picturesquely put it – 'lit *outta* there like m' shirt tail was afire'! To which we could all attest!

"And I want to thank *you*, Pat," he said, shakily. "I don't even want to *speculate* what might happened if you hadn't dragged me back! I am purely beholden. But at least I know now what come of Emily, Annie and Arthur – Tom Hillyer murdered 'em. And I reckon that could explain your hants, Derek. Because the bodies are still *there*, I can feel it – still in that blamed cottage. You have to *find* them, Derek – let their family give them decent burial. Then maybe you fit get shuck your hants, and your place fit be clean and healthy for your kids."

Now Derek obviously has a high regard for Dan – but he hadn't actually *experienced* most of what Dan was claiming, and he wasn't *totally* convinced! "But, Dan," he said carefully, "what you're saying here is we have three axe-murders! And nobody even *suspected*? And I can tell you now, there is nowhere in that cottage where three bodies could possibly be hidden – I mean, we stripped the place *bare*! Where would you suggest we *look*?"

"All I can say," said Dan, a little stubbornly, "is they felt *close*. In that very *room*, most like. I can't swear to Emily and Annie, but Arthur's body, at least, is still there, you may lay to it. I can't say *where* – I didn't see the room the way it is *now*, only the way it was *then*. And I have me this bad feeling that if I did screw myself up to go back, I'd likely see the same thing all over. You don't happen to have photos, do you?"

"No – but I've got a Polaroid camera," said Derek. "If you want, I could go and . . . d'you fancy a little stroll over there, Dad?"

I had to smile to myself, but I took pity and went with him. We photographed the back room from all angles, and took some pictures of the rest of the house for good measure. When we got back, Dan studied them earnestly, concentrating almost exclusively on that one room. "It's all real different," he commented. "But – who put in the electric fire? It was a ***real*** fire when I – when ***he*** – was there. Did ***you*** do that?"

"We ***changed*** the fire," Derek admitted. "There was a really old rusty wreck of an electric fire when we came here – God, State of the Ark! But the chimney was already blocked off."

"Why anybody fit ***do*** that?" Dan persisted.

"Well, that's no mystery!" Derek cried. "Electric fires are so labour-saving, and . . . "

"Labour-saving, I grant you," cut in Dan. "But – in ***these*** parts, where you fit get wood for the taking – why would ***anybody*** pay for electricity? ***You*** burn wood. I swear, Derek – ***that***'s where they are – he hid 'em in the blamed chimney, then blocked it off!"

Derek is not often stuck for words, and I know I am mean but I couldn't help quite enjoying the show. He didn't want to offend Dan, or appear to disbelieve him, but he obviously had no intention of ripping out that chimney-breast and damaging the decoration of the whole room. Dan, however, picked up on it quite quickly, and kindly let him off the hook. He stood up and said, "It's time I got back to what I came to do – I'll trim that hedge, then give the lawns a quick cut – that'll hold things 'til I can get back again. As for your offer of letting me live in the cottage – you'll likely not be ***too*** surprised if I don't take you up on it. Thanks anyway."

And off he went. Pat went after him to try to persuade him to go home and rest rather than carrying on with the gardening, but he insisted it would help him to 'settle his mind, he fit only chase it round his head like a squirrel in a cage', so in the end she let him please himself. He did join us for a belated lunch, but Kyle was there and we stayed off the subject.

After lunch, Pat had a long talk with Mabel while Derek took Kyle outside to let off some of his pent-up energy, then he went to pick up the other two from school. I am very glad that all happened while they were safely out of the way, but we can't be sure it won't happen again. I mean – we haven't actually solved anything, have we? We still have absolutely no control over these 'phenomena'.

I have spent the whole evening on this record of events, and I am actually in bed now. I can hear Pat and Derek talking quietly in the room above me. Pat, I think, is trying to persuade Derek that they have to open up that chimney, but I think she's got her work cut out! Personally, I'm not sure who is right. Do Dan's 'feelings' justify the outlay of what could turn out to be quite a lot of money? Derek has already invested a *lot* in that cottage, in time, effort and expense. On the other hand – *could* that fireplace be concealing a makeshift tomb? It's a horrible thought! I believe **Dan** was convinced – I can **not** imagine him putting on that performance for the fun of it! – but am *I*? I honestly don't know **what** to think. I mean – even if Dan is right about the bodies, would the mere fact of them not having been 'properly' buried be enough to cause this sort of 'haunting'? And if they were removed, would all this unpleasantness stop? I find it impossible to get my irreligious mind round that! And maybe it's best if I stay out of it, anyway. If I **did** express an opinion in favour of demolishing the fireplace, it would probably only make Derek more determined **not** to! My brain is reeling, and I am absolutely shattered. I haven't managed to record everything, but I think I've covered the main points – any more will simply have to wait for another day. As will any con- clusions. I am going to pack up now, and see if I can actually get a decent night's sleep. I don't usually resort to sleeping-tablets but – damn it! – I think I'm going to tonight. Oblivion – here I come!

Thursday, 20th June

Well, I'm not sure whether I have to thank the sleeping-pills or just sheer ex- haustion, but I dropped off to sleep almost as soon as I put out the light, and I slept like a log until I was awakened by Derek and Pat moving around up- stairs. I nearly said 'slept like the dead' there, but after recent events, I'm not sure just how accurate that simile is! It is quite a cloudy and overcast morning, but not actually raining, and I'm sure Chris would have phoned by now if he meant to call off our expedition, so I am filling time while I wait for him.

Fortunately, Kurt and Kirstie didn't seem to pick up on the rather-strained atmosphere, which we couldn't quite seem to dispel. They got ready for school quite happily this morning, and Derek and Pat have both gone to drop them off, then they are planning to go and do some shopping, taking advan- tage of Derek's unexpected time off work. I'm sure Pat will be glad to have him around for a few days – I think the events of yesterday actually upset her quite badly, even though she coped remarkably well at the time. They have taken Kyle with them, and they weren't very happy at the idea of leaving Mabel here all alone, even though everything seems quiet at the moment. But Dan turned up quite early, and has begun clearing out that old wreck of a barn, which is full of lord-knows-how-many years of junk, not to mention piles of rotten old hay and straw. He is planning to stay for the whole day, so Mabel ought to be all right until Pat and Derek get back. He has already made several journeys with a big wheelbarrow from the barn to the level ground at the top of the hill, where he is planning to have a bonfire. Rather him than me! He suggested that Mabel might like to keep the doors closed, just in case the rats he expects to disturb might fancy a change of lodgings! He has Judy and Droopy with him, but I don't think he is really optimistic that he will get much help from *that* direction! We do, of course, also have four cats, but I'm not sure just how good they are at ratting – Dan obviously doesn't feel they have exactly been earning their keep!

I don't know about the *cats*, but the dogs certainly kept well out of the way yesterday! Mabel says they both came bundling into the kitchen as soon as the screaming started, desperately trying to hide under the dresser. But, after the courageous display of that trained police dog, maybe we shouldn't blame them too much – even if it is 'their' property, and you might expect them to make *some* push to guard both it and their owners! 'Man's best friend' obviously draws the line at 'ghosts'.

I still can't make up my mind just how much of that story of Dan's I actually *believe*. I believe *he* believes it. And it certainly linked up in many ways to my own experiences, and to what the children claim. But is it objectively *real*? And what exactly do I mean by 'Reality' anyway? Oh . . . socks!

Never mind. Chris is just driving in at the gate, and maybe I can have a rest from all this total insanity!

Later – *8.30 p.m.*

What was that I said about having a rest from the insanity? I seem to have spent most of the day talking about it!

I still couldn't help feeling a little concerned about leaving Mabel, but she waved that aside, saying, "Never you mind that, Sir – off you go, it'll do

101

you good!" So I reassured myself that she wouldn't hurt with Dan around, and no doubt Derek and Pat wouldn't be away too long – and I can't pretend I was reluctant to get away for a while. Chris had to help me into his vehicle, which I find just a shade **high** to be able to get into easily, but once I **am** in it is quite comfortable, and gives a good view over the hedges. He asked if I had any preference as to where we should go, but I told him I would leave that up to him – he knows the area much better than I do. So off we drove, and he asked if I wanted to tell him about what happened yesterday, or if I would prefer him to mind his own business. I couldn't help being a little curious as to exactly how the local 'grapevine' actually works, and he said Helen had been at her W.I. meeting yesterday afternoon, along with Amy Moffatt – wife to Constable Moffatt, of whom I still have fond memories! Quite a few people had seen and heard the police vehicles racing through the village with sirens blaring, which naturally occasioned more than a little interest! P.C. Moffatt had been able to confirm to his wife at lunchtime that they were on their way to Manor Farm House, although more than that he apparently managed to keep to himself – *if* he actually knew. I'm almost sure he wasn't among the officers involved. So speculation was rife about what had really happened, and all sorts of wild stories were doing the rounds. Helen had told Chris about it when she got home, and naturally they were worried about us – he hoped we didn't mind him ringing to find out if we were OK. I assured him we were grateful for their concern, but told him it was a little difficult to explain exactly what had happened, as we were having severe credibility problems ourselves.

"Ah!" he said grimly. "We couldn't help being afraid it might have been something like that. Look, George – we've been wanting to talk to you about it for some time, only *we* didn't know *you* and *you* didn't know *us*, and – well, it *is* a bit of a touchy subject, isn't it? We weren't sure just what your attitude might be. I did try to speak to young Derek about it when they first moved in, only – well, I suppose it was only natural that he should see it as interference. I mean – he didn't know me from Adam! But we *have* been worried – especially when the gossip started up again. Just how much do you actually know about that place, George?"

Well, I was absolutely flabbergasted! I had been arguing with myself about how much I dared tell him – if I dared actually mention the subject at all – and here he was, sounding as if he knew all about it! So I decided to jump in with both feet and give him the unabridged version of what has been going on since I arrived. He listened solemnly, nodding his head occasionally. When I finally wound down, he gave a great sigh and said simply, "Oh dear."!

At that point he stopped the vehicle in the middle of a narrow lane – I had been so engrossed in my own recital that I hadn't really been paying any attention to where we were going. "Excuse me a minute, George," he said, climbed out and crossed the lane to open a five-barred gate into a field of what looked to me like potatoes. "We go off-road for a while here," he explained, climbing back in and driving into the field. I felt pretty useless as he had to climb out again to close the gate behind us, but he assured me that he always has to do that anyway. Usually he is alone, but even if Helen is with him she finds it such a struggle that he prefers to do the job himself. "Good job I'm well in with the local farmers," he said. "There's a footpath across here, but it's rough, and a bit far for you to struggle anyway. But they know I don't do any harm, and always close the gates, so they don't mind me bringing the jeep in. Sometimes I want to bring my gear – spades and things – and it's a bit far to have to hump it. But I think you'll agree it's worth the trip . . ."

He stopped the jeep at the far end of the field, and helped me out. The view was absolutely breath-taking – we were right on the top of a hill, with a wide panorama of open countryside all around. The clouds which had shrouded the early morning were beginning to break up and allow the sun to shine through, and there was a pleasantly fresh little breeze, stirring the foliage of the little wood which ran down the hill on our right. Somewhere, high above us, a lark burst into song, which somehow only served to accentuate the surrounding silence. In the far distance, I could see the sun reflecting off the traffic on what was obviously a major road – probably the A46 – but it was far enough away for the noise of engines to be completely lost. We were on the edge of a totally prosaic field of potatoes, and yet, somehow, the isolation was almost awesome. For a few minutes we simply stood and breathed it in. Then Chris said, "If I hold your arm, d'you think you can manage to get down to that next ridge? There's something I want to show you. I've got a folding chair for when we get there . . ."

The distance was not more than about fifty yards, and the slope was not too steep; with Chris supporting me under my good arm I coped without too much difficulty. He opened up the chair, and managed to find a level spot where it could stand, on the banks of a small stream that chuckled cheerily down the hill. The view from there was really beautiful, too, even if a little more enclosed, looking back the way we had come, down into the valley which surrounds Gorsey Hallowell. The grass was rough, but painted golden with buttercups, purple with thistles and sweet with clover; and the only sounds were the rustle of leaves and the drone of insects. Chris made another trip back to the jeep to fetch a chair for himself, and a large cooler that contained our lunch. He set his chair beside mine, and for a while we were both silent, looking at the view spread out in front of us. "Can you see those roofs on the hill right away in the distance?" Chris asked after a while. He handed me a pair of binoculars and pointed in the right direction. "That's Manor Farm."

I adjusted the focus and gazed at the miniature buildings far across the valley, trying to imagine Mabel hanging out the washing, and Dan humping the wheelbarrow up the hill. "You know," I said, "sitting up here like this makes what happened yesterday seem even more unreal and like a nightmare. I can hardly believe it happened. From here it looks so – *normal* – so ordinary."

"Doesn't it?" agreed Chris. "Can you see the village, down there in the hollow? That looks pretty ordinary too. But – look again, George. Can you see a very vague dark cloud over that whole area – from the village up to Manor Farm? A bit like smoke or fog?"

When he mentioned it, yes, I could – a faint, purplish smear in the air, centred, it seemed, almost directly over Manor Farm.

"Dan was going to have a bonfire," I commented, "but I wouldn't think he would have started it yet . . . and the smoke wouldn't spread *that* far, surely?"

"No, it's not a bonfire," said Chris. "It's always there. It's even harder to see when the weather is overcast, but you can just about make it out if you really look. And not only from *this* hill – but from all the hills round about. I noticed it about four or five years ago, and it took me a while to convince myself I was really seeing it. If we were in Los Angeles, or even a much smaller built-up area, you could put it down to air-pollution. But there is no industry for miles, and precious few houses; and at this time of year, not many of those have fires burning. And how many cars would you estimate go up and down Banebrook Lane in a day? And, unless my Physics are completely all to pot, you'd expect smog to sink down into the hollow, wouldn't you, not hang around on that hillside? And the thing that worries me most, George, is – it seems to be spreading. It's awfully difficult to quantify something as nebulous as that, and I would love to be able to believe I'm imagining it. But I can't."

"What on earth do you think it *is*, then?" I queried, and my voice sounded almost as scared as I felt. Suddenly, the beautiful morning felt somehow *ominous*. For some moments, Chris didn't reply. Then he sighed, and said, "George – this must be one of the hardest things I've ever had to say. I know how *ridiculous* it sounds, but I promised myself – and Helen – that I would *not* chicken out. Helen has seen it too, by the way, and we've talked it over and worried at it 'til we're blue in the face. I even went up on that hill and took a sample of the air – I sent it off to a chemist friend of mine in London and got him to analyse it. And the answer came back that it was *air* – cleaner and purer than most, these days! Nothing out of the ordinary showed up in the lab. *But*, George – what if it were something for which they have no tests, no instruments, no formulae? Something for which they have never learned to look? Daft as it may sound, what Helen and I think, George, is – it's the damn' De Coursey curse, somehow becoming active again after all these years. Don't tell me - I *know* it sounds crazy! But, you see, *you're* not the only ones, George: other people – people who live in the area covered by that 'cloud' – have been 'seeing things', too – apparitions, people who are known to be dead, that sort of thing. I don't know *how*. And I don't know *why*. But I do know it scares the *hell* out of me, George! It freezes my very *liver*! And after listening to your story – oh my God! We are going to have to *do* something – it's obvious we can't just sit here and twiddle our thumbs any longer, telling ourselves we don't *believe* in such rubbish! At least you didn't laugh in my face – that's something, I suppose. But what are you *thinking*, eh, George? What are you *thinking*?"

"What I am thinking," I replied slowly, "is that you are making me even more scared than I was yesterday, and I never felt less like laughing in my life. I have always rather prided myself on being a born sceptic, Chris – for many years I have congratulated myself on being 'rational' and 'scientific' and all that jazz. If you had told me this six months ago – or maybe even six *days* ago! – I am ashamed to say I would have felt pitying and superior, and wondered how anybody could be so gullible and benighted. Wonderful what a little *experience* can achieve, isn't it? I am still having great credibility problems, but mostly, I think, because I am simply floundering around out of my depth, and I haven't the first clue just what is going on – or what, **on** this earth or out of it, we can **do** about it! So – first, can you please tell me a little more about this 'curse' carry-on, and secondly, tell me how we go about patenting a little product called 'Curse Buster' or 'Spook Away', or whatever it is we'll need if we're going to do a little psychic spring-cleaning?"

Chris chuckled at this. "Glad you've got a sense of humour," he said. "You just might need it! I'll do my best with the explanation, but you have to realise, George, that the information that Helen and I have been able to gather is somewhat unreliable and out-of-date – by at least a few centuries! – or pure extrapolation and guesswork on our part. But I think we have dug out **some** pieces that fit together to make a kind of weird sense – and that's another reason I brought you up here. See this stream? This is called 'the Thornbrook'. If you look just a little further up the hill, you can probably just make out the source it springs from. It runs down into the hollow where the village stands, into the pool that is generally known as the Holy Well. But Helen and I believe that pool is actually only part of what you might call the 'complex' of the **ancient** holy well. It is actually fed by five streams, running down off five different hills –Acbrook, Alorbrook, Hollenbrook, the Bane-brook, which flows down past your place, and this one. Many years ago, Helen took a degree in Medieval History, and when we started looking at the place-names around here, she realised that all the brooks except the Banebrook were named for trees in Anglo-Saxon – thorn, oak, alder, and holly. She spent quite a lot of time on research, and she found some old documents written in Anglo-Saxon which, at the time, we didn't take very seriously. But it seems that, at one time, the Banebrook was actually called the 'Wiccebroc', or the 'brook of the wychelm', which seemed to tie in nicely with the tree theme. The 'Banebrook' appellation only began to be used after the curse was laid on the De Courseys, and it is interesting to note that the stream actually flows around the site where their castle used to stand. And I'm sure you don't need me to tell you that 'bane' and 'curse' are not all that different in meaning! This seemed to imply that the Banebrook was somehow instrumental in bring-ing about the fate of the De Courseys. Anyway – I was hooked on the story by then, and took a few field-trips to see what I could still see of the topog-raphy. And as I followed each stream to its source, I found a large tree, of the designated species, growing right over each spring. Look – you can see the big hawthorn hanging over this one! Now – all this happened so long ago, that it seemed impossible that these particular trees were here in Saxon times. And yet – here they stand, although the wychelm is very nearly dead now, with only a few sickly-looking leaves growing each spring. I decided that maybe the original trees had self-seeded, and that the present trees were the descendants of those that were growing there when the streams were named. Now, I'm sure you know, George, that five is thought of, by the superstitious, as one of the 'numbers of power', as are three and seven, of course. And certain trees were also considered to have magical properties in pagan religions. And springs, wells and pools were all thought of as sacred places by the Celts, and probably many other ancient peoples. So we began to wonder whether the whole **area** had actually comprised the sacred 'well' – five hills, five trees, five springs, five streams and the central pool. So we looked at relief maps of the area, and – do you know what we saw, George? We saw a **star** – a five-pointed star! The streams, and the valleys and channels down which they flow form an unmistakable star-shape. Then Helen had another inspiration: as you know, we both grew up here, and the ground surrounding the pool which **we** were always taught was the 'holy well', was called 'the Tangle'. I never could understand why – I mean, look around! The whole landscape round about, even the wilder parts, is exceptionally tame and orderly. But, when you're a kid, you simply accept these things, without ever really questioning them, and I had never bothered to think about it since. But, looking at that map, Helen suddenly clapped her hands over her mouth, and her eyes grew huge. 'It's not The **Tangle**, Chris,' she whispered, 'it's The **Tungol**!' In Anglo-Saxon, 'tungol' was a word meaning 'star'! And then we **knew** we were right – this whole landscape was a religious site! It felt a bit like discovering a new continent, that nobody knew was there! How those ancient people managed to **see** the star, I don't know – maybe the view was more open then, with fewer trees; or maybe they just deduced it from the streams and the contours of the land – I can't say. But I've been up in a hot-air balloon and taken some aerial photographs since, and it's there, George – just look!"

He pulled a packet out of his jacket pocket, and handed me some photographs. And sure enough – a star – a five-pointed star spread out across the ground! I was fascinated.

"So you think the site was actually *pre*-Saxon?" I asked.

"Oh, most definitely!" he cried. "I've poked around a bit since, and – as you saw in the museum – I've found a few flint arrow-heads and a broken neolithic hand-axe, so there were *people* here, way back into prehistory. Whether this was a sacred site to *them*, of course, I can't say. I've found only a couple of bits of pottery dating back to the Bronze Age, but Iron Age stuff is more plentiful, and during a really bad drought I found a few Roman coins, which looked as if they might have been tossed into the main pool of the well, probably as an offering to the goddess. The pagan Romans would have had no problem with accepting local gods and goddesses. The Angles and the Saxons were originally pagan too, of course. When they came to Britain they took over a lot of existing sites, and renamed them in their own language – as, of course, did the Danes and the Vikings. But now I'm going to tell you something really strange, George, and you'll probably think I'm barking mad. You said you read about 'The Guardians of the Well', yes? Well, we still have several families with the surname of Wardwell living in the area. Helen and I traced them back through the old records, and the name began as 'Weardwael' – meaning 'Guardian of the pool' – or 'well'. And, whilst most of the family tend to laugh it off these days, the – can I call her the 'Matriarch'? – still claims to be the successor to a line of well-wardens stretching far back into prehistory. Oh, yes! She maintains that her grandmother taught her the sacred rites for worshipping the goddess of this site, handed down by word of mouth through untold generations, and even an ancient language in which the rites were conducted! Not being a linguist, I couldn't begin to vouch for that, of course. Now – I'm not saying that what she says is *true* – but I'm absolutely certain that *she* believes it. And as you're being so sympathetic, I'll pluck up the courage to admit that *I* believe what she says. It seems *unlikely* that any sect could have survived that long, but – especially in a secluded place like this – I suppose it's not actually *impossible*. Up until very recently, I had come to the conclusion that the more prosaic parts of the story *could* be true, although I must admit I pooh-poohed the 'supernatural' aspects. But I am fast becoming a convert – especially after *your* experiences!"

For several minutes I sat silent, considering the implications of what he had said. "So," I replied at last, "what exactly are you implying here, Chris? That maybe this old lady could be responsible for – what can I call it? – 'updating' or 'renewing' this curse? Following, for some unknown reason, in the footsteps of her distant ancestor? In which case – if she could lay *on* a curse, could she, perhaps, also take it *off*?"

"To be honest with you, George," he sighed, "I'm not totally sure *what* I'm implying. I still can't, for the life of me, begin to imagine a little old lady like Lira Wardwell being *able* to lay a curse – it's so utterly fantastic! And – although she can be a little sharp and tetchy in her manner – I definitely can't believe she would dream of doing anything so downright *evil*, even if she could! But I *do* think that we ought to have a talk with her, and see what she has to say about it – don't you?"

"It couldn't hurt," I agreed. "Even if it didn't *help*, we'd be no worse off than we are now. I wonder if this sort of thing could account for why the Church was so ready to brand the so-called 'miracle healings' as works of the Devil rather than of God? And another thing that has been puzzling me is – do you know what actually happened to the De Courseys, Chris? I mean – did they die particularly horrible or untimely deaths, or did their punishment have to wait until *after* death? I know life could be rather short and bloody in those days, anyway, but did the members of the family suffer exceptionally nasty ends, or what?"

"To be honest," he said, "I never really looked into that angle too closely. You see, until very recently, I never took that 'curse' business at all seriously. My own view was always that what finished the De Courseys in these parts was most likely the Black Death – the timing seemed to fit in quite nicely. I'll ask Helen to see if she can find out any more if you like, but things were pretty chaotic at that time, and records were pretty sparse and unsatisfactory. If I remember right, the land was sold off around 1370. The castle, which stood on that earthwork behind the house . . . "

"That's an *earthwork*?!" I interrupted. "I thought it was just a hill!"

"When the Jeffries owned the farm," said Chris, "they let me have a look around, and that 'hill' is definitely man-made – what they called a 'motte', as in 'motte and bailey' – yes? The castle was probably originally of timber-construction, which was later replaced by stone. Anyway, by the time it was sold, the castle was already in bad repair. It was demolished, and a fortified manor-house was built on the site, re-using a lot of the stone. They still kept the moat, for which the water came from the Banebrook, until that building was gutted by fire in the early 1600's. When the place was rebuilt, they filled in the moat, and – as you know – the present house is built at the foot of the earthwork, and mostly of brick, although some of the original stone was incorporated, as well as some very old oak timbers. So the place you're living in has *quite* a history! Although, the way things are at the moment, I'm afraid I can't say I envy you! There's one thing I keep meaning to ask you, though, George – did Kirstie say she had actually *seen* this 'spider' she mentioned, or was it just something she had heard about?"

"I'm afraid I'm not sure," I confessed. "I couldn't get her to talk about it, and it didn't seem worth upsetting her any more by pushing for answers. All she would say was that Arthur would explain it to me. Do you happen to know what she was talking about?"

"All *I* know," he said, thoughtfully. "is that up until you told me that, I had always considered the 'spider' to be one of the more ridiculous and far-fetched parts of the legend. Which states, by the way, that the 'Soul Trap' was originally *constructed* by a great spider – like a sort of invisible, intangible *web*, I assume, through which souls could not pass. And this is reflected in the names of the villages round here which, along with the spring at the wychelm, the source of the Banebrook, were supposed to be the 'anchor points' of the web. There's Saltrap, of course – from the Old English 'sawol træppe', meaning 'soul trap'. Then we have Lobbesden, and Copsford – both 'lobbe' and 'cob' or 'cop' being old words for 'spider', hence 'Spider's Den' and 'Spider's Ford'. The beast itself was supposed to hang out in the tangle of caves on Rodden Hill – which Helen thinks, by the way, may be a corruption of 'rotten hill'. It's riddled with very dangerous caves, and a lot of people who have gone in there over the centuries have failed to come out. There were a couple only a few years ago – trained potholers – who had a cockamamie theory that there was a way right through the hill. They went to test out this idea of theirs – in perfect midsummer weather, and equipped with all the proper gear – and that was the last anyone ever saw of them. When they failed to report in, a cave-rescue team went in after them, but they couldn't find them, and in the end they gave it up as simply too risky. The bodies were never recovered. Personally, I think the caves are simply dangerous caves, and *I* wouldn't set foot in there at gunpoint! Since that incident, the entrances have been sealed up anyway, to prevent any more tragedies.

But I'm sure we don't need look to look for anything as unlikely as a super-natural *spider* as the cause of *that* trouble!"

"That's quite a relief, actually," I said. "When Kirstie came out with that, I couldn't imagine where she got such an idea from. But if it's well-known local folklore, she could easily have heard someone talking about it and got the wind up. Not a *nice* thought, is it?"

"Damn' right, George!" agreed Chris forcefully. "Tell you what – let's forget about spiders, or any kind of spooks, for a bit. Are you ready for some lunch?"

At the mention of food, I realised I was absolutely famished. Helen had packed us up a delicious spread, and we certainly did it justice. Chris didn't have to carry any of it *back* with him, that's for sure! After lunch we felt too lazy to move for a while. I sat looking over the valley at that strange dark cloud hanging above the village and Manor Farm, and trying to come to terms with the fact that I, George Hanson, lifelong sceptic and unbeliever, was actually giving credence to all this utter nonsense. Because, try as I may to deny it, I *am* giving it credence. It comforts me to know that both Chris and Helen are doing the same. They are both sane and intelligent people, not normally, I'm convinced, given to lurid flights of fancy. They obviously didn't *want* to believe it, but they have been backed into a corner and forced to a very unpalatable conclusion. A thought suddenly popped unbidden into my mind, and I said, "Chris – did you say that five streams flow into the pool in the hollow? What happens to the water *then*? Surely there must be *out*lets as well as *in*lets!"

"Sorry – I obviously didn't explain it very well," he said. "Actually – the Hollenbrook runs into the Acbrook, and the Alorbrook and the Banebrook join just before they flow into the pool. So there are actually three inlets, but from five sources. Then two streams flow *out* of the pool – one of them is still called the Banebrook, and that flows down to Copsford, and then on into a larger stream which eventually becomes a tributary of the Avon. The second is our 'Chatterbrook' – officially known as the Stanbrook – and that joins with the Banebrook only just outside the village. So we still have the 'five' motif. I'll show you on the map, if you like – it might be easier to understand." Luckily it wasn't too breezy – we managed to control the map well enough for me to make out what he meant.

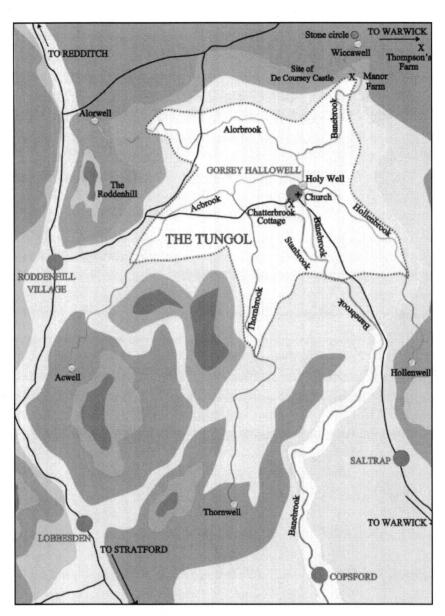

THE TUNGOL AND THE COMPLEX OF THE SACRED WELL

"Do you see," he asked, "how the Banebrook runs right through the area we're talking about? Like a central channel, if you like. Like a main artery, through which the poison could spread?"

I couldn't quite repress a small shudder, even though the day was bright and warm. "Sorry, George," Chris was obviously concerned. "I shouldn't be putting you through all this – I keep forgetting you're convalescent. Maybe I ought to talk to Derek about it instead – he might be more receptive to these crazy notions after the fun-and-games yesterday. Would you like me to take you home?"

I assured him that I was fine, and that 'convalescence' had never really held much charm for me – although I couldn't lay my hand on my heart and swear that I would have chosen this particular cure for boredom! I did feel, however, that we both ought to talk to Derek – *and* Pat. They need to know all the 'facts' we have – and we all need to decide what the next move ought to be. I felt strongly that Derek ought to be told about the weird 'cloud', and maybe see it for himself if he couldn't take our word for its existence. So Chris helped me back up the hill and into the jeep, and we headed back to Manor Farm.

When we arrived, though, Derek was attired in his oldest clothes, helping Dan with the barn-cleaning. The stench coming off the lower layers of that old rotten hay and straw was appalling! Pat had taken Mabel home on her way to pick up the kids from school, but she got back only a few minutes after we arrived, and quickly shepherded us into the lounge out of the smell. She put the kettle on, and made us all tea, but it was obviously not the best time to try to have a serious discussion – *she* had the dinner to prepare, and Derek was both busy and filthy. So Chris and I put the telly on and watched a bit of cricket, which was a welcome change of subject! He left about five o'clock, with a promise that he would try to arrange for us to have a meeting with Lira Wardwell, and would phone me tomorrow.

When Dan left, Derek headed straight upstairs for a bath, then we all had dinner. After the children were in bed, he asked me if I had enjoyed my day out, so I plunged in and explained all that Chris had told me. I'll give him credit for hearing me out, but I could tell he wasn't totally convinced. "But Dad," he said patiently, "Dan had a *fire* going – right?"

"It wasn't *smoke*, Derek," I persisted. "Chris says it's *always* there – has been for several years that *he* knows of – and . . ."

113

"Chris *says*," he said, "but *you* only saw it on a day when Dan had a fire, Dad. Tell you what: I'll go up there tomorrow morning – *before* Dan starts the fire again! – and take a look for myself. You can come with me, if you like – fair enough?"

I had had a feeling he wouldn't take it on trust. Well – to be fair – I'm pretty sure *I* wouldn't have, either. But I think I can remember the way to get there, so we'll go and see what we can see.

We discussed the whole issue a little more, and I could see that poor Pat was *very* unhappy about it all – especially the bit about the spider! I hated upsetting her, but I'm afraid there's no way to avoid it. Suddenly she said, "What about your Mum, Derek? We're going to *have* to tell her what's been happening. And Jenny might not want to bring Elizabeth down, not with all this going on. You or Dad ought to ring them – tonight."

I let Derek make the call and do the initial explaining. Finally he handed the phone to me, with a rueful look, saying, "Sorry, Dad, but I think you're in trouble! Mum wants a word – *now*!"

I put the handset to my ear rather gingerly. "George?" said Mary, in a reproachful tone, "what on *earth* is going on? How *could* you keep me in the dark about something like this? You *know* you're supposed to be taking it easy, but what do you do as soon as my back is turned? You go chasing around after – *what*, George?! I couldn't make head nor tail out of what Derek was telling me!"

"Mary," I said, placatingly, "I haven't been 'chasing around' as you put it, after anything! I've been doing my best to avoid believing in *any* of it – and most of it only came to light yesterday or today, anyway!"

"So why didn't you phone *last* night?" she persisted. To which, I'm afraid, I had no valid answer! I lamely explained that we hadn't wanted to *worry* her, at which she nearly exploded! I don't think I have ever known her so angry!

"Not *worry* me?!" she cried. "George Hanson – we are a *family*! Do you know what that *means*? It means that anything which affects any *one* of us affects us *all*! We are all in this *together*, George – whatever 'this' may actually *be*! How could you dare to *patronise* me by 'not worrying' me about something which involves so many of my family?"

What could I do but offer an abject apology? "Very well," she said, more calmly, "but – no more of it, George – do you understand me? Take off your cave-man suit, and stop assuming that you have to protect your women like that – if you males can cope with it, George, I'm sure *we* can! I want to know *exactly* what is going on, every last *detail*! Now – let's leave it for tonight – I want you to go and get some rest, before we have you ill again. Jenny, Elizabeth and I will all be down tomorrow evening as planned, and you can explain things a little more clearly then, to Jenny and to me. It'll save repetition. You can tell Pat to expect us as usual, and you can tell Derek that I am amazed that he would suspect for a minute that we would choose to be *anywhere* but with our family at a time like this! Goodnight, dear – do look after yourselves, won't you? I hope you all have a peaceful night."

She's quite a woman, is my wife! And I think I had better pack up now and try to obey orders, before I get into any *more* hot water!

Friday, 21st June

Well, this has been another somewhat unusual – not to mention busy! – day. Things are happening so fast that I am having real problems trying to keep a record of them. And – that being so – I had better do as little 'waffling' as I can, and get right down to it!

It was a really pleasant morning again, with clear air and bright sunshine. Derek and I headed out directly after breakfast, making sure we had his binoculars with us. I managed to find the way to the gate into the potato field, but I was a bit worried about going in without Chris. Derek, however, was not in the mood to fuss about niceties, saying, "There's no-one in sight, Dad – we'll worry about it *if* anyone sees us and complains. We're not doing any damage, anyway!" So he drove in, and carefully closed the gate behind us. Derek's is not an all-terrain vehicle but luckily the ground was dry and firm around the edge of the field, and there was no danger we would get stuck in mud. We parked in the same place as yesterday, and Derek helped me down the slope to the banks of the stream. I pointed out the direction in which he should look, and he peered intently across the valley to the opposite hill. He didn't move or speak for several minutes, then lowered the binoculars and looked at his watch. "Ten to nine," he remarked. "Dan said he'd come about nine, so it's highly unlikely he's got a fire started already, even if he arrived early."

115

"I take it you *can* see the cloud, then?" I asked.

"I can see *something*," he admitted slowly. "It's obviously not smoke, or fog, and it doesn't look like any ordinary cloud that I've ever seen. I don't know what the hell it *is* – but I don't like the look of it one bit! Sorry, Dad – I suppose I was *hoping* you and Chris were wrong. Because – if it *is* what you seem to think it is – what the heck are we going to *do*? I mean – we've tied up everything we've *got* in Manor Farm! And how could I sell it, knowing what I know now – or maybe I should say 'suspecting what I suspect'? I don't like to think that the Jeffries had any idea of all this when they sold it to *us* – and yet – it seems to be pretty common local knowledge, doesn't it? I can't help feeling they *had* to know! By the time Chris tried to warn me, it was too late anyway – we'd already bought the place. And I honestly can't pretend I would have believed a word of it! I thought he was a real *nut*!"

He looked more defeated than I have ever seen him since that Julia girl left him in the lurch and almost broke his heart. Derek is usually one of the most optimistic and ebullient people I have ever met – his grin and his whole-hearted enthusiasm for life make the whole world seem a brighter and more cheerful place. I felt awful for him.

I put my hand on his arm and said, "We're not beaten yet, son. OK, we've never come across anything like this before, and I haven't the foggiest notion how we can begin to tackle it. But there must *be* a way. At least we have finally allowed ourselves to think the unthinkable. And surely, 'knowing your enemy' – or accepting that you've got one! – has got to be the first step in the battle – right? You're not alone. As your mother said so forcefully, your whole *family* are right with you in this. And *Dan* obviously doesn't need any more convincing. And Chris and Helen have been doing their homework for some time, and they know the place and the people. Maybe this Lira Wardwell can give us some answers – it's worth talking to her, anyway. We all know what Manor Farm means to you and Pat and the kids, Derek, and we won't let you lose it without a fight. OK?"

He turned and looked directly into my eyes for a few moments. When he is serious like that, he looks incredibly like my father as a young man, even though he has Mary's colouring. Then he gave a crooked smile, and said, "You're a game old dog, Dad – you know that? And with *Mum* on our side

116

as well – spooks watch out! Come on – let's get out of here before we get done for trespassing!"

The field and the lane remained quiet and empty, however, and no irate farmer came to bawl us out. We made sure the gate was shut behind us, and headed home.

"Actually – it's quite handy I'm home today," said Derek. "You know that security firm I contacted? They're supposed to be turning up this morning, and I'd rather be here to talk to them myself than leaving it all to Pat. I'm afraid they won't do spook-alarms, though, *or* ghost-proof fences! Pity!" At least he seemed to be regaining his sense-of-humour, which was a relief. There was a plume of perfectly ordinary smoke hanging over the top of the hill by now – we could smell it as we got close. Dan had obviously got his bonfire re-lit.

We went inside, and Pat was just making coffee. "That was nice timing," she said, handing Derek a mug. "Would you take this out to Dan? The thought of all those *spiders* he's disturbing makes my skin crawl – never mind the rats! I don't know how he can *do* it!"

"Would you like me to catch a few for you?" Derek teased, tickling the back of her neck with a tissue. "You could keep them as pets!"

Pat squealed, and very nearly spilled the coffee. "Brute!" she cried, "Don't you *dare* bring any of them in here, Derek – I *mean* it! I'll never *speak* to you again! Go on – take this to Dan before it goes all over the place!"

Derek grinned wickedly, took the mug and headed out of the back door. Pat was just going to close it firmly behind him, when he pushed it violently open again. The grin had completely disappeared, and he literally threw the mug into the yard, where it smashed to pieces. "Dad!" he yelled, "Get out here, quick!"

I put my mug down on the table, and joined him in time to see Dan staggering across the yard towards us, in the same uncoordinated way as on Wednesday. We rushed over to him, and managed to sit him down on the old mounting-block before his knees gave way.

"What *is* it, son?" I asked, "Here – put your head down between your knees for a few minutes – you're going to be all right. Derek – go and get a glass of water!"

Derek turned to go, but Pat was already bringing one. Dan took it, and managed a few sips. He seemed affected less deeply than the last time, and was already starting to pull himself together. He took some deep breaths, and shook his head as if to clear it, then said thickly, "Thanks. Sorry 'bout that – I fit be fine now – honest . . ."

"What brought *that* on, dare I ask?" said Derek, quite pale himself. "I have a nasty feeling it was more than just the rats or the spiders!"

"Yeah – sorry!" said Dan, "I finished clearing the place – that's the last load burning now. There no wind, so I figured I could leave it for a spell – ain't nothing to hurt up there. Heck – what a mess *that* was! There were *two* old busted baby-carriages, a gazillion empty feed-sacks, paint-cans, such, and even the skeleton of a long-dead cat, not to mention all that rotten hay and straw. How folks fit ever let a place get in such a *mess* is more than I can figure! Couldn't nobody have cleaned out that place, seemingly, in fifty year, maybe more! Howsomever, I was just sweeping up some, and I come on a sort of concrete block over in the far corner – I was real puzzled what the purpose of it could ever been. But it was all cracked and busted up, and wasn't no use for anything, so I lifted the bits, and went to smooth off the earth underneath. And that's when I found . . . maybe you best come see . . . " He hoisted himself upright with an effort and led the way back across the yard and into the shadowy interior of the barn. The three of us trailed reluctantly behind, Pat clinging tightly on to Derek's arm. I wouldn't have minded copying her myself!

The barn was now completely empty, and looked much bigger with all the clutter gone. Dust motes danced on the golden beams of pale sunshine which forced their way through every crack in the wooden sidings, as Dan made his way over into the far corner. There he stopped beside a wheelbarrow containing pieces of cracked cement, and pointed to a hole in the earth floor. It took a moment for our eyes to adjust to the dim light, but suddenly my gaze focused on the contents of the hole – my stomach muscles clenched involuntarily, and I heard a sharp intake of breath from either Derek or Pat. Lying in the earth was an axe – an axe covered in rusty brown stains, not just on the metal of the blade but on the wooden handle, too.

"Dad," said Derek, in a hoarse whisper. "Is that – *blood*?"

"Almost certainly," I said, as normally as I could manage. "Not necessarily *human* blood, though . . . "

It didn't sound convincing, even to me, and Dan cocked an eyebrow in my direction, as much as to say, "Who do you think *you're* kidding?"!

"Sumpun else," he said, quietly, picking up his spade and scraping away a little more of the dirt. Lying under the axe was something which, as I squinted at it, resolved itself into the reinforced corner of a suitcase.

"The clothes they went to London in, Doc?" asked Dan, looking at me ironically. "You know a good reason why anyone would want to bury a suitcase, Sir, and a perfectly good axe covered in blood – human *or* animal? Sorry, Derek, but – like I said the other day – he killed 'em. They never *did* go to London – they never had no *call* to go to London, there *was* nobody belonging them in London. They died right here. He murdered them, and the bombing-raids were just a good cover for their disappearance, so folks didn't commence to asking questions . . ."

"OK – that's it!" said Derek, letting out a deep breath. "I'm going to call the police!"

"The po-lice?" echoed Dan. "What *they* fit do?"

"According to you," said Derek, "I have three axe-murder victims hidden in the chimney of my cottage. What, pray tell me, am I *meant* to do with three bodies, *except* call the police?

"Derek," I said, warningly. "Hadn't you better think this through? I mean, wouldn't it be a good idea to make *sure* there really *are* bodies there before we . . . "

"Fine, Dad!" he snapped, "Maybe *you'd* like to go and grab a pickaxe and take a look for me! It's obviously no good sending *Dan* in there, not after what happened the other day, and *I* have never even *seen* a dead body, not even someone who died peacefully in their sleep, never mind someone who has been murdered with a damn' *axe*, for pity's sake! And I would rather like to keep it that way! Call me squeamish if you like – I *am*! And I don't think I'd like to call in some poor, unsuspecting tradesman, either! That's what the police are paid for – dealing with dead bodies!"

And off he marched. The three of us stood looking after him open-mouthed for a moment, then followed him back to the house, where he was already on the phone. And just at that moment, the doorbell rang. Pat went to answer it, and came back saying it was the men from the security firm, come to assess the property!

"Damn and blast!" yelled Derek, slamming down the phone. "Talk about *timing*!" He charged off to the front door, and came back saying he had sent the poor chaps packing. He'll probably have to pay for the call, but there really was no way we could cope with them as well! We had got quite enough on our hands, and there *are* priorities!

Maybe because of the goings-on on Wednesday, the police were a little less sceptical than they might otherwise have been. Derek explained what Dan had found in the barn, and they sent someone out straight away. Pat and I waited inside, while Dan and Derek went to display the grisly discovery, and Derek told us afterwards that when they understood the background story of the disappearance of Emily Hillyer and her two children during the London Blitz, they immediately saw how *convenient* that might have been. When they opened the suitcase, they found it was, indeed, stuffed full of clothes in the style of the 1930's – 40's, suitable for a woman, a girl and a little boy. They also began to wonder where the bodies might be hidden, and Derek was able to suggest Dan's theory about the chimney. Before we knew it, we had a full SOCO team on the premises – the yard was full of vehicles, and the barn and the cottage were cordoned off with yellow tape.

Good old Mabel came up trumps again, as usual. She had carried on with both minding Kyle and preparing lunch while we were otherwise occupied in the barn, although I'm afraid none of us had much appetite for it. And she kept the kettle on the boil all afternoon, providing cups of tea for the invasion of police and technicians. About 2.30, Derek, who had been outside with the police, rushed into the kitchen looking as white as a sheet. He flung himself down with his head on the kitchen table, covering it tightly with his arms, and his shoulders shaking with sobs. I can't even remember the last time I saw him cry, but it must have been a *very* long time ago. Pat rushed to him, holding him fiercely and stroking his hair. At last he took a deep breath and raised a tear-streaked face. "Oh, God, Pat!" he gasped, "It's *real*! Boy, is it *ever* real! They're there – all three of them – stuffed in the damn *chimney*! I'm so *sorry*, Pat – I honestly never thought they were *really* . . . oh, *God*!"

"Don't be silly," she comforted him. "How *could* you know? I didn't *really* believe it either. And we've found them *now* – the police will take them away, won't they – and Dan's family can bury them, the way they wanted to. It'll be OK now, you'll see . . ."

He soon pulled himself together, once the initial shock was over, and they both went to drop Mabel home and pick up Kurt and Kirstie from school.

I was glad that by the time the kids arrived, the bodies had been removed, but they really coped with the situation remarkably well. They had, after all, already been convinced that Arthur and his mother and sister were dead. They seemed relieved, if anything, that their bodies had been found and could be buried decently. Pat and Derek had explained everything as well as they could on the way home, so seeing all the police and vehicles was no great shock – Kurt, particularly, found it quite exciting! And little Kirstie cannot be persuaded that it was not all due to her kind and brilliant grandfather's intervention on Arthur's behalf! I tried to tell her that I, personally, had precious little to do with all this, but she put her arms round my neck anyway, kissed me and whispered, "Thank you, Grampy!" Modesty was never one of my overriding faults, so I gave up trying to disillusion her. *I* don't mind being viewed as a Great and Noble Dispenser of Blessings, if that's the way she wants to see it! I just wish I could believe that this means our problems are over. But I can't quite understand why removing some old bodies should be the whole answer, even though I would like very much to believe it will be.

Mindful of my lecture last night, as soon as I was sure she would be home from collecting Elizabeth from school, I called Mary to warn her of what was going on here. She was, naturally, shocked, but assured me that they would leave as soon as Jenny got home. They arrived about six o'clock, by which time most of the police team had departed, having finished their photographing, etc. Obviously, after over forty years, there was going to be precious little other evidence left – the whole house had been decorated and renovated. And the principal suspect is long-dead himself, anyway. I suppose they will have to do their best to confirm the identities of the bodies, but I'm not sure what conclusive proof there can be. At least it must be obvious that the crime took place so long ago that no suspicion can possibly attach to any of *us*!

I'm not sure how the media got hold of the story – I suppose it must have been via the police – but by five-o'clock we had a mob of reporters and photographers, not to mention some television cameras, crowding around the gate and almost blocking the lane. The police have left a constable to keep them from swarming all over the property, but I'm not sure just how long we may be the subjects of the unwelcome attention. Probably not for too long, once they have taken their photos of the 'murder cottage', but we shall probably be pestered by sight-seers for quite some time to come.

121

Little Elizabeth seemed to take it all in her stride when *she* arrived, and she and the other three were quite thrilled at the thought of Manor Farm being on the television! What it is to be young! We had dinner, and finally managed to get the kids calmed down enough to get them to bed. Then Derek, Pat and I settled down to try to explain the situation to Mary and Jenny – as far as we understand it ourselves, that is! Luckily, they are both very calm and practical women, and we were never in any danger of having to cope with hysterics. Obviously, they have no more idea than the rest of us about what is really going on, and whether the removal of the bodies will actually change anything. From the look on Mary's face, I think she is as dubious as I am about that. She has been very patient about me scribbling down these last few notes – fortunately I managed to jot most of it down this afternoon, in the midst of the chaos! But she is now insisting that I pack up and get to bed, and I can't pretend I shall be sorry to switch off for a while. It has been *quite* a day!

Saturday, 22nd June

Well, I'm afraid it was a forlorn hope that the removal of those bodies would improve the situation. In fact, it seems to have made things worse – with a vengeance! I have never before made any entries in my diary when Mary was here at the weekends. But I showed her my notes last night, and with the go-ings-on *still* going on, she seems to feel that this record of events may be valuable, and has agreed to my making the effort to keep up to date. With so many completely outrageous and incomprehensible things happening in such quick succession, it would be impossible to keep up sides with recording them otherwise. So let's see if I can get my thoughts organised enough to be clear and coherent.

We adults all went to bed about eleven o'clock, and I fell asleep more quickly and easily than I had expected after all the excitement. All was peaceful until about quarter-past-two, when we were violently awakened by what sounded like an *explosion* right outside. Even before I was properly awake, I found I had sprung out of bed, disoriented and desperately trying to fathom what had happened. Mary was still in bed, but was sitting up clutching the bedclothes to her, her eyes wide and startled. "George – what on *earth* . . .

122

?" she began, but then our eyes were drawn to the side window of our room – which faces towards the cottage. Even through the curtains, we could see flashes of light. My first thought was that the cottage was on fire, and I raced across the bedroom to look out, with Mary right behind me. As I drew back the curtains, I hardly knew *what* to think: I had never seen anything like it before in my life – nor had I ever expected to! My brain simply couldn't seem to make any sense of what my eyes were trying to tell me. The cottage was not on *fire* – but it was completely enveloped in a sickly yellowish-greenish glow – a pulsing light, which leapt up then fell back, almost like the phosphorescent breath of some unimaginable mythical creature! While I was still trying to make some sort of sense of the phenomenon, Mary had run to the foot of the stairs, calling to Derek. I think he was probably already on his way – there was no chance that anyone in the house could have slept through that massive percussion of sound! Mary dragged him into our room, and I beckoned him over to the window. "Dad – what *is* that?" he demanded, although I can't imagine why he thought *I* would know any more than *he* did! "Sorry – no idea!" I said.

"It sounded like an explosion!" he cried, "I'm going to call the Fire Brigade!"

He dashed out into the hall, grabbed the phone and dialled 999. But he didn't speak. He took the receiver away from his ear, frowned at it, shook it, replaced it, then lifted it to his ear again. He jiggled the little thingummies the handset sits on, went through the performance again, then slowly replaced the receiver in its rest. "The line's dead," he stated in a flat voice, giving me a look I simply cannot describe. By this time, the whole family were gathered in the hallway, in pyjamas or nighties and bare feet, all staring at him with big, frightened eyes.

"I don't think the place *is* on fire, actually," I said. "And even if it is, it's not close enough to cause any danger over here. Luckily there isn't much wind. We should be safe enough at this distance."

For a moment, nobody spoke. It was almost as if we were collectively holding our breath. Mary was the first to pull herself together. "We're doing no good standing here getting chilled!" she said firmly. "Pat – will you pop and get Jenny and the children their dressing-gowns and slippers? And put your own on while you're up there, love! Jenny – go and put the kettle on, and we'll all have some hot chocolate. You children will come in the lounge with me – I'm going to light the fire, and we'll get warmed up. Derek – hand me my dressing-gown and slippers, will you, dear, then wrap up a bit yourself? George, put yours on, too, then we'll have . . . "

I never got to hear the end of what she was going to say, because suddenly there was the unmistakable noise of smashing glass – as if someone were throwing bricks through each of the cottage windows in turn. Kyle began to cry, frightened by the noise, and probably by the expressions on our faces, and the dogs began a terrified yelping from the scullery where they sleep. Mary pulled herself together again, clapped her hands, and said, "Come along, now! Everybody do what I told you! Jenny – while you're in the kitchen, will you let those poor animals in?" She picked up Kyle, and shepherded the other children through the door into the lounge, shutting it behind her. Jenny headed for the kitchen, and Derek put his arm around Pat as they went off upstairs together. I went back into the bedroom, and took another look out of the window. The weird, unearthly glow was still pulsing, brighter and more rapidly than before. Suddenly, with another loud smash, the glass in the landing-window of the cottage, which is on this side, broke into smithereens, followed by the window of the bathroom next door. I went cold all over. Dan only cut the hedge on Wednesday, so I had a clear view of the whole side of the cottage – and there was no *sign* of anyone throwing bricks. No sign of *anyone* - anyone *visible*, that is!

I dragged myself away from the window, and began to fumble for my clothes. I felt that I would cope much better with this situation if I were properly dressed – I always feel far less capable and in control when slopping around in pyjamas and slippers. By the time I had pushed my feet into my shoes and found a warm jumper in my drawer, Derek was back. He had had the same idea, and was fully dressed, too. We both went over to the window again, and I saw that my remark about the wind was no longer true: the wind was now quite strong, and seemed to be rapidly growing stronger – the trees all around were thrashing in frenzy. In fact, I had a vivid mental vision of the tornado-scene in 'The Wizard of Oz'! In my head, I kept hearing, "It's a twister! It's a twister!", although I knew, of course, that it couldn't possibly be. Tornadoes do not simply spring up from *nowhere* on a calm June night in the middle of England! But the *wind* seemed not to know that, and began whirling around the cottage, roaring and shrieking ever more loudly. The air was full of flying litter – leaves, straw, paper, pebbles – anything the wind could find to seize and hurl about. Then the slates on the roof of the cottage began to be ripped off, whirling about the cottage like a swarm of demented bats. I *know* Derek had locked up as usual after the police had departed, because we were concerned about the reporters trying to get in to take pictures of the room where the bodies were found, but suddenly the cottage doors burst open simultaneously. They began to bang wildly to and fro, so violently that the back door was ripped away from its hinges, and joined the cloud of debris hurtling around in the wind. The noise was horrendous, and the scene like something out of a horror film, with the corpse-light around the cottage pulsing more brightly and more rapidly than ever. Derek and I seemed rooted to the spot, almost mesmerised by the chaos and the total incomprehensibility of what we were seeing, until suddenly one of the slates from the cottage roof came crashing through the window where we were standing. I'm not sure how we both escaped major injury, but we were showered in flying glass, and our hands and faces were bleeding from what seemed like hundreds of small cuts, which burned like wasp-stings. Derek grabbed my arm, and yelled, "Let's get out of here!" We raced for the door into the hallway, slamming it behind us. Pat opened the lounge door and peered out, then, seeing the blood, she rushed into the hall. "Derek! Dad!" she cried, "What on earth . . . ? Are you badly hurt? What's *happening?*"

"It's OK," Derek grabbed her shoulders, trying to sound calm and in control. "The wind's just ripped the roof off the cottage, and one of the slates came through the bedroom window. It's only scratches – at least, *mine* are! Are *you* OK, Dad?"

"More shaken than hurt," I confirmed. "Let's go and get rid of the blood before anyone else has to see us."

"But – the *wind?!*" poor Pat was completely bewildered. "The *wind* ripped the *roof* off? Derek – should we go down into the cellar? What about *this* roof . . . ?"

"I can't positively *swear* to it," said Derek, "but I think it's the *cottage* that's under attack, not this place. I damn-well *hope* so, anyway! *I* think it's old Hillyer, throwing a paddy because we took those bodies away! What do you say, Dad?"

"Well, that is no normal storm!" I agreed. "Incredible as it may seem, I can't think of any other explanation for what we just witnessed. How far he can take it, of course, I really don't know. But if the phone's dead, we can't summon help, and . . . "

"*I* know – I'll get the car!" cried Derek. "I can drive down to the Thompsons' and phone from there!"

Pat begged and pleaded with him not to go, but when we looked out of the kitchen window the wind seemed to have abated considerably, and he gave her a quick kiss, promised to take care, and dashed out of the back door with the car keys in his hand. Pat was obviously very unhappy about it, but occupied herself by getting a bowl of warm water and the first-aid kit, and beginning to clean up my cuts. They were sore, as those sorts of small nicks always are, but none of them was dangerous. I was soon bathed, disinfected and ornamented with sticking plaster. Apart from a few blood-spatters on my sweater, I looked more or less respectable again. We were just discussing whether to rejoin the others in the lounge, when the kitchen door opened again, and Derek strode in, his hair tousled by the wind, and his mouth grim. "Damn car won't **start**!" he yelled. "I'll take yours, Pat!"

He grabbed another set of keys off the board, and rushed out again. Pat and I looked at each other – I think we were both thinking the same things, and I'm sure neither of us was surprised when Derek returned in only a few minutes. Pat flew into his arms, but he looked at me over her head and said quietly, "That one won't start either. **Both** of ours are completely dead. I haven't got the keys to Jenny's but I'll bet you anything you like that *it's* dead too. We'll just have to sit it out."

The flashing and the banging were still going on unabated, although the wind had now died away almost completely. Pat and I cleaned up Derek's wounds, and we all trooped into the lounge. Pat and Derek always keep kindling laid in the hearth, ready to light at a moment's notice, and Mary had got the fire burning brightly by this time. It was a good job, because suddenly the lights went out, and at least we weren't plunged into pitch darkness.

"Light the candles, please, Pat," said Mary calmly, as if all this were all perfectly normal. They had a row of candles sitting on the mantelpiece, and a box of matches beside them, all ready for action.

"I'll do it, Mum," offered Derek, and soon the room was aglow with flickering flames. Derek and I sank down gratefully into the easy chairs, and Jenny made us mugs of chocolate, with milk which they had had the forethought to keep warm for us in a pan over the fire.

"I had a feeling we might lose the power," Mary explained, "so we made sure we were all ready, just in case! Now, just relax, George, and drink your chocolate!"

If it hadn't been for the sharp stinging of my cuts, I could almost have believed I was dreaming, it was so strange sitting there in the early hours of the morning, in the soft glow of the fire and the candles, drinking sweet milky chocolate and surrounded by the shocked faces of most of my family. I could still hear the frenzied banging coming from the cottage even though, in the lounge, the sound was muffled. The curtains blocked most of the pulsating glow from outside, although flashes of light were just visible around the edges. For a while, no-one spoke – the children were snuggled up on the sofa, clinging tightly to the women, who had obviously done a nice job of comforting them, even though they must have been pretty scared themselves. The trembling dogs were cringing against their legs, ears flat and white rims showing around their wide eyes.

"Derek," said Pat quietly, trying not to let the children hear her, "you don't think he can . . . get in *here*, do you? I mean – that window being broken, and there's no lock on the door, and . . . "

"I'm not sure that would make a whole lot of difference!" Derek whispered back, looking worried. "The *cottage* was all locked up, tight as a drum, but you can *hear* the front door still banging. The *back* door got ripped right off its hinges! Not to mention that every window in the place must be smashed, and the roof gone to hell and back!"

"It's all right, Mummy," piped up Kirstie, who had heard despite their lowered voices. "He can't come in *here*." She sounded quite confident of her assertion.

"How can you be so sure, Poppet?" asked Derek.

"*Arthur* told us," she pronounced. "It's only his Mummy who can come in the house – his Daddy has to stay outside."

"Yeah – there's like . . . still *rules*, see," Kurt put in. "Arthur's Mum was let to come in, 'cause she had to do the housework – like Mabel does now. But when you're dead you can't go where you weren't let to go when you were alive. Arthur and Annie were allowed to come into the kitchen, some-times, but their Dad had to work *outside*, and he always had those big dirty boots on, so they never let him come in. So he can't now, either. If he could of, I'd *never* have gone to bed – not with *him* around!"

Derek and Pat were looking dumbfounded by these revelations! "Why didn't you tell us all this before, Kurt?" asked Derek wearily.

Kurt sighed, and raised his eyes dramatically to heaven. "We *did*, Dad!" he said scathingly. "You just weren't *listening*! *You* said it was all a load of twaddle, and *you* said you didn't want to hear any more about it!"

Derek did have the grace to look ashamed, and gave the children an un-reserved apology. But *I* couldn't find it in my heart to really blame him – I mean, it *did* all sound a bit far-fetched, didn't it? His children, of course, had *never* blamed him, and did their best to reassure him.

"You were really *brave*, Dad!" said Kurt magnanimously. "I was so scared I nearly p . . . no, p'r'aps I better not say that with Grandma here!"

"Very wise!" agreed Mary, but her lips twitched, all the same! "Have you children got any *more* words of wisdom from Arthur? Anything that might help us to stop all this?"

Kurt and Kirstie looked at each other and shrugged. Kyle had gone fast asleep on Pat's lap, with his thumb in his mouth.

"I don't think Arthur *knew* how to make his Daddy stop," said Kirstie at last. "He was really *scared*, wasn't he, Kurt? And so was Annie. Their Daddy was a bad, bad man. Are they still here, Grampy, or have they gone now? We haven't been able to go outside to see, since the policemen left."

"I really don't know, sweetheart," I told her. "I have a feeling they may still be around, but I'm honestly not sure. We'll have to wait and see."

"I hope they're not in the cottage, with their Daddy getting so mad!" she whispered, her eyes filling with tears. It was *not* a nice thought, and I think it upset us all pretty badly. Unfortunately, none of us had any reassurance to offer. If, indeed, there *are* 'rules', as Kurt claims, I have yet to discover what they are! But it would seem that I may have had *Emily* Hillyer to thank for the incident with the books, if she is the only one who can enter the house – not Arthur, after all.

After that, nobody seemed to be able to find much to say, and we all sat looking into the fire and listening to the temper-tantrum going on next door.

I suppose, objectively, the whole episode lasted only a couple of hours, but it seemed much longer.

I have never really believed in the efficacy of 'cock crow' before, but maybe there is, after all, some truth in the power of the dawn, as described in all the old fairy-stories. The dead darkness outside, relieved only by that awful glow from the cottage, gradually began to lighten to grey, and with the coming of the natural light that foul illumination seemed to fade. One moment it was night, and the horror was strong. The next, we heard – faint, but clear in the distance – Farmer Thompson's cockerel begin to crow his greeting to the coming day. At that very moment, the banging and thumping abruptly ceased, and into the deafening vacuum a chaffinch began to pour his liquid notes. As if they had been awaiting his signal, other birds joined in, and soon a full dawn chorus saturated the air around us, just as if the terrors of the night had never been. At that moment, too, the electric power cut back in, and when Derek checked the phone, we had a dialling-tone!

"Do I call anyone?" he asked, looking around rather helplessly at the rest of us. "If so, *who* – and what on earth do I tell them?"

The general consensus was that whatever had happened seemed to be over for now, and there didn't seem much point in sending for help at *this* point. Derek sighed, put the receiver back on its cradle, then heaved himself wearily out of his chair, and went over to open the curtains. A wonderful torrent of early sunlight flooded in, and we could see the pale, clean blue of a windless, cloudless sky, still tinted with the rosy glow of sunrise. Absolute magic!

"Right," said Mary. "Let's get these children back to bed. I think we should *all* turn in for a couple of hours – it's Saturday, and we haven't got any deadlines to meet, thank goodness. Come along, George. Don't worry about those mugs, Pat – I'll wash them up a little later."

"I'd better just pop out and see what the damage is," began Derek, but she cut him off short.

"You will do no such thing, Derek!" she said decisively. "What you *will* do is to take your wife and children back to bed, and get some rest yourself. You'll cope with the rest of the day much better if you're sensible, believe me! What damage is done is already done, and you can't change it, so there is no point in worrying about it. Off you go! Come along, George!"

Can you believe that my wife has, on occasion, actually had the nerve to accuse *me* of being a 'steamroller'?! I'm not even in the same *class* as she is! Anyway, we all did as we were told – Jenny carried a heavy-eyed Elizabeth, Pat a snoring Kyle, and Derek followed Kurt and Kirstie, with a hand on each of their shoulders. The dogs both followed, close on Derek's heels, and nobody ordered them to stay downstairs.

It wasn't until we actually went back into our bedroom that Mary and I remembered the damage that had been done to it – there was a gaping hole in the window, and the slivers of glass to which it had been reduced had been thrown liberally all over the room. There was no way we could sleep in that bed! "Never mind," said Mary staunchly, "the sofa in the lounge converts into a double bed – we can use that for a few hours. Gather up some cushions, George, and I'll go and get some blankets out of the airing-cupboard."

We made ourselves as comfortable as possible, and it wasn't too bad at all, all things considered. I've slept on worse.

Actually – looking back on it – I think that we, as a family, handled that traumatic episode rather well. Nobody got hysterical, or made any kind of unnecessary fuss. And considering how terrifying it was – being completely cut off from the rest of the world in this isolated farm house, with no electricity, and with the phones *and* the cars out of commission – I feel every one of us deserves a pat on the back!

I think we were so exhausted from the strain that all of us managed to drop off, but I don't suppose anyone else's sleep was any more refreshing than mine. We struggled out of bed at about nine o'clock – Kyle was wide awake by then, and full of beans as usual, which makes it almost impossible for anyone else to sleep in the same house! I let Mary shower first, then I stood for quite some time under the sprays of hot water, trying to summon up enough energy to face the day. I haven't felt so totally *drained* for quite some time – which just goes to show, I suppose, how much my condition has actually *improved*, despite all the mayhem! If *tiredness* is the worst of my problems, I defy *any* man of my age to come through what we experienced last night in much better shape! I finally turned off the water, got dry and dressed, and went to join the others in the kitchen. There was a wonderful, mouth-watering smell of cooking, and Jenny was soon handing me a heaped plate of bacon, eggs, tomatoes and fried bread. There is nothing like a good meal to revive you after an ordeal like that, and I had to be strict with myself and resist the temptation to ask for a second helping. I'm not as active these days as I used to be, and if I allow the old waistline to spread *too* much, I may never get back into shape.

As soon as we had finished eating, Derek, Pat and I went out to take a look at the damage, while Jenny and Mary washed up. Mabel was having the whole weekend off, for which we weren't too sorry – the place was a *mess*! If there had *really* been an explosion, it could hardly have done more damage. There was broken glass everywhere, and the slates from the cottage roof were scattered all around. But the really strange thing was how *localised* the damage actually was – centred exactly over what remained of the cottage. Its utter ruin brought back vivid memories of buildings shattered by German bombs during the war. And Derek and Pat had something of the same bleak look on their faces as the survivors of those air-raids, who had to face the reality of the destruction of their homes. None of us had been killed, or even badly hurt; and none of us were homeless – but the devastation was still so overwhelming, and so unexpected, that I think the comparison is excusable.

"What do we do *now*, Derek?" asked Pat.

He took a deep breath. "First," he said, "I think we had better call the police. I know they can't *do* anything, but they need to see this. They need to *know*, at least. I think *some* of them will have an idea about what happened, although perhaps we'd better tone it down a bit – I don't think we had better try blaming old Hillyer, do you? I mean – we don't actually *know* it was him, do we? It's only guesswork, and we couldn't begin to prove it. I'm not sure *how* we stand about insurance – does this classify as an 'Act of God', do you suppose? Whatever – we've got to get this mess cleared up as quickly as we can, particularly the glass. It's a good job I *didn't* try driving out here last night, after all, or I'd be having to shell out for four new tyres, as well! I think I'll give Dan a ring – he told me to call if we needed him in any way. And we'll have to get a glazier to mend that bedroom window before Mum and Dad want to go to bed! No doubt the police can recommend someone who does emergency work. That's if you and Mum are staying after all this, Dad?"

"Don't be silly, Derek!" I said. "Of course we're staying. Do you honestly think we are merrily going to drive back to town and leave you to cope with *this?* Although perhaps Pat and the children ought to go and stay with her parents for a little . . . "

"No way!" said Pat stubbornly, decisively shaking her head. "If Derek stays, so do I! And I think the kids will feel the same. Now we're all agreed about what's going on, they seem to be handling it better than you'd suppose. We'll stay. We *can't* let him drive us out of our own home!"

I expected Derek to argue with her, and insist that she left, but he didn't. Whether they have made the *right* decision, of course, I have no idea. I can only hope so. And admire their guts. Pat was right that Kurt and Kirstie voted to stay at home, and Kyle is a little young to have a valid opinion. Mary and Jenny were quite determined to stay put, as was little Elizabeth. So, having reached a unanimous decision to give old Hillyer a run for his money, we got down to the practicalities of cleaning up.

The police arrived, and were initially certain that *we* must have blown the place up! They seemed to think that probably we didn't like the fact of those bodies having been concealed there, and preferred the insurance money! Anyway, *they* sent for the Fire Investigation people, who sent for some bods from the army bomb-disposal squad, and *they* had to check that there were '*no more explosives*' before they would let anyone near the place. It was a toss up whether we all had to be evacuated, but they finally decided that the house was far enough away from the cottage to be safe, as long as we all stayed indoors, and on the far side. Once they had reassured themselves that it was unlikely there would be any more 'earth-shattering *kabooms*', they took in a dog trained to sniff out explosives – or *dragged* the poor creature in, might be more accurate: *it* was no more eager to go near the place than the police dog had been! Anyway, it gave none of the responses they use to indicate that explosives are, or have been, present, and got out of there as fast as its handler would allow. In the end, after lengthy and serious discussions, and after listening several times to our account of how it happened – in which, as Derek had suggested, we did *not* stress the 'supernatural' angle! – the experts came to the conclusion that freak weather conditions must have been to blame! One of the policemen had reported that he had seen 'sheet-lightning' flashing over in this direction during the early hours of the morning, and that seemed to clinch the matter. I suppose it was really the best we could hope for. The insurance company has promised to send an inspector to assess the situation, but whether they will actually pay out, I have no idea. Somehow, just at the moment, it seems like the least of our worries!

After taking copious photographs, the police allowed Derek and Dan – who had kindly dropped everything and rushed right over – to start clearing the shards of glass from the driveway. Mary spent most of the morning contacting all our nearest-and-dearest about recent events, just in case they do happen to see it in the papers or on the television news. They were all suitably shocked, even though I think she was careful to keep to a simplified version, namely that Derek had decided to open up the old fireplace, found the bodies, and then called the police – which hangs together quite well, and will, we hope, also satisfy the media. Our 'freak storm', coming so close on the heels of all the other melodrama, is rather stretching credulity, but I don't know what we can do about **that**! Some of the reporters, I suppose, are bound to talk to the locals and hear some lurid stories about the ghostly goings-on at Manor Farm, but most readers will treat that as poppycock anyway. Before all this, I would have snorted in disbelief, myself! We have an even bigger crowd of journalists clogging up the lane today than we did yesterday. "Before" and "After" pictures of the poor cottage are obviously going to be splashed all over a few front pages! No doubt it will be a nine-days-wonder. (I hope!) It rather amuses me to speculate what the meteorological chappies will make of it!

Once Mary had spoken to all the people we felt had any right to know, and had marched off to make a start on cleaning up the bedroom, I called Chris. He was very relieved to hear from me, and said they had been hearing wild stories since yesterday afternoon, but felt that, even though he had promised to ring me, it was best not to pester us with phone-calls at a time like that. They had, of course, been very anxious for us, but were sure I **would** contact them as soon as things calmed down a little. When I told him about last night's little shenanigans, he simply didn't know **what** to say! "God, George," he managed at last, "this is getting really ugly! It's way beyond anything I ever expected – although, as you know, I **have** been worried! To bring you up to date on our end, by the way, I did go to see old Lira Wardwell, but I'm afraid she isn't having **any**! I did tell you that some people down in the village have been having weird experiences too, didn't I? Well, some of the local yobs have decided that poor old Lira is a 'witch', and that **she** is responsible for what is happening. They've been yelling abuse, and throwing stones

133

through *her* windows! I only wish I could catch 'em at it! Under the circumstances, you can't blame the old girl for being more than a little upset, and she wouldn't agree to a meeting with you, no matter how Helen and I pleaded. In the end, she shut the door in our faces. But I'll have another try, and tell her what you've been going through up there. Maybe she'll think better of it. Mind you – I can't promise she'll be able to help much, even then – I wouldn't want to give you any false hopes! I'll call you back, and let you know how I get on – OK?"

He did ring back, about half-an-hour later, sounding defeated. "Sorry, George," he sighed. "She still refuses to talk. Look – if nothing else untoward happens in the meantime, how about you and Mary coming down for lunch tomorrow? Or would you prefer not to leave your family?"

"I'll clear it with Mary," I said, "but I think you'll find she'll be as keen as I am. And the rest of them *ought* to be all right in broad daylight. I'll let you know for certain, but I'll say a provisional 'yes, please'!"

As I predicted, Mary felt it should be safe enough for us to accept the invitation, and is very much looking forward to seeing Helen again. Derek, Pat and Jenny all assured us that they would be fine, and encouraged us to go, so that is a pleasant prospect for tomorrow.

When I went outside to have a break from writing and to see how Derek and Dan were getting on, an aged pick-up truck wheezed its way slowly up the hill, nudged through the crowd of reporters, and pulled into the gateway. As soon as it had drawn to a halt, out jumped Mabel from the passenger seat. She stopped a moment, clapping her hands to her mouth in horror when she saw the wreckage of the cottage, then drew a deep breath and marched on towards the house. "'Morning, Sir!" she said grimly as she passed me. I was sure that she was going to give Pat her notice, and my heart sank. The man who had been driving the truck also got out, and stood staring in disbelief at what, only a few hours before, had been a cottage. He was a stocky, red-faced man, with a chin covered in white stubble, wearing a cap, an open-necked work-shirt, corduroy trousers and lace-up boots. I assumed he had to be Mabel's husband, and went over to speak to him.

"I'm George Hanson," I said, smiling and holding out my hand. "Derek's Dad? You must be Mr. . . . . er . . . " I suddenly realised that I had completely forgotten Mabel's surname – always assuming I ever knew it!

"Potts, Sir," he said, taking my outstretched hand in a firm, rough grip. "Albert Potts. Pleased to meet you. By gum, though – looks like you *'ave* been 'aving trouble! What was it – a bloody earthquake?"

"Something like that, Mr. Potts!" I agreed with feeling, hoping he wasn't going to ask too many questions. Constable Moffatt was holding back the news-hounds, but they were obviously straining to catch every word!

"Aaah!" he said. "We 'eard you'd been 'aving even more trouble up 'ere! Nothing would do for Mabel but she must come up and see if you was all all right. Nobody 'urt, I 'ope?"

"No, nobody hurt, Mr. Potts," I assured him. "That was very kind of Mabel – and good of you to bring her!"

"Aaah!" he said again. "Well – you up 'ere, you'm allus been good to both the missus and 'er Dad. If there's aught we can do to 'elp, I 'ope you know you oney 'ave to say the word! Well – I'll be leaving you now, Sir. I'll be back for Mabel about four or five – looks like there be plenty to keep 'er busy – aaaah!"

"I'm glad you're still allowing her to come," I said. "I know we'll be glad of the help *today*, and I'm not sure how we would go on without her as a general rule."

"Aaah, a right good worker, Mabel is," he agreed. "As for me 'allowing' 'er to come – I'd like to meet the man as could stop 'er, when she 'as 'er mind made up! That *would* be a sight, that would! Aaaah."

And he climbed back into his truck, performed an ungainly three-point turn in the gateway, and chugged off down the hill! It was a great relief to know that we weren't losing Mabel after all. Not *this* time, anyway! When I went back into the house, she had her sleeves rolled up and was energetically helping Mary to clear all the glass out of our bedroom. She really is a treasure – a downright good-hearted, honest woman – and her husband is quite right about what a good worker she is!

Derek said that the glazier the police recommended was only willing to board up the window over the weekend, but Jenny slogged through the entries in the Yellow Pages and finally came up with a young chap, just starting his own business, who was willing to come and do the job properly straight away. So Mary and I now have a new pane of glass in our bedroom window, and a glass-free bed that we can sleep in. Mary and Mabel have done their *best* to ensure that all the splinters of glass have been got out of the carpet, but Mary suggests I don't walk around without my slippers on – just in case! So the house itself is more or less back to normal.

The cottage, though, is a complete wreck. After all our variously-uniformed friends had departed, Dan and Derek went and had a good look around the outside, although the building is now so dangerous, structurally as well as 'spiritually', that they didn't venture inside. I asked Derek later just what Dan had made of it, and he said, "He pointed out something quite interesting that I hadn't noticed – the windows had all been broken from *inside*. The glass had all blown *out*, not *in*, as it would if there had been someone throwing rocks. He also thinks that the noise we *thought* was an explosion might have been the chimney-pots falling, and crashing down through the roof. It ties up, somehow, doesn't it, for it to start with the chimney? And the holes that were made in the roof would have let the wind under to rip the tiles off. Dan has no doubt at all that it was old Hillyer, showing us what he thought of our interference! And I'm not sure if I told you, Dad – Dan also suggested we go and check on the cars, and they both started first time. I flicked the keys, and away they went - just like they usually do. Spooky, eh?"

Definitely spooky, Derek! Most *definitely* spooky!

Anyway – it was a busy and chaotic day. I've been frantically scribbling on and off, trying to keep abreast of events. This evening, hardly surprisingly, it took a little longer than usual for the kids to settle down and drop off to sleep. I think we're lucky that they have coped so well – it's strange how kids are seldom as fragile as you expect them to be. Anyway, Jenny read bedtime stories to Kirstie and Elizabeth, who share a room, and Derek read to Kurt, until one by one they finally succumbed to exhaustion. Once they were sleeping, we adults gathered in the lounge and treated ourselves to a glass of rather nice wine apiece.

"Right," said Mary, after we had sat sipping quietly for a few minutes. "I think we had better discuss what we can *do* about this situation. We can't just sit here like dummies and let these sorts of things keep on happening, can we? Has anybody got any suggestions?"

"What about the Church?" suggested Pat tentatively. "They *do* deal with this sort of thing, don't they – casting out spirits and things like that?"

"We could try it, I suppose," I said dubiously. "But I don't think they get involved lightly. It could be hard work to convince them. And never having had any real dealings with this sort of thing, I honestly don't know if they could cope with the sheer *intensity* of this, even if we could persuade them to try. Why don't you have a word with Olly, Pat, and see what he says? It's an avenue we may have to explore."

I could see from Derek's face that he wasn't much more optimistic about it than I was, and was probably carefully *not* saying that attempted exorcisms can sometimes make matters worse.

"What about parapsychologists?" suggested Jenny. "We could probably find some if we tried. Is it the 'Society for Paranormal Research' I'm thinking of? *They* must have quite a bit of experience with this kind of problem."

"See if you can contact them, dear," agreed Mary. "*My* only suggestion is a lady I know slightly who claims to be a medium. But I'm rather afraid to involve her. I mean, old Mr. Hillyer – if that *is* who we're dealing with – seems very strong and very aggressive, judging by the display he treated us to last night! I wouldn't want poor Mrs. Henderson to get *hurt* in any way . . . "

"Why don't we keep her in reserve for now?" said Derek. "We'll see if we can get any joy from the church and the parapsychology wallahs first. *I* haven't got any more bright ideas, I'm afraid, but Dan is convinced that the person we really need is that old Mrs. Well-whatsit down in the village. Are you sure we can't persuade her to talk to us, Dad?"

"She shut the door in Chris and Helen's faces," I said, "Doesn't sound too encouraging to me! Do you know what Dan has in mind? I mean – does *he* think she has had some part in causing all this trouble, like some of the people in the village? Or what?"

"I'm not sure, to tell you the truth," he admitted. "He just said she might have some suggestions – I didn't get the feeling that he thought she was in any way responsible."

"I should think not, poor old soul!" cried Mary indignantly. "What a terrible thing to be accused of – she must be *so* upset, and probably *terrified*, if those louts are breaking her windows! It sounds positively Medieval! No wonder she's not keen to talk to strangers. But I'm going to get Helen to take me round to see her tomorrow – perhaps if I could meet her myself, I could persuade her that we're really not hostile. The thing I'm *most* afraid of, I think, is that she may agree to talk to us, but not have any more idea than *we* do what to do about it! Still – if **Dan** thinks she can help, he must have a reason, and I think we must do all we can to get her to **talk** to us, at least."

"Thanks, Mum," said Derek. "If anyone can talk her round, it has to be you. Now, how about we head for bed? I'm **hoping** we're going to have a quiet night tonight, but maybe we better not count on it! It didn't start 'til well after midnight last night, so let's make the best of it before he decides to clock on again!"

And on that comforting thought, we dispersed and began to get ready for bed. Mary has been very patient about me jotting down these last few notes, but I'm sure we shall both be glad to call it a day. I only hope old Hillyer is worn out, too – he jolly well ought to be! Where on earth did he find the sheer *energy* required to cause all that destruction? I have never come across anything like it before – although, let's be honest, I would have dismissed it as bunkum if I had! I think some serious research into psychic phenomena is called for – *if* ever I can find the *time*!

Sunday, 23rd June

Well, old Hillyer must have recharged his batteries *somehow* – although I am puzzled as to just how a ghost would go about doing that! I mean – *we* might have a good night's sleep, or put our feet up for a bit, or have a good meal and a cup of coffee or a stiff drink to revive us, that sort of thing. Surely a non-corporeal entity can't indulge in any of those homely measures? **Can** they manage the equivalent of sleeping, I wonder? Strange thought! None of *us* got much sleep last night, but at least there was no actual damage, like the night before. I think the worst thing was not knowing the extent of his powers, or what we might have to contend with next. We simply don't know what to **expect**, and the unknown is always scary.

When I got into bed, it took me a long time to actually drop off – I simply couldn't relax, and my ears were focused sharply on every tiny sound. I lay there in the dark, wondering if Mary was awake too – she was lying quite still, and breathing deeply and evenly, but I had the feeling that she was really as alert and as tense as I was. I didn't like to ask her, though, just in case she really was asleep. Eventually, I did dissolve into slumber, but it didn't last long. I suppose it must have been about 2.30 again, when we were rudely awakened by the most appalling chorus of howls! For a moment, I was absolutely petrified – I simply couldn't imagine what it could possibly be! Mary and I sprang up in bed at the same moment, urgently trying to identify the source of the noise.

"Oh, God!" cried Mary, "it's the dogs!"

As soon as she said it, I realised that of *course* that was what it was – Judy and Droopy had been reluctantly closed in the scullery as usual at bedtime, and the sound was coming from that direction. But even when I knew that it was only our pet dogs, not a pack of slant-eyed wolves or even marauding Demons from The Pit, the sound still froze the marrow in my bones!

Mary had immediately jumped out of bed and shoved her feet into her slippers. She grabbed her dressing-gown, and started towards the door, but I caught her arm as she passed, and said urgently, "No, Mary – wait! Lord only knows what's happening now, but leave it to Derek – he can handle it better than we can. Put your dressing-gown on, and we'll go and act as back-up . . . "

I bundled into my own dressing-gown and slippers – I didn't dare take the time to dress until I knew what was going on – and Mary and I headed out into the hallway. Derek had just got downstairs, and was warily opening the kitchen door. His face was grim, but he gestured to us to go back. "Wait 'til I find out what's the matter!" he ordered, and disappeared through the kitchen doorway, flicking the switch as he passed and flooding the place with light.

The dogs must have heard him, and the mournful howling changed to frantic yelping, as they pleaded to be rescued, scratching desperately on the door. I wasn't really aware of moving, I was so focused on Derek and the dogs but, arm in arm, Mary and I had made our way to the kitchen doorway. Derek hesitated for a split second, then turned the handle of the scullery door. As soon as he had released the latch, the frantic animals burst through, and came charging across the kitchen, claws scrabbling madly on the tiled floor. But before they reached the table, they seemed to catch sight of something on their right that terrified them even more, and both of them suddenly swerved to the left, and almost slid over – it was really strange. I have seen *horses* shy – but I've never seen dogs do it before! They desperately untangled themselves and regained their feet, but the momentary delay gave Mary and me time to make room so they could pile out through the kitchen doorway without bowling us over. They fled full-pelt along the hall, and thumped off up the stairs, leaving us staring after them, open-mouthed.

Derek recovered his balance – they had nearly knocked *him* flying! He took a deep breath and flicked the hair out of his eyes. He cautiously peered around the scullery door, looking into all the corners. Then he went in, snapped the light on, and tried the back-door, which was still firmly locked. I noticed he had a large torch in his hand – he wisely did not want to get caught out there in the dark if the power was suddenly cut off again!

"What the hell was all *that* about?" he demanded, coming back into the kitchen. "I can't see anything out of place – what on earth got *into* them? Damn, but it's cold in here!"

Mary and I made our way into the kitchen, and stood looking around rather blankly. Derek was right – it had been quite a warm night, but now our breath was smoking in the air, and we had begun to shiver. I couldn't help being curious about what had made the dogs swerve so violently, and headed towards the pantry to take a look over there. "Did you see the way they . . . ?" I began, then stopped short in utter disbelief. Faint and indistinct, huddled in the corner, were three almost-transparent figures. I recognised them immediately – Emily, Annie and Arthur Hillyer!

"What is it, Dad?" hissed Derek, and Mary hurried over to take my arm.

"Look!" I whispered in awe, pointing into the corner. *Look*!"

Mary and Derek both peered where I was pointing.

"*What*, Dad?" said Derek, frowning. "I can't *see* anything!"

"I'm not sure, but I think I *almost* can!" said Mary softly. "Oh, George – it's the Hillyers, isn't it? They're taking refuge in here, where he can't come! Look, Derek, they're – no, they keep fading!"

But no matter how hard he looked, Derek simply couldn't see a thing. I am convinced *I* could see them better than Mary could, although even for me they were wavery and faint. It must have been one of the strangest experiences of my whole life. I could have stood for hours, simply staring at this manifestation of something that I had always maintained was no more than moonshine and bunkum. But it was obvious that these were sentient beings of some description, even though one could hardly call them 'human' – and they were obviously in great distress. I'm not sure what the social conventions for such encounters *are*, but obviously an open-mouthed stare is hardly good manners in any company!

"Can we help you?" I asked, although I could hardly recognise my own voice, I was so overcome. "Is there anything we can do for you?"

I don't honestly know if I actually expected an answer, although it would appear that Arthur had been able to communicate in some way with the children. But it seemed as if the apparitions were running out of energy, and they began to fade away in the same way the light of a torch dies when the batteries are exhausted.

"They're gone!" said Mary, in an awed whisper.

"Not necessarily *gone*," I said, "they're probably still here, even if we can't see them. Mrs. Hillyer – Emily – " I felt rather silly addressing what appeared to be an empty corner, "if you can hear me, I just want to say that you are welcome to stay, if being in the house keeps you safe. If there is anything we can do, will you please try to find a way to let us know."

At that point, Pat put her head round the kitchen door, looking absolutely terrified. "*Derek?*" she said shakily, "What *is* it? What on earth is happening *now*? Jenny's minding the kids – and the dogs! – but I just couldn't bear to stay upstairs any longer – I'm sorry, I *had* to come – we have to *know*! Are you all right?"

"Just cold!" he reassured her, with his teeth chattering. "It's OK – but it seems we have visitors! Or so Mum and Dad say – *I* can't see anything! Seems Emily, Annie and Arthur have come to us for sanctuary, or something, where dear old Tom can't get 'em! And *Dad* just invited them to stay as long as they like! I'm not sure I'm too happy about that, Dad! I mean – is he tamely going to *let* us shelter them? We could be endangering our own kids – not to mention the rest of us! I'd rather like *this* house to be still standing in the morning! Unreasonable of me, perhaps, but there it is!"

I honestly hadn't stopped to think about what sort of danger I might be putting *us* in – at the time, my only thought had been to protect the Hillyers!

"God, I'm sorry, Derek," I groaned, "I simply – it's just – they looked so scared, and . . . "

"Derek, *you* didn't see them, dear," put in Mary. "I don't know just what Mr. Hillyer can actually *do*, but I think it's a risk we've got to take. We did decide to see this through, whatever it took, didn't we?"

Derek pulled a wry face. "I'm not sure just how we would have gone about evicting them anyway!" he said. "Don't worry about it, Dad. Come on – let's go somewhere a bit warmer, I'm *frozen*!"

We all trooped into the makeshift fortress of the lounge, and found that Jenny had brought all the children and the dogs down, and already had the fire lit. The candles were standing on the hearth, just in case we lost the power again, and the women had taken the precaution of bringing all the makings for hot drinks – not to mention the biscuit tin! – in to the room before we went to bed. Talk about Emergency Rations! Derek checked the phone, and found that it was still working at that point, and there was nothing unusual to be seen or heard, but we were all still in a state of high nervous tension. Mary, Derek and I sat close to the fire, trying to thaw ourselves out, while Jenny put some milk on to heat and made drinks all round. This time we had Horlicks, but I could really hardly taste it, I was so tense, waiting for something to happen.

We sat sipping our drinks and cuddling our mugs, while Derek began to tell the others what had happened. He had just explained how the dogs fled from the kitchen, when suddenly there came a knock on the window. Everybody froze. The only sounds in the room were the quiet ticking of the clock and the crackling of the fire. From outside the window came a voice – a reedy, child's voice. "Kurt!" it called, "Kirstie! Let us in – *please*! Please help us – we're so scared! Kirstie, let us in!"

"It's Arthur!" cried Kirstie, jumping off the sofa. "Daddy, we've got to help him!"

Derek grabbed her, and pulled her into a close embrace on his knee. Pat reached out for Kurt, and held him tightly, too.

"It's *not* Arthur!" Derek assured them. "Arthur and his mummy and his sister are all in the kitchen. You said yourselves that *they* could come in there, but Arthur's Daddy couldn't – well, they came. That's what frightened Judy and Droopy so much. Grandma and Grandpa *saw* them, and they told them they could stay. I think someone's trying to trick us – to get us to *invite* him in, by pretending to be Arthur. It's all right, sweetheart – if he *could* get in, he would have done it, wouldn't he?"

The children looked relieved, and relaxed in their parents' arms. "Grandma – you *saw* them?" asked Kirstie, wide-eyed. "I didn't know *you* could see them! Didn't *you* see them, Daddy?"

Before Derek could answer, the knocking on the window began again, louder than before. This time the voice outside was screaming, as if in mortal agony, "Kurt! Kurt! Kirstie! Help me, help me, help me – let me *in*!" over and over again.

"It's all right, Kurt," said Kirstie, as her brother pressed his hands to his ears to shut out the voice, squeezing his eyes shut in an attempt to hold back tears. "It isn't *Arthur* – it really isn't! Can't you hear – it's not his voice!"

She sounded so sure of it herself that her certainty was very convincing, and Kurt relaxed again. Elizabeth was clinging around Jenny's neck, with her face buried in her mother's shoulder. Kyle was huddled on Mary's knee, pale and big-eyed, but probably not totally sure just what was going on; his rumpled hair was standing on end, and a half-eaten biscuit was clutched in his chubby little hand. The dogs were huddled in the alcove between Derek's chair and the fireplace, trembling and whimpering in an agony of terror.

"Go away, you bad old man!" Kirstie shouted suddenly, making me jump. "*You're* not Arthur, you can't trick *us*, we *know* you're not Arthur! You *can't* come in, you can't, you can't! We won't *let* you!" Her little fists were clenched, and her face was blazing with anger – our normally shy, timid little girl was a picture of defiance! For a moment, we all held our breath, amazed at her temerity and wondering what sort of response her challenge might bring, but we heard nothing but silence from outside. It was awful, sitting there waiting for something to happen. We were under siege, and all we could do was wait. Suddenly, a veritable torrent of bangs rattled the window in its frame. Not knocking, now, but violent *banging*. Elizabeth gave a little cry and covered her ears with her hands, and Derek half-rose from his seat. I'm sure we were all wondering how long the window could withstand that onslaught – and what would happen if it didn't!

"How about a song?" suggested Jenny suddenly. "What about 'Row, row, row your boat'? We all know that, don't we?" And she began to sing, just as if nothing out-of-the-ordinary was happening! One by one, the rest of us joined in. Our voices were a bit quavery and scared at first, but quickly became firmer. The electric light suddenly went out, but we still had the firelight, and I immediately got up and lit the candles. The room grew cold at our backs, but I put another log on the fire, and we had bright, comforting heat at our faces. The banging continued, but the window-pane still held. And we went on singing.

143

The very *act* of singing, our family all singing together, somehow helped to unite us even more strongly, and the atmosphere in the room gradually seemed to change – to become warmer and cosier and safer. We sang and we sang. We sang song after song. We sang 'Lavender's Blue', and we sang 'Mr. Fox went out on a windy night'. We sang 'All things bright and beautiful' and we sang 'Froggie went a-courting'. We sang 'Morningtown Ride' and we sang 'Little Brown Jug'. Each time a song came to an end, one of us started up with a new one, and the rest joined in. The dogs stopped shivering, and crept out of their corner to lie in front of the blazing fire. And the banging gradually grew less violent and more spasmodic.

After what seemed an eternity, once more the greying of the eastern sky aroused the fearless cockerel, and with his crowing the banging instantly ceased. We had survived another night, and it was Sunday morning. The daylight broadened as the sun climbed slowly into the blue. And as the sun got up, the birds took over the singing, and we could give *our* hoarse voices a well-earned rest. The rest of the world woke gladly to a new morning, but *we* all went back to bed.

For a few hours, I slept the sleep of sheer exhaustion and over-stretched nerves. But Kyle had managed to slumber through most of the noise during the night, and was his usual rumbustious self by nine-o'clock. As we congregated around the breakfast table, we were all pale and heavy-eyed, and we yawned more than we spoke. However, the kitchen was normally warm again, and we could only assume that our house-guests had departed, although I cannot even speculate where they had departed to!

Having *two* stressful nights like that on the trot was pretty exhausting, and we still have no idea when we may get relief from the disturbances. How much more of this can we tolerate? I think we were all depressed at the prospect, and the rest of them probably felt as impotent as I did. While I have come across patients with quite a few *delusionary* spirits, caused by anything from hysteria to alcohol to brain lesions, *this* kind of 'ghost busting' is not a subject I was ever trained in!

The telephone rang several times during the morning. First Dan called, to see if we were all right and if we needed him for anything. Derek told him about our impromptu concert and the reason for it, but assured him that we were all fine, and there was no need for him to give up his Sunday. Then

Helen called – she and Chris had obviously been worried sick about what might be happening here, so she was very relieved when Mary promised we would be down for lunch, as planned, and would explain it all to them then. The next call was from Mabel, who apologised for disturbing us but said she just had to ease her mind. If we were OK, and didn't need her for anything, she would see us all tomorrow. It's cheering to know that so many people are so concerned about our welfare, and so willing to offer practical help as well as emotional support.

Mum rang, too – a little miffed because she had been trying to get through for quite some time, and our phone was always engaged! Of course, *she* didn't know any good reason why we should have had any more trouble, and was simply ringing to see how the children were coping, and if we were all getting over the double traumas of the finding of the bodies and the demolition of the cottage. Luckily, Derek took the call, and soon reassured her – he always can wrap her round his little finger! *He* can get away with things that I would have got into real hot water for! She reported that she and Dad are both fine, just a little at a loose end. Derek said later that he got the impression that she was angling for an invitation to come over for the afternoon – the pair of them are probably bursting with curiosity to see for themselves what has actually happened to the cottage. They *did* see it on the News, yesterday, and I can't help suspecting that the 'freak storm' story isn't going to convince either her *or* Dad! But *now* is not a good time to have them here, and Derek did some quick thinking and pleaded a prior engagement!

Actually, he, Pat and Jenny are thinking about taking the children over to the Dassett hills for a picnic, so it wasn't an outright lie. And it is perfectly true as far as Mary and I are concerned, of course, and it's time I went and started getting ready to go to Chris and Helen's – we wouldn't want to let a good dinner spoil by keeping it waiting! No doubt I will have some more to report later.

Later:

That throw-away remark is truer than I realised at the time, and I feel quite daunted at the thought of how much more there *is* to report! Still, the only

145

way is to get stuck in, I suppose – maybe enthusiasm for the job will grow on me, although writer's cramp is a distinct possibility!

The smell that greeted us as we arrived at Chatterbrook Cottage was mouth-watering. Helen had prepared roast pork and apple-sauce, which I haven't had for some time – succulent, tender meat with crisp crackling, cooked to perfection, and absolutely delicious. I resolutely forgot about my waistline, and abandoned myself to gluttony. The plum pie and custard that followed were also irresistible, and it was with a comfortably bulging stomach that I followed Chris out to sit on the patio while the women washed up.

Chris and I *did* volunteer to help, or to do it for them, but they determinedly shooed us out of the kitchen, and I confess we didn't fight the eviction too hard. Both Helen and Mary are very neat and efficient people, and the job seemed to take them no time at all. When they joined us outside, I had brought Chris up to date on our early morning ructions, and Mary had obviously done the same with Helen. Chris sat blinking like an owl in daylight as I recounted the improbable tale. "God, I wish I had some bright suggestions to offer!" he groaned. "But this – it's just – well, it's beyond *me*, I'm afraid!"

"Well, Mary and I are off to see if we can get round Lira Wardwell," Helen told him. "You two stay here – it's just possible she may respond better to *women*."

"Worth a try!" Chris shrugged. "I wish you luck!"

Off they went, on foot, and Chris and I sat chewing over the problem between us – but we were only going over and over the same old ground, and neither of us had anything new to contribute.

"I respect your courage, all of you," said Chris at last, "but I'm not sure you should stay there any longer. This thing seems a lot stronger than any of us had bargained for, and it might be best to cut your losses before anybody gets hurt. We could carry on trying to find a way to make the place safe, and then you could come back . . . ."

"It may have to come to that," I admitted, "but I don't think Pat and Derek are ready to go that far, yet. And if *they* stay, Mary and I can hardly leave them, can we?"

"No, I suppose not," he sighed, "but . . . ah, excuse me, a minute, George – there's the phone!"

SoulTrap

He was gone for such a short time that I assumed the call must have been a wrong number, but he came back calling, "Come on, George – that was Dan! He says to get ourselves over to Lira's – she wants to talk to us! Looks like your Mary did the trick!"

"But – what's **Dan** doing there?" I asked, puzzled.

"Haven't a clue!" he said, shrugging. "Do you want me to take the car, or can you manage? It's just round the corner there, next door to the church . . . "

"I'm getting stronger all the time," I assured him. "I've no doubt I can make it that far!"

So off we went on foot. I don't know why, but I had imagined that Lira Wardwell would live in one of the little crooked old thatched cottages, of which the village boasts quite a few. Instead Chris opened the gate of a largish, quite modern bungalow, nicely maintained, and with well-stocked gardens. Dan's van was parked outside. A name-plate on the wall of the bungalow said, "Saran Ata", which I tended to assume was one of those rather twee anagramatical names that people sometimes feel moved to bestow upon their houses, but I had no time to make any sense of the words before the front door was opened – by Dan!

"Sir – Doc," he greeted us. "We all had the same notion, seemingly! The poor lady allows maybe she better see us, or she fit get no peace whatever. Come on in . . ." He led the way into a lounge on the right of the hallway – a light, airy through-room, giving a view of gardens both front and back, but with one pane of the back window boarded up. The carpet and curtains were a soft green, the walls were papered in white embossed with small golden flowers, and there was a beautiful painting of a woodland scene on the chimney-breast, and a couple more on the facing wall. A tapestry screen covered the open fireplace, the hearth gleamed with well-polished brass fire-irons, and a few brass ornaments stood on the mantel. Mary and Helen were sitting side by side on a chintz-covered sofa, and two elderly ladies occupied the matching easy chairs on either side. One – who I immediately assumed to be Lira Wardwell – was a tiny, fragile-looking lady, with bird-like bones, soft grey hair and rather faded blue eyes. The other was taller, but almost skeletally thin – with her long limbs, a long neck and a long, sharp nose, she reminded me of a heron! Her bright silver hair, which was pulled into a large bun at the back of her head, had obviously been jet-black in her youth, and her rather swarthy

147

face was a maze of leathery wrinkles. But when she turned her head to look at us, she had the brightest, beadiest, fiercest, black eyes I have ever seen – they positively snapped as she looked me up and down!

"This is my husband, George, Mrs. Wardwell. George, Mrs. Wardwell has very kindly agreed to talk to us after all," said Mary, indicating the heron-woman. (Wrong assumption again, George!) "And this," indicating the woman *I* had taken to be Mrs. Wardwell, "is Mrs. Millicent Campbell – Dan's . . . er . . ."

"Stepmother's aunt!" supplied Dan, grinning, as she got stuck on the relationship. "Emily Hillyer's sister."

We went through all the usual 'pleased to meet you' routine, although I must confess that Lira Wardwell neither looked nor sounded very pleased to see us. She looked angry and impatient.

"Well – pull out some chairs!" she snapped, waving a long, bony hand in the direction of those tucked in around the dining table at the far end of the room. "You're making the place look untidy, standing there, and you're a bit old for sitting on the floor, I reckon!"

Dan handed a chair each to Chris and to me, then turned his own around and sat leaning on the back of it. I have got so used to seeing him dressed for rough work, that I find it strange to see him all cleaned up and smartly dressed in a shirt and tie.

"Right!" said Lira Wardwell when we were all seated. "Now, let's get this nonsense sorted out once and for all. *I - can't - help you*! I know you don't *want* to believe it, and I'm not saying I wouldn't help if I could – but I *can't*. That's the plain fact of it, and you're going to have to accept it. It's too late. It's gone too far. I'm too old, and too weak and too tired. And even if I were young and strong, I could *never* have done it all on my own. It needs a lot more than one, oh yes! I've done my best, over a lot of years – over my whole life, and I'll be 96 next week, if I live to see it! And I'm *tired*, and I have failed in my duty. So now maybe you'll go away and leave me in peace, and stop rubbing my nose in my failure and my shame!"

Despite the wrinkles, I would never have guessed she could be *that* old! Mary was looking as disappointed as I felt, and I knew I couldn't simply give it up that easily and walk away – obviously, this old lady knew *something*, but she seemed to be talking in riddles. I needed to understand what she meant, and I had to try to come up with an argument to counter what she had just said, but I wasn't sure how to begin. Before I could open my mouth, however, Dan said quietly, "Meaning no disrespect, Ma'am – I know that none of would wish to be a trouble to you, but it's real hard for us to just give up and go away. You say you fit not *help* us – but *you* understand a whole lot more than we do, seemingly. And no way is this just idle curiosity, Ma'am – we got *real* trouble, *big* trouble, and we have us no notion how to fight it. And I reckon that you could teach us some about that. We don't expect you to fight it *for* us – but maybe you could tell us how to fight it ourselves. *Please*, Ma'am?"

Even Lira Wardwell was not immune to the old Dan charm, although she fought hard against it! Her determination obviously wavered, and Millicent Campbell pressed home the advantage.

"My dear sister," she said, in a voice thick with suppressed tears, "and her innocent little son and daughter were not only brutally *murdered*, but more than forty years later they are still in torment! Thanks to these kind people from Manor Farm, we have found their bodies at last. Finally, we can at least give them a decent burial. But what good is paying respect to their bones when, in their very essence, they are *still* not free of the monster who tortured and killed them? I would do anything – *anything*! – to help them! I'm not as old as you, Mrs. Wardwell, but I *am* 84, and I'm not very strong, or very brave. But I would do my best, if only I knew *how*! I think Danvers is right, that *you* know something – you said yourself, you tried for many years but couldn't manage it alone. Please – tell *me* what to do!"

(*'Danvers'*?! *I* thought 'Dan' was short for 'Daniel'! When she said his name, Dan winced and closed his eyes – I think I see now why he kept saying 'Just call me Dan'! I don't think he's too fond of his full name! Wonder what his surname is? I still don't know!)

After Millicent's outburst, Lira pursed up her lips, and sat looking into the middle distance for a few minutes. None of us moved or spoke. Then she gave a deep sigh, and her shoulders slumped.

"When that young man came a-ringing my doorbell," she said at last, in a softer voice, nodding towards Dan, "I told him I was sick of trying to contend against so much *ignorance*. My family has been struggling against it for centuries – we have been mocked and scorned, we have been persecuted and tortured and killed, because of it. Even *now*, I get stones through my windows, and people blame *me* for a problem which exists because of their own *ignorance* – a problem which *they* are making worse every day! My family has fought, generation after generation, to maintain the balance – but we have failed at the last, and now the scales have tipped too far, and I am afraid it is too late. But this young man looked into my eyes, and he said, 'Yes, we *are* ignorant. But, if you will teach us, we will *try* to learn.'! Maybe I am a lonely old fool, but I think he meant it. It has been so long since anyone has been willing to learn from me that I couldn't send him packing, as I had intended. My own daughter is long dead – *I* raised *her* daughter Orilla, my grandchild, and I tried to teach her the things my own grandmother taught to me – the Old Words, the Old Ways, the Old Wisdom. I trusted that *she* would take my place when the time came, but she was flighty – she married the baker, Ben Bowman, and took *his* name, instead of taking the Wardwell name to her marriage, as all her foremothers have done for generations. So my great-granddaughter didn't even bear the name from birth – although her mother did at least have the grace to call her Athaney – great among the Old Names! She spent a lot of time with me when she was small, and I taught *her*, too – but her friends laughed at her, as the ignorant always laugh. Finally, she began to pull away – from me, and from her heritage. She lives in London, now, with a mob of young heathens, with her pink spiked hair and her black nail-varnish and her pop music. She's even changed her name – her beautiful name! – she calls herself Anthea, now. It's more 'normal', she says – more 'accepted'. So *I* am the last of the line – the last of a long, long line. The Guardians of the Well have failed. Maybe we really failed a long time ago, and we were just dying a long, slow death. But it's a sad, sad thing, to be the last. So sad, and so lonely! And how shall I face my own foremothers in the Shadowland when *my* time comes, as soon it must?" Her eyes clouded for a moment, with the sheen of unshed tears. Then, with an effort, she controlled her emotion, and drew herself upright in her chair. Her voice hardened again as she went on, "Then, suddenly, here are all *you* people, claiming to *want* the Old Wisdom, all of you badgering me to teach you! Can you wonder that I find it hard to *believe*? But I need you each to tell me now – is the young man right about you? If I force myself to make the effort to teach you – will you *really* learn? Will you *accept* the teaching? For I know it will not match with what you have

been taught by others, all your lives. And I warn you, I have little **comfort** for you – I truly believe it is too late."

"Mrs. Wardwell – may I call you Lira?" said Mary gently, breaking the silence that descended on the room as the old lady's impassioned speech came to an end. "I know that I speak for my whole family when I say that we had never realised before just how **very** ignorant we are in some areas. Suddenly we find ourselves faced with a whole new dimension, the existence of which we were unaware. **I** always thought that ghosts and spirits were merely the stuff of horror films and stories. Now I find they are very **real**, but I have no **knowledge** of how deal with them – either to help those of them who need help, or to fight those of them who are attacking us. If you can teach me **anything** which will enlighten my ignorance, then **yes** – I will gratefully learn. And so will all my family."

Lira Wardwell's black button eyes scrutinised Mary keenly for a long moment, as if to read her mind and her soul. Then the old lady nodded her head slightly, as if satisfied with what she saw, and turned to Chris. "What about you, Christopher Wainwright?" she demanded, with a curl of her lip. "You're not in this as deep as the others, seems to me. Can **you**, Mr. Clever Professor, learn something from an old woman who left school when she was twelve years old? Who learned, not from books, but from the words of her foremothers? An old woman you were taught to laugh at when you were a boy, and maybe feared as a witch? Can you truly learn from crazy old Mother Wardwell, with her crack-brained notions? Or will you despise her, deep down in your heart?"

Chris looked her full in the eyes, and gave her a crooked smile. "Lira," he said, "there **was** a time when I placed all my faith in the knowledge that could be gained from books, and in some ways I still do. Books are fine, but I know now they do not contain the **whole** story. There was a day when I revered academic degrees from prestigious universities, and diplomas hanging in glass frames on office walls. But that was a long time ago. If I have learned one valuable lesson in my life, it is to recognise how **little** knowledge these symbols actually represent; how little knowledge I, and most of my colleagues, really possess, and what vast quantities of knowledge will be forever out of our reach – quite often because we **do** wilfully and arrogantly reject it when it is offered to us. If, when I was young and foolish, my bad manners and my thoughtlessness led me to offend you, then I hope you will accept my sincere apology – I know better now. And if you will forgive me and include me in the lesson, I will try to be a humble and respectful pupil. And I am not making fun, Lira – I mean it. I think you know Helen too well to even doubt *her* good intentions. So, please, Miss – what time does school begin?"

The old lady frowned at him, but I don't think she was really displeased. She sat back in her chair, and folded her bony hands in her lap. "If we are to begin at all," she said, "it is very late, and we had best begin at once. Now pay attention, because we have little time. In the Distant Times, when people first came to these lands, they chose to settle *here* because they recognised it as a Place of Power. Because that is what this valley is – a Place of Power, a channel and a storehouse for the energy that comes from the very Earth itself. In those days, people were closer to the Earth, more in tune with all of Nature, and they *felt* the Power in a way that modern people have lost, and they learned to use it, just as they had learned to use fire, and stone and metals. But it is hard for humans to understand the Great Forces of the Earth and the Universe, so they gave the power a name and a face – they *humanised* it, and worshipped it as a goddess, whom they called Urtha. She was a goddess of Life – of fertility, of birth and of healing. And channelled through the goddess, the Power was used for *Good*. But a Power is just that – power – in itself neither Good nor Evil, but able to be used for either purpose, just as the powers of Science, the modern god, can be used today. It is not the Power that is good or evil, but the intent of the *user*. And in the Old Times, the Power was Urtha, and Urtha was a power for Good. Do you understand me so far? Can you *accept* this basic concept?"

I needed more time to fully explore it, but I was able, without too many reservations, to nod with the rest of them – now, when we had finally persuaded the old lady to begin, was no time for quibbling!

"Very well," she went on, after scanning all our faces with her fierce, dark gaze. "In case you are unaware of it, this valley is surrounded by five hills – and five is a magical number. On those hills rise five springs of clear water, which run as streams down to the pool in the bottom of the valley. This gives the valley the shape of a pentangle, or a five-pointed star, and because of this configuration, they called the place, in the Old Words, 'Saran Ata', which means 'Place of the Star'."

"The name of your house!" I burst out, before I could stop myself.

"Ah! You're a noticing one, are you?" she said approvingly. "That's good. Have you ever noticed, Medical Man, what is the difference between Magic and Science?"

"To be honest," I replied, having no answer to her question, "I have never believed in Magic, in the sense you seem to mean – only Science. But I would be glad if you would tell me?"

"Magic," she said, smiling slightly at my response, "is when human beings learn *how* to make a desired thing happen, but they do not understand *why*. Magicians perform certain actions, or recite certain words, or concoct certain potions – and a certain result will follow. They don't understand *why* it works – they simply know it does, and they are content, and they hand on the rituals to their descendants. Scientists want to find out *why* certain actions produce certain reactions – they perform 'experiments' instead of rituals, and they call the words 'formulae' instead of spells, and they feel very superior to their benighted counterparts. And they have learned many things – but they cannot simply *accept* that these things are so, and let *be*. They have pried into a lot of dark corners that would have been better left unexplored. And there are many things that they have only partly understood, or even misunderstood completely, but in their pride and arrogance they think that they have uncovered most of the great secrets already, and that revealing those that remain is just a matter of time. But in their quest for *new* knowledge, there is much *old* knowledge that they have forgotten, and much of the Old Wisdom has been lost. Do you disagree?"

I think her question was actually aimed at me – and maybe at Chris, as well – but before either of us could answer, Dan spoke up.

"I don't reckon Science will *ever* truly get to the bottom of what make the world tick," he said thoughtfully. "Like – take electricity. Most folks can *use* it – heck, even *I* can use it! - you push a plug into a socket, and you flick a switch, and – presto! Your toaster toasts, or your vacuum-cleaner sucks up dirt, such. Just so you've paid your bill to the utility company, that is! But I never yet come on anybody who could explain me what electricity actually *is*. Oh, sure – they fit spout a whole lot of jaw-cracking words, but I would lay to it there aint one man alive who *really* sees clear what that kind of force *is*! The answers only go so far, and there are always more questions behind the answers – like when you get to the top of one hill, and see the road leading

153

to a whole range of *more* hills. Questions like 'What was before the Beginning?' and 'What will come after the End?' I've read the Good Book, and I know the story of Creation told in Genesis. And I've heard guys, all educated up, explaining on tv all about the Big Bang, and how all the matter in the universe was created in a split second in one gosh-a-mighty explosion, and how it's all still hurtling apart through Space. But I'm still no closer to truly *understanding* about Creation, or Eternity, or Infinity, or Time or Space, for all of Religion, and for all of Science. And I reckon, if'n they was to tell the truth, no more are most folks, even top scientists. So maybe Science is closer kin to Magic than you might suppose – yeah?"

(I have to confess both Dan and Lira Wardwell were giving me quite a few surprises! I had obviously badly underestimated both of them!)

Lira nodded her approval, and went on, "So do we agree that there are Forces and Powers that we can *use*, even if we don't really understand them? Very good. So – the Old People evolved magic rites to allow *them* to use the power of this site, even though I cannot tell you how or why these rituals worked. They used the power of the magical number five. They used the power of the stars in the heavens, and the symbolic star laid out in this place on the earth. They used the power of the cycles of the moon, which symbolise birth and growth, decline and death, followed again by birth, in never-ending circles. They used the power of the water, springing purified from the earth and running downhill. They used the power of trees – at each water-source they planted and cared for a sacred tree – a thorn, an oak, an alder, a holly and, at the north-facing apex of the star, a wychelm. They used the power of human speech, to invoke the goddess and ask her to bless them with health and fertility. And they appointed Guardians – women, because fertility and reproduction are female mysteries, although, of course, they require a male principle to bring them to fruition. The Guardians were appointed to ensure that the knowledge was passed by word of mouth from mother to daughter, down through countless generations. And also to perpetuate the trees – for trees, as well as people, have an allotted life-span. When a parent tree died, it was the Guardians' duty to ensure there was a new seedling waiting to take its place, and the circle of Magic could continue to turn – to complete the circuit of power, if you like. People came to the goddess to beg for healing, to pray for fertility for themselves, for their herds, for their flocks, for their crops. And all this drew on the Power, and the Power was used for good things, and in the process it became Positively charged, and Good begat Good as dog begets dog. But all of life is *change* – nothing remains the same. *New* people came – people who worshipped other gods, people who used metals for swords instead of ploughshares. And more new people followed *them*, and they brought new customs and new languages, and new philosophies. The Old Words were replaced with foreign tongues. The Old Ways were changed for different customs. The Old Wisdom was lost, and new ideas took its place. The Old People were slaughtered, or died of pestilence or old age; some intermarried with the new folks, and forgot the old meanings. Only the Guardians clung to these things, against all the ravages of time and the persecution of conquering tyrants, and the domination of new religions, even though, to survive at all, we have had to pay lip-service to the new ways and try to blend in and not be noticed. It didn't really matter – Power is Power, no matter what you *call* it; worship is worship, no matter what the name of the goddess or god. *But* – as the old ways of life disappeared, and the Power ceased to be drawn upon for Good, its polarisation began to swing from a Positive charge to a Negative – which could be used by, and for, Evil and Destruction. And that is what happened. There came a time when one old man – *not* one of the Guardians, no matter what lies you have heard! – one powerful, wicked old man, full of hate and malice, found a way to tap into the Power, and he drew upon it to aid him against his enemies, the De Courseys. And the Power was corrupted, and an abomination was loosed upon the valley – an abomination which twisted even the natural cycle of life and death. The very spirits of the dead, instead of leaving the earth for realms of which I can tell you nothing, were trapped – in modern parlance, in a sort of force-field – unable to escape. Souls are delicate things, and they could not overcome the pull of the Power, just as a leaf thrown into the air will be dragged back to earth by the force of gravity. First of all, people – in their ignorance – blamed the Guardians, and persecuted *us*, not understanding that our only power is in Good, and that the goddess Urtha would *never* allow herself to be used for such foul deeds! Finally, in desperation, when no-one else could aid them, they turned to us for help. And somehow, my foremother at that time – called Athaney, like my great-granddaughter! – summoned up all her knowledge and strength, and with the help of the whole community – in secret, because such things were forbidden by the church – she managed to wrest the force from Negative to Positive again, and re-align the Power. 'So what has gone wrong *now*?' you are asking yourselves. 'Has some new Magician conjured up a new Curse?' And my answer to you is 'No'. This is not a *new* curse. I believe the old one was never de-activated completely, but only deprived of Power, enough to render it weak and ineffectual. But now, because of the ways of the world we live in, there is insufficient use of the Power for Good. People don't respect or understand Nature – no-one prays to Urtha any more. And while Positive forces thrive upon Goodness, Negative forces feed on violence and cruelty and selfishness and apathy and ignorance! And there are plenty of all of those around! But nobody *believes* in these things nowadays – not even my own daughters' daughters! And the Power is swinging from Positive to Negative again, and the negative energy, trapped in this valley that used to be so pure and sacred, has revived the old Evil. The streams that flow from the sacred springs were so clear when I was a girl that I could drink my fill and take no hurt. Now the farmers drench their fields with pesticides, which drain and leech into the brooks, and I would no more drink that polluted water now than I would drink from a bottle marked 'Poison'! I recall the days when the waters of the brooks and the pool were teeming with life – frogs, toads, minnows, sticklebacks – and the jewelled kingfishers flashed and darted in the sun! The goddess's pool lay in the valley like a crystal mirror, reflecting the pure arch of the sky; and the leaves that danced in the realm of air danced also in the realm of water! Now . . . ah, *now* . . . come with me, all of you! I will *show* you!"

Suddenly, she heaved herself out of her chair, and disappeared out of the door. Looking around at each other in surprise, we all trooped after her – along the hall, through her kitchen where the windows were also boarded up, out of the back door, and down her long garden. She strode ahead of us, surprisingly quickly for a woman of that age, her long legs again reminding me forcibly of a heron. At the bottom of her garden was a high hedge, through which a gate led into a space of grass surrounding a pond, and enclosed by tall trees.

"*Look*!" she howled, flinging out her arms, "Look what the 'sacred pool' has come to now!"

It was, indeed, a sight to sadden your heart. The grass was rank, and smothered with litter – crisp packets, soft-drink cans, plastic bottles, pieces of tattered paper and polythene bags, and even some used condoms. The water looked stale and lifeless, mostly covered in a vivid green pond-weed, with what looked like the frame of a rusted bicycle poking up through the surface. Over beneath the trees lay about half-a-dozen old car-tyres, and a couple of 12-volt batteries, rusting, and probably leaking acid. Some wooden packing-crates lay around, smashed, with their boards streaked red from the rusted nails. Some of the branches of the trees had been broken, obviously deliber-ately, and hung down limply displaying their raw, pale wounds, the leaves on them dying and turning brown. A holy well?! It was the epitome of squalor! Looking around, I felt physically sick.

"The Church took our Well," said Lira Wardwell, in a husky voice. "They declared *themselves* its official guardians. And you can see how well they do the job! They changed its name – and looking at it now, I cannot be sorry! How could we ask Urtha, the pure, clean, gentle, wholesome mother Urtha, to dwell in a place like *this*?! And this is just part of the desecration and the destruction! The wychelm is dying – it is nearly dead – and *I* have no new sapling to plant in its place. The Old Words are no longer spoken by any tongue but mine. The Old Ways are changed, and if *these* are the *new* ways, I want no part of them! The Old Wisdom is scorned and cast aside, and mankind and Nature are no longer working towards the same ends. Even the Earth that gives us life is no longer good enough – men despoil and disrespect even that, their own mother, and now they plant their polluting footsteps on the clean face of the moon! *I*, too, am dying, and I have raised no new Guardian to take my place. The Positive energy is being corrupted, and the Negative energy is growing, feeding upon itself, and becoming stronger and stronger. And the dead can no longer fully die, just become disembodied, lost in limbo, at the mercy of the Evil – and, with Death staring *me* in the eye and beckoning me to come, it is a prospect I do not know how to face! But I have no strength to combat it – it needs the combined strength of many, not the feeble efforts of a failed old woman!"

Listening to her, I felt infected with her hopelessness. What on earth were we going to *do*?! What *could* be done to repair this desecration? But into my melancholy reverie broke the practical voice of Dan.

"Meaning no disrespect, Ma'am," he said, "but I can't help but feel you're rolling over before you're whupped! OK – we got us a big problem, you'll get no argument from me there! But you aint *alone* no more. What we have to do is to find a way to recharge the Positive Power in this geological battery, seemingly – and, to my mind, we have just the people who can do it, if anybody can. Just answer me a couple questions, if you will, Ma'am – first off – *you* still know the Old Words, yeah?" Lira Wardwell nodded, frowning and chewing her bottom lip. "OK," Dan went on, "so maybe, if needful, you could teach the rest of us? But – *is* it needful? I mean – surely it aint the *words*, is it? Surely it has to be the *meaning* of the words that matters, and the feelings behind them, not the language they get spoken in! Couldn't we charge the Power just as good in plain old English – even *my* brand of it! – if the good intention is there? As for *this* mess – heck, I can soon do sumpun about that! It aint half so bad as Derek Hanson's barn!"

I could see the beginning of a new spark in Lira's eyes as she considered this. "You're right, son!" she said at last. "But – it would take a lot of people, all with strong intent for Good, and I'm pretty sure we couldn't convince this village in the time, if ever!"

"Wouldn't the number matter less than how *strong* they were?" persisted Dan. "Besides – I reckon we already have us a good core of volunteers! I swear, that Hanson family, they some of the strongest folks for Good I ever met – 'specially *this* fine lady!" He lightly touched Mary on the shoulder. "Ma'am – couldn't you act as Recruiting Officer, and get us the help of those fine folks I met at Derek's party? With that old Miss Flora along for the ride, I reckon we fit kick ass!"

Mary both smiled and blushed, but her eyes began to sparkle with new hope. "I think I could persuade them!" she said. "They are old, but they are all very wise, and I am sure I could make them understand the need. And they would fight to the *death* in defence of their Family!"

"So that's - five of *them* – and you and the Doc is seven – and Derek and family makes twelve, and Jenny and Elizabeth is 14. Then there's Millicent here, and me – that's 16. And – I reckon we fit count on you, Sir, Ma'am?" he asked Chris and Helen, who assented eagerly.

"That's 18!" declared Dan. "Then there's Mabel – and I suspicion her husband and her Pa might help out also. That's 21 I can think of, right off pat. Not forgetting *you*, of course, Ma'am!" he bowed slightly to Lira. "Every army needs a General, but I'm just numbering the troops you fit count on!"

"You're forgetting we have another daughter," put in Mary. "With Pauline and her husband and daughter, that makes 24! 25 counting Lira."

"And 25 is 5 x 5!" cried Dan. "A magic number multiplied by a magic number!"

"Powerful," agreed Lira, doubtfully, "but possibly still not enough!"

"I reckon none of you folks was ever at a tent-meeting?" asked Dan. "You know – a Revival, yeah? You maybe seen 'em on tv? But I reckon you fit lose a lot of the impact that way. When it's live – whoooeee! – can those red-hot gospellers ever cook up a storm! The energy they can generate, heck, I swear it like to frizzle yo' hair! And if *they* can do it, aint no reason on God's green earth why *we* shouldn't!"

"But – hang on a minute, Dan," I said. His enthusiasm was infectious, and I hated to be a party-pooper, but I did feel obliged to voice an objection. "You can't include the *children* in this! Kyle is only two years old, and . . . "

"His very innocence would be his strength," said Lira. "if he can be helped to understand, even vaguely, what it is we would need him to do. The others would all need to be willing, too – no-one can help unless they are committed, heart-and-soul, to the cause of righting the balance."

"But – that's just it!" I complained. "What exactly *would* you need them to do? We can't have them put in danger . . . "

"George," interrupted Mary determinedly, "it seems that those children have been in danger every minute they have lived at Manor Farm! And you *know* how much they want to help Arthur and the others. Obviously they will have to be consulted, and decide of their own free will. But I am sure I know what that decision will be – and so do you!"

"I can't promise you that it *won't* be dangerous," said Lira, looking me challengingly in the eye. "It will be dangerous for all of us. But exactly how dangerous I cannot tell you – I have never *done* this before! It is many hundreds of years since *anyone* has done it! But I do know that it *was* done. Athaney and her daughters achieved their purpose, although it is told that Athaney herself died from the drain on her energies. But death is the least of *my* worries! The rest of you will have to make your decisions for yourselves! Now – go away, all of you! I have to think – I have to recall many things, and there is no-one to remind me! Although – it is possible that Orilla *may* remember some of the things I taught her, even if she has got fat and lazy! Christopher Wainwright – go and call at her house and tell her I need her – *now*! I'll talk to you again when I have decided what we must do!" With that, she turned and strode back through the gate into her garden, muttering to herself as she went, and leaving us speechless.

From the expressions on their faces, I think the rest were as dazed as I was! I felt as if I had been swept clean out of the familiar world in which I had spent the whole of my life, into a place in which I had lost my hold on reality and any pretence of control over my own destiny, or that of my family. Dan, as usual, was the first to break the silence. "Phew!" he whistled, "aint she a caution! That is purely one spunky old lady! Come on, Millie – I think you've had enough for one day, let's get you home!" He took her arm, and began to lead her away. Helen, Mary, Chris and I followed after – back through the garden, around the side of the house, and back out to the road. Dan was unlocking his van when Helen called to him. "Dan," she said, "I'm sure your aunt would be glad of a cup of tea – I know *I* need one! Please will you both join us for tea?"

"I'm sure she would be beholden, Ma'am," said Dan, and went back to confer with Millicent Campbell. She was obviously pleased by the invitation, and we turned to head back to Chatterbrook Cottage. "Hang on a minute!" cried Chris, slapping his forehead. "I better not forget I've got an errand to run! The rest of you carry on – I'll just go and tell poor Orilla Bowman she's got to leave *her* Sunday tea and get over to her grandmother's – pronto! I'll join you in a minute!"

Away he swung with his own long, easy stride, and the rest of us went at the pace of Millicent Campbell, which I could easily match. It was rather nice not to have everybody slowing down for *me*, for a change! We had only just got sat down on the patio when Chris rejoined us. "Poor woman!" he said, "She's got her work cut out with that old girl, eh, George?" I agreed wholeheartedly!

Helen and Mary somehow found the energy to make us all very welcome cups of tea, and to cut a load of ham and tomato sandwiches, and we all tucked in with a right good will. Helen had a lovely fluffy sponge-cake in her tin, and there was not a lot of it left by the time we had finished!

Old Millicent Campbell was beginning to look very tired by this time, but asked to use the bathroom before Dan drove her home. Helen led her off to show her where it was, and as soon as she was out of earshot, Chris said urgently, "Dan – I don't want to put the mockers on, or anything, but – don't you think we're pushing our luck with all these old people? *I'm* no spring-chicken myself, but I feel positively *young* beside your – can I *call* her your aunt, just to simplify things, even though I know she's not? – not to mention old Lira! And – no of-fence intended, Mary, but – if these others you're including, Dan, are actually George's and Mary's *parents* – well, not to put too fine a point on it, they can't be exactly in their *prime*! This is one darned nasty situation we seem to have got involved in – do you really think they can handle it?"

"Me," replied Dan, "I would say that if they have managed to survive to eighty/ninety years old in good shape, they fit cope with most things! They purely have to be tough as whip-leather! It aint no *physical* battle, Sir! That *would* be a horse of a whole different colour! This one is down to the sort of *soul* you have. I take it you never met Doc. and Mizz Hanson's folks, yeah? Well, I did. And I reckon they could teach most of us a thing or two when it comes to holding to good principles and living right. And Millie may be frail physically, but she's brim-full of spunk – 'specially where her sister's con-cerned! She'd face down a cage full of grizzly b'ars if'n it was needful! Same goes for the kids – they're all real gutsy little people, and I think you would be doing them no service to leave 'em out of this, when they been involved right from the start! What do you say, Mizz Hanson, Ma'am?"

"I would much prefer it if *none* of us had to be involved," said Mary, with feeling. "But we don't have that luxury, do we? We couldn't walk away with a clear conscience, or with any kind of *honour*. And that being so, I think Dan's right. In this battle, I think the weak may fight as bravely as the strong, and it may even be that 'a little child shall lead them'. Where does that come from? It sounds Biblical! Remember Kirstie last night, George? The way she shouted at old Mr. Hillyer – the way she defied him? We've always said that Kirstie wouldn't say boo to a goose, haven't we? But she said more than 'boo' in defence of her friends! As Lira said, it has to be their choice, all of them. We need to explain it to them – as well as we can! – and leave the decisions to their own free will. Here's Millicent coming back – let's say goodbye, George, and go and make sure things are all right at home!"

So the party broke up. Helen and Chris waved to us all from the gate, then had a pile of washing-up to look forward to. Dan helped Millicent into his van, and headed off towards Warwick. Mary and I drove back to Manor Farm, where we found Derek feeding the dogs while Jenny and Pat bathed the children and got them into their night clothes. They were all happy and flushed from an afternoon racing around in the sun, and it seemed awful to spoil the joyful atmosphere and the childish laughter, but we decided that the sooner we explained to everyone just what Lira Wardwell had told us, the better.

I realise I have omitted to note that Mary and Jenny have decided that, under the circumstances, there is no way they can go home as normal, with the way things are here. Jenny has to go to work, but it is not totally beyond commuting distance, and she has decided to see if she can transfer Elizabeth to the village school with Kurt and Kirstie on a temporary basis, pleading a crisis within the family. (You *could* put it that way!) If not, Elizabeth will just have to miss school for a while, and play with Kyle instead. Academically, she's well up-sides with her age-group – way ahead of most of them, in fact – so a couple of weeks off won't hurt her. (Or however long this may take!) That will leave Mary free – she has decided to go home tomorrow to pack whatever the three of them will need for a protracted stay, then they can all sleep here with the rest of us. Derek's 'stomach-bug' is due to be cleared up by tomorrow, and he should be back at work, too. Always supposing we can get through the night in fairly good shape, that is!

So – once more, we congregated in the lounge and, between us, Mary and I tried to recount as exactly as possible what the old lady had said. Everyone listened gravely – even Kyle sat still and paid attention, although I wasn't sure how much of it he was actually taking in; it all seemed a little heavy for a two-year-old to understand. But when we finished, and for a moment nobody spoke, he suddenly piped up, "If we can zap the bad man, will Arthur and Annie be able to go to Heaven?"

I have obviously been underestimating *him*, too – he had certainly got the gist of it!

"That's what we *think*, darling," said Mary, beaming with pride.

"Then let's zap him!" yelled our young tearaway, all ready for the fray! "Pow! Pow-pow-pow-pow-POW!"

It was such a welcome anticlimax, that all of us simply burst into fits of laughter, and rolled around until our sides were sore.

"It's not going to be quite that *easy*, I'm afraid, Sunshine!" said Derek, when we had finally got ourselves under control again. "We can't do it with ray-guns, or anything like that. And it could get *very* scary! You don't *have* to do it, any of you. Nobody is asking you to – and nobody will think any less of you if you don't want anything to do with it. I haven't had chance to discuss this with your Mummy yet, but if any of you are really *sure* you want to help, then *I* don't think we should stop you. You've all been really brave and strong so far, and we're proud of you. With what *we've* been through recently, a whole lot of grown-up people would have done a lot worse! So *I* think you've earned the right to make your own decisions on this. What do *you* say, Mummy?"

"I suppose you're right," conceded Pat reluctantly, biting her lip. "But – if you *do* decide to do it, will you all please help *me* to be brave, because the thought of it scares me to death!"

"Don't be frightened, Mummy!" said Kurt, throwing his arms around her. "We'll look after you! Won't we, Kirstie?"

"Me too!" yelled Kyle, not about to be left out.

"I'll try," said Kirstie, looking pale but determined. "It's just – Daddy, will we have to fight the *Spider?*" Her voice tailed off into a whisper.

"I don't think there is a *real* spider," Derek reassured her. "I think it's more like – well, just a way to explain something nobody really under-stands, something that nobody had a name for. This 'soul trap' thing seems to act a little bit like a spider's web – it traps souls like a spider's web traps insects, right? So, all those hundreds of years ago, people thought it was made by something like a giant spider. But I don't think it was *really* a spi-der, sweetheart."

"I think it *was*, Daddy," she persisted. "Arthur said it was. But it doesn't matter, anyway, does it? Something *like* a spider might be worse than a really, truly spider. And we *have* to kill it, or make it go away, or poor Arthur will never be free, and a whole lot more people might get caught. So I'll try to be brave, Daddy."

"You *are* brave, Poppet!" said Derek, hugging her tight. "You're the bravest little girl I know! What about you, Jenny? It looks like Dan's planning to rope in you and Elizabeth, too, but it's not really your problem . . . "

"It sounds to me as if this is *everyone*'s problem!" retorted Jenny. "*My* main difficulty has been trying to work out what on earth is happening, and why! But I like Lira Wardwell's explanation – somehow it makes more sense to me than I thought any explanation *could*. In a way, when you come to think about it – we actually practised a little bit of that sort of magic ourselves last night, didn't we? We all supported one another, and when we started singing, and thinking about *good* things, I believe it helped to erect a barrier against him. We shut him out, didn't we? Kirstie started it – she told him he *couldn't* come in – and she meant it so much that it was the equivalent of raising a drawbridge and dropping a portcullis! And we got stronger, didn't we, the longer we kept it up? I think *that's* the sort of battle Lira means we have to fight – only we shall not only have to put up our mental and emotional *defences*, but we shall have to hurl those feelings outwards, too – we shall have to *attack*, just like shooting arrows from the castle walls. Chris says there was once a real castle on this spot. Well, we haven't got a *real* castle, but we have got a castle in our minds, haven't we? Our *family* is a castle, and we help to shelter and protect each other. So you polish up that imaginary ray-gun, Kyle – it could be as effective as any weapon we've got! Anyway – count me in. Elizabeth, of course, has the same free choice as anyone else. Do you want to think and talk about it a bit more before you decide, sweetheart?"

"Can I pretend to be a warrior princess, like in that book you read me last night?" queried Elizabeth, all big eyes. "If I can – and if I can stay right by *you*, Mummy – I think I could do it . . . "

"Good girl," said Derek approvingly, "that's the spirit! But we don't know *exactly* what it is we are going to have to *do* yet, so I don't think we can take anybody's decision as final or binding. There's plenty of time to change your minds – OK?"

Kirstie had obviously been doing some hard thinking. "Daddy?" she put in suddenly, "that spray stuff you have to kill flies and wasps, the stuff we mustn't touch – does it kill spiders, too? 'Cause if Kyle is going to have his zap-gun, and Elizabeth is going to be a warrior-princess, *I* could imagine a great big can of that stuff, and go 'Shhhh! Shhhh! Shhhh!' all over the Spider!"

"I think that's a wonderful idea, Poppet!" cried Derek, and the rest of all applauded.

"What about *me*?" demanded Kurt. "Can I have a flame-thrower? That would shrivel a spider up in no time, wouldn't it?"

Maybe the way that children *think*, the sheer *breadth* and *scope* of their imagination, is exactly what we need, after all! *If* we are right about this thing at all, that is!

Anyway, it seemed a good point at which to stop the discussion and get the children to bed. Derek and Jenny both got story-duty again, but the children dropped off much more quickly than we had expected. While Mary and Pat have been busy re-stocking our lounge-cum-castle with everything they can think of that we might conceivably need if we have to fend off another attack tonight, I sat down with my pad and pen. It seemed a forlorn hope that I would *ever* be able to record all that had happened since lunchtime. Luckily, when Derek came down, he took pity on me, and provided me with a little dictaphone that he uses for work. So – talking being so much faster and easier than writing – I have just about managed to get up to date. Now Mary is chivvying me to get ready for bed, and I shall not be sorry to obey! Wonder what sort of fun and games old Hillyer may have in store for us tonight? I shall not even try to speculate, but simply wait and see! So, let's to bed.

Monday, 24th June

Old Hillyer took a night off last night, but of course we couldn't be sure of that until it began to get light, so none of us got a very good night's sleep. Even though I tried my best to relax, *I* lay awake for hours, on the twitch, all psyched up, waiting for *something* to happen. When nothing did, it seemed almost like a form of psychological warfare – he doesn't even have to actually *do* anything now, purely because we know he *might*! And when I did finally drop off from sheer exhaustion, I woke with a start from a horrible dream about spiders! Still – it's no good moaning – that's not going to help, is it? "Think Positive" is evidently the order of the day, so I'll do my best, even though I feel like a wrung-out piece of ratty old rag after all the excitement of the last few days, on top of very little sleep. At least Derek and Pat had allowed the dogs to spend the night upstairs with them, so we didn't have any problem from *that* quarter!

It's a pleasant day again, so I'm out on the lawn, and the fresh air is very welcome. Jenny and Derek have gone off to work, although Derek has promised to ensure that he is not sent off on any jobs which will involve staying away overnight. Mary has driven home to fetch more clothes and to make arrangements about the milk and the papers. Linda next door is always willing to keep an eye on the place for us, although I think Mary is planning to make fairly frequent trips to collect the post, put the dustbin out and water the plants. Luckily, it isn't too far, and I'll probably go with her next time, when I'm not feeling *quite* so tired. It's been a long time since I walked through my own front door! Pat and Mabel are busy with the housework, Kurt and Kirstie went off to school without any fuss, and Kyle and Elizabeth are playing near me on the grass

Chris phoned first thing to check that we were OK, and was relieved to hear that we had had a quiet night. Dan called in for the same reason but, when he found we had no new disasters to report, he said he would get off and make a start on clearing up the Holy Well – I wish him joy of the job! Pat suggested it might be diplomatic just to check with Olly first, as the site does technically belong to the Church, and lies right behind the churchyard. Dan assured her that he would smooth it over – just say that he had noticed what a terrible state the place was in, and offer to clear it up just for the sake of the village. I don't see Olly refusing! Not often you get an offer like that, is it? And seeing as Dan already helps to keep the churchyard tidy, it won't seem *too* strange. You have to admire the chap's enthusiasm – he certainly doesn't intend to lose the momentum, but is getting stuck in right away!

Pat has just told me something rather disturbing. She brought out some drinks – fruit juice for the children and coffee for us. She pulled up a chair beside me and flopped down. "Did Derek tell you, Dad?" she said, "The cats have all disappeared! Every one of them! We haven't seen them now since – it must have been Friday morning, I suppose. They didn't come to be fed as usual on Friday evening, but we thought maybe it was just all the coming and going, with the police and everything. But they haven't been back since – and I've never known them to miss dinner-time before! What do you think can have happened, Dad?"

"I shouldn't worry too much, love!" I said, trying to sound reassuring. "You know what cats are! They probably did take exception to all the disturbances – I don't blame them one bit! Since Friday, we haven't exactly had much *peace* around here, have we? Cats are more independent than dogs, and they're far more likely to just look out for themselves. They shouldn't have too much difficulty in catching something for their *own* dinners, if they're really hungry! They'll probably turn up again, as soon as all the fuss dies down!"

"I wonder when *that's* going to be?" she sighed. "Sorry, Dad – I hope you're right! Only, I've had Tinker since she was a kitten, and when she gave birth to Rascal, Ripper and Scamp, the kids each had a special kitten of their own. They keep asking me about them, and I keep telling them what *you've* just said. I only hope we're *both* right! At least the weather hasn't been cold or wet – they shouldn't exactly die of exposure! And *I* had better go and give Mabel a hand upstairs! I've been trying to explain to her what Lira Wardwell said – I only hope I'm getting it all right! I *think* she'll be willing to help – she's promised to pass it on to her husband and her father, and she says she's fairly sure they'll want to help too, but of course she'll have to ask them first!"

I hope we're right about the cats, too! But I must admit I don't like the sound of it – it gives me a nasty feeling deep down in the pit of my stomach. Still, there's not a lot we can do about it, so we shall just have to wait and see.

The two children have just dragged out the dressing-up box, and Elizabeth is busy turning herself into "Zelda, the Warrior Princess of Zandar", and Kyle has become "Captain Blade, the Guardian of the Galaxy"! He is wearing the strangest assortment of clothes – a Zorro-type mask covered by a space-helmet, a cloak, a pair of shorts and a pair of open sandals, and he is armed with not only a large pink-and-green-plastic space-gun, but a six-gun *and* a pirate's cutlass for good measure! He is racing madly round the garden, yelling at the top of his quite-considerable voice, "POW! ZAP! POW-POW-POW! DIE, SPIDER, DIE! I'M CAPTAIN BLADE, THE GARDEN OF THE GALAXY! DIE, SPIDER, DIE! POW! ZAP-ZAP! POW!"

It ought to be enough to frighten the Dreaded Arachnid right out of the county! I can only hope it's just as deadly to Negative Energy, and with those yells reverberating through my head, I can hardly doubt it!

Now Elizabeth is trying to deprive him of the cutlass – evidently Warrior Princess Zelda has to be armed with a sword, and we can only find *one* in the box. There has to be at *least* one more somewhere, but *I* can't find it! Ah! She's finally managed to make a trade with him – the cutlass in exchange for Kurt's rifle – and what passes for peace around these parts reigns briefly once more. Now *she* is yelling, "Die, Spider, die!", too, with her own addition of "Death to all spiders!" and expending an awful lot of energy in chopping off imaginary spider-legs with her hard-won cutlass! I am *almost* beginning to feel sorry for the beast! What chance can it possibly stand against two little monsters like these?! They have certainly cheered their Grandpa up, if nothing else!

Initially, I was a little worried about them seeing this situation as a *game*. But I have reminded myself that all young creatures use play as a means of learning and practising the skills they will need in later life. So maybe this *is* the right way for the children to come to terms with it, after all. Perhaps it is the best way for them to handle it – certainly, dwelling on the *horror* of it wouldn't help. In fact, I think we're back again to this same "Positive versus Negative" thing. Surely, if this 'Spider' *is* a Negative Force, or something which is producing a Negative Force, then their sheer Positive exuberance just *may* help to counter it in some way!

My main trouble, I think, is that I am finding it difficult, at my age, to get to grips with a whole new mind-set – a whole new world view. I suppose I have actually been rather arrogant in my certainty that I understood exactly how the world worked – the physical world as described by the Laws of Physics and Astronomy, etc., and I truly believed that was all the world there *was*. Now I suddenly find myself plunged into realms which I had always considered to be pure Fantasy and Nonsense. And yet – I can no longer deny that *I* – rational, pragmatic George Hanson the Realist, the oft-proclaimed Sceptic – actually stood and spoke to three ghosts the other night! Well, technically 'morning', I suppose, but I can never really think of it as morning until it begins to get light! Anyway – exactly *when* is beside the point. The point *is* that I saw for myself beings who were once alive in the way that *I* am alive; who once inhabited human bodies, with human brains – just like me. Now they appear to be some sort of – what? – 'energy', perhaps? But energy with *emotions* – energy which can experience sorrow and terror! Perhaps 'disembodied human *minds*' would be as good a description as any.

And there is something intrinsically wrong – something *unnatural* – about that. In no way have Emily, Annie or Arthur Hillyer threatened us or tried to make us afraid. And yet their very *presence* is frightening – witness the blind terror of the dogs! The drop in temperature, I have always heard, is caused by the drain of energy required to fuel an 'apparition', but even that, in itself, is most unpleasant. These beings obviously do not belong in our world – and just as obviously they would prefer not to *be* in our world! Somehow, they *must* be 'trapped', even though I find this whole 'Soul Trap' concept very difficult to swallow! And if that is the case, then I suppose we do have to direct our own energies to trying to release them.

What about old **Tom** Hillyer, though? Now, *he's* a whole different proposition, isn't he? He is unmistakably *malevolent* – he seems to have been a nasty piece of work while he was alive, and he is still a nasty piece of work now he's dead. And he is pretty darned strong! It must take an incredible amount of sheer energy to create the physical effects which *he* has caused! The sight of that ruined cottage is a constant reminder of that! I always had the notion that if there *were* such things as 'spirits' floating around, they would be unable to function on the physical plane, and I have always thought that supposed examples of psychokinesis-by- ghosts were clever fraud, pure and simple. I can hardly dismiss what happened *here* as fraud, though, can I?! I suppose that what old Lira Wardwell said does make some sort of sense in that respect. If this truly *is* a 'Place of Power', and that power *can* somehow be tapped into by someone with evil intentions, it could just provide the tremendous amounts of energy which would be required. That is a point that has been really puzzling me – where on earth was he getting the *power*, and how was he 'recharging his batteries' afterwards? Lira's explanation provides some kind of answer to that question.

I also want to try to think out another point – just when did all this 're-newal of the Curse' business actually *begin*? I wonder – this is just a thought, but perhaps I can toss it around a little – could the onset of World War II have had anything to do with starting to change the polarisation of the Energy to Negative? Or even World War I? Both certainly caused a great up-swell of negative emotions – of fear, suffering, pain and death. Could that have swung the balance? Maybe it has been a long, slow, gradual process. It would have had to be strong enough to activate the 'Soul Trap' at least as far back as 1940, when Hillyer murdered his family, even though the actual sightings of them do not seem to have started until much more recently. Could that, perhaps, be because while Hillyer himself was still alive, and on another plane of existence, they were safe from him, and hence quiescent? Then, when *he* died, eight or so years ago, he was able to resume terrorising them?

If the stories I have heard are accurate, and the Curse was initially aimed at the De Coursey family, then it would make sense that the force of it **would** be felt most strongly right **here**, in the place where their castle once stood. It would, perhaps, also follow that someone like Hillyer, a natural bully and petty tyrant, would be able to feed on that negative energy more easily **here** than in the rest of the valley. And by 'plugging in', if you like, to that enormous source of raw power, he could accumulate the strength he now possesses. I think that theory holds together well enough to satisfy me for now.

There is, however, one aspect which, more than any other, fills me with dread. He appears to know an awful lot about what is going on here! The point that worries me most is that the other night he was playing upon Kurt's and Kirstie's sympathy for Arthur. He **knows** how much they care. He knows they have been able to communicate with Arthur, and that they see Arthur as their friend. He used that knowledge to try to trick them into inviting him in. How vulnerable does that make them? **How** does he know it? Obviously, he is not always visible. Is he watching us at this very moment? What is he planning? Where **is** he, right now? I suppose we did the equivalent of declaring war on him when we recovered the bodies that he had hoarded, like trophies, for all those years. And I cannot convince myself that he will be satisfied with the punishment he has already inflicted and the damage he has already caused! But I have no idea at all just what his next move might be!

Another thing I keep wondering is – where are Emily, Annie and Arthur right now? They are obviously not still in the kitchen – their presence is always quite unmistakable, and while the dogs are still nervous and on edge, they are not displaying the utter terror that overwhelmed them the other night. Those dogs are probably the most accurate indicators of the presence of anything supernatural that you could find! Speaking of which – I am beginning to appreciate just how much **courage** it took for Judy to actually spring at the apparition of old Hillyer when he got close to Kirstie and Kyle in the meadow! Despite her own terror, she did her best to protect the children. And what might have happened if she hadn't, eh, George? Maybe we had better not think **too** hard about **that**!

It also makes me feel pretty guilty when I remember how none of us believed Kirstie when she told us about it! Poor little girl – she must have felt so **alone**, when none of the adults, on whom she was relying for help and support, would believe a word she said! Damn, though – no matter what Dan or Lira Wardwell say, I still wish we could keep the children out of this!

I wish I could understand why there is such a difference in the ability to perceive these phenomena between one person and another! It appears that *dogs* have a remarkably acute perception of these things, and a well-developed terror of them! The children – maybe because they are still so open-minded – seem to be able, not only to *see* the apparitions, but also to communicate with them! And they seem to distinguish between the good and the evil ones, whereas the animals are equally afraid of them all! Of the adults, Dan seems to be the most susceptible to them, while I am slightly less so. I wonder if I have always had the ability to see these things? Is it just that I have never actually come into contact with them before, or is it that my head injury somehow altered my perception? I shall probably never know the answer to that one! Mary was able to see the Hillyers, albeit faintly, but Derek couldn't see a thing, no matter how hard he looked! Very strange. Although, I suppose our normal senses do vary greatly – eyesight, hearing and smell can vary a lot between one individual and another. Perhaps this isn't so very different!

Right – Mary has just driven through the gate, and Pat is calling that lunch is ready. I feel I have managed to clarify a few points in my own mind – as well as I am able – so I will probably pack up and give it a rest for today. Unless, of course – which may kind Providence forbid! – something *else* happens!

Later:

Talk about 'tempting Fate'! We *have* had a couple of incidents which I feel I ought to report! About half-past-two this afternoon, when Mary, Pat, Mabel and I were sitting on the patio with cups of tea, discussing the topic which is currently claiming all our attention and watching Kyle and Elizabeth playing ball, the phone rang and Pat went in to answer it. She came back looking harassed.

"Crikey!" she said, pushing her hair back from her face, "The pressure doesn't intend to let up, does it? That was the school – Mrs. Blakemore, the headmistress, wants me to go down there immediately. It seems both Kurt *and* Kirstie have been *fighting*! It's crazy! Can I leave Kyle with you, Mum?"

"Don't be silly – of course you can!" said Mary at once. "Off you go, dear – but drive carefully! I'm sure they're both all right!"

As far as any of us could remember, Kurt has only ever been in *one* play-ground fight before – he's not an aggressive lad, although I think he can stand up for himself enough to deter any potential bullies from picking on him. But *Kirstie*?! Oh, come on!

Anyway, there was nothing we could do but try to field Kyle's and Eliz-abeth's excited questions, and to contain ourselves in patience until Pat got back. Luckily, it was no more than half-an-hour before we heard Pat's car returning, and she had both Kurt and Kirstie with her. They both looked a little flushed, and Kirstie had a graze on her cheek, but they didn't appear to be significantly hurt. The explanation went as follows – when they got to school this morning, they were initially the centre of a lot of attention, be-cause of all the media-coverage of the events up here on Friday and Saturday. Some of the interest was just natural, childish curiosity and quite good-na-tured. Some of it was less so. But I think, on balance, they quite enjoyed their moments of fame! Then, during this afternoon's playtime, Kirstie saw some of the older boys with a packet of chewing-gum, and they were both dropping the wrappers and spitting the gum out on the ground. She – very unwisely! – went over and asked them not to do that, but to put their litter in the bin. When they demanded to know what it had got to do with *her*, she said, "Don't you know that, when you do that, you make the Badness worse?" I don't suppose for a minute they understood what she meant, but they took exception anyway, and started pushing her around. Kurt heard the fuss and looked round to see what was going on, just in time to see Kirstie pushed to the ground, so – giving not a moment's thought to his own welfare – he raced over and piled in to protect his sister. Luckily, the teacher on duty was close by, and put a stop to it before any real damage was done to anybody. *But* – the headmistress, with whom Pat has always got on very well, was quite nasty about it, saying that, just because their house had been shown on the television news, Kurt and Kirstie needn't think they could be 'uppity' in school!

"The worst of it was," sighed poor old Pat, "that I couldn't begin to ex-plain what's been going on, could I? And I'm a little strung-up myself, after all this, and I just wanted to *scream* at the stupid woman! Only I thought that might not be a good idea in the long term, so I just dragged the children away, before I lost my temper, and left her to it!"

Oh – dear! I think I can understand how she felt! Anyway, she went in to make a start on the dinner, while Mary drove Mabel home – Pat usually drops her off on her way to pick the kids up, but that didn't apply this afternoon, of course, and it's a fairish walk, especially on a hot day. Kurt and Kirstie changed out of their school clothes, and raced out to play with the other two, and I went inside to see if I could find a reasonably-recent newspaper, to find out how the rest of the world was jogging along. Just as I walked into the kitchen, Pat came staggering in from the hallway, looking so pale I was afraid she was going to faint! I quickly pulled out a chair from the kitchen table, and guided her into it. "What on earth's the matter, love?" I demanded, quite worried.

"I'm all right, Dad – really!" she assured me, in a shaky voice. "It's just – I know where Emily and her children are hiding! I've just seen them – well, sort of . . . "

"Where are they?" I asked, intrigued.

"In the cellar!" she said, the colour beginning to come back into her cheeks. "I knew the dogs weren't happy – they've been sort-of *scooting* through the hall, with their tails between their legs! – so I suppose I should have thought of the cellar, with the door opening off the hall! Anyway, I was doing a salad for tea, and I thought I'd fetch the last jar of pickled onions we put up last year – Derek really enjoys them! So I put the light on and went down – it was cold down there, but I thought it was just the contrast with the heat up here. And I had just picked up the jar, when I suddenly felt there was something behind me. I turned round, and – over in the corner, right in that dark alcove by the boiler, there were three – well, they were sort of glowing lights, shaped roughly like people – one about as tall as me, one slightly shorter, and one only about as big as Kirstie. I couldn't see any faces, or anything – only shapes – but I just *knew* who it was! I was – well, I *was* scared even though I wasn't *really* scared, if you can work out what I mean! They didn't *do* anything, they were just there – and – maybe I was imagining it, but I got the feeling they were saying 'Thank you' – not in words, not in voices – just in my head! Only it made me jump – I wasn't expecting it – and, like an idiot I dropped the pickles, and the jar smashed all over the floor! And I sort-of squeaked, 'You're welcome!' – my voice wouldn't seem to work right! And I ran up the stairs faster than I've ever run up stairs before! God –

I do feel a fool! Derek will just have to do without his pickled onions. Do you think ghosts can **smell**, Dad? I hope not, or those poor souls down there will be **choking** on the smell of vinegar! I'll have to go and sweep up the mess, but I better stop shaking, first!"

By the time she had got over her fright, Mary was back, and **she** nobly took a dustpan, a bucket of soapy water and a scrubbing-brush – plus a can of air-freshener! – and went down into the cellar to clean up. Pat and I stood in the open doorway at the top of the cellar steps and kept an eye on her – just in case! – but she was totally calm throughout. We could hear her talking quietly, in a perfectly normal conversational tone, although we couldn't catch the words. When she came back up, we asked her what she had been saying, and she replied, quite matter-of-factly, "Oh, I just explained that Pat wasn't expecting to see them, so it made her jump, but it didn't mean they were unwelcome. I told them to stay there as long as they wanted to, be-cause we don't really have to go down there very often – the boiler doesn't need stoking at this time of year, or anything like that. It's a good place for them – they're much less in evidence there than they would be in the rest of the house. I know they don't mean to, but they do upset the dogs so! Mind you, of course, now we **know** they're there, it won't be such a shock another time."

I can't help smiling when I compare **my** wife with Mrs. Magee!

"There's one thing I don't understand," I said, when she had finished. "**I** thought the children could only come into the kitchen, and weren't al-lowed into the rest of the house!"

"George, dear," sighed Mary, with exaggerated patience, "**you** were the one who issued the invitation to them! Did you actually mean to imply that they could stay **only** in the kitchen? Because, if you did, it shows a total lack of consideration! We have plenty of **bed**rooms, we have three **bath**rooms to choose from, and we have a couple of sitting-rooms, but the kitchen is the one room in the house that we simply cannot do without! To have three **ghosts** cluttering it up all the time would be quite intolerable! I don't think Mavis would like it – not to mention the havoc it would cause with the poor dogs! Pat, we'd better remember to **warn** Mavis, just in case she does decide to pop down there for any reason!"

When she comes out with pronouncements like that, Mary reminds me forcibly of my mother! I know there is no genetic link between them, but sometimes I could *swear* she takes after Mum!

Derek and Jenny got home within ten minutes of each other, and Jenny assured us that the journey was no worse than she usually has to face at that time of day. Once she got through Warwick there was very little traffic, and she didn't seem too tired, even with the heat. She reported that she had explained to the headmistress of Elizabeth's school that we had a bit of a family crisis and would be out of town for a while. The woman – having seen the news broadcasts, and knowing that Elizabeth's grandparents are called Hanson – had been all agog to hear the inside story! Anyway, *she* was quite sympathetic, and has no objection to Elizabeth temporarily changing schools if the village school will take her, so Jenny is planning to take an hour or so off tomorrow morning and go down and see the headmistress here. I'm not sure what sort of reception she will get, after the contretemps this afternoon, but she says she will give it a try, anyway.

That was a funny attitude for this Mrs. Blakemore to take, though, wasn't it? As Derek so aptly put it when he heard the story, "What's *her* problem?"! Still – we shall see what we shall see! We have had a pleasant evening, and the children are now all in bed and fast asleep. I shall put my pen away for the moment, with sincere hopes that we may get another peaceful night!

Tuesday, 25th June

Well, 'peaceful' would hardly describe our night! It would seem that no physical *damage* was done, though, so I suppose we should be grateful for that much. We took all the usual precautions before we went to bed, and we turned in about ten o'clock because we were all pretty shattered. It was just on midnight when I was awakened by a banging noise. Even though I had probably slept for at least an hour-and-a-half, it felt as though I had only just dropped off. The sound seemed to be coming from the cottage, so was a little muffled by distance, and Mary was still sleeping. I debated whether to waken her, but decided I would wait and see if anything else developed. I sat up in bed carefully, trying not to disturb her, and listened. I concluded that the noise was probably one of the cottage doors being slammed repeatedly. After a few minutes, I heard someone getting out of bed in the room above, then cautious footsteps on the staircase. I managed to slide out of bed without waking Mary, grabbed my dressing-gown and crept out into the hall, where I came face-to-face with a tousled Derek, just about to tap on our bedroom door.

"Ah! I wasn't sure if you were awake, Dad," he whispered. "What about Mum?"

"Still sleeping," I said. "What about Pat and Jenny and the kids?"

"Pat's awake, and I'm not sure about Jenny, but I couldn't hear any movement in her room," Derek reported, "but the kids are still fast asleep. Do you think we ought to wake them, Dad? Could you *see* anything from your window?"

"I didn't look," I confessed, "I didn't want to disturb your mother. It sounds like a door slamming, over in the cottage. If that's *all* it is, it seems a shame to wake everybody up, doesn't it? Tell you what – I'll keep watch for a bit, and call you if it starts to develop into anything nasty. You've got work tomorrow – *I* can catch up on some sleep in daylight, if necessary."

"Thanks, Dad," he said gratefully, "but I'm wide awake now, anyway. I think I'll make a cup of tea while I'm up – want one? I bet Pat'd be glad of one, too – I'd better go and let her know what's happening – or *not* happening, or whatever!"

But as we made our way along the hall, we could see Pat peering over the top of the banisters, so Derek beckoned to her to come down. We put the kettle on, and sat around the kitchen table. With just *us* in there, and no ghostly visitors, the kitchen was still pleasantly warm with the residue of heat from the hot day, and we were quite comfortable. Physically, anyway! We could still hear, "BANG! BANG! BANG!" from the cottage, and when we looked out we could see the greenish light again, although this time it was much fainter, and almost still, with just an odd, sudden flicker. It glowed eerily through the empty window-frames although, strangely, it didn't seem to actually illuminate anything outside. Very weird! Obviously, Hillyer was active, and we had no way to know whether he was just getting warmed up, or when he might suddenly erupt into mad violence. But we drank tea and ate biscuits, and did our best to stay cheerful, in the hope of putting up some sort of psychological barrier.

"What are we going to *do* about the cottage, Derek?" Pat asked suddenly.

"You know I never did *like* the place, but now I can't stand looking at it!"

"I know, love," said Derek. "What I'd *like* to do is send for a demolition crew tomorrow morning, and flatten the damn' place to the ground! And that's just what I *will* do, as soon as this is over. But I daren't try to do it now, Pat. Look how he reacted about the bodies! While he's still hanging out there, I wouldn't dare to send in unsuspecting workmen, even armed with bulldozers! And if we *did* demolish the place – would he have to find a new home? And if so – where? I wish I understood all the ins and outs of this kind of thing! But I think we'd better wait. I'd rather he was banging doors over there than banging on the windows over here!"

"Oh, God – me too!" agreed Pat. "Sorry – I hadn't really thought about all that! You're right – we'd better leave well alone for the moment. I just wish Lira Wardwell would hurry up and let us know what it is we can *do* about all this! This *waiting* is really getting me down!"

I concur, wholeheartedly! But, having met Lira Wardwell, *I* wouldn't like to be the one to try to rush her! I think we shall just have to wait until she is good and ready! I had so much to report on Sunday, that I realise I have forgotten to mention that Pat did manage to have a word with Olly after she and the children had been to the morning service, but he was not very encouraging! Seemed very doubtful whether his bishop would want anything to do with it, but still gave Pat a 'friendly word of warning' about getting mixed up with Lira Wardwell! *Somebody* has obviously been taking note of Chris and Helen's visits to 'Saran Ata' and associated them with *us* – and tongues have evidently been wagging! So it seems the Church isn't very interested in our problems, but they would prefer it if we didn't seek help anywhere else! Nice of 'em! We've decided we're not going to involve the Parapsychology brigade until we've given Lira's methods a try – best not to get too many irons in the fire at once!

Though the banging continued, there was no sign of other activity, and by two o'clock Pat was starting to yawn like a cavern, so Derek decided they might as well go back up and *try* to get some sleep. I promised to stay awake, and to call immediately if anything changed, so off they went, and I settled down with the newspapers that Derek had brought home with him.

I found it rather hard to take any serious interest in the doings of the outside world – somehow they seemed far away and unimportant. I did, however, manage to immerse myself in the crosswords, and that kept my mind occupied for a while. It was still difficult to concentrate, because sometimes the banging would stop for a few minutes, which put me on the alert. But it resumed each time, until the steady "BANG! BANG! BANG!" became almost as monotonous as the ticking of the clock.

Once I had finished the crosswords, I desperately wanted to go back to bed, or at least to move to an easy chair, but I was afraid that if I did make myself comfortable I would have a job to stay awake. It is not nearly so easy to 'sleep on duty' on a hard chair at a kitchen table, even though my eyelids still kept trying to close. So I made myself another cup of tea, which helped to revive me, and eventually I heard the blessed crowing of that wonderful cockerel, telling me my vigil was over. I stumbled gratefully back to bed, but though I took great care as I slid under the quilt, it still roused Mary. "Is anything wrong, George?" she mumbled, blurred with sleep.

"Not a thing, love!" I assured her. "It's just getting light – go back to sleep!"

Oh, the bliss of snuggling down into that comfortable bed! I was asleep almost before I had chance to appreciate it fully. When the rest of the family got up, Derek must have told Mary that I had been on sentry-duty most of the night, and they all tiptoed around trying not to disturb me. But I still awoke around eight, frouzled and a bit out of sorts, feeling unable to sleep any more. A long, hot shower managed to refresh me a little, and a good breakfast finished the job, so I was able to stop feeling quite so sorry for myself.

It's a little cloudier today, with more of a breeze, but I found a sheltered spot on the patio, where I could still enjoy the fresh air without my papers blowing away. Derek had left for work, and Mary had gone with Pat to take the children to school – Kyle was with them, and they were planning to pick Mabel up on their way back. Jenny had taken Elizabeth, and was going to see if Mrs. Blakemore would allow her to attend the village school for the last couple of weeks of term. I had assured them that I would be fine on my own for the short time they would all be away – but I had no idea of the horror which was just about to be revealed!

I had no sooner sat down outside than Dan came hurrying round the corner, looking pale and grim. At the look on his face, I automatically jumped out of my chair. "Sir," he said, "Sorry to trouble you, but do you happen to know where I could find a garbage sack? I usually carry some in the van, but

I used 'em all up yesterday, and I need one in a big hurry – before Pat gets back. Is Mizz Hanson in the house? I couldn't see her in the kitchen . . . "

"She went with Pat," I said. "They were going to pick Mabel up on their way from taking the children to school. What's wrong, Dan?"

"It's . . . it's the cats," he said, looking green. "I need to move 'em before the ladies and the kids see 'em. They must have missed them when they were leaving, but I guess the hedge sort-of hides them on the way out. I wish now I hadn't chopped it off so short! But they can't miss seeing 'em, coming back the other way. And I wouldn't want for them to have to see that! Damn, I feel sick to my stomach!"

"What's happened to them, Dan?" I asked, **needing** although not **wanting** to know. "I assume they're dead?"

"Oh, are they **ever** dead!" he said, closing his eyes. "They're hanging up in the front window of the cottage, right in full view. Can we look for that sack, Sir – the ladies could be back any time . . . ?"

"I have a feeling they may be kept under the sink," I said, racking my brains. "Let's go and look."

Fortunately, for once, my memory had managed to do its job right, and we quickly found a whole roll of black plastic bags. Dan ripped one off, and headed for the cottage, with me in hot pursuit.

"Hang on, Dan!" I cried, "You can't go **in** there – that's probably exactly what he wants, to lure us in!"

"Sir," he said, looking pale but determined, "I **have** to. You know how much store that family set by them cats – we can't **leave** 'em there, like that! I **think** I fit do it, if I can just get my mind set right, ward him off for long enough. You best stay here, Sir – no call for **you** to see this, neither."

"If **you're** going, Dan," I said, "then **I'm** coming with you! Come on – we haven't got time to stand around here arguing about it."

"But, Sir," he said doggedly, "they aint just dead – they been . . . mutilated! Bad."

"Dan," I persisted, "may I remind you that I trained as a doctor? I **have** seen dead bodies before – dead, **and** mutilated! Now let's go!"

I think he could see that my mind was made up, so off we marched, down the drive and into the front garden of the cottage. Doctor or not, I still felt my gorge rising when I saw the row of pathetic, bloody corpses hanging in what used to be the front window. Now it reminded me forcibly of the window of an old-time butcher's shop, hung with the lifeless bodies of rabbits and game-birds, pierced with large, shiny steel hooks. Except that these were domestic **cats** – my grandchildren's pets! The rage I felt at that moment helped to fortify me, and I managed to overcome the nausea. I felt a momentary annoyance that I had forgotten to pick up the keys to the cottage, but then I realised we didn't need them – the lock was smashed, and the door hanging half off its hinges.

Dan paused at the step, fumbled in his pocket, and drew out a large handkerchief which he proceeded to tie around his face, covering his nose and mouth. He had also brought a pair of heavy gardening gloves, and he had tools in the belt he usually carries around his waist. He put on the gloves, then drew a deep breath. "I need a **song**!" he said, incongruously. "A song about good things, happy things, that don't suddenly bring in death or loneliness, such . . . OK, I got one! Sir – you stay right here, so if anything should go wrong you fit get me some help, yeah? **Don't** come in – not for any reason! I'll be right back – I **hope**!"

From the way his eyes crinkled up, I could tell he managed to summon up a grin when he said that! Then he began to sing, 'Morning has broken, like the first morning . . . ", resolutely stepped through the front door and disappeared into the house!

Even at a time of such stress and horror, I was enthralled by what an incredibly and unexpectedly beautiful singing-voice the chap has! The sound grew fainter as he moved away from me, then increased in volume again as he approached the front window. He was somehow managing to sing calmly and absolutely in tune, which is a thing **I** can never achieve at the best of times! He appeared to be sure of all the words to all the verses, and when he finished, he began again. I was able to see him now, through the side window of the bay. As he began to reach for the cats' bodies, the flow of his singing was briefly interrupted, and my heart almost stopped too. But it was only momentary – with an obvious effort, he resumed his song, and grabbed the four bodies, cramming them into the bag. Then he gave a brief glance over his shoulder, and suddenly vaulted right out through the big front window of the bay, just missing some jagged shards of glass still attached to the frame like wicked, grasping claws. He landed neatly on his feet, and yelled, "**Move,**

Doc! *Go*! Get outta here!"

I didn't need telling twice, believe me! Even so, Dan caught me up before I was half-way to the gate, put a strong, supporting hand under my arm, and helped me back out on to the road, just in time to meet Pat's car coming over the brow of the hill! She slammed on the brakes when she drew level with us, and she and Mary jumped out and hurried over to us. Mavis, sensibly, stayed in the back with Kyle and Elizabeth, to make sure *they* didn't manage to jump out on to the road.

"George – Dan – what on earth . . . ?" cried Mary.

"Dad – Dan – are you all right?" gasped Pat simultaneously.

"It's OK, we're fine!" I assured them, trying not to sound as breathless as I felt. "Let's go inside, shall we?"

Mary took my arm, saying in an ominous tone, "George – what *have* you been getting up to now? Honestly, it seems as if I can't take my eye off you without you getting into some sort of trouble!"

"Beg pardon, Ma'am," said Dan, wincing and looking guilty. "Reckon it was *my* fault – I should-a . . . "

"Dan," said Mary, in an exasperated tone, "George really ought to be old enough to look after himself, without you having to nanny him! And who is looking after *you*, I'd like to know – you look a little peaky to me! Come on – let's get the kettle on!"

Dan shrugged and gave me a rueful look, as if in apology, as Mary swept us all into the kitchen. "Sit!" she ordered, and we both obeyed on the instant!

"Auntie Pat – can we go and play outside?" asked Elizabeth, and my heart gave a lurch of utter dread. From the way Dan stiffened, I could tell he was thinking the same awful thought!

"Maybe you could go and watch some television for a while?" I suggested. "It's . . . er . . . it's a bit breezy outside today . . . "

Both the children protested, but Pat gave me a questioning look, then said firmly, in a tone that brooked no argument, "I'll get you some milkshakes and some biscuits, and you can have a picnic on the family-room floor. Come on, now!" And she shepherded the pair of them off out of the kitchen. When she returned, Mary had just finished making the drinks. She placed them on the table, and said, "Sit down, Pat – and you, Mabel. Right, George, will you please tell us all exactly what has happened now?"

It was not a pleasant task, and I was careful not to stress the mutilations.

Even so, all of them, especially Pat, were naturally upset. She managed to handle it very sensibly, though, and controlled herself well.

"George," said Mary thoughtfully, "are you sure this was old Mr. Hillyer's doing, or could it possibly have been some thugs from the village, or something like that?"

"I don't think there's a person in the village, thug or otherwise, who would *dare* set foot in that cottage, to leave the bodies there!" I said. "If it *had* been someone else, they would have maybe left them lying in the garden where we couldn't help but see them, or something like that – but *not* in the cottage."

"Ma'am," added Dan, "it was him, for sure. I didn't have chance to tell the Doc this yet, but – well, I wasn't for sure just how he had hung 'em up there, so I took some tools with me, to cut or pry 'em loose, such. But I didn't need any tools – they weren't nailed up, or strung up – sorry, Pat! – they were just hanging there in the air, with *nothing* to support 'em! It like to fazed me, for sure – I never did see the beat!"

"Was that what made you pause in your singing?" I asked.

"Heck, you may lay to it!" he confirmed. "Only – then it was like I could *feel* somepun behind me – just nerves, mebbe, but I wasn't fixing to stick around to find out! I wouldn't turned round and come back the way I went in, not for a million dollars, so I come out through the blamed window like all the devils in hell was after me! Could you see any *more* through that window, Doc?"

"My name is *George*, Dan," I said, "You make me feel like an escapee from a Bugs Bunny cartoon – or one of the Seven Dwarfs! And I was rather busy watching *you* – what else did you have in mind?"

"You didn't notice the *walls?*" he persisted. I assured him I hadn't been worrying about the walls at the time, and had noticed nothing unusual. He was obviously reluctant to explain what he was talking about but, as he *had* mentioned it, we all insisted it was only fair for him to tell us what he meant. He sat, deep in thought, for a few moments, then sighed and ran his fingers through his hair.

"I wish I had the *words*," he said, finally. "But it's real hard for me to make plain just what I fit mean. But they were all . . . you know that black mould, that grows on walls that get real damp, such? Well, they was all covered with stuff like that – black, all over the walls – *and* the ceiling and the floor.

And then there was a whole lot of . . . like, *fungus*, yeah? You know them big, like, *plates* of fungus, that grow on trees – I don't know its rightful name. Big clumps of it, here and there, all over the walls. And the air, also, was full of like – little black particles – maybe fungus *spores*, I can't be for sure. How-somever – it was real creepy! Like being slap in the middle of a horror movie. When you fixing to get shuck that place, Pat?"

Pat explained to him that they were impatient to have the place demolished, but didn't quite dare to at this time. He sighed again, and said, "Sorry – I have this bad habit of letting m' tongue wag on without hitching m' brain up to it first! Look – if you folks fit be OK, I best be leavin' – I got work to do for Lira today. She fit be getting impatient, and I don't relish the rough side of her tongue – she sure do scold a body fierce! I'll – uh – dispose of the bodies, yeah?"

"No," said Pat decisively. "Thanks, Dan, but the kids are going to have to know that the cats are dead. And I know they're going to want a funeral. It might just help them to cope. I've got some old shoe boxes we can put the bodies in, and we'll bury them in the garden when Derek gets home."

Dan looked worried – and, having caught a glimpse of the mangled remains, I was worried, too. Derek is already under a lot of stress, and he freely admits how 'squeamish' he is. He would *not* enjoy having to handle those poor little corpses!

"Tell you what," said Dan. "If you fit lay your hands on them boxes, I'll turn 'em into coffins before I go – save Derek the bother. Mizz Wardwell can wait a few more minutes, I reckon!"

So Pat went and dug out the boxes, and Dan went off into one of the outhouses with them, along with the garbage bag containing the bodies, and three spare bags, as well as a roll of tape. When he had finished, all that was visible were four neatly sealed boxes, each marked in felt-tip with the name of its occupant. He then came in and asked Pat where the grave was to be, and went and dug a huge hole underneath the big apple tree. He left the spade, so Derek could fill it in when the interments were concluded. He began to stride away, then stopped dead, slapped his forehead, and said, "Heck, I 'most forgot what I come here for! Pat – would you and Derek allow me to store all the truck out my van in one of your outhouses for a few days? The one with the lock fit be best, then we be sure the kids fit not get in there. See,

I cleared up all that truck from round the Holy Well, yesterday, only I can't tell what to do with it, not right away. Some of it I can burn, but other stuff I'll have to try and find a dump will take it, and nobody wants old tyres, such, seemingly! And I don't have too much time, right now, to go trailing round with it. So I straight off thought of you! I'll shift it, I swear, just as soon as things slacken off some . . . "

Pat told him that of course he was welcome to leave the stuff here, so he backed the van into the yard, unloaded an assortment of junk and an incredible number of black rubbish bags – no wonder he had run out! – and locked the outhouse door behind him. Then he waved to us, and off he went to face the sharp tongue of Lira Wardwell.

He is quite a character! And a darned brave fella. He was perfectly well aware of the danger this morning, but he went ahead anyway, for the sake of Pat, Derek and the kids. I can't help feeling, though, that my invitation to call me George will **not** have the desired results – I am probably going to be 'Doc' to the end of the chapter!

When I asked how Jenny got on with Mrs. Blakemore, Mary and Pat exchanged exasperated glances. "I don't understand what's got into that woman!" said Pat. "She's always been so nice – firm, of course, as a headmistress would have to be, and not familiar, but always kind and fair and understanding. I don't know exactly what she said – we waited out at the gate – but it had obviously really **upset** Jenny! And you **know** what a lot it takes to make **her** get angry! She must be the most tolerant person I know! But she was absolutely seething, and poor little Elizabeth was almost in tears! Jenny just said, 'I wouldn't leave her **there** if it was the last school in England! She'll just have to stay at home, that's all! I **can** leave her with you two, can't I?' Well – Elizabeth is more help than hindrance to us, of course – she helps keep Kyle occupied, and she's such a sweetheart, anyway! No doubt Jenny will give us the full story tonight. I would have had a job to believe that Mrs. Blakemore could actually **be** like that, if I hadn't had a taste of it myself, yesterday afternoon. Dad – do you think we are really going to have to keep the children **inside**, and not let them out to play, even in the garden? Do you think he really might . . . oh, God! Maybe we ought to just pack up and leave, right now! I would never forgive myself, if . . . "

Mary, Mabel and I managed to calm her down between us, and we decided that it ought to be safe enough to let the children play in the garden as long as we have a couple of adults with them at all times. If we keep the dogs with us, we should be able to count on getting early warning if Hillyer *should* approach, and we could grab the children and head for the house immediately. So Mary and I took Kyle and Elizabeth outside, leaving the french doors into the family-room wide open in case we needed to beat a hasty retreat, while Pat and good, solid old Mabel went and got stuck in to the housework.

I've been alternating between jotting down these notes and keeping a weather-eye open, but the dogs seem quite happy and relaxed, and they have given us plenty of reasons to trust *their* senses above our own. Mary is sitting knitting, outwardly as placid as ever, although I find it impossible to believe that is how she really *feels*.

We heard the phone ring, and Pat came out to say that Chris would like to talk to me. She volunteered to stay with Mary while I took the call, so I went in and settled myself by the phone.

"How *are* things up there, George?" Chris asked. "Did I detect an unusual level of *stress* in young Pat's voice? Have you been having more trouble?"

"You *could* call it that!" I said, and explained what had been going on.

"Oh, Lord!" he exclaimed, when I wound down. "I was *hoping* – not too optimistically, I'm afraid! – that it wouldn't escalate to Violence Against The Person – or, in this case, Cat! It was bad enough when it was inanimate objects! Look – it's Tuesday, today, isn't it? What would you say the chances are that you can hold out 'til Friday night? Lira has decided that would be the best time for us to try this ritual she has in mind. She's not entirely happy about it, because she would have preferred to do it on the night of the new moon, but we're too late, that was on the 18th. And Midsummer's Day, which would evidently have been another good time, is gone, too. She says we can't afford to wait for the *full* moon, which isn't due 'til 2nd July, but the night of Friday 28th through into Saturday morning, is about half-way between the quarter and the full moon, and seems the best time available. How does it sound to you?"

"You want the truth, Chris?" I sighed. "It sounds to me like an awful lot of hocus-pocus! But I haven't got any better ideas, so I suppose we have no choice but to trust the lady – or *try* to! What about you, buddy?"

"Hail, Fellow Unbeliever!" he said. "I am *trying*, George – I'm trying very **hard**! But I've never been one to work on blind faith, and it's not something I enjoy. It's nice to have a bit of company in the Doubters' Brigade! But you're right, George – we **must** trust her. Wish I was as sure about it as **Dan** seems to be! I tell you, though, George – you will be amazed when you next see that Holy Well! It's **never** looked so good, not in my time! Damn, I wish I knew where that chap finds his **energy**! If we could bottle some of it, we'd make our fortune! He's cleared all the rubbish, he's cut off those broken tree-branches, he's cut the grass – he and Lira even planted some flowers! He was having problems with the pond, but I managed to come up with an honest-to-goodness coracle, borrowed from an old guy who builds them in the traditional way, and **I** paddled it while Dan scooped all that weed out with a leaf-rake! We were at it until dark – **and** we got jeered at by the local yobs, who started to congregate in the evening. But Dan went and had a word with young Pike, the ring-leader, and they didn't hang around long after that. I have a feeling Dan can probably handle himself and, even though there were five or six of them, they didn't seem too keen to try him on for size. Thank God! I'm afraid I'm a little old to provide the help he would obviously have needed! Not to mention being a confirmed coward where physical violence is concerned! I tell you, though, George – I don't like the atmosphere in this village, these last few days. Everybody seems . . . angry, and unfriendly . . . almost aggressive! I'm not sure if it's because they're **afraid**, or what, but I don't like it! "

I told him of the uncharacteristic behaviour of Mrs. Blakemore, and he seemed a little upset by it, but not exactly surprised.

"We'll stay in touch, George," he concluded. "If you need us for **any** reason, just give us a ring and we'll be up there on the double! Don't hesitate – **please**!"

I promised their number would be first on my list in any emergency, and we hung up. Friday night, eh? Well – with a bit of luck, we **might** be able to hold out that long! I just wish we didn't have to have all that mumbo-jumbo about the moon! Still, Mary and Pat seemed quite relieved – just to have a date to work to seemed to help their morale.

All is still quiet and apparently normal, and I suppose every hour of respite we have brings us another hour closer to Friday. Exactly what happens **then**, of course, I still have absolutely no notion! I suppose all will be revealed when Lira feels like telling us. Meantime, we sit tight and keep our eyes and ears **skinned**!

Later:

Well, the rest of the day passed uneventfully, which was a good thing, because I'm not sure how many more nasty surprises our jangled nerves can stand! When Jenny and Derek came home, we had the unenviable task of telling them about the fate of the poor cats. I can't remember when I ever saw either of them look so cold, hard **angry**! We decided we might as well wait until after dinner to break it to the kids – there seemed no point in upsetting them before we really **had** to. But after the meal, Derek sat Kirstie on his knee and put an arm around Kurt's shoulders, while Pat cuddled Kyle and Jenny held Elizabeth. He quietly told them that the cats were dead, giving no more detail than they absolutely had to know.

"That **wicked** old man!" cried Kirstie, even though no-one had mentioned how the animals had been killed – all the children seemed to intuit it straight away. "I hate him! I **hate** him!"

"That's playing **dirty**!" said Kurt, grim-faced and tight-lipped. "What did the cats ever do to **him**? I'd like to **kill** him, only I can't because he's already dead. But I'll find a way to . . . to . . . what's that word, Dad, for what you do to ghosts to send them to Hell?"

"Exorcise?" suggested Derek.

"Yeah. I'll find a way to **exorcise** him, if it's the last thing I do! Do you think old Mrs. Wardwell could tell me how?"

"I bet my Ripper scratched him!" shouted Kyle, "I bet he scratched his eyes out!"

"Is that what that big hole is for – the one that Dan digged?" asked Elizabeth. "So that we can bury them?"

"That's right, sweetheart," said Derek. "Shall we all go and do it now?"

"Can we put up some stones – like in the graveyard?" demanded Kurt, "Some stones with their names on?"

"And can we put a jar of flowers on them?" cried Kirstie.

Once they were reassured on these points, we all trooped off into the garden to have a very touching funeral. They have obviously picked up an idea of the usual funeral procedures from the television, and were insistent upon following the ritual as closely as they could remember it. Kurt, Kirstie and Kyle each carried the box containing their own pet, and Pat asked if Elizabeth would carry Tinker for her. So the sad cortege wound its way down to the apple-tree, and the children solemnly laid the pathetic boxes side by side. Then we had to sing the first verse of "The Lord is my Shepherd" – which was all that the children could remember. They made up for it, however, by singing, "Little bird, I have heard/What a merry song you sing . . . " which may not have been strictly appropriate, but seemed to satisfy *them*. Then Kurt said a prayer, which he made up on the spur of the moment, and was actually very emotive – it brought a lump to my throat, and I saw Mary surreptitiously wipe away a tear. Then all the children dropped a rosebud from the garden on top of the tiny coffins, and the rest of us dropped in handfuls of earth. Only then was Derek allowed to spade back the soil, and the boxes disappeared from sight.

"*Can* we put up stones, Dad?" asked Kurt.

"Sure," said Derek, "but not tonight! For a start, I haven't got any stone, and secondly, you need to think about what you want to put on them. How would it be if we had one big stone, for all four, and you were to make up a verse to put on it?"

That idea seemed popular, so the kids said a last goodbye to their pets, and we started to make our way back to the house. I waited for Kirstie, who was still standing looking down at the grave, her eyes brimming with unshed tears. I put my arm around her, and she looked up at me, whispering, "Do kitties go to Heaven, Grampy? It's so dark down there, with all that soil! Scamp might be scared."

"Cats see much better in the dark than we do!" I offered, in a dazzling display of meant-to-be-comforting illogic. "But it's only their *bodies* down there, sweetheart – it's not *really* Scamp and the rest of them. I'm not quite sure what a cat-heaven would be like, but I would think they might have soft, sunny places to lie and doze, and butterflies to chase, and they can probably have chicken and best cream three times a day, and never get fat! And nobody can ever hurt them, ever again. And they've got each other! I'm sure Scamp will miss *you*, just like you'll miss her, but at least she's with her mother and

188

her brothers, so she won't be too lonely!"

It didn't seem the time for cold reality, and the child is only five. The picture I had painted for her seemed to comfort her – it even made *me* feel a little better! She took my hand, and together we followed the others into the house, where the routine of getting ready for bed helped to restore some sort of Normality to the end of this god-awful day.

In the way of children, they quickly fell asleep, and their grief was sublimated for a while. The rest of us congregated in the family-room, with the doors still open to the fresh air. None of us felt like watching television, so we simply talked disjointedly about this and that. I repeated what Chris had said about holding this 'ritual' on Friday night/Saturday morning.

"That's – what? – three more full nights to get through?" Derek calculated. "Think we can hold out, troops? You don't *have* to, Pat. If you feel we ought to get out, then we're on our way, no matter what – OK? I don't know where we'd go, or what we would do for money – I mean, we'd still have to carry on paying the mortgage on this place! But we'll still have each other, and that's all that really matters. Let the rest of the damn' village take care of themselves!"

"But that includes Chris and Helen, and Mabel and Albert, not to mention old Harry," objected Pat. "And Shirley, my hairdresser, and – oh, all sorts of decent people! I think I'd feel like a traitor for the rest of my life if we ran out on them *now*! We just won't leave the children alone outside for a *minute*, OK? It's only three days . . . "

"Why don't we take it a day at a time?" suggested Mary. "Or even an *hour* at a time? *I* think we ought to *plan* to stay, but be ready to leave at a moment's notice, just in case!"

"Sounds like a good idea to me!" I agreed. "Jenny – just as a matter of interest – what exactly happened with that Mrs. Blakemore today?"

"I don't really want to *repeat* it," said Jenny, looking uncomfortable, "but the gist of it was that she didn't want any *more* of our family in her school, being disruptive and giving themselves airs! She actually said – and I could hardly believe I was hearing it! – that she had no great opinion of people who consorted with old women who thought they were witches – which tends to make me assume that your visit to Lira Wardwell on Sunday was seen and noted, and that the village grape-vine has been busy! Anyway – it was so . . . peculiar . . . and so unlike a headmistress, that it gave me the creeps! I almost

189

wanted to drag Kurt and Kirstie out with me as well, but I was afraid it might make things worse. Do you think it might be a good idea if they were to suddenly develop a bad case of chickenpox or mumps or something, Derek? I didn't like the look in that woman's eye!"

"Damn it – *no* way are they going back there!" snorted Derek. "She can keep her precious school! I'll find another school, even if I have to pay to send them to a private one! Looks like summer holidays start early at Manor Farm! Sorry, Pat! You do agree, don't you?"

"*I* was going to say it if *you* hadn't!" Pat assured him. "We'll cope somehow!"

"I feel so sorry for that poor old Mrs. Wardwell!" put in Mary. "It must be so awful for her, with people saying things like that about her. No wonder she feels rather bitter – I'm sure I would! Right – come along, everybody! Let's get ready for bed – we don't know what we might have to face, and we could all do with some sleep! And if anything does happen tonight, George, you are to wake me – do you understand? You are not to sit there all on your own for hours, like you did this morning! You are supposed to be taking it easy, even though I cannot seem to make you realise it! I hope you have remembered, too, that you've got your check-up with Dr. Hayward at 9.45!"

Damn! I had forgotten all about that! Well – not 'forgotten', exactly, but I just hadn't realised it was tomorrow! I have had a few other things on my mind! And with Mary in her bulldozer mode, I had better pack up and get to bed! I've got a nasty little headache, and I won't be at all sorry to lie down and switch off!

Wednesday, 26th June

Well, back to the old dictaphone! Events have been so fast and furious again today that it would be downright impossible for me to *write* it all! And – having come this far with it – I would rather *like* to complete my record of these events, if I can actually survive to do so! Although how I am going to get this transcribed is a mystery – Derek volunteered the services of his secretary, but I don't think that would be a good idea, somehow! We wouldn't want to send the poor girl into violent hysterics!

It would appear that Hillyer decided to take another night off – at least, we all managed to sleep through. I'm not one hundred percent sure whether that was because there was nothing to hear, or whether we were just too plain exhausted to hear it! In some ways, I mistrust the silence – it feels a little like the lull before the storm – but we did badly need a break, and I think we all felt a little stronger and more alert this morning because of it.

Derek and Pat had definitely decided that they were not going to send the children to school under the circumstances. Derek had to leave for work before the school would be open, but he made a note of the phone number. He promised that, as soon as Mrs. Blakemore was likely to be in her office, he would ring to inform her that the children would not be back this side of the summer holidays, if ever.

In one respect, it was lucky that it was raining this morning, as it meant that the children had no expectation of being allowed to play outside. Mary was insistent that I keep my appointment with Hayward and, as she was planning to drive me to Warwick, it would mean that only Pat and Mabel would be there to keep an eye on the children. We all felt they would be safer indoors.

Mary and I left about nine-o'clock, to be sure of arriving before 9.45, and it was a miserable journey in the pouring rain. Try as I might to control my imagination, I kept having visions of all the awful things that *could* be happening back at the farm. I am definitely going to cancel any further physio. appointments, though. I am getting *plenty* of exercise, my limbs are coming along nicely – almost back to normal – and with all this other mayhem going on, it is simply too much.

As per usual, of course, arriving on time in Out Patients meant that we had to wait – Hayward wasn't even in yet. Luckily, it seemed that most of the other patients were scheduled to see Hayward's juniors, so when he finally did stroll in, (delayed, of course, by that useful old standby, 'an emergency on the wards'!) I was first on his list. In the usual, inefficient way of the N.H.S., he *then* sent me off for x-rays, where – of course! – there were daunting numbers of people in front of us. We finally got *that* out of the way, and returned to Hayward, photos of the 'inner man' in my hand.

He greeted me like an old friend, which annoyed me a little, because, really, we are nothing of the sort. We're no more than colleagues at the very most, and have never really had much to do with each other at that, as we work in different A.H.A.'s. He came across as oily and unctuous, and a bit patronising, although he did generously allow me to study my own skull-series with him – big of him!

We then had a barrage of questions about my general health and mental welfare. "You've put on a few pounds, George!" he said, in that awful, jovial – almost mocking – tone. "This lovely lady's obviously been feeding you too well!"

He is in no position to talk! He would probably tip the scales at 20lbs. more than I do! Actually, I am a few pounds *under* what I weighed before the accident, and I have only put back some of what I lost whilst being fed via a damn tube, so there was no call for the sarcasm! And I do not need *him* to give me lectures about weight-control and physical fitness, thank you very much!

"And I'm not too happy about your b.p., George!" he commented, putting away his sphygmomanometer. "We'll have to do something about that! "So – anything else you want to discuss, Old Boy?"

If there *had* been, I would have changed my mind by that time! I wonder what sort of shape *his* b.p. would be in if he'd just been through what we have?! But I bit my tongue, assured him there were no problems of which he was unaware, thanked him kindly, and made sure he discharged me from his clinic, even though he insisted he ought to see me at least once more! Not flipping likely! I decided I would cancel the physio. appointment by phone – I simply couldn't wait to get *out* of that place!

However, as Mary and I made our way out into the waiting-room, we saw Chris, sitting on a chair by the door, looking miserable and worried – which immediately got us worried, too! We couldn't imagine what he was doing there – what on earth could have happened now? I went cold all over, and Mary muttered, "Oh, *God*, George!" Chris jumped up when he caught sight of us, and came striding over, looking the picture of rude health in that place.

"Chris – tell us quickly – what is it?" begged Mary.

"It's OK – calm down! Everybody's all right!" he said, taking her arm. "Let's go somewhere where we can talk, and I'll tell you all about it. Shall we go and get a cup of coffee?" He led us to the Coffee Shop, and we found a vacant table while he went to the counter, and came back with three steaming cups.

"I tried to phone you," he began, "but Pat said you were on your way here. I told you yesterday, didn't I George, how things seemed to be turning rather nasty down in the village? Well, this morning they turned *really* ugly! The first we knew about it was when Helen was cooking the breakfast. She suddenly said, 'Blow! I've burned the toast!' but when she pulled it out, it was hardly golden, never mind burnt! Well, we could both smell smoke, and it wasn't in the house, so she turned off the cooker to keep it that way, and we both ran out to the gate to take a look. There was *smoke*, all right – *and* flame! Lira Wardwell's cottage was all a-blaze – really well alight! I don't think we made any conscious decisions – we just started running! To our utter relief, Lira and Orilla were in the front garden – Orilla with her arms around her grandmother. But in the road were a whole mob of people – we thought at first they had come to help, or simply to gawp. But then we realised they were actually throwing stones at the two women, and shouting, "WITCH! WITCH! BURN THE WITCHES!"!! One of the stones hit Lira on the fore-head, and her knees buckled. Before I could stop her, Helen had dashed through the gate and was trying to help them, even though the mob was still pelting stones. I did what I could to stop them, but – oh God!" He covered his eyes with a shaking hand, and his voice shook, too, as he went on, "Mob violence is a *horrible* thing! I never thought I would witness anything like that – *ever* – never mind in my own village, where I was born and brought up, from people I've known all my life! Anyway – I have never felt so *impotent* – I couldn't seem to make any impression at all, and they were throwing stones at Helen, now, and I couldn't make them *stop*, and she couldn't back *away* because of the flames, and . . . "

His eyes filled with tears, and he squeezed them shut. Mary took his large hand in both of hers, and held him tightly. He took a deep breath, then a gulp of coffee, and somehow he managed to regain control.

"I just couldn't handle it!" he croaked, "and I was just wondering whether my best course would be to run for the police – although I couldn't understand why they hadn't heard the racket! But then I saw both Fred Grimshaw and Bill Moffat in the crowd. *Not* trying to control it, mark you – but shouting with the rest of them! Well, at that, I just about panicked! But then – damn, it was like the arrival of the 7th Cavalry! Up drives *Dan*, seems to take in what's happening in a split second, bumps his van right up on the pavement, and forces his way in between the crowd and Lira's wall! Then out he jumps, grabs hold of Sam Pike – who, by the way, is the father of the leader of that gang who came giving us grief on Monday evening. Pike is a lazy, ignorant, drunken slob – and if there is ever any trouble in the village, you can bet your life's savings he's right in the middle of it! He's a *huge* brute, and you know how thin Dan is – but Dan just grabs him by the shirt, and lands him a real hard punch, right on the point of the chin! I'll bet Sam's *still* seeing stars and hearing cuckoos! Anyway – down he went in a heap, and naturally, everybody stopped to look. 'That's *it*!" yells Dan, at the top of his lungs, "Fun's over! All of you *go home* – get out of here, **NOW**! Go on, **MOVE**! There's plenty more where *that* came from!' He started pushing the people at the front of the crowd – who were, of course, the worst trouble-makers – turning them round and *shoving*! And – how can I describe it? It was almost as if people . . . woke up! As if they had been in a trance, and they suddenly realised what they were doing! There were a lot of black looks, and a lot of ugly muttering, and for a moment I think it was a close thing. After all, he was only *one* man against – God, I don't know how many! But he had managed to break it up, somehow, and gradually people began to move off. Gary Pike and his cronies hauled old Sam to his feet and dragged him away, and I was finally able to get to the women. They all had cuts and bruises, and we were afraid Lira had concussion, but it could have been a hell of a lot worse! Anyway – sorry this is such a saga! – Dan went to call the emergency services in Warwick, and I took the women back to our place. Luckily, it wasn't too long before the police and a couple of fire-engines arrived, but it was way too late to save Lira's cottage, I'm afraid – it's burned to the ground. An ambulance was right behind, and to be on the safe side, they decided they had better bring all three of the women to the hospital, and I brought Dan in my car because I thought he might have broken a bone in his hand. Seems it's only badly bruised, though. So *they're* all over in Casualty, and I came looking for you two. I told Pat it might be a good idea if she went and got the kids out of school, but she said they hadn't gone in today anyway, which is a very good job – I don't trust that village! Dan backed them down, but I don't think it's necessarily over. I wouldn't be surprised if it were to break out again at any time. I think it's *got* to them – the Curse, or whatever you want to call it. The worse elements of them, anyway. *You* saw that cloud hanging over the village, didn't you, George?"

The poor chap was starting to get really upset – small blame to him! I think the impact of that awful incident was just starting to hit him.

"I certainly did see it," I reassured him. "And so did Derek. Look, Chris – you've had a nasty shock. Why don't we all make our way over to Casualty, find out how the rest of them are doing, and then we'll think about how we're going to get you home. OK?"

"I've got to give a statement to the police, yet!" he groaned. "They held off for a bit, with us coming to the hospital, but – what the hell am I going to *tell* them, George? They'll think I've gone screaming bananas! Especially if I tell them about Grimshaw and Moffatt!"

"We'll worry about that later," said Mary soothingly. "Come along – Helen is probably worrying about you!"

So off we trolled to Casualty, where we found Lira lying on a trolley, Orilla her granddaughter, and Helen sitting beside her, and Dan standing leaning against the wall of the cubicle. Helen introduced us to Orilla – after her grandmother's description of her as 'fat and lazy', I had expected to see a stout person, but instead I found she is just comfortably well-covered, with quite an attractive figure. She has dark brown hair, and very dark eyes – a softer version of her grandmother's – altogether a pleasant, middle-aged woman with a really pretty face, which was temporarily disfigured by a purple bruise under her left eye. Considering the traumatic experience she had just undergone, she seemed to be coping admirably and was well in control of herself.

Helen had a bruise on the right side of her jaw, and a nasty gash on the back of her right hand, where she had fended off a stone which would obviously have caused a lot of damage if it had hit her in the face. She looked pale, but remarkably calm – on the surface, her normal quiet dignity seemed almost unruffled, although I think she was having to work hard to keep her hands from shaking!

Dan had a very nasty bruise across the knuckles of his right hand, but if I could interpret his emotions at all, they seemed to be a mixture of cold anger at what had happened, and slightly amused satisfaction when he thought of how he *got* the bruise. I have a feeling that old Sam Pike's chin will be sore for quite some time, and that that very fact will afford Dan not a little pleasure!

Obviously, I was happy that none of them had suffered more than super-ficial injuries, but perhaps I can be forgiven if the one I was *most* concerned about was Lira! After all, we *are* rather depending on her, and the poor old soul *is* nearly 96 – it can't be much fun to have your house set on fire around you, and then to be stoned by a howling mob! We had really begun to pin our hopes on only having to hold out until Friday night, but if Lira was in no state to instruct us in the 'ritual', *then* what?! There was no way we could continue without her.

When I first entered the cubicle, she was lying quite still, with her eyes shut and a dressing on her forehead, and my heart sank. But after we had done a whispered check on the condition of the other combatants, her eyes suddenly sprang open, and were as sharp and alert as ever! The heron evi-dently wasn't dead yet – nor even hors de combat!

"Oh, so he's found you, has he?" she snapped, sitting bolt upright. "Good – then let's get out of this place, I don't think much to it!"

"Gran," objected Orilla gently, "you know the doctor wants you to stay overnight for observation! They're just trying to find a bed for you on the ward, and . . . "

"If that young whippersnapper of a doctor wants to '*observe*' something," interrupted Lira, "he can go and study his own navel, if he likes, but he won't be observing *me*! *I'm* not concussed – I was never unconscious, I'm not dizzy, I'm not seeing more than one of any of you, thanks be, and I'm not feeling sick. I've got a bit of a headache, but who wouldn't have, after a couple of hours in this atmosphere?! Now – are you taking me out of here, or do I have to get up and call a taxi?"

"But, Gran," persisted Orilla, valiantly, "where are you going to *go?* You can't go home, and I'm afraid Ben's not going to want us at our place, not with the mood folks are in."

"You'd be very welcome to come to us," said Chris, gently but firmly. "but I don't think it would be wise for either you or Orilla to go *near* the vil-lage at the moment, Lira."

"We'll go to a hotel, then!" said the stubborn old woman, undaunted.

"You won't do any such thing!" put in Mary. "You and Orilla will come to Manor Farm House with us. It's right out of the village, and there's no reason for anyone to even know you're there. We have plenty of room, and you'll be very welcome. Now – how are we all going to get home? Chris – are you up to driving?"

"I'm fine, Mary," he assured her, and he did seem to have regained his usual composure. "Helen will come with me, of course, and I can take Dan, if he wants to go and reclaim his van. Or would you rather we dropped you at home, Dan? You could rest up a bit today, and I'll call for you tomorrow, if you like?"

"Heck," drawled Dan, seeming amused by the suggestion, "no time for resting *this* week, Sir – I have me a whole boiling of things to get done! I aint *tired*, nohow! If you fit drop me back, I'd be beholden. I just hope m' van and m' traps are OK – I didn't really ought to of come and left 'em, mood them folks was in!"

"Lira and Orilla can come with us, then!" said Mary. "George – will you go and inform the Sister, or whoever, that you are a doctor, and Mrs. Wardwell can safely be discharged into your care? I'll go and phone Pat, and let her know to expect us!"

What was that I said about a bulldozer?! *I* wasn't at all sure about any of this, but it seemed to have been decided without me, and was now moving under its own momentum. I went and had a word with the young doctor, who looked doubtful but resigned, and I even signed to confirm that *I* would take responsibility for the discharge! I must be mad!

When I got back to the cubicle, I found we had been joined by a couple of police persons – one male and one female. The male one looked somehow familiar. "D.S. Hopper," he introduced himself, "and this is my colleague, D.C. Grant. Haven't I seen you somewhere before, Sir?"

"George Hanson," I said, "Manor Farm House, Gorsey Hallowell?"

"Of course!" he cried. His face was a picture. "The cottage that got blown up!"

"The cottage that was demolished by a freak storm, Detective," I corrected, and he rolled his eyes.

"A freak *storm*, Sir – of course!" he repeated. "May I ask – what are you doing mixed up in . . . I mean, what are you doing *here*?"

"I happened to have an appointment with Mr. Hayward at 9.45," I said, a little pompously, I'm afraid. "All these people are my friends, and Mr. Wainwright – knowing that my wife and I were at the hospital – kindly came to let us know what had happened. As Mrs. Wardwell would appear to have no home left, she and her granddaughter are coming home with us. If you have any more questions, I'm sure we could answer them much more comfortably at Manor Farm, and let this Casualty Department have the full use of its over-stretched facilities back?"

The police officers seemed to suspect that something strange was going on, but they obviously had no idea just *what*, and couldn't think of any objections that would hold water. So they arranged to come at two this afternoon to take statements from Lira and Orilla, and to call in with Chris and Helen afterwards. Dan said he would likely be up at the Wiccawell for most of the day, but would call in to the police station in Warwick on his way home, if that would suit them. They decided it would, and departed.

Once all the arrangements were completed, Lira hopped off that trolley with the agility of your average healthy fifty-year-old, and declined the use of a wheelchair to take her out to the carpark with such vehemence and determination that nobody had the audacity to argue too hard! Having blithely broken most of the cherished rules of an N.H.S. hospital, she clambered into our car, and sat there as perky as you please. You would never have guessed that her lovely home and the possessions of a lifetime had just gone up in flames, or that she had narrowly escaped what sounds as if it amounted to a lynch-mob! She told us that Orilla had been staying with her for the last couple of days, as Ben Bowman the baker, Orillas's husband, was not very happy about her having any involvement in what he still sees as 'witchcraft'. "The customers don't like it, you see!" explained Orilla, matter-of-factly! Mary and I both got the feeling that the marriage was probably in deep trouble anyway, and that this was just the last straw. So a good many of Orilla's clothes, toiletries, etc., had also been destroyed in the fire. I only wish I could believe *I* could be so philosophical in the face of such disaster!

At least I was able to comfort myself with the knowledge that, when Mary phoned Pat, all was well at Manor Farm, the children were playing happily although it was still pouring with rain, and Pat was quite willing to take these poor souls into her home. She was, of course, pretty shocked to hear what had been going on down in the village. "Thank Goodness we didn't send the children to school!" she said.

Amen to that, Pat! Amen to that.

Pat really must be a daughter-in-law in a million! She welcomed Lira and Orilla as warmly as if they had been invited guests, and she and Mavis had already got two rooms ready, and two beds made up. They had managed to squeeze a single bed into the little room that evidently used to be called the 'buttery', to save Lira having to climb the stairs. Obviously, they had no luggage to unpack, so we went into the lounge, where Pat had lit the fire – more for comfort than warmth, I think – and made ourselves comfortable, while Mavis took orders for tea or coffee, and came back with a loaded tray.

While the rest of us were sipping our drinks and helping ourselves to biscuits, Lira was sitting perched on the edge of her chair, with her eyes shut and her head cocked on one side, as if she were listening intently.

"Are the children being too noisy?" asked Pat, looking worried. "I can tell . . . "

Lira opened her eyes, in the sudden way that I am coming to think of as characteristic of her, and said, " Not at all, gal! It's good to hear childish voices and innocent laughter! Let 'em laugh while they may! No – I was just *feeling* the place. I can't recall when I was last in a place that felt so saturated with the good strength of a family! *Now* I understand why you were able to keep that old devil out! If you can manage to do this well come Friday night, there's a chance . . . just a *chance*, mind you! . . . that we can make it!"

Seemingly satisfied, she reached for her cup and settled down to the quiet enjoyment of her tea. Orilla caught my eye, and gave me a surreptitious half-smile, shaking her head slightly in what looked like affectionate exasperation. Chris was right – the poor woman must indeed have her work cut out, trying to handle Lira! She is not what I had been led to expect at all, and I like the woman. The adjective that springs to mind is 'wholesome'. I can just *imagine* her in a bakery – she is a bit like freshly-baked bread herself!

We had a sandwich lunch, by which time the police were ringing the doorbell. As none of *us* had any first-hand knowledge of what had happened in the village, we left Orilla and Lira to make their statements in the lounge. It didn't take long, as evidently all they could say was that while they were washing up their breakfast dishes, they heard a terrific smash of glass, and assumed someone was throwing stones at the windows again, although this time it was at the front, not at the back. On running to investigate, they found the lounge was ablaze, and could only suppose that this missile had been, not a rock, but a fire-bomb – probably a bottle filled with petrol. Anyway, the blaze was already way beyond control, and all they could do was run to the door to get out of the building. Then they found themselves confronted by a howling mob, and met by a barrage of stones. Very nasty. As we know, Helen and Chris came to offer assistance, closely followed by Dan, who managed to put a stop to the insanity. The detectives wrote it all down, asked whatever questions came to mind, and departed, saying they would be in touch when they had completed their investigations. They were very non-committal, and I have no idea what they actually made of the story.

Once they had gone, Mary said, "Orilla, dear – would it be a good idea if you and I went and did a bit of shopping? From what Chris told us, it doesn't sound as if there is much of your grandmother's bungalow left, and what has survived is bound to be soaked! The firemen probably wouldn't let us in there anyway. But you're going to need a change of clothes and some night things, at least – *I* could probably lend *you* some stuff, but I don't think any of us have anything that will fit Lira!"

So off the two of them went, using the back lanes instead of going anywhere near the village. Lira scorned our suggestion that she might like a little nap, and insisted that she wanted to go and take a look around outside. I offered to go with her, but she gave me a withering look and said, "I don't need a body-guard, young man!" (It's quite a while since anyone has called me *that*!) The rain had let up by then, although the whole place was drenched and dripping, so I left her to it, and went to give Chris a ring and find out how he and Helen got on with *their* Statements.

He answered promptly, saying that he was sitting in an easy chair right by the phone, and Helen had gone to lie down for an hour or two. The detectives had just left them, and I asked, "What did you say about the local police, Chris?"

"I told them what I saw," he sighed, sounding drained, "but Grimshaw and Moffatt had already got in ahead of me. *Their* story was that, yes, they were in the crowd – doing their best to break it up! Yes, of *course* they were shouting – but in that mob there was no way that anyone could have heard *what* they were shouting! Well, that's true enough – and I admit that I'm no lip-reader! But I couldn't have mistaken the *way* they were shouting and shaking their fists in time with everyone else in the crowd! I'd like very much to believe it *was* my imagination – but they were part of it, George, I know it! But I can't prove it. Nobody else can back me up. Helen didn't see them – which is hardly surprising! – and I'm pretty sure Lira and Orilla didn't, either. The detectives say they didn't mention them, and they were having to shield their faces from the stones, not to mention the smoke! So I let it go. I got it put on the record that I *thought* they were part of it, but I know the police aren't going to believe me. I mean – they would obviously prefer *not* to believe it of two of their own! I think it's the same with the others – we're going to have a job to prove that *anybody* was part of that mob! They'll all back each other up. I only hope they don't try to turn it round so that it winds up being *Dan*'s fault for hitting old Sam Pike! At least they'll find traces of the accelerant that started the fire, and Lira's garden has to be full of stones, but that's about all the evidence we've got. At least she did report the other stone-throwing incidents to the police, and I would suppose that Grimshaw and Moffatt must have written it down. I *hope* so, anyway! George – this could be a *long* couple of days coming up!"

You never said a truer word, Chris, old son! Actually, I'm quite worried for him and Helen, down there in the village. What if the mob decides to have a go at them, next? They have made it perfectly plain where their sympathies lie! I was on the verge of suggesting that they should pack a bag and come and join the rest of us, but I suppose I had better have a word with Derek and Pat first! This is a big house, but it is starting to get just a little crowded!

Pat had rung Derek, to let him know we had a couple more guests, and he took it in very good part – better than I had anticipated, actually! I think this business has got him really worried, and he feels so out of his depth that he is willing to try almost anything! And, despite that flippant exterior, he is really what Jenny describes as 'solid marshmallow' – he would never see anybody stuck. *He* had managed to contact Jenny, so neither of them was surprised to find Lira wandering around in the yard when they got home. I went out to meet them, just as they were introducing themselves to the old girl. Derek told her she was welcome, and said, half-jokingly, "Do you think you could put up a psychic barrier round the house, so we can get a good night's sleep without having to worry about what old Hillyer's up to?"

"I wouldn't waste my time!" she snapped, in her usual sharp fashion!

Derek had obviously not anticipated that sort of response – his mouth fell open, and he looked completely taken aback! "Oh! Well – just as you like!" he said at last.

The old woman's face broke into a wicked grin, and she said, "Got you on the raw, did I? Boy, that wasn't how I meant it! What I meant was, I don't need to waste my time doing any such thing – you and your family have already done it, and done it well! He can't get past the barriers you've already made – you don't need any help from me! Don't mind my tongue, boy – pure vinegar, I know, but I'll not be changing at my time of life, so you'll just have to put up with me! Now, if that pretty wife of yours has got dinner ready, I'm getting hungry!"

And off she marched towards the kitchen! Derek and Jenny exchanged surprised glances, shrugged their shoulders and followed, both amused and mystified. I don't think they have come across anything quite like Lira before – not too many of us have!

I was beginning to feel that Mary and Orilla were taking an awfully long time over the shopping, and little niggles of worry were making me edgy. Then Mary phoned to say that they were fine, but would be late, and there was no need to keep any dinner for them. Pat had already made enough for everyone, of course, but with Judy and Droopy around there is never any need for food to go begging, and they polished off the extra helpings in no time.

Mary and Orilla finally arrived about eight o'clock – to my great relief. Mary explained that they had managed to buy all the necessities, and had also taken the opportunity to call first on Mum and Dad, and then on Dennis, Kathleen and Flora, to let them know what was going on and ask if they would be willing to help in the ritual!

"Time is running out fast, George," said Mary firmly, "so it's no good you looking like that! *They* have to know what is happening here, and *we* need to know which of them we can count on! It seemed like a good chance, and Orilla was able to answer all their questions."

"So – what did they say?" I asked weakly. The thought of trying to explain something so incredible to them – particularly to Dad! – has been preying on my mind since Sunday! I simply could not imagine their reaction!

"Do you really need to ask, dear?" said Mary, almost smugly. "They coped with it very well, didn't they, Orilla? And of course they will do whatever is necessary. We've promised to let them have full details, just as soon as we know them ourselves."

"Good people!" commented Orilla. "Strong. Well-principled. A little *surprised*, maybe, but what could you expect? They'll be wonderful support!"

Well, I'm very glad to hear it! Because *I* am feeling banjaxed!

Thursday, 27th June

We had another quiet night, and the sun was shining from a clear sky this morning, so we started the day feeling as cheerful as anyone could under the circumstances. Initially, the children had all been a little overawed by Lira, and on their very best behaviour, but they had soon realised that her sharp manner is only a thin veneer over a kind personality, and they soon relaxed and chattered away as usual.

It was still a little wet underfoot for them to be able to play outside first thing, but Lira took them off into the family room, and we soon heard excited voices and shrieks of riotous laughter. I have no idea what she was saying to them, but it certainly caused gales of merriment! They had obviously cooked up some kind of secret between them, and the kids went around whispering behind their hands and giggling for the rest of the day. The dressing-up box was again in evidence, but for once there was very little argument about who was to have what, which made a refreshing change!

While Lira was taking care of the kids and the women were doing the housework, I went into the lounge to call the Wainwrights – I was very anxious to know that they were OK. Helen answered, but handed me over to Chris, who was able to assure me that they had had a quiet night and that all still seemed peaceful in the village, although there still seemed to be a strained, brooding atmosphere – "Just as if a big thunderstorm were on the way!" was how he put it. Well, all we can do is to hope that the storm will hold off for another couple of days. What will happen if our 'ritual' is unsuccessful, I don't want even to speculate!

Just as I was putting the phone down, I caught sight of Dan's van pulling in at the gate, so I went out to ask how he had got on with the police, and if he had found his van undamaged when he got back.

"I'm one powerful lucky guy, seemingly," he said, with a dead-pan expression on his face, "That Pike guy I slugged has real generously decided not to press Assault charges against me! But I best watch my step in future, not be so handy with my fists – the po-lice have their eye on me! Comforting, aint it, to know they watching out for bad dudes like me? As for m'van – well, scraping it up agin that wall of Lira's didn't improve my paint-job half so much as you might suppose, but – heck, what's a little paint, more nor less? If we get through this in one piece, I'll check it into the body-shop, give it a make-over! Now – if things are OK here, I'd best make tracks . . . Oh! Just one more thing – do you happen to know, Doc, who owns that land the Wiccawell lies on? I reckon it may be Derek's, but I'm not for sure if old Thompson may pay him rent for it."

"Sorry – I can't tell you," I said. "I suppose it could be Derek's land, but I'm not sure. As for Thompson . . . maybe Pat might know, I'll ask her, if you like. Do you need to know *now*, or will it wait?"

"It don't have to be this *minute*," he conceded, "but it's sumpun we need to find out soon as possible. If you would ask, I'd be beholden. Now, I best . . . "

"Dan – before you go," I put in, "just satisfy my curiosity – what is up at the Wiccawell to keep you so busy yesterday, and why does it matter who owns it?"

"What's up there," he said, "is a flat space on a hilltop, and a spring of water and a big old tree they tell me is a wychelm, whatever *that* may be! Up to yesterday, aside from that, all you could see was a whole lot of rough grass and a huge old briar patch. Following orders from General Lira, I went and cut down and cleared all the briars, and strimmed the grass. *Now* what you fit see is a circle of real old standing-stones, mebbe knee high, all growed over with moss, such, that had been hid real good by the brambles! Mizz Wardwell allowed that the place we *really* did ought to hold this ritual is that pool down behind the church, only I don't reckon folks fit give us much peace, yeah? So – second best spot, seemingly, is the Wiccawell, and the stone circle. Would you be so kind, Sir, to tell her the place is all fit for action, now?"

"You mean – right up on that hillside?!" I cried. "But Dan – how on earth are we going to get everybody *up* there? By my reckoning, four of them are over *ninety*, and another four are in their eighties! And – if I'm understanding this right – this is supposed to take place after dark? It's crazy!"

"Not just what you would *choose*, Doc," he agreed wryly. "Always supposing you had a choice! If you think you prefer to face them folks in the village – with respect, Sir, *you* didn't see 'em all fired up! And if you care to argue it out with Lira – heck, be my guest! *She*'s in charge of this ho-down – me, I'm just the lootenant, and general jack-of-all-trades! Now, if I fit get to London and back, I have to hustle!"

London?!! What on earth was he off to *London* for?! But before I could ask him, he strode away, climbed into his van, and drove off, waving through the window as he disappeared. I'm not at all sure *I* would care to drive that van all the way to London and back!

He left me more overwhelmed and out-of-my-depth than ever. Surely these crazy happenings couldn't be *real*? I have never felt so much like Alice in Wonderland in my life! I *must* be dreaming – but I can't seem to wake up. And I have *never* in all my days had a nightmare as vivid as *this*!

Later:

After Dan had departed, things seemed to settle down to something resembling normality again, and I was beginning to hope that we were going to have an uneventful day. Fat chance! The Nightmare goes on.

By afternoon, the sun had mopped up any remaining dampness, and we were all glad to be able to get out of the house for a while and sit in the fresh air. The children, having been cooped up all day yesterday, were able to release some of their pent-up energy by running races across the lawn, doing handstands and cartwheels and other gymnastic feats that *my* poor old bones have forgotten. We felt reasonably safe, with so many of us watching them, and I was able to relax more fully than for some time, soaking up the welcome sunshine. Mary was knitting, as usual, and had managed to find some spare pins and wool for Orilla, who is making a start on restocking her depleted wardrobe.

Those poor women had to leave the house without even grabbing their handbags, so have no money or chequebooks, or any of the necessities of everyday life. Mary footed the bill for the shopping they did yesterday, and

Orilla has promised full repayment as soon as she can get access to their bank accounts. She got in touch with the Fire Department this morning, to be given the glad tidings that very little could be saved from the bungalow, the fire was so fierce, and had been burning for so long before the fire-engines could get there. It hardly seems worth the risk of going into the village on a salvage-mission at the moment and, fortunately, Lira keeps her important papers at the bank, so she will be able to produce her insurance policies, etc. Anyway, there is no rush. Let's cope with this other business first – that is more than enough to be going on with!

Anyway, as I was saying, we had a nice little respite this afternoon – before all hell broke loose again! Pat dropped Mabel home at the usual time, then she and Orilla went to begin preparations for dinner – there are eleven of us now – quite a few mouths to feed! The dogs had followed Pat to do a bit of begging, and things seemed so peaceful that none of us thought twice about it. The children had tired themselves out a little by now, and were sitting in a group on the grass, Kirstie and Elizabeth making daisy-chains. I may have closed my eyes for a moment, I can't be sure, but suddenly Mary put her hand on my arm, whispering, "Oh, George – *look!*"

Little Kyle was trotting across the grass towards us, a beaming smile on his face – and a *cat* in his arms! "Look, Gammar! Look, Gampar!" he called, "It's Ripper – my Ripper's come back!"

My whole body went deathly cold and prickled with goose-flesh. Ripper was *dead* – we had buried Ripper! My mind was racing, desperately sorting through possibilities – had Dan made a mistake, and assumed that *another* cat was Ripper? Or had the cat been unconscious, but not dead, and clawed its way out of the grave? No. Not possible. Those corpses had been torn and bloody and stiff – there was no way any of them could have been alive! For a long, long moment, Mary and I both sat immobile, frozen with horror and confusion.

"It's *not* Ripper, George!" Mary forced out a hoarse whisper, "Look at its *eyes!* Quick – catch him! Don't let him take it in the house!"

She was trying to scramble out of her chair, entangled in her knitting wool. I managed to force my stiff limbs into action and started running in desperate slow-motion, calling, "Stop, Kyle! Wait!"

The cat in his arms was staring full at me, and – no! – the eyes were *not*

206

the eyes of a *cat*! They were an incandescent red, and blazing with malevolent triumph, as the little boy kept trotting forward, shouting, "Mummy – Mummy, look – it's Ripper!" unwittingly carrying the enemy towards our only stronghold.

I made a final gargantuan effort, and managed to grab Kyle just before he crossed the threshold. I spun him around, and as I tore the 'cat' out of his arms it leapt for my face, spitting and screeching, with wicked claws unsheathed. I flung up my arm to protect my eyes, and the creature dug its talons into my scalp and neck, scrabbling and gouging, while its teeth fastened themselves into my right ear. The pain was indescribable, as I fought to take hold of the awful beast and tear it off me, but my hands could not seem to get a grip, and I was being ripped to shreds. Suddenly, in the midst of the hot agony, I heard Lira's voice shouting in a strange tongue, "SARAN SAHANTHA! AR FENNA TARLAGHIR, SHU PALYNSHARA SHANA!"

The writhing body literally dissolved beneath my fingers, the yowling snarls faded into silence, and the wicked claws and teeth detached themselves from my cringing flesh. The world around me was spinning in sickening circles, and my boneless legs buckled beneath me. Through the roaring in my head, I was vaguely aware of Mary, on her knees beside me, her arms around me, crying, "George! Oh, George! Is he all right?!" and other words to that effect. I tried to reassure her, but I was so sure myself that I was *not* all right that I was probably not very convincing! I could feel the warm blood streaming down my face and neck, and I was very reluctant to open my eyes and actually face the damage. I have never been startlingly handsome, or anything – even a little homely, perhaps – but I have become accustomed to my face over the years, and I did *not* want to see what that brute had done to it!

Then there was a different hand on my head, and Lira's sharp voice cut into my self-pity. "Come along, there, George Hanson!" she said briskly and – I couldn't *help* thinking – unfeelingly. "You're still alive to tell the tale! Get up, and we'll make the hero a nice cup of tea!"

Shock-treatment can sometimes work, and hers certainly helped me to pull myself together. Bravely I opened my eyes and took my hands away from my face. I expected to see them dripping red – but there was not a trace of blood to be seen! In disbelief, I felt my torn scalp and shredded ear – and they felt whole! I inspected my hands again – still no blood, not even a smear!

I looked up at Lira, who was staring back at me with her left eyebrow cocked. "*Psychic* wounds, doctor!" she said dryly. "Painful – but they don't bleed! You'll be fine, once you get over the shock. That was quick thinking, and quick moving – and it took a lot of courage. Well done! Now, come on in, for goodness sake! *I* could do with that tea, even if *you* don't need it!"

Her astringent tone helped all of us, I think. I looked around to see the rest of the party all crowded round, gaping at me wide-eyed. Their faces were all pale with shock, and Mary, Pat and the children all had tears streaming down their faces. For their sakes, I had to make an effort, so I led the way inside, and managed to sit down on the sofa without looking *too* much as if I were collapsing. The children all piled up around me, hugging me and burying their faces in my shirt, which was soon rumpled and soggy – and it felt wonderful! Mary sank into a chair, covering her face with her hands, and Pat was shaking so badly that Orilla forced her down into the other chair, saying, "Stay there, love! I'll go and make that tea!" And off she bustled.

"It wasn't Ripper, was it?" whispered Kirstie, after a moment.

"No, love," I said. "I think it was old Mr. Hillyer, up to his tricks again, trying to get us to bring him into the house. It's OK – he's gone now."

"I *thoughted* it was Ripper!" cried Kyle defensively. "It looked like Ripper! I'm sorry, Gampar, I'm sorry he hurted you!" He burst into tears again, and I cuddled him tight, assuring him that it wasn't *his* fault. Eventually the sobs subsided, and he lay against me in a damp, exhausted little heap.

"Did it hurt a lot, Grandpa?" asked Kurt. "It *looked* like he was hurting you *bad* – I thought I could see blood, I did honest!"

"I was scared!" said Elizabeth, in a little shaky voice.

"I think we were all scared!" I said. "I was actually more scared than hurt – I *thought* it was hurting me, so it did. And *I* thought there was blood, too!"

"Convincing, isn't it?" put in Lira. "But there is *one* good thing about it – it may give you a bit better idea what we could be up against on Friday night! It *seems* real – and in a way, of course, it is real. There are just different kinds of Reality. You have to remember the right way to fight it. There was no way your Grandpa could pull that thing off with his *hands,* you children – you have to do it with your *minds*! Do you understand?"

The children all listened earnestly, and nodded, although I'm not sure exactly how much they really *did* understand – or, even if they did, how they can be expected to put it into practice! What *have* we got involved in?!

"Good!" snapped Lira, "Then let's make sure we remember it! Eh, George?"

At that moment, Orilla brought in the tea-tray, and the fragrant brew was more than welcome! We all finally stopped shaking, although I think it will take us a while to get over the shock. I still feel trembly inside. Once I felt my voice was under proper control again, I asked, "Lira – I assume that was an example of what you call 'the Old Words'? Would you mind telling me exactly what you said?"

"Well," she said, with that wicked grin of hers, "what I actually yelled was, 'By the Power of the Star, get off his head, you evil old – ' no, maybe I'd better not translate that word with kiddies present! Esoteric, eh?"

I couldn't help laughing! "Would you write the words down for me?" I asked, trading on her good mood. "I'd rather like to make a record of them, if you wouldn't mind . . . "

"*I* don't mind," she said, "only you'd better remember it's a spoken language – not one that was ever written down, so I can't guarantee the spelling! Still – there's no-one to contradict me, so it doesn't really matter!"

Anyway – she obliged, which is how I was able to include the actual words in these notes, in case anyone ever reads them and wonders. My verbal memory is good, and I can usually remember conversations pretty accurately – but only in a language I *know*!

Pat and Mary soon recovered sufficiently to go and have another attempt at getting the dinner, and the children quickly got fed up of sitting still and got down on the floor to play. I took the opportunity to pass Dan's message on to Lira – it had rather slipped my mind earlier! – and to ask her if there were no place easier of access where we could hold this ceremony, or whatever it was. For once, she was fairly mellow, and answered me without her usual impatience.

"We have to call Urtha," she explained. "Now, I think Dan is right about the language, and that English will work just as well if we can send the right *meaning*. And *you* could be right, too, and it *might* be possible to make Urtha hear us in other places – but I have never tested the theory, and we shall only get one shot at it. So I would prefer to err on the side of caution, and use a *sacred* place, a place where the Power is strong, and the echoes of the ceremonies of ancient days may still linger and give us an extra boost. In the Old Days, when these Rituals were formulated, a whole *tribe* of people would take part, each with a lot more faith than any one of us has! Yes, son, even *me*! *I* believe, because I was *taught* to believe, and I have faith in the teachings of my foremothers. But I have never witnessed these things for myself – Urtha has never been called upon in *my* lifetime – there was no point in disturbing her! All I really have are memories of words, passed on from people long dead. I have never *used* them, never tested my *own* powers! I am trying to cling to my faith in myself, but I *must* use all the help I can get. Sacred places are not to be found just anywhere – there is the Pool, which would be best, but I *dare* not try to perform the rites on the very doorsteps of those who have already been infected by the Evil! They would tear us all to pieces, if they found us involved in such practices! The springs are the only other option, and of those, the Wicca is the most powerful. It is at the apex of the star. The wychelm was revered as the most potent of tree-spirits, although it worries me that it is so nearly dead. And there is the stone circle, which must still contain great energy, even after all these centuries! *All* the springs are high on hills – but the Wicca is the closest and easiest for us to get to unnoticed. And – unless the boundaries were changed at the time of the sale – the land is part of *this* property, and should belong to your son. In which case, we shall have the permission of the land-owner to be there, and cannot be accused of trespass. Do you understand now, George Hanson?"

"I suppose I must *accept* it," I groaned. "But I *cannot* be happy about it, Lira Wardwell! With so many elderly people . . . "

"Are they infirm, then?" she asked. "Are they confined to wheelchairs, or do they still have the use of their limbs?"

"Yes, they can all walk," I admitted, "but hill-climbing is a different matter!"

"I think you underestimate them, young man!" she replied. "Desperate undertakings require desperate measures, and *I* intend to climb that hill, with all my 96 years upon me!"

At that moment, the doorbell rang, and we heard voices in the hall as Pat ran to answer it. I groaned inwardly, wondering what new problems we might be confronted with, but suddenly the door of the family room burst open and a young girl of about 18 came in. The pink, spiked hair gave me some inkling of her identity, and she rushed over to Lira and dropped to her knees beside the chair. "Oh, Gram!" she cried, throwing her arms around the old lady, "Oh, Gram, are you all right? I couldn't believe it when Mum told me – I *had* to come, I had to! Where is Mum?"

"Right behind you, dearest!" said Orilla, having hurried in from the kitchen when Pat told her who had arrived. The girl jumped up and hugged her mother as if she would never let her go, and so missed the rare sight of her great-grandmother actually having to reach for a tissue to wipe her eyes!

"You found her all right, then?" Orilla asked, looking over at Dan, who, I now saw, was standing grinning in the doorway.

"No sweat!" he assured her. "We didn't make bad time, considering the traffic."

Evidently, Orilla had phoned her daughter from the hospital to let her know about the fire, and Athaney had wanted to leave immediately, but hadn't got the train fare! So – Dan to the rescue – again! He volunteered to fetch her – *and* all her belongings! – and got her address from Orilla. It was a touching reunion, and it looks as if the young lady may have had enough of London, and is not planning to return!

"That makes 12!" said Pat, pushing her hair back from her flushed face. "Or are *you* staying for dinner, Dan? There should be enough, if you don't mind sitting down 13 to a meal!"

"Thanks, Ma'am," said Dan, "but Millie will have mine all ready on the table! She worries if I'm late, so I best be on my way. Oh – if you don't have room for her here, I can come back and fetch Athaney, and she can sleep at Millie's – we have a spare bedroom . . . "

"Orilla's got a double bed," said Pat, "so you two can sleep together, if you like . . . ?"

"Fine by me!" said Orilla.

"Thanks, Pat," said Athaney. "Mum, I hope you don't still *snore*!"

So Dan drove off to ease Millie's mind – actually, I imagine it must be pretty nerve-racking for her, all alone in Warwick, wondering what on earth is going on over here! It's not much *fun* being in the thick of it, but at least we know what's happening!

Derek and Jenny arrived to find that our merry band had now grown to twelve. Derek seemed to find the whole thing quite amusing, and greeted Athaney with, "Hey – dig the *hair*, chick!", with an exaggerated leer and wiggle of the eyebrows, which made her giggle.

Mind you, it soon knocked the smile off their faces when the children heard their voices and came racing to tell Jenny and Derek about the incident with 'Ripper'! I have never been acclaimed as such a hero before! Mind you, it's an experience which I would have been more than willing to forego – I would certainly *not* like to make a habit of it, plaudits from my family or not!

After dinner – for which we used both the table in the kitchen *and* the table in the dining room! – I remembered to ask Derek whether he owns that piece of ground. He said, "What – that flat bit, right up on the top of the hill back there? Yes, we do, come to think of it! Which I don't very often – it's not good for much! Too brambly!"

"Not any more!" I informed him. "Dan has disposed of the brambles, in favour of an ancient stone circle! We're supposed to be holding this 'ritual' effort up there . . . "

"*What?* Up *there?*!" screeched Derek. "Dad, you've *got* to be joking! We'll *never* get all those old codgers up there!"

It's not often my son and I are in wholehearted agreement, but this would appear to be one of those occasions!

"Derek," I said, in a mock-shocked tone, "Where is your respect for your elders? I shouldn't say that in front of Lira, if *I* were you – I already got a rocket for 'underestimating' them!"

"Right!" he said, closing his eyes. "OK – I see. Just a few practical considerations, if I may? For one – how long is this session supposed to last, and what happens if one of the old dears needs the loo in a hurry? Are we really meant to lug them up and down that rough hill in the *dark?*"

"Don't ask *me*, sunshine!" I told him. "Ask Lira! Only don't say I didn't warn you!"

"Oh, never mind," he sighed. "Tell you what – why don't *we* just stay mum and leave the logistics of this thing to *Dan* – *he* seems to have a talent for it! *I* don't know what's going on – I think the whole world's gone *mad*!"

Once again, he and I are in complete agreement! And he assures me that that particular piece of land was never included in Thompson's lease, so we can, at least, do what we like – if we *can* ever get everybody up there!

Now *I* am jolly-well off to bed!

Friday, 28th June

We had no disturbances from *outside* last night, but even though Hillyer was not in evidence – in *any* form! – I kept jerking awake in a cold sweat, reliving vivid memories of that awful, yowling, biting, clawing *thing* clinging to my head. I suppose it was bound to shake me up pretty badly, but I still feel as if I ought to be able to control it better. It's not so bad when I'm fully awake, but as soon as I dropped off to sleep – oh boy! Anyway, I struggled through the night somehow, but as Mary was just beginning to stretch and yawn, I had a sudden awful thought.

"*Pauline*!" I cried, shooting up in bed. "We haven't told Pauline! If she and Roger and Paula don't come, Dan's 'magic number' will be all to pot!"

"George, *do* calm down, dear!" said Mary placidly. "Try not to get yourself in such a *state* – there is so much to do today that it's going to be very important that we should stay calm and organised. And I *wish* you would listen to what I tell you – I went to see Pauline when I was over at home on Monday, and she rang back that same evening to say that she had explained it to the others, and of *course* they will all be here! They are quite determined to give the family all the support they can. They're going to drive over after Roger gets home from work, and Pauline has promised they will have their dinner before they come – Pat has got *quite* enough people to feed, as it is! And don't say I didn't *tell* you, George, because I *did*! I even asked if you wanted a word with Pauline when she was on the phone, but you were stuck in those notes of yours, as usual, and you just grunted at me. I had a strong suspicion that you hadn't heard a word I said! As for the number – now that Orilla and Athaney have joined us, that has changed, anyway. There are 27 of us now – but Lira assures me that 27, being 3 x 3 x 3, should be just as powerful, if not more so! Now, come along – we must be up and doing! Although, perhaps it would be best if *you*, George, just do your best to keep out of everybody's way and not confuse the issue! And *try* not to worry yourself into a state, or you'll be fit for nothing by tonight!"

Well, that's telling *me*! I shall do my best to oblige on the 'staying out of the way', but I am giving no guarantees on the 'not worrying' bit! I *am* worried! I am *darned* worried! I think I have every *reason* to be worried! But I will do my best to hide it, and maybe my notes will help to keep me out from under everybody's feet, and occupy my mind to some extent.

Anyway – all the time she was talking, Mary was sorting out the clothes both she and I were going to wear today. With her parting shot she headed for the bathroom, softening her words a little by patting me on the shoulder as she passed, and planting a kiss on the top of my head! Once she had finished showering, I followed, and breakfast was all ready when I arrived in the kitchen, although there was not much room at the table!

Derek and Jenny were on the point of leaving for work, Derek cramming a final slice of toast into his mouth as he grabbed his briefcase. "I'll *try* to get off early!" he promised – at least, I *think* that's what he said, although it wasn't easy to be sure with his mouth full of toast. "*I'll* pick up Gran and Grandad Hanson on my way home, then call in Warwick and pick up Dan's Aunt Millie, or whoever she is! (*Where* did I put that address?! OK, here it is!) Then Jenny's going to call for Gran and Grandad Rogers and Aunt Flora – right?"

Jenny gets off early on a Friday, anyway, so at least that will take care of the transport for the Oldsters and save any extra journeys. Jenny and Derek both kissed the kids, Derek planted a buttery kiss on Pat's mouth, and they departed, relieving the kitchen of *two* of the bodies that were crammed into it. It's a damn' good job that Emily & Co. *did* find lodgings in the cellar – there is certainly no room for them up here!

I was feeling slightly sick with nerves already, but I managed to get *some* food inside me – enough to satisfy Mary, who was keeping a watchful eye on me! Dan arrived early, having called for Mabel on his way, and they were both relieved to find we had had no new disasters during the night. Dan declined breakfast, claiming that he had already eaten. (Thank Goodness for small mercies!) He said he had a few 'messages' to run, but they shouldn't take long, then he would be back and spend some time with the kids. *I* was somewhat puzzled by this, but *they* seemed to know what he was talking about! "Polish up our act – yeah?" he grinned, giving them a big wink! Kurt was the only one who could actually wink back with *one* eye, but the others screwed up both eyes, in what was obviously *intended* as a conspiratorial response, and off he went again! Lira got up from the table and followed him outside, where she grabbed his arm and engaged him in what looked like a serious discussion, punctuated by a lot of arm-waving – probably detailing a few more 'messages' for him to run! It's a good job he seems to take it all in good part!

"Right – we'll just clear up these breakfast things, if everybody's finished," said Pat, "then Mum and Orilla and I are going to shoot off to Warwick to do some *serious* grocery shopping! Can you think of anything else we need to put on our list, Mum?"

"Don't you worry about the washing-up!" put in Mabel, "I'll soon take care of that! You get off now, and get restocked. You *have* got butter on that list, haven't you? This is the last, and there's barely a scraping left! Dr. Hanson, Sir – can you keep an eye on the kiddies for a bit?"

"*I'll* play with them for a while," offered Athaney, "Let's go and give you all a wipe down, first – we seem to have got as much marmalade, or whatever this sticky stuff is – outside as inside!" She whisked them off to the bathroom, then they all piled into the family room where, judging from the noise, they were soon having a high old time. Well – she's got more energy than I have!

Lira grabbed a tea-towel and started drying up for Mabel, while the other three women set off on their shopping expedition. That left me free to come into the lounge and give Chris a ring. It was good to hear that *they* had had a quiet night, too, although Chris was pretty horrified when he heard about my tangle with the cat look-alike!

"Lira *really* thinks that's the sort of thing we may have to contend with?" he groaned. "God, George – I tell you, I am not looking forward to tonight!"

"You're in good company, Chris!" I assured him. "I only wish I felt I really *understood* all this – even after all that's happened, I feel as if I still only have the vaguest, fuzziest notion of what is really going on! As for us being able to *take on* this 'Power', or whatever it is, and actually *lick* it – Ha! *I'm* simply groping around in the dark! And Lira may make light of it, but *I'm* still worried sick about how we're going to get all those old folks up that hill!"

"Well, that's one problem I *can* do something about!" he said, rather smugly. "Worry no more, old son! That four-wheel-drive of mine can get up there, no problem! It's rough, but it isn't actually that steep – not if you go up the west side. How do you suppose *I* got up there on my previous visits? You didn't think I *walked*, did you?"

Well – actually, *yes* – in so far as I had thought about it at all!

"She seats seven," Chris was continuing to enthuse about his beloved vehicle, "so just a few trips will do the job – depends if the youngsters feel up

215

to the climb! I can get us *all* up, if need be! Actually, George, I had better go – Dan's waiting for me. We're just off up there now with a few things. Keep your chin up, George, and we'll see you later! Let's just hope the weather-forecast's right, eh?"

Well, *that's* a load off my mind! To be honest, I was at least as worried about how *I* was going to manage to get up there as about any of the old folks! My walking has improved no end, but I couldn't feel exactly happy about hill-climbing!

At the moment, it is drizzling and overcast but, from Chris's remark, it sounds as if the forecast must be good – *I* haven't got round to anything as normal as listening to the news or the weather forecasts recently! It would certainly *help* if it were dry tonight, and preferably not too windy. I can't lay my hand on my heart and claim that I would *choose* to spend the night up on *any* bare hill-top, even in delightful weather *and* without all the rest of this insanity!

At that point, I had nothing more to report, and I couldn't simply sit there, with my thoughts running riot, so I gave way to a sudden impulse to call Dad. I needed to hear his reaction to all this for myself – I mean, he has always been so scathing about the 'Supernatural', or – to quote his own words 'load of utter bunkum'! So I was finding it hard to take in that he was tamely going to go along with this. The phone rang for so long that I thought they must be out, but just as I was about to put the receiver down, Dad's voice growled, "Yes? If it's double-glazing, we don't want any!"

"It's George, Dad," I told him.

"George? George who?" he snapped. "Oh! *George*! Is that *you*, m'boy? Just the fella! Your mother and I were just having an argument – maybe you can settle it! That woman . . . int'resting woman! . . . the one who came round the other evening with Mary? Know the one I mean? Yes, well – your mother – always *was* a feather-headed creature, memory like a sieve! – swears blind that woman's name was April! *I* say it was Oprah – I'm right, aren't I?"

"Actually, you're both wrong!" I told him, just a little maliciously. "Her name is Orilla."

"Never heard of it!" snapped Dad, "Are you *sure* about that, George – you know what a one you are for pickin' things up wrong! What kind of name is *that* to go to bed with? *Dor-is*!" he bellowed, and I quickly moved the receiver six inches away from my ear! "***Doris – George says that woman's name was*** . . . what was it again, George?"

"Orilla," I said patiently. "O – R – I – L – L – A . . . Orilla."

"As in 'gorilla' eh!" quipped Dad. "***Told*** you it wasn't April, didn't I?! So, George – to what do we owe the pleasure of this call? You're not calling to say it's all off, are you? Or that Derek can't pick us up? I suppose we could get a taxi, but it'd cost a bit, all ***that*** way!"

"No, Dad," I said, beginning to regret my folly at having recklessly put myself in line for this conversation in the first place! "It's still 'on', as you put it, and Derek's all set to pick you up. I was just calling to make sure you do understand this is going to be an all-night session, Dad, so you'd better wrap up warm, and . . . "

"Go teach your grandmother to suck eggs!" he retorted. "George, Mary explains things a site more clearly than you do, if you don't mind me saying so, and ***she*** gave us all the gen! Long time since we were out all night! Rather looking forward to it!"

I groaned inwardly! "Dad," I ploughed doggedly on, "I honestly don't think it's anything to look forward to! I know you've never ***believed*** in this sort of stuff – well, neither have I, of course! – but you'd better be prepared for things to get really nasty. It's been sheer mayhem here for the last week or so, and . . . "

"You always were too set in your ways, George!" he interrupted. "You have to keep an open mind, try for a bit of liberal thinking! If these phenomena are all Mary and that Orla woman cracked 'em up to be, it should be quite an experience! We haven't had much excitement recently, your mother and I, and it sounds as if ***somebody*** has to do something about all these goings on – it's not good for the children! Not to mention Derek's property values, eh! I'm looking forward to meeting this old priestess, or whatever she is! Did you want a word with your mother while you're on, George, or shall we just see you this evening?"

I simply didn't feel up to coping with Mum as well, so I said "'bye, Dad – see you later!", put the phone down very gently, closed my eyes, took a deep breath and counted slowly to twenty. Whilst I'm glad my parents aren't exactly ***terrified*** of the prospect facing us, I could wish they were taking it a little more seriously! But it was no good trying to explain any more – I would have been simply wasting my breath! It *would* have been nice to be able to have a serious discussion about some of the points that I still don't understand, such as – why should it be that the poor *cats* were actually killed, and physically mangled, but that *I* only got 'psychic wounds'? *And* how old Hillyer could become such a realistic cat! I can't seem to get my head round this 'incorporeal' business. Maybe, if you are not blessed – or encumbered? – with a rigid, physical body, perhaps you *can* appear in any form you choose, but it's the realism that still amazes me! That not only looked but *felt* like a real cat – the fur felt just like real fur, never mind the claws and teeth! Maybe it has something to do with the brain experiencing what it *expects* to experience – because the brain is fooled into thinking that it is *looking* at a cat, it then deludes itself into thinking that the object under scrutiny also *feels* like a cat? Oh, *I* dunno! Maybe it doesn't really matter anyway – but it would just be nice to feel I had *some* rudimentary understanding of these things! I suppose Dad wasn't really the best candidate to discuss it with – I don't suppose *his* ideas on the subject are any better-formulated than my own. Although when he *does* settle down and put his mind to it, he is a formidable debater! He actually has a brilliant brain – rapier sharp. He picks up instantly and infallibly on the slightest flaw in an opponent's argument, and his insight and deductive powers are amazing. He has had many papers published in medical journals over the years – very controversial, some of them! – and has always been in great demand to speak at medical conferences. His reputation is known and respected not only nationally, but internationally, and he has always been rather a daunting act for a son to follow! But you would never *guess* it, when he's in the sort of mood he was in today! I suppose the person I really ought to clarify these points with is Lira – but I'm not sure if I am feeling quite *robust* enough at the moment! Maybe when all this is safely over? He who lives *may* learn! And he who stays sane is doing darned well!

Good old Mabel brought me in a cup of milky coffee at that point, and it was quite a relief to speak to somebody so solid and sensible and down-to-earth! I can *cope* with Mabel! I know I have never been quite up-sides with the rest of my brilliant, quick-silver family – I have always been poor slow George, plodding along step by dogged step, while my parents and my two brothers leapt carelessly and effortlessly from conclusion to airy conclusion. Derek is far more like them than *I* am – *he* never really had to work at things, either – not for **him** the hard, slow grind and the long slog. Anyway – I am what I am – a conscientious, slightly fussy, elderly chap who worries a lot, especially about the safety of his family – but that **is** what I am, and I'm afraid I'm stuck with it! My epitaph will probably damn me with, 'He meant well,' or some such faint praise!

It looks as if the drizzle has stopped, so I think I'll take a little stroll around the garden and see if the fresh air will help to dispel this fit of maudlin introspection!

Later:

As I went out of the back door, I met Dan just returning as promised. He was carrying three long, knobbly poles of polished wood, about six feet long and all different shades, from pale to almost black. "What on earth are you planning to do with those?" I asked, absolutely mystified.

"Hand 'em over to Lira, merely!" he grinned. "She sent me to fetch 'em from her place – hoo! what a mess **that** is! The roof's fell in, and the whole place is gutted, and what the fire didn't get, the water finished – it looks almost as bad as your blamed cottage! Lucky she had these stored in the garden shed, not in the house, and the flames didn't reach that far! They're magic staffs, seemingly – one of hazel, one of holly and one of – oh heck, I disremember what! And they are real **old** – she allows they been in the family for centuries, so she was some worried if they had survived! If you want to know what **she's** fixing to do with 'em, you'll have to ask **her** – me, I'm just the messenger boy!"

"How did you and Chris get on?" I asked. "Did you get up the hill OK?"

"Sure – sailed up!" said Dan, then added – as if taking pity on me! "We just went to take up one of them camping-toilet affairs, in case the ladies should feel the need, and a bunch of folding chairs. It could be a long stand, and folks might be glad to set a spell. Right – I best deliver these to Mizz Lira, ease her mind, then I have to look out a large can or tub or jar, such . . . I **think** I saw one in one them outhouses . . . then I best get round to them kids . . . "

By now he was obviously talking to himself and had forgotten my existence, so I left him to his riddles and carried on with my stroll. I stood for a while gazing at the top of the hill where I believe the Wiccawell stands, and tried to imagine what on earth we would be doing up there tonight – I have never taken part in a pagan ritual before! My imagination, however, was quite unequal to the task – the only images I came up with seemed so innately silly that I almost blushed at the very thought! I only hope I am going to be able to summon up the right kind of attitude once we actually get started!

One encouraging sign, though, was that the clouds over the hilltop seemed to be breaking up, and a glimmer of sunshine was forcing its way through. If I knew any prayers or invocations to the Weather Gods, I'd be reciting them now!

The fresh air and the exercise helped to cheer me a little, and I came back to my sanctum in the lounge in better spirits. Mary, Pat and Orilla have just returned, loaded down with vast quantities of assorted groceries – and they *did* remember the butter, thank Goodness!Dan and the kids are still in the family room, laughing like hyenas and making the *strangest* noises! What they are up to is anybody's guess! Kurt just raced in here, yelling, "Grandpa – Grandpa! Can we have some of your big paper, please? I've only got little bits, and we need a *lot*! And I need four pencils – no, three! Kyle can't write!"

I supplied several sheets of paper as requested, and off he dashed again! Oh well – I suppose it's keeping them occupied, whatever they're doing, and helping to stop them getting frightened. No doubt there will be *plenty* of time for that later!

Later still:

We had sandwiches for lunch, and when I sat down afterwards, I must have dropped straight off to sleep! I suppose I have had a lot of less-than-restful nights recently, and a nap was probably what I needed most. When I woke up, Mary was sitting beside me, knitting. As soon as I roused, she got up and brought me a really good hot cup of tea, and I was amazed to find that it was actually quarter-to-five! That was *one* way of passing the afternoon! Jenny and Derek and their passengers should be arriving shortly. Mary tells me that she took Mavis home about 3.30, so that she could get dinner for Albert and old Harry, and that Chris and Helen are going to call for them and drive them up here about seven o'clock.

Derek's car has just driven through the gate, so the mustering of the troops has begun! I suppose I am going to have to pack up for now, and **hope** to conclude this record tomorrow. What will I have to report, I wonder? I've just had an idea, though – I'll see if Derek will let me take that little dictaphone to help me keep tabs on exactly what does go on! It runs on batteries, and I know there are some brand new ones in the bureau drawer. I obviously won't be able to take written notes, but that just might be an invaluable aid to memory. If the kids can pretend to be warriors, etc., maybe their old grandpa could pretend to be a war correspondent! It just might help **me** to cope! Right – here goes nothing! Put the pen away, George, and report for duty!

Sunday, 30th June

Well, I **did** survive the ordeal, so once more I take my pen in hand! I was too shattered to even think of lifting the damn' thing yesterday, but I feel a little stronger and more in control of myself today, so here we go again! I **never**, in all my life, expected to have an experience like **that**! I could never have imagined it, either! But let's stop waffling, and, with the aid of my trusty dictaphone, try to keep it chronological: back to Friday evening, which seems light-years away, not just a couple of days!

As soon as Derek arrived and had ushered Mum, Dad and Millicent Campbell into the house, Kirstie – hearing his voice – rushed out to lay claim to him. "Come **on**, Daddy!" she cried, dragging him by the hand, "you've got a lot of **learning** to do!"

Derek shrugged and raised his eyebrows at us as he was hauled away, and the family room door closed behind him.

"Why don't you all go in the lounge with George?" suggested Mary. "Dinner isn't quite ready yet, but I'll bring you in a cup of tea, and we'll tell you when to head for the dining room. If you happen to need the bathroom, Millie, there's one just over here, dear . . . "

A bright notion struck me as the old folk were trooping into the lounge. "Mary," I said, "Wouldn't it be a good idea to take some food and drinks up there with us? We could be glad of something before morning! I know it's all more work, but . . . "

"George, love," she said, "don't worry – it's all taken care of! Helen is kindly seeing to that side of it – she felt Pat had *quite* enough catering to do! And *she* is in charge of the catering for the W.I. and the Pensioners' Club get-togethers and the church socials, so she has plenty of experience, *and* plenty of equipment. She keeps it at home, because she says it *walks* if she leaves it at the Church Hall, so there was no problem about getting hold of it, and no awkward explanations! Now, do go and look after the guests, George, please!"

Too slow again, George! Another case of "He meant well"! Outmanoeuvred on all flanks!

So off I went to try to entertain Mum and Dad and Millie. The poor old girl was looking very pale, and almost on the verge of tears. I said, "It's quite a prospect, eh, Millie? Try not to worry – I'm sure it'll be all right!"

"Oh! Oh, it's not *that*!" she assured me. "It's just . . . well, being so close to where it *happened* . . . my sister, I mean! I've only ever been here once – not in *here*, of course, but in the cottage! – but her Tom made us so unwelcome that my husband would never come again. I never could abide that Tom Hillyer, even when we were childen! Whatever possessed Emily to *marry* him, I can't imagine! So this is the first time I've been near the place since he . . . He certainly made an awful mess of that cottage, didn't he? I saw it on the news, but it looks even worse when you actually see it for yourself!"

Poor old soul! I hadn't considered that angle! I couldn't help wondering if Emily, down in the cellar, had any inkling that the sister she hadn't seen for so many years was actually sitting right above her! I had no idea whether Dan had told Millicent about our squatters in the cellar, but I decided I had better keep my big mouth *shut* – I wasn't sure exactly how she might feel about it!

Derek must have been telling them about my experience with the pseudo-cat, and they were all suitably concerned about me – it was really quite flattering, even if a little embarrassing! I mean – I hadn't *intended* to do anything *heroic* – *I* didn't know at the time what was going to happen! I just couldn't let poor innocent little Kyle actually carry that thing into the house, or *none* of us would have had a place of refuge, not the living nor the dead! Still – it was nice for old fuddy-duddy George to have impressed Mum and Dad so favourably for once, with my apparent bravery, so I didn't disclaim any harder than modesty dictated!

By that time, Jenny had arrived, and Dennis, Kathleen and Flora came to swell our ranks in the lounge. Right behind them came Lira, who, it seemed, had already been introduced to them on their way in. "Ah, Lira," I said, "I'd like you to meet my mother, Doris Hanson, and my father, Michael – another **Dr.** Hanson! Millie, of course, you already know! Folks, this is Lira Wardwell, the current Guardian of the Holy Well, and the lady on whom we are pinning all our faith!"

"Come and sit over here by my wife!" said Dad, gallantly getting up and giving her his seat. "I've been looking forward to meeting you, Mrs. Wardwell – your . . . is it your granddaughter . . . Orilla? She gave you quite a build-up! When are we going to learn just what it is we have to do? I'm fascinated!"

"Well, you'll just have to be patient!" said Lira firmly – she is not **that** easy to impress! "I'm only going to say it once, and there's not enough space here to get everybody into one room, so we'll leave it 'til we get up to the Wiccawell. Anyway – the more spontaneous it is, the better. I don't want you all to have too much time to prepare!"

This sounded a little ominous, but we didn't have chance to worry about it because Mary came to tell us that the dinner was ready, and there were places for all of us at the table in the dining room. I honestly hadn't much appetite, and the food all tasted like cardboard – the fault of my nerves, I must stress, and no reflection on the cooking! But I managed to get **some** down me, telling myself I needed the energy and I would be glad of it later. The children and the rest of our merry band, including Dan, ate in the kitchen. By the time the meal was over, Pauline, Roger and Paula had arrived, so the family contingent now had a full complement. Paula and Athaney gravitated towards each other immediately, and seemed to be getting on like a house on fire. (Ouch! Pardon the unfortunate simile!) They were the only two there of that sort of age-group, and both seemed very glad of teenage company! God, though, our Paula is growing into a real beauty! That long, dark, naturally-waving hair of hers is quite spectacular, and whilst her face is, of course, changing as she matures, it is obviously always going to be poignantly lovely. And she has those gorgeous deep-brown eyes, like Mary's and Pauline's and Jenny's, with lashes that need no mascara, they are so naturally long and thick and dark! Her one ambition in life is to be a photographic model, and I would imagine she has everything it takes, with a tall, slender figure to add to the rest of her attributes. I only hope that, if she does make it, they won't spoil her too much! To my mind, they would find it difficult to improve on the way she is already! But, then – I *am* her Grandpa!

While Jenny and Orilla cleared the tables and washed up, Pat and Mary tried to get the rest of us organised. "Can we go and get dressed now, Mummy?" cried Kirstie, her eyes bright with excitement!

"All right – but calm down!" said Pat. "If someone can give Kyle a hand, I'll go and get your coats and things!"

"I'll keep an eye on them!" offered Pauline, picking up Kyle. "Come on, big fella – let's go and get you dressed! Ooof! What on earth have you been eating? You weigh a *ton*!" And off they all trooped into the family room!

"Right – has everybody got a warm coat?" demanded Mary of the rest of us. "Ladies – hoods or hats – yes? Dad and Dad," she looked from my father to her own, "did you bring your caps? Good. George, pop and get yours! Chris and Helen will be here in a few minutes, and Chris will start ferrying us up to the hilltop. Now, has everybody got everything? And I know you're all too old for me to need to tell you, but I think it would be a very good idea if everyone uses the toilet before we leave! They *have* put a Porta-loo up there, just in case, but it will be much more comfortable and civilised down here!"

"Yes, Miss!" said Dad, putting his hand up in the air. "Please, Miss – shall we take a clean hanky as well, Miss?"

"That's a very good idea, Michael," said Mary, playing along. "Then you can all go and sit down quietly, and recite your multiplication tables until it's time to go!"

I think you could say Morale was holding up pretty well! We were all a little surprised, though, when the children trooped out of the family room, all dressed up in different costumes! Kyle was wearing his space helmet again, although this time without the Zorro mask, with a pair of long corduroy trousers instead of shorts, and red wellington-boots instead of sandals. He was still clutching that ray-gun tightly, though! Elizabeth had refined upon her Warrior Princess outfit, and had managed to acquire a sword which looked more like a rapier than a cutlass, and somehow suited the part rather better. Kirstie was wearing a long, white, shiny dress, with a long red cloak, a little tiara on her head, and was, incongruously, carrying one of those old-fashioned spray things that people used to squirt their roses with to rid them of greenfly!

I did ask where she got it, but she just said, "Dan brought it for me!" Where *he* found it, Lord only knows – I haven't seen one in years! Kurt was dressed in camouflage army gear, like a commando, with a plastic helmet on his head, and with a contraption strapped to his back which looked like a rucksack with a vacuum-cleaner hose coming out of it! The hose was draped around his waist, and he was clutching the nozzle as if his life depended on it. Being the eldest, he probably realised the gravity of the situation more deeply than the others, and his knuckles were white. My heart went out to him – he *is* only seven, and this was a lot for a seven-year-old to cope with.

"Oh dear!" said Kathleen, looking a little taken-aback when she saw them all. "Are you sure it's all right to dress up like that? I mean . . . "

"It's not a dull-as-ditchwater, droning, po-faced service in a cold, stone *church*!" put in Lira, overhearing her. "Urtha is a goddess of *Life* – of joy, and singing and laughter! *She* won't mind! She likes little children to enjoy themselves. And you may be surprised by what powerful magic can spring from a child's imagination! Children are *strong* – in energy and imagination, in life-force and in faith – children can *believe*, when adults doubt and falter! I *hope* I'm wrong, but I have a feeling we're going to need their protection yet, because *I* can't think of anything else with a hope of doing the job! And it's best to be prepared for any eventuality!"

Well, I was glad that *I* wasn't the only ignoramus around! Kathleen looked quite taken-aback, and even *Mum* was completely stumped for an answer to *that* one! Old Flora chuckled a little, nodding her head. "I wish I'd met *you* a little sooner!" she said to Lira. "Never could stand the cringing and whining, and the disapproving old men who usually run religions! Never could see why the act of worship had to be so deadly and apologetic! And you're right about children being the strong ones – they're *survivors*, are kiddies – far less timid than adults!"

Well, I was glad that *they* were so sure of it, because *I* couldn't claim any such certainty myself! I could see what they meant, in a way, *but* . . . ! I would have *much* preferred not to test the theory in practice!

By this time, Chris and Helen had arrived, bringing Harry, Mavis and Albert. It amused me a little, I have to admit, to see Albert and Old Harry in their Sunday-go-to-meeting clothes! I had never seen either of them in a shirt and tie before! Anyway, we were now all Present and Correct, and the operation to ferry us up the hill began in earnest. The Lounge Brigade all sat down again for a while, awaiting our turns – as Mary said, we might as well be comfortable as long as possible. But gradually the numbers left at Manor Farm dwindled, and the numbers on the hilltop swelled. Derek stayed until the last load, of which I was one, to lock the place up after us.

"What are you doing with the dogs?" I suddenly wondered.

"I've put them in Kurt's bedroom – which is the place they seem to prefer," he said, looking worried. "Kurt has a bed they can hide under! I've left them food, and plenty of water, so they *should* be OK, and I've put down plenty of newspaper, although I bet they manage to miss it! I only wish I could explain it to them better! It's not ideal, but it's the best I could come up with – we can't take them with us, we obviously can't leave them in the *cellar*, and all the people I *could* have left them with are going *with* us! Fingers crossed, eh?"

Well, *I* didn't have any brighter ideas, so that was how it had to be. But knowing the abject terror to which they had been subjected on so many occasions recently, and having no idea what might happen down at the house in our absence, I felt really sorry for the poor creatures.

When we had finally bumped and bounced our way up to the flat place at the top of the hill, I couldn't help thinking that we looked like a cross between an Old People's Outing and a Fancy Dress Parade! But Dan and Chris had certainly been hard at work – there were enough folding chairs for everyone, and they had even had the forethought to put the portable toilet up on a sort of wooden platform, to raise it a little. Those things are always too low for comfort, for people whose knees are not quite what they once were! It was surrounded by a canvas screen for privacy, and toilet-paper was provided. They had set up a barbecue, which was already alight, and a couple of big kettles were heating over the glowing charcoal. Helen had several large cool-boxes standing by, along with a trestle-table laden with mugs and plates and a large tea-urn. It looked like a party rather than a Ritual!

Chris simply couldn't wait to drag me over to show me the stone circle – he was as excited as a little child at Christmas! "Just look, George!" he cried, "I had absolutely no *idea* it was there – I thought it was just a scraggly old heap of brambles! Just think of the *age* of it! Stone Age, George! What did I tell you? Damn, but I think I can actually feel the *power* of the place!"

It **was** rather awesome, to think of the many long centuries of wind and sun, snow and rain, of days and nights, of springs, summers, autumns and winters, that had passed since these moss-and-lichen-covered stones had been placed there. I tried to imagine the people who had brought them to the site and set them up, and what was going on in their minds to make them go to all that trouble; but my imagination fell far short. It was just a ring of short, weather-worn stones, eaten away by plants, by Time and by the elements, but it was very impressive, nonetheless. And – yes! – whether it was just the power of suggestion, I can't say – but there did seem to be a faint, almost electric, tingle in the air around it.

Stuck into the ground, at regular intervals outside the stone ring, were the sort of torches you see in films set in Medieval times. "Nice touch, eh, George!" cried Chris, proudly displaying them to me. "Got 'em from the old chap who makes the coracles! He swears they'll burn for hours, but we'll leave off lighting them 'til the last minute. They'll give the whole thing more atmosphere than any electric lighting we could have rigged up! Lucky the weather's cleared up, though!"

It was, by now, a still, balmy evening, with hardly a cloud in the sky, and a huge, blood-orange sun slowly dipping towards the hills and making way for twilight. Apart from ourselves, there was hardly another living creature to be seen or heard. A few late bees were blundering homeward, but the world around us seemed hushed and expectant, and a pale, white, moon was climbing up the sky, still several days away from the full.

I looked around for Lira, and saw her standing gazing up at the old wychelm on the edge of the plateau. Orilla and Athaney were with her, each carrying one of the staffs I had seen earlier in the day. It made them look strange and uncanny, even though they were wearing perfectly ordinary clothes. Lira and Orilla were dressed in the sort of flower-print, cotton summer dresses favoured by middle-aged and elderly ladies, with cardigans over the top. Athaney was wearing denim jeans and jacket, with open sandals on her bare feet, and her vivid pink hair glowed in the sunset. Instead of her usual bun, Lira had set her hair free, and as it cascaded in waves of rippling silver past her shoulders, she truly had the look of an ancient sorceress of olden times. As I watched, they all flung their arms high in the air, as if paying homage to the huge tree, which was, indeed, as good as dead. The trunk was hollow, and only a very few of the bottom branches had twigs bearing a few sparse leaves; the upper branches bore not even a twig, but reached bare and stark into the sky, gnarled like arthritic fingers. I felt a wave of sadness, looking at that former monarch of the hillside, long past its days of glory, and already in the process of decay. I shivered. Somehow, it seemed like a bad omen.

I wandered over to take a closer look, and just over the edge of the slope, I saw a spring of water trickling out of the hillside – the Wiccawell, the source of the Banebrook. It flowed into a little pool, almost surrounded by the roots of the old tree, then lipped over the brow of the hill, disappearing behind a hump in the ground, to re-emerge at intervals as flashes of silver in the distance. It followed a winding course around Manor Farm House, then away down into the valley to join with the other streams in the sacred pool behind the church.

With the suddenness that seems to characterise all her movements, Lira turned her back on the tree, and stalked, with her heron-like gait, across the grass towards the stone circle, her descendants one behind each shoulder. It seemed as if some subtle change in the atmosphere took place, and silence descended on the rest of the party as they all turned to watch her approach. She strode to the northernmost stone of the circle, which was a little taller than the rest, and turned to face to the south.

"Take the places I assign to you," she ordered, not even having to raise her voice, the silence on the hilltop was so complete. "Stand inside the ring of stones, facing towards the centre, spaced so that you can link hands with those on either side of you. Orilla Wardwell – on my right hand. Michael Hanson . . . " she pointed to the spot on Orilla's right, and Dad moved obediently into position. "Doris Hanson . . . Roger Dennison . . . Pauline Dennison . . . Kurt Hanson . . . Derek Hanson . . . Kirstie Hanson . . . Patricia Hanson . . . Kyle Hanson . . . Jennifer Morris . . . Elizabeth Morris . . . Mary Hanson . . . Danvers McReady . . . Millicent Campbell . . . George Hanson . . . Helen Wainwright . . . Christopher Wainwright . . . Mabel Potts . . . Albert Potts . . . Harold Swale . . . Flora Rogers . . . Dennis Rogers . . . Kathleen Rogers . . . Paula Dennison . . . and Athaney Wardwell on my left hand. The circle is complete, the number is made up – three times three times three. In the sacred circle of my foremothers we are gathered, as the earth turns from sunset to moon-rise, to call upon the goddess Urtha, to beg her to lend us her power and her protection, that we may have the strength to fight the Evil that surrounds us. I do not know how many times the moon has risen and set, waxed and waned, since last the goddess was called from her sleep – it is many, many, many! But in the name of you all, I will call her now. Christopher – Dan – light the torches!"

The last sliver of the setting sun had just slid behind the hills in the west, darkness was thickening around us, and the rising moon now glowed silver in an indigo sky. Standing in our allotted places, we seemed almost to have passed into a different dimension from that in which we lived our normal lives – a place that seemed poised between the earth and the sky, standing outside the realms of Past and Present and Future. There was only here . . . only now. We all stood as if entranced, the children big-eyed and solemn, clinging to the hands of their parents. As if from somewhere outside myself, I mused that Lira had obviously given our placings a lot of thought, and carefully arranged that the children were each placed between close and trusted relations. Kurt was between Pauline and Derek, Kirstie between Derek and Pat, Kyle between Pat and Jenny, Elizabeth between Jenny and Mary. Even Paula had been placed between Kathleen, her mother's mother's mother, and Athaney, closest to her in age. It was a good arrangement, although, if I could have had my own choice, I would have *preferred* to be standing next to my Mary and holding *her* hand. But *my* needs were not the primary consideration here, and I resolved to do my best to help Dan to care for Millicent Campbell.

Lira had obviously also gone to some trouble to find out and learn all our *names* by heart! And at *last* my curiosity was assuaged! At last I knew Dan's name . . . Danvers *McReady*! A *good* name. A *strong* name. He had no need to hide it!

While all this was passing through my mind, Dan and Chris were making their way around the circle, lighting the ring of torches at our backs. The flickering flames added an extra air of mystery to the scene, as the last glimmer of daylight died away completely and the darkness crept stealthily nearer, enclosing us in the haven of a small circle of light. As the two men returned to their places, Lira, holding her ancient staff in her right hand, raised her arms and began to speak, her voice clear and crisp in the stillness.

"Oh, dear Mother Urtha, goddess of Life and Procreation, goddess of Healing, Comforting, Joyfulness and Laughter – awake from your long slumber and hear your daughter calling! While you have slept, men have again corrupted the Power of this sacred place, and Goodness has again turned to Evil. The spirits of the dead can no longer complete their journey to the Blessed Lands, but are bound to the earth, here in this valley, where they have no purpose, no place and no rest, and are at the mercy of evil tormentors. The force of the Evil is infiltrating the hearts of the living, causing them to hate and revile their neighbours, and to defile the very land on which they live, until the Earth itself cries out in protest! Dearest Mother, forgive our neglect of your ways and our rejection of your wisdom – in your mercy, hear us and help us! Awaken! Give us the light of your Star for our protection! Ita bueta – so may it be!"

"Ita bueta!" repeated Orilla and Athaney, and the rest of us, unbidden, joined in with, "So may it be!"

As Lira's impassioned prayer drew to an end, Dan left the circle for a moment, and came back with a guitar slung around his neck. He began to strum a simple, lilting melody, then raised that beautiful deep, rich voice of his in a haunting repetition of the prayer. He sang softly and effortlessly, and I felt the tears starting to my eyes as the notes rang out over the hilltop:

> *'Urtha, awaken*
> *Gently from slumber,*
> *Pity thy children –*
> *Rise from the deep!*
> *Thou, who hast helped us*
> *Times without number,*
> *Once more we need thee,*
> *Rouse from thy sleep!*
>
> *Sweet, tender Mother,*
> *Kind and forgiving,*
> *Since from thy wisdom*
> *We wandered afar,*
> *All are in peril,*
> *The dead and the living,*
> *Send to protect us,*
> *The power of thy Star!*

Urtha, awaken!
Darkness is falling,
Strong is the Evil
That shadows our way!
Bring us thy blessing!
Answer our calling!
Lead us in safety
To the new day!'

As the music faded away, I glanced at Lira, and her face was radiant with a light that had nothing to do with the moonlight or the flickering torches. "Urtha has heard us!" she cried triumphantly. "Look! Look, all ye doubters! Look, all ye unbelievers! Oh, look, and *believe*!" She was pointing in the direction of the mighty wychelm, beneath whose rugged roots arose the Wiccawell. There should have been no source of light over there, away from the torchlight, shaded from the moonlight by the huge tree, and yet – from the pool below the spring rose an unearthly golden glow. A collective sigh of wonder went up from our circle, and as we watched, the light slowly grew in brilliance, spreading like a halo, like an earthbound star, and causing the old wychelm to cast a stark, black shadow over the grass. *This* light was nothing like the foul, toxic greenish-yellow light that had illuminated the haunted cottage, but a delicate, pure, soft gold, glowing like dew-kissed primroses on a fresh spring morning.

I had no frame of reference for dealing with this. My mind was struggling vainly with the very concept. It *could* not be. And yet it *was*. My *head* was seeking suspiciously for fraud and trickery, but my *heart* joyfully accepted it as undisputed truth. I wanted to laugh, and I wanted to cry. My fear was at war with new hope, and the conflict between them was immense and overwhelming. Were we – could we *really* be - in the presence of a *goddess*? Utter incomprehensibility!

For long moments we stood in awed silence, watching the wondrous light rippling gently, as the waters of the spring, through which it seemed to be shining, lapped and splashed. Then Lira's voice cut into our reverie.

"Good!" she said softly, "We have wakened the goddess, and she is listening. Now we must convince her that we are worth helping, and try to strengthen her Power, which has been weakened by centuries of disuse. Working round the circle in the order in which we joined it, each one of us must pour out our own beliefs into the storehouse of the circle – *good* things to give the Positive Power strength. I do not want you to *think* too hard – just speak what is in your hearts. Let your tongues express the things that *move* you and stir your emotions, the things that make you happy – your dearest memories and your most precious dreams. Don't worry if you repeat what someone has said before you – what *matters* is the strength of the *feelings* behind your words! *I* will begin – but just a word of warning! The Negative Power will not give in without a struggle, and we are bound to be attacked. By now, Urtha's presence will have been detected, and the Evil will try to defeat her before she has regained her full strength. But remember – we are dealing with phantoms, apparitions, delusions – you cannot fight them with your hands! Your only weapons are your hearts and your minds – and particularly your love for each other! Do not let doubt and fear defeat you! Think *good* thoughts, pour forth *good* vibrations, and be strong! Let us begin:

I believe in Urtha, and I believe in the power of Goodness. I believe that our Mother Earth will protect and sustain *us* if we protect and care for the Earth. I believe that whatever blessings we demand from, and whatever goodness we take *out* of the Earth, we must return and repay, so that we do not deplete the resources and upset the Balance. I believe in a partnership and a compact between Mankind and the Powers that gave existence and awareness to both the planet and ourselves. I believe in the Old Words and the Old Ways and the Old Wisdom. I believe in the Way of Urtha! Ita bueta."

As the old lady's heartfelt declamation ceased, Orilla, smiling at her grandmother with tears in her eyes, began: "*I* believe in my grandmother, the wisest and bravest woman I have ever met. I believe in the Wisdom which she spent so many hours bestowing upon me, and I believe in all our blessed foremothers, who passed that Wisdom, from mother to daughter, down to her, to me and to my daughter. And in this sacred place, in Urtha's sacred presence, with all these people to bear witness, I solemnly swear that from this night I will do my best to follow her teachings, and to be worthy at the last to follow in her footsteps, and continue the line unbroken. I also believe in the selflessness and the courage that causes people to risk their own safety to defend others, as all of *you* are here tonight to fight in the cause of us all. And particularly

Helen, Christopher and Dan, who put themselves in great danger to protect my mother and me when the mob were attacking us. Also, the kindness that caused the Hanson family to take us in and shelter us when we were homeless. And I want all of you to believe in our eternal gratitude. May Urtha bless and protect us all!"

It was Dad's turn next, and I was curious to hear what he would come up with – not to mention floundering around in my mind, wondering desperately what *I* could come up with when *my* turn came! Dad cleared his throat, hesitated for a fraction of a second, then began: "*I* believe in the secrets of Life, for ever beyond our understanding. I believe in the double-helix – the continuous spiral of deoxyribonucleic acid, passed from one generation to the next in endless new combinations, connecting us to both our ancestors and our descendants, unbroken from time beyond memory, to time beyond imagination."

It was short and succinct, but impressive. I felt so proud of him, and happy in the fact of being his son, and sharing *his* DNA! Now, what could *Mum* come up with?

"*I* believe," she began, in a voice that shook just a little, "in the skills and crafts of human minds and human hands: the wonderful illusions that artists can create with paint on canvas. The varied and satisfying shapes of pottery, fashioned from mere lumps of clay by the turning of a potter's wheel and by the potter's clever hands. I believe in statues, cast in bronze, or patiently sculpted, chip by careful chip, from blocks of lustrous marble, the talent of the sculptor freeing his mental vision from the stone so that all can share it. I believe in the rich, deep colours of glass – the sun shining through the rainbow panes of church windows, or beautiful, fluted vases blown from incandescent molten glass. I believe in the craft of the carpenter, and the shining beauty of tables and chests and dressers, polished to a satin sheen by loving hands, and passed as treasured heirlooms down through many generations. I believe in the roughened fingers and the patient feet that draw fleeces into yarn upon a spinning-wheel. I believe in weaving and knitting, and crochet and macrame, and embroidery and tapestry, and the care that goes into every stitch and every knot. I believe in elderly ladies with cushions on their laps, interweaving their little beaded sticks to make delicate lace. And I believe in the love embodied in the creation of all these things!"

Oh, Mum! I was almost choked with emotion, and my eyes were overflowing as she spoke. And Lira, with a satisfied smile, nodded her head and said, "Good! Very good! Look!" I followed her pointing finger, and saw that the stones of the ancient circle were beginning to glow faintly around their bases! They *couldn't* be, but they *were*! *We* were doing it – we were starting to recharge the battery! We were actually working Magic!

Then everyone tensed a little, as out of the darkness a chilly wind began to blow, seeming to send probing fingers questing around our circle. The wayward torches flared and flickered. "Go on!" ordered Lira, and Roger – my solid, dependable son-in-law, Roger – began to speak in a steady voice:

"*I* believe in music," he said, "in all its many forms: the glorious swell of a mighty church organ; the lilting strains of a violin; the deep sweet song of an oboe, or the crisp, clean notes of a piano – not to mention the haunting melody of Dan's guitar! The urgent call of trumpets can rally us to a cause; the strident beat of drums can order our steps as we march together, keeping us to the same beat and rhythm; and the heart-rending melancholy of a bugle calling the 'Last Post' gives a voice to our wordless grief for the fallen. All music gives expression to our emotions – songs of joy or sorrow, soothing lullabies or choral exaltation, or the excitement of a lively tune we can dance to – Music has a power all its own."

I have always known that Roger *liked* music, but I never even suspected that he had such a deep passion for it! But his expression of that emotion helped to charge the emotions of the rest of us, and the lights around the bases of the stones glowed a little brighter still!

But the wind outside the circle had continued to grow stronger, and was now beginning to toss our hair. I glanced around, worried, and to my consternation, on the southern horizon, huge black storm clouds were massing, and I thought I caught a flicker of lightning. Oh God! Not *another* 'freak storm', with us all caught on this open hilltop, with no shelter in sight! Above us, all was clear and still – I could see the diamond pin-pricks of stars piercing the dark sky, and the moon glowed brighter as it rose higher – but the storm was obviously approaching fast.

"Prepare for some bad weather!" called Lira. "Everybody go and get your coats on, while we still have light to see – then back to your places. Quickly – quickly – we must reform the circle!"

Nobody needed to be told twice! The women had obviously been prepared for just such a contingency, and had all our outdoor gear ready to hand
out. Jenny, Pauline, Pat and Derek bundled the children into raincoats, and
tied hoods firmly under their chins. We were back in our places in a remarkably
short time. "Close the circle!" cried Lira. "Move closer, huddle, huddle! Into
the centre, crouch down, if you can, put the little ones in the middle, and
hold fast to one another! Keep faith! Now – let us continue!"

And over the wind came the soft voice of my elder daughter, Pauline. "*I*
believe in Hope." she said. "Like a beacon in the darkness, or a lifeline in
stormy waters, Hope can give us the strength to struggle on when it would
be so much easier to let go and give up the fight. Hope tells us that though
the battle may be only just beginning, and a long, hard tussle may lie ahead,
there *will* eventually be an ending to the strife. Hope assures us that the steep-
est hill will lead to level ground, and that the stoniest, roughest road will give
way to soft grass at last. Hope promises us that the blackest clouds will roll
away, the heaviest rain will cease, and we *will* see the sun shine again. And
Hope makes us certain that the longest, darkest night will draw to an end,
and give way once more to morning."

What she said was very appropriate and topical! I have never seen clouds
move with such appalling speed. From a small band on the horizon at the
south, they were now racing towards us, pitch-black, roiling, boiling, filling
the sky and devouring the moon and stars. The wind that swirled around us
had now penetrated our circle, its voice rising to a screaming roar, extinguish-
ing our torches and nearly bowling us over with its onslaught. Impossibly, it
grew stronger and wilder yet, buffeting us from every side, and suddenly down
came rain, in such a deluge that I felt just as if someone had flung a pail of
very cold water right over my head! We were instantly drenched and dripping,
and hats and caps were torn from our heads and whirled away into the raging
darkness. Right above us, a streak of lightning tore the sky apart, and the si-
multaneous crash of the thunder sounded like the end of the world! I was disoriented, and absolutely petrified! The thunder and lightning seemed almost
continuous, and the very ground shook under our feet, with the sheer power
and volume of it. We all crouched in our pathetic huddle, while the wind
whipped us, and the rain assaulted us, and the ground beneath our feet became a quagmire. Even the lights that had formed at the base of the stones

seemed to be extinguished, and the darkness was utter and impenetrable. Then into the maelstrom came Lira's voice – I could just make out her words, and they struck me as so incongruous that I felt I wanted to laugh hysterically. She said, "Magic, Danvers! A little storm-calming music, if you please!"

Storm-calming music!!! Oh, come on! I would have bet good money that *nothing* could calm *this* storm!

"You'll have to let go of me, Millie!" shouted Dan, trying to extricate himself from our rugger-scrum. "Hold on to the Doc – he'll look after you!"

I very nearly *did* burst into a bray of hysteria at *that* one! Oh, sure – the *Doc* will take care of things, *not* a problem! The Doc was having quite enough trouble of his own! But I wrapped my arm around Millie's trembling shoulders as tightly as I could, and did my best to seem confident. I was just able to turn my head enough to see Dan, struggling against that vicious wind, lurch over to one of the standing stones and perch himself on top of it. Bracing himself as well as he could, and clinging on to his guitar, which was doing its best to take flight, he plucked a few notes which I could hardly hear, and began to *sing*!!!!! Strangely, even through the tumult around us, we could all hear his words – which, in itself, *had* to be magic! What he sang was a very simple little ditty, with almost nursery-rhyme type words, and it went like this:

> '*Pitter-pitter-patter,*
> *Feel the raindrops splatter!*
> *But there's no need for fear, now –*
> *Dark clouds soon will clear now!*
> *Winds may rush and tear, now,*
> *Tossing clothes and hair, now,*
> *But stormy winds are dying*
> *To breezes gently sighing!'*

And – absolutely incredibly! – as he sang, it seemed his words truly did contain some irresistible, suggestive power, and were fulfilled! The rain stopped as suddenly as it had begun, the angry clouds broke ranks and began to tatter and move away, and the raging tempest abated! Instantly! Impossible, but it happened! The thunder and the lightning, however, were still rampaging around us, and the song continued, addressing itself to them:

> *'Rumble-bumble-bumble!*
> *Hear the thunder grumble!*
> *But never fear the roaring –*
> *It's just an old man snoring!*
> *Sudden flash of lightning*
> *Can be kind of frightening,*
> *But, honey, don't be frightened –*
> *Skies will soon be brightened:*
>
> *Shining through the raindrops,*
> *Moonbeams paint the cloud-tops –*
> *Rainbow's archway bending,*
> *Rainbow colours blending!'*

I have never, ever seen – nor ever expected to see – a rainbow caused by moonlight before! But there it was – glowing with iridescent colours, calm and clear and incredibly beautiful! I could hardly swallow for the lump it brought to my throat. I'm not sure whether the following verses were meant to comfort *us*, or to convince whatever Power had caused the storm that it was actually defeating its own objects and causing Good instead of Evil, but I *did* find them comforting, whatever their intention!

> *'What the storm is doing*
> *Is but Life renewing –*
> *Cleaning dusty air, now,*
> *To make the world more fair, now.*
>
> *Racing down each hill now,*
> *Foams many a sparkling rill now!*
> *Dried-up streams will spring, now,*
> *With regained voices sing, now.*
> *Sleeping seeds will wake now,*
> *Buds will swell and break now,*

Down reach thirsty roots now,
Up spring tender shoots now.

'Sweet new grass will grow now,
Flowers will bloom and glow now,
And at each puddle's brink, now,
Critters fit come drink now.
Water in the ditches,
All the land enriches;
So when the storm is over
Bees may feast on clover!'

The last clear notes dripped into the silence like the last sparkling raindrops of a summer shower. Once more, all the night was still around us: high above, the arch of the sky was brilliant with stars, and among them the moon swung, calm and unperturbed. Our torches were drenched beyond resurrection, but the stones that formed the ancient sacred circle were glowing once more with a bright silver radiance; and with their other-worldly light and the wonderful aura rising bright above the pool, we had all the illumination we really needed. We were soaked, dripping and battered, but unhurt, and Lira roused us from our stunned lethargy by clapping her hands sharply and calling, "Time for a tea-break, don't you think? Let's have a cuppa and a breather, and re-group! Well done, all of you – and thank you, Dan!"

Dan gave her a grin, and sketched a little bow. "Glad to be of service, Ma'am!" he said. "Does anybody know any magic for drying out gee-tars? I have me a suspicion that getting soaked like that may not do 'em half so much good as you might suppose!"

Personally, *I* didn't think hot tea was going to be on the agenda, much as I wanted a cup – that rain and wind **must** have doused the barbecue! But – as, perhaps, I **might** have expected after our experience with the 'storm' at the cottage – the effects were strictly confined to one small area, and the barbecue had been set up far enough away from the circle not to have been touched. Even the screens around the toilet were still standing, despite those vicious winds which had raged only a few yards away! And the hats and caps we had lost during the onslaught were soon recovered, having fallen to earth not far from the edge of the circle! I doubt if I will *ever* become accustomed to the way in which Magic blithely manages to override all the Laws of Physics and the Dictates of Common Sense!

Helen and Mary rummaged in bags and handed us all towels to dry our sopping hair, and once we had taken off our soaking-wet outer garments, we found the night was once again balmy and warm, and my fears of contracting pneumonia quickly receded. Chris and Derek tended and refuelled the barbecue, and soon we all had mugs of steaming hot tea, which was very soothing to my jangled nerves. Once the kettles had boiled, they were replaced on the grills with hamburger patties and sausages, and we were soon tucking in to hot-dogs, hamburgers and sausage-rolls. I discovered that I was absolutely *famished*, and went back for not only second but *third* helpings! The food tasted wonderful!

At last we were all replete, and Lira called us to order once more. "We have done well so far," she said, "*Very* well – you are even stronger than I expected! But we still have much to do. We must go back to recharging the energy, so I want you all to return to the circle as before, and we will continue where we left off when we were so rudely interrupted! Places, everybody!"

So back we trooped to our circle of ancient stones, and I couldn't help wondering if it had been as casual as this in the Old Days, with barbecues and things! Or the prehistoric or medieval equivalents, anyway!

"Kurt Hanson – it is your turn next," instructed Lira once we were all in place. "Do you remember, son, what I want you to do?"

"Yes, Ma'am," Kurt assured her – a phrase I assume he must have picked up from Dan! "Shall I start *now*? OK – *I* believe in the way I felt last winter, when we had really heavy snow. When the snow stopped falling, the whole world was covered in white, as far as I could see. In the morning, the sun came out and made the snow sparkle, and the sky was really blue, but the lanes were all blocked, so we couldn't go to school, and my Daddy couldn't go to work. So he said, 'Let's build a toboggan, and try the Cresta Run!' So he showed us how, and we took our sled up to the top of the steep hill behind our house, and when I was sliding down I felt . . . I felt like I could truly *fly*, and I felt like I could live for ever and *ever*! And I believe it was one of the best feelings I ever had, or ever *will* have. And I believe *that* was a sort of Power – a really good sort!"

The lights around the stones appeared to agree with him. And there was hardly a dry eye in the house! Derek, whose turn was next, was so choked with pride that he had to swallow hard a few times before he could get his voice back in proper working order! When he finally managed it, he said:

"I believe in the power of *mothers*, and the gentle strength of *women*, that can bring forth new life, and tend and nurture a new baby. The careful hands that can soothe all your hurts and bathe your cut knees. The soft voice, that can somehow control your worst impulses, or outbursts of temper, better than any amount of shouting and threatening. The sure knowledge that, however bad you may have been, your *Mum* will forgive you – however illogical you may be, your Mum will understand what you mean and sympathise with how you are feeling. And whoever else in the world may hurt or betray you, your Mum will *never* let you down!"

Well, Derek, you were lucky in *yours*, son – you were blessed with a good one, and I'm glad you appreciate her! Mary always could manage him when I was at a loss!

"Kirstie Hanson," said Lira gently, "can you tell us what makes *you* happy, now?"

Kirstie has always been the shy and timid one of our brood, but she has demonstrated recently that she has a lot of hidden strength. Now she stood up straight, drew a deep breath, and said in her little, piping voice:

"*I* believe in butterflies! They start out as funny little wiggly caterpillars, and I don't know how they do it, but they have a Power, and one day they go to sleep, and while they are asleep they change themselves into beautiful, flying jewels! And I believe that *angels* may be a bit like that."

She finished breathlessly, leaving us all astounded. And the lights around the stones beamed brighter than ever, in approval.

"My turn . . ? " said Pat, a little nervously. "Oooh – well, then – umm – *I* believe in flowers! I believe in gorgeous velvet roses, with their rich, sweet perfume that smells of summer. I believe in tiny, white daisies, like soft drifts of snow across the lawn. I believe in the glorious gold of buttercups swaying among the lush meadow-grasses, stirred by every smallest passing breeze. I believe in the sweet kitten-faces of pansies, and the deep, purple carpets of aubretia. I believe in snowdrops – so delicate, yet strong enough to triumph over the last days of winter, and the trumpet-call of daffodils heralding the spring. I believe in bees, frantically burrowing for nectar into pink and white clover, and the amber honey dripping from the comb. I believe in fat, furry bumblebees, cramming themselves into foxgloves, and backing out sparkling with pollen like little flakes of gold-dust. I believe in pollination, and the miracles hidden inside little dry seeds, that look so dead but are really tiny time-capsules, full of Life, and bursting with the promise of next year's flowers."

Once she got started, she was quite carried away with her own beautiful visions, and carried the rest of us away with her. And now the Power within the circle was beginning to tingle in the air – almost to hum!

"*My* turn, *my* turn!" cried Kyle, jumping up and down – he always does enjoy being the centre of attention, and has always got plenty to say! "*I* believe in my Mummy and my Daddy, *and* my Gammars *and* my Gampars, *and* my sister Kirstie *and* my big bruvver Kurt, *and* in my dogs Judy and Droopy *and* my little cat Ripper, who's dead now and we buried him under the apple tree, *and* my fluffy teddy called Cuddles that my Gammar Rogers made me for Chrismus when I was little, and comes to bed with me." (Deep breath, start over!) "And I believe my Mummy and my Daddy keep me safe, and my Daddy wont let *any* monsters come in my bedroom in the dark while I'm sleeping, because my Daddy is big and brave and stronger than *any* silly old monsters!" (Another deep breath! Thumb into mouth, to demonstrate that he really had finished!)

The Power was literally starting to hum now, the lights were running riot, and the rest of us couldn't decide whether to laugh or cry, but *tried* not to laugh in case we hurt his feelings! The level of raw emotion was like nothing I have ever felt before! They say 'A trouble shared is a trouble halved', but I swear that that sort of *emotion* shared is an emotion multiplied by factors that are simply off the scale!

Jenny's turn was next. She gave a little wry smile, and said, "*That* was a very hard act to follow! And, really, the sentiments I want to express are very much what Kyle just said, but I think they can stand repeating! I believe in our Family, and the close ties of blood through the generations. I believe I am fortunate, because for some years now I have lived in a four-generation family – including both my mother's and my father's parents. I have revelled in the love and support that offers, and welcomed the opportunity to offer love and support to the children of my brother and sister, as they love and support my own daughter. I believe in our intertwined roots of blood, and the strength of many strands woven into one. I believe in our innate knowledge and understanding of one another that comes from shared genes, and the intimate sympathy that comes from a shared childhood environment. I believe in the safety and security within one unit made up of many, and many individuals both providing and sharing in the security of that whole."

Oh, my Jenny! Why, oh *why*, could she not have found that kind of love and understanding with David Morris, so that her *own* daughter could have experienced that same warm security? But *that* young lady was not feeling sorry for her*self*, but standing straight and speaking clearly in her turn.

"*I* believe in puppies and kittens, with their round fat tummies, and baby lambs and soft, fluffy little chicks. I sawed some baby piglets once, when I went to a farm for a day-trip with my school, when I was little. They were all pink and new, and they raced around all over the place, and they squealed, and they drank milk from their mummy's tummy. And inside them was a Power, so that they could grow big, and one day they could have little piggies of their own, just like their mummy. And I believe I have that same Power in *me*, so that I can grow to be like *my* mummy, and one day have a little girl of my own, who will be just like me."

Mary smiled down proudly at her little granddaughter, and squeezed her fingers in congratulation. "*I* believe," she began, in the gentle voice that I have loved since the day I first met her, when *she* was little more than a girl herself, with deep eyes full of secrets, both wise and merry in equal measure. "I believe in the contented sleep of babies, cradled safe in the warm haven of their mother's breast. I believe in the way that a satisfied stomach, full of natural milk, can make the eyelashes flutter down to rest upon the downy cheeks, and the tiny fingers uncurl and relax. I believe in the untiring strength of the arms that support, the body that gives of itself to nourish and provide, and the depth of the indomitable love that will defend and protect against any threatened danger. And is it my imagination, or can I feel something nasty happening behind me? Would somebody please look and tell me I'm imagining it?"

She said this last in the same tone of voice, and it took a moment for us to register what she had said. She, Dan, Millie and I were all standing with our backs more or less to Manor Farm House, far below us at the bottom of the hill; but when we turned our heads to look, we could see that the ruins of the cottage were heaving again with that sickly greenish glow, flaring, then dying down, then flaring again.

"*Uh*-oh!" said Dan. "Brace yourselves, folks – I reckon we fit have company in a minute!"

"Remember!" cried Lira, "Delusions! Apparitions! Fight them with your *minds*! They can only hurt you if you allow your senses to accept them as real – defy them! Dismiss them! Do not allow them in!"

While she was shouting, I was peering into the darkness behind me, and suddenly, silhouetted against the glow from the cottage, I could make out a swirling, airborne mass. I suddenly went cold as I realised what they were – bats! Huge bats! And heading straight for us! Now, it is all very well in *theory* to say, 'Don't believe in them, they're only apparitions!" but when the things are hurtling straight for you, appearing real in every detail, it is not so easy for your brain to put that advice into practice! As the bats swooped in to the attack, I think most of us screamed, and automatically put up our arms to protect our faces from their claws and teeth. "Hold the circle!" yelled Lira, "Join hands, do not let go!"

"It's OK!" shouted Flora, who had obviously learned the rules of this game more quickly than some of the rest of us. "They're not *bats* – look! They're only leaves, blowing in the wind! Only *leaves*!"

"*Leaves*!" seconded Lira, "Only *leaves*!" and the rest of us held hands tightly again (*I* had my *eyes* shut tightly, as well!) and began to chant, "Leaves! Only *leaves*! Leaves! Only *leaves*!" over and over again. Gradually, the shrill cries, almost beyond the range of our hearing, stopped, and the choppy wind from the beating of the leathery wings around our heads, died away, and I dared to risk a squint through half-closed eyes again. Believe it or believe it not – suddenly they *were* just leaves! Just a flurry of dead leaves, that faltered as the breeze failed to support them, and circled down to land in drifts around our feet!

"Nice bit of Magic, Flora Rogers!" said Lira approvingly. "Back to work, now! Dan – your turn!"

"Yes'm!" said Dan, grinning. I was glad it wasn't *my* turn – I was still shaking from the shock, and my mind was in a turmoil!

"*I* believe in trees!" said Dan, and *his* voice didn't seem to be shaking!

"I believe in the many different kinds of trees that clothe the earth with their varied shapes and colours; the smooth, grey skins of beeches, the great spreading fans of their leaves, and the dappled patterns that they cast in the sunshine on the forest floor. I believe in the dainty limbs of birches, and the fluttering of their tiny leaves in the slightest of breezes; the rich, deep smell of pines and cedars, and the rugged strength of the gnarled trunks of mighty oaks. I believe in the beauty of *leaves*, from the fresh, new green of springtime to the golds and reds and russets of leaf-fall. I believe in the rushing music that they make as they dance in the currents of the air, mimicking the sounds of the sea-shore as the waves roll in; or the rustle as they lie on frosty ground, scurrying away, in ones and twos or hundreds, from the unfriendly wind. I believe in the patterns that bare branches make, silhouetted against a winter sky, when the leaves are only a memory and the new spring is but hope and imagination. I believe in the inner *joy* of trees, and the hidden column of Life that flows between their deepest-seeking rootlets and their topmost leaves, returning to the sky the moisture that they have drawn from deep in the dark soil. I believe in the homes and sanctuaries that trees provide for so many critters – for squirrels, for birds, for insects. I believe in the bounty of food that they offer, bringing the forests alive with hogs rooting for beech-mast, squirrels hither-thithering with acorns, fluttering birds that come to feast on the glut of brightly-painted berries, and insects that burrow beneath the bark or chomp upon the leaves. I believe that trees are just as alive as we are, and maybe just as aware – they just do a whole lot more quiet *being*, and a whole lot less fussing and fighting and rushing around. I believe they were on the earth before us, and I believe we best *hope* that they fit still be on the earth when we are gone. I believe in the Power of trees."

All our eyes were fixed on his rapt face as he was speaking, but when his voice ceased, and silence closed in once more, I suddenly noticed what looked like a tongue of golden flame running down a far-off hill to the south-west. My heart gave a sudden lurch, as I anticipated some new, unknown form of attack, but somehow the clear, pure colour of the phenomenon seemed to tell me that it was not *evil* in origin. "Look!" I cried. "On the hill over there! What is it?"

Everyone craned their necks to see, and Lira, her face a mixture of joy and triumph, said, "It is the Oakbrook! Now that *this* well is saturated with energy, Urtha is spreading her power across the Star – the Oakbrook is flowing golden, as it did during the ceremonies of the Ancient Days! Oh, that I should have lived to see it! Quickly – quickly – back to our work! Let us try to make *all* the brooks run golden! Millicent Campbell – your contribution, please!"

I could feel Millicent's frail old hand trembling in mine, but her eyes were shining and her body erect as she began to speak:

"*I* believe in the warm feeling of *gratitude*! For more than forty years, the surviving members of my family have been haunted by doubt about what *really* happened to my dear sister Emily and her two young children. We *knew* there was something badly wrong with the story we had been told – we felt that something *terrible* had happened to them, something far worse than a quick, impersonal death from a bomb. We *suspected* murder, but we had no proof, and we could not find out – the authorities were not interested in our *suspicions*! Until recently, we had no idea of the sheer horror of what was *really* going on, but, because of the help and support of all you kind, brave people, I truly believe that *all* my family may find peace at last. My sister Harriet and her daughter, my namesake, and *her* daughter, Heather, are far away in America, but their hearts and their prayers are with us, and they have asked me to express their gratitude on their behalf. And especially to this young man – Danvers McReady – who has no links of *blood* to our family, yet has committed himself so wholly to our welfare that he could not be more a part of us under *any* circumstances! No words can ever truly express our gratitude, to him, and to you all, but we *do* thank you, from the bottom of our hearts!"

As we looked around, the genuine emotion behind her words had topped-up the energy still more, and now two *more* streams were glowing brightly through the darkness – the Hollybrook and the Alderbrook were rippling streams of gold! It was awesome!

"Good! Good!" cried Lira, "keep it up! Keep it up!"

Now it was my turn to speak. Could *I* actually supply the power to light up the one remaining hill with a streamer of flowing gold? What could I say? Somehow, my mouth outstripped my thoughts, and I was aware of my own voice, echoing as if in the distance, and saying:

"I believe in *Dawn* – in the Power of cock-crow, and the song of birds welcoming the light of the returning day. Before you can be really *certain* that the dawn is breaking and the power of evil forces is on the wane, the triumphant voice of the cockerel will confirm it, and tip the Balance in your favour. The first bird will begin its song, and before you know it, the whole jolly lot of them are pouring liquid joy and beauty into the cool, dewy air. I believe their chorus is an expression of the wonder of Life and the glory of each new sunrise, and that *they* are rejoicing in it as much as I, but with much better voices to tell it to the world!"

Crikey! Did *I* really say that? It didn't matter – the Alorbrook was pouring down its hillside in radiant splendour, like a river of molten lava! *Five* golden streams – *five* points now to the Star!

I was so awestruck that my senses did not immediately register the ominous creaking noise that had begun behind me. I was totally confused and bewildered as I heard people screaming, and saw our circle breaking up. Then Dan lunged at me, grabbed my arm and flung me around, pushing me ahead of him at a stumbling run! Suddenly I realised what was happening – the roots of the rotten wychelm had finally loosed their precarious hold – but instead of falling *down* the hill, as gravity dictated it *should*, it was going to crash right where we were standing! For a few awful moments, Time shifted into slow-motion – it seemed impossible that everyone could get out of the way in time to avoid being crushed by those enormous dead branches! Then I saw a sight which will, I believe, be burned into my memory for the rest of my days. Our three Guardians of the Sacred Well did not run away, but stepped into the centre of the circle, with Lira in the middle. They raised their staffs – staffs made of nothing but wood, and yet imbued with the mighty Power of the faith of these women – and pointed them at the falling tree.

"URTHA SAHANTHA!" they cried, as one. "SARAN SAHANTHA!" Even before the words were ended, from the tip of each staff shot a shaft of pure, blinding blue energy – more like a bolt of lightning than anything else I can think of. The three streams of energy intermingled and intertwined, racing towards the tree, and as they reached it there was a massive, dazzling, although almost-silent explosion, as if the soundwaves had been absorbed and stifled by the Magic. The solid wood blew apart, and disintegrated into tiny, incandescent fragments that were hurled in every direction through the disrupted air. The shock-wave knocked me over, and the glare of the explosion was so bright that the after-image was imprinted on my retinas for quite some time afterwards, making it difficult for me to see properly.

Suddenly, the action was all over. There were a few of us still standing, but most of us were sprawled on the ground, trying to gather our wits and get our breath back. The shattered air reeked of ozone. For a few moments of paralysing shock, no-one moved or spoke. *I* was so dazed, I could hardly even *think*! Then into my trance broke Kyle's childish voice, from where he sat clasped safely in Pat's trembling arms. "Pretty fireworks!" he cried, his eyes round with wonder!

"Don't be such a dumb-head!" said Kurt, in the scornful way of older brothers. "Not *fireworks* – it was Magic!"

"Pretty Magic, then!" amended Kyle. "Athey – do the pretty Magic some more!"

"Sorry, Kyle!" Athaney replied, with a slightly hysterical giggle. "*One* like that is plenty! God, my legs feel like chewed string! Can we sit down a minute, Grams?"

"I think I *have* to!" admitted Lira. "Good job we'd got such a good charge built up, and plenty of energy to draw on! But it is still *draining* – let's have a rest and another cup of tea, shall we? Plenty of sugar in mine, please! But will you all please be very watchful, and hurry back into our circle at the first hint of trouble?"

Somehow, we all managed to haul our exhausted bodies upright again, checking on one another's safety as we began the mundane tasks of making and drinking tea, and handing round sausage rolls and cakes.

"George!" cried Mary, carrying a mug of tea for each of us to where I sat, collapsed upon the chair where Dan had gently deposited me, panting, and with my head bowed almost to my knees. "Oh, George, dearest, are you *really* all right? When I saw that tree start to fall, I thought for a moment . . . oh *God*! You were one of the closest to it, and right in its path, and you can't move so quickly now, and . . . "

She put her hands over her eyes, which were brimming with tears. "I'm fine!" I assured her, hurriedly pulling myself together. "Thanks to Dan! *He* hauled me out of the way, and then Lira did her stuff. What about *you*? Were *you* hurt at all?"

"Not if *you're* all right!" she gulped, wiping her face with her hanky. "Oh, George – you do *know* how much I love you, don't you? If *you're* all right, then I'm fine too!"

I am a very lucky man! Of all the women in the world who might have loved me, *I* wound up with Mary! And that very *fact* is truly magical!

The only one of the party who had actually sustained any real injury was Helen. Chris had done his best to drag her out of the way, but the tip of one of the topmost branches had gouged her face and neck quite badly. When I had got over my preoccupation with *myself* enough to notice other people's problems, she was still bleeding quite profusely, and Mabel, Flora, Dad, Jenny and a few more were gathered round her, all busily trying to staunch the flow of blood and offer advice. Mabel was pressing a pad of lint over the cut, and Jenny was rummaging in the First Aid Kit that Mary had had the forethought to bring with us, while Chris was hovering anxiously, getting in everybody's way.

"It needs *stitches*!" Dad was insisting. "Someone – her husband, I suppose – should take her to the nearest Casualty Department right away!"

Then Lira, noticing what was happening, came quietly over and pushed her way through the group. "Come along, dear!" she said. "Urtha will take care of it!" She took Helen by the hand, and gently led her over to the brow of the hill where the roots of the wychelm were now lying on their sides, pulled completely out of the ground. The pool below was still lit with a golden glow, although it was fainter and paler now. I looked around, and found that the streams were only just visible as faint, winding ribbons of light on the hillsides. The Power had been depleted, but was still not totally spent – it had proved sufficient for the need, with a little left to spare.

"Bend down over the water," Lira urged, and Helen obediently sank to her knees.

"Lira Wardwell!" scolded Mabel, "Don't you go a-bathing that poor woman's face with that there water! Who knows *what* might be in it?"

"Don't be more foolish than you have to be, Mabel Potts!" retorted Lira with spirit. "*I* know what's in it – *Urtha* is in it, and that means it is purer than any other water that you could find! And Urtha is Healing, and if we ask her, Urtha will *heal*! Bow your head over, Helen Wainwright . . . "

She began to scoop up handfuls of water, splashing it over Helen's injured cheek and neck. All the time, she was muttering in a low croon in the ancient tongue. She spoke too softly for her words to be picked up by my voice-recorder, so I have no record of them, but it was obviously a prayer to the goddess, begging for healing. The two of them knelt there for several long minutes, then . . "It doesn't hurt any more!" cried Helen, sounding surprised.

"And yes – I think the bleeding has stopped . . . "

Mabel ponderously clambered down into the little hollow and, by the glow of the pool, inspected the injury.

"Oh, my stars!" she gasped in a hoarse whisper, "it's closed up! Why – I can hardly see it any more! Oh, glory be!"

Chris had jumped down after her, and he, in turn, avidly inspected his wife's face. "She's right!" he cried, "Helen – I don't think you'll even have a scar! Not a *trace* of a scar!"

"Humph!" said Dad, rather sceptically. But when Helen came back up on to the hilltop and allowed him to look for himself, his expression changed immediately! "George, m'boy!" he cried, "Come and look at this! You too, Flora, Dennis! You won't believe it – there's new tissue there already! Well – did you *ever*! I beg your pardon, Mrs. Wardwell – your Urtha certainly beats our cosmetic surgeons all to pot!"

With that little incident safely concluded, Lira insisted that we take our places again in the circle, even though we were, by now, thoroughly exhausted and emotionally wrung-out. Little Kyle had given up the unequal struggle, and was fast asleep in Pat's arms! He would normally have been in bed hours ago, of course, and had held up remarkably well, considering. The other children were looking pale, and a little bruised around the eyes, but were still wide awake – fuelled by adrenalin, I would imagine.

Lira looked down at Kyle and laid her withered old hand tenderly on his soft baby hair. "Can you hold him in the circle?" she asked. "He may be needed before the end, but for the present he has no part to play – let him sleep while he can."

"Here – give him to me for a bit!" said Derek, holding out his arms. "You can take over if I get too tired, OK?" So Pat transferred the limp, relaxed little body to his father's arms, and the movement didn't rouse him in the least. Then we all straggled back to our places in the circle. Obviously, with Kyle in his arms, Derek couldn't hold hands, but Kurt clutched his jacket, and Pat put her hand on his shoulder, so the contact was maintained.

"Helen Wainwright!" called out Lira, when we were all back in place. "Are you fit enough to make a start at replacing the energy we were forced to expend? We must try to get back what we have lost as quickly as possible!"

Helen gave a little smile. "I'll do my best!" she promised, and continued in a firm voice, "*I* believe in the Power of Companionship. Whatever task has to be undertaken, it is easier if performed by many willing volunteers. Whatever fears we have to face, they are less terrifying with someone standing beside us and holding tightly to our hand. No pain or sorrow is so great or so overwhelming if we have a friend who truly understands and freely offers their love and their sympathy. No road is so long or so weary if we have company along the way, and are certain that there is a welcome awaiting us at journey's end. One of the most precious Powers we can have in our lives is that of Companionship and Love!"

Already, the far-off streams were discernably brighter, and it was reassuring to have a visible measure of our success. As Helen's voice faded into the vast silence, Chris cleared his throat and began:

"*I* believe in the special joy of **Home**. There is a great big wonderful world out there, crammed full of an incredible variety of environments, creatures, people, their customs and their history. But, in the middle of all that, every one of us needs a special place where he truly belongs – a place made dear by ties of birth, or of family or friends. And I believe that *my* home is right **here**, and that it is as beautiful and as precious as any place in the whole Universe! I believe it is worth fighting for, and I thank all of you for coming here to help me to do just that!"

The streams were almost back to their previous pinnacle of brilliance, and the down-to-earth voice of Mabel took up the task. She drew a deep breath, and her formidable bosom heaved.

"I believe in Cleanliness!" she declared forcefully. "I believe in the good feeling when I step out of my bath, and I'm clean all over. I believe in the energy I get from putting on a clean apron, and rolling up my sleeves to give a place a really thorough going-over. I like the comfort of a room that has been tidied and vacuumed, where every surface and every ornament has been polished 'til it shines. I believe in the joy of newly-washed sheets, dancing on a line in a stiff breeze, and the warm, fresh smell as the creases melt out of crisp fabric under a hot iron. And, best of all, when I climb into a clean bed at night, I believe in the comfort of having a clean conscience, and the knowledge that all my dealings throughout the day have been clean enough to stand up to scrutiny by any Inspector, even the highest!"

Lovely! And as I peered over little Elizabeth's head, I could see a faint golden aura filling the valley where the sacred pool lay, hidden by the hillside.

"Yes!" cried Lira, following my gaze, "The Pool is turning golden, as has not happened for many centuries! Redouble your efforts – we may need every fragment of energy we can store!"

"Reckon it's up to me to do my bit, now, then," said Albert. "Me, I believe in honest rich earth, and the good fresh smell of it after the rain. I believe in things I can understand – things that I can make to grow. I don't understand the Mystery of *'ow* they do it, o' course, but I do know 'ow to give 'em what they need so they can grow *right*! Aaaah! I believe in carrots and cabbages and taters – good, solid, wholesome things that can fill an empty belly! I believe in plantin' 'em, and 'elping 'em grow – and the good soil underneath my fingernails! Aaaaaah!"

"Right for you, Albert! Aaaah!" agreed Old Harry, obviously in complete sympathy with his son-in-law! "Well, then – *I* believe in the old familiar things – my old cottage, with its dear old memories of my good old gal; my old tweed jacket that *sits* on me right; my old pipe, and my old carpet-slippers, not them new-fangled leather ones my blasted daughter keeps buying me for Christmas, even though I've told her times out of mind that I wont wear 'em! I believe in things that are conformable to my shape, and have my own smell on 'em!"

The glow in the valley was now so bright that I said, "Lira – don't you think they'll notice it down in the village?"

"With their heads under the bedclothes, snoring?" she replied scathingly. "Well, if they do, they do – *I* can't do much about that! But I doubt they'll want to leave their comfy pits and trail up here to investigate! Let's move on!"

"*I* believe," began Flora, in that confident tone of hers that always seems too big to issue from her tiny frame, "in the Power of the knowledge to heal. When we don't have goddesses and miracles at hand, it is down to ordinary men and women to learn to ease the sufferings of the world. To set broken bones so that they can knit right and grow straight again. To know the right medicines to drive out fevers from the flesh, to absorb poisons, or to fight infections. To know how to suture gaping wounds, to hold the torn flesh in place until it can join itself together once more. I believe in learning how to help the body to heal itself. And I believe, when the body is too sick, too injured or too old to constitute a viable container for the soul, that we *will* step out into the Light."

The springs at the source of each of the streams were now shining and twinkling more brightly than the stars in the heavens, and the power in the stone circle hummed and crackled – it was like standing in a ring of high-voltage cables! And *still* there were four of us to go!

"*I* believe," said Dennis, in the deep, jolly voice that I always think would be just the voice for Father Christmas, "in hot buttered toast! I believe in warm kitchens, full of the wholesome smell of baking. After a long walk on a bitter cold afternoon, I believe in sitting beside a glowing fire and toasting crumpets for tea, where the butter oozes out and runs all down your chin! I believe in rich, dark fruitcake, full of raisins and spices. I believe in home-made shortcake and parkin and mince-pies! I believe in crusty loaves and cheese and pickles!"

No wonder he is a little portly! But his ingenuous, boyish enthusiasm caused the lights to shine ever more fiercely.

Now it was dear Kathleen's turn. "*I* believe," she said, "in Renewal! I believe that each time a mighty volcano belches out lava and ash and deadly toxic gases to destroy the life all around, that as soon as the new black rock cools, the wind will carry in the tiny seeds of plants to colonise the barren places. Although the giant has laid all to waste, the small invaders infiltrate unseen. The rain falls, and the sun shines, and once more the miracle begins! Delicate white roots probe down into the cracks and crannies of the bare, dead rock, and questing green shoots stretch upwards, hungry for the energy pouring from the sun. And before long, the devastation and the desolation are healed and gone – Nature has covered the scars in lush, new green; insects, birds and animals quickly follow, and once more Life is brought forth out of Destruction."

"This may sound a bit silly," said Paula rather shyly, as her great-grand-mother finished, "but – *I* believe in rainbows! When I was little, I was told there was a crock of gold hidden at the end of a rainbow, but to *me* it always seemed that a rainbow was actually a beautiful bridge leading to Fairyland! When I was a little girl, I believed very strongly in fairies, and I would read any story I could find about them – and I always hoped that one day I would see one! I never did – and yet – I still have a soft spot for fairies. After tonight, I think maybe I was *right* to believe in them, even if my idea of what a fairy actually *is* isn't quite so simple any more! But I can still see their beautiful bridges, and one day – who knows? – I may even find the way to follow the Rainbow Road and discover the way to Fairyland!"

It was lovely to hear her talk like that, and to know that she is still not too grown-up and sophisticated to have such innocent dreams! By now the Power was so strong that I could feel its vibrations through the soles of my shoes! Just Athaney to go now. Her pink hair was standing up on end and literally quivering with static electricity as she said:

"*I* believe in learning by your mistakes! When *I* was just a little girl, I was enthralled by what my great-grandmother told me. Maybe it was similar to how Paula felt, in a way, but instead of fairies, *I* had a goddess! But as I grew older, it all seemed to change – it seemed stupid and old-fashioned, and *I* wanted to be modern and with-it, and not have my friends and everyone laugh at me and call me names. Trying to live in the Old Ways seemed a burden, and I wanted to have *fun*, I wanted to *live* while I was young! But I found out the hard way that the lifestyle my friends live isn't *really* fun – and it isn't really *living*. In fact, it's a fast-track to hell, with smoking, and alcohol and drugs and careless, loveless sex! I realised that I was existing under fluorescent tubes and flashing disco-lights rather than clean, fresh daylight. I was breathing tobacco-smoke, and carbon-monoxide from traffic-fumes, instead of pure air. I was poisoning my system with alcohol and nicotine rather than good wholesome food, although – thank God! – I did at least have the sense to stay off the other drugs! I suppose I have *really* hated it for some time, now, but it was hard to *admit* what a fool I had been and come home! But then I realised that I was pregnant – and I had no real idea who the father was! And that changed things. I *couldn't* carry on with that lifestyle when I was carrying a baby. I *should* say – now that I *am* carrying a baby! Now that *I* am responsible for a new life, I have to *act* responsibly. I have to give my baby the best start I can in life, because the world outside isn't going to do her too many favours! She has to be able to count on her *mother* – and I want her to know her grandmother and her great-great-grandmother, too – right from her birth. I was a little afraid of what Mum and Gram might say when I told them, but I plucked up courage yesterday afternoon – and – you know what? They said, 'Oh, isn't that *wonderful*!'! They will be delighted to welcome my daughter into the world, they long to hold her in their arms, they *love* her already!

When I heard about the fire, and I realised how easily I could have lost them, and that I might never have seen them again, I soon found out what was *really* important in life! I couldn't get home to them fast enough, and I am so grateful that Dan came to fetch me, and so *glad* to be home! And I want all of *you* to know about my baby, and to be as happy for me as I am for myself. I was a little afraid that my gram might want to insist upon one of the Old Names – which, OK, they're lovely in their way, but they do get you teased rotten at school! But she was really understanding, and we finally decided we will call her 'Linna', which *is* an Old Name – it means a deep pool – but it doesn't sound *too* peculiar! While she's little, we can call her 'Linn', and nobody will think anything of it! I'm going to change my surname officially to Wardwell, and so is Mum, and my daughter can be a Wardwell right from the start! And we will tell *her* the Old Stories, and teach her the Old Wisdom, and maybe one day she, in her turn, will be a Guardian of the Sacred Well, and pass it all on to *her* descendants! And, after tonight, I will *never* doubt or think it 'stupid' again!"

The tears were streaming down Lira's leathery old cheeks as her great-granddaughter was speaking. And when Athaney finished, both Orilla and Lira left the circle and clasped her in their arms. It was a truly emotional climax to our ceremony. Or so I had the temerity to think! Unfortunately, the Evil hadn't finished with us yet, and was just about to clobber us again!

"Lira," said Dan, who had been looking warily around, "I hate to break up the party, but I think we may be about to have a gate-crasher!"

Lira instantly put aside her emotion, and was all business again. "Look over there," Dan said, pointing out the direction. "Way over, between the Alderbrook and the Oakbrook – further back still, over the Roddenhill. Is it my eyes, or can the rest of you see it?"

My distance-vision isn't all it once was, but I *could* just make out a paler glow against the sky. As I watched, it grew stronger and clearer – and I knew at once from the evil colour – like rot and corruption and decay – that *this* time the light signified great Evil. Then I realised, to my horror, that the light was moving towards us – fast!

"Sweet Urtha protect us!" breathed Lira. "It is the Web-Spinner! This is what I was afraid of!"

I looked over my shoulder again, and the light was moving at such impossible speed that it had already covered almost half the distance between the Roddenhill and where we were standing! And it was heading directly towards us, growing larger and more distinct with every second! Now I could see that it was not *just* a light, but silhouetted within the light – the core from which the nauseous light was pouring – was a creature of Nightmare. A gigantic spider. *The* Spider! The ancient Evil, coalesced by Magic and the malice of an insane human brain, into the hideous form of a gargantuan arachnid! There was no deviation in its course, and it was *still* heading straight for us. We gazed at it in horror and despair – what kind of Magic could we use against *this* foul abomination?! "It's a *delusion*!" I kept trying to assure myself, "Just an *apparition* – don't *believe* in it!" But my brain was more inclined to believe what my *senses* were screaming than to listen to such idiotic nonsense! I desperately wanted to turn and flee – *anywhere* away from this overwhelming terror! – but my family were all here, and I couldn't leave them! And, anyway, I was totally *paralysed* with fear, and I don't think I could have moved a muscle if *they* had all run off and left *me*!

"So we try Plan A, yeah?" queried Dan, his urgent but controlled voice cutting through my panic.

"I think we must," decided the old lady, squaring her shoulders. "If *I* am to have the strength to disperse the Web, I must keep myself in reserve, and husband the Power! Will you take over?"

"Thank you, Ma'am!" Dan snapped her a salute and marched briskly over to where the children were standing. By this time Kyle was awake again, and saw him coming. Pat had taken him from Derek, but now he started wriggling to get down. "Is it time, Dan?" he shouted excitedly. "Where's my *gun*?"

"Spider-Killing Brigade . . . " commanded Dan, in a parade-ground voice, "For-ward! Captain Kyle . . . Princess Elizabeth . . . Fairy Queen Kirstie . . . . Commando Kurt . . . Slob Derek . . . all present and correct. *Pre*-sent – *arms*!"

At that command, the children all held out their 'weapons' – a green-and-pink plastic space-gun, a plastic sword, an empty, old-fashioned green-fly-spray, and a make-believe 'flame-thrower' contrived out of a rucksack and a vacuum-cleaner hose! Derek had quickly scrambled into a tatty old cowgown that he uses for painting, and a pair of wellington boots; he had crammed a battered old hat on his head, and now held out for inspection a broom and an empty metal container that looked like a cut-down, rusty old oil-drum! There was yellow writing around the sides of this strange object which, I could see when he brought it nearer, was done in yellow wax-crayon and said, "**ACME STICKYACKY GLUE! BEWARE – ULTRA-GOOEY! DO NOT TUTCH IF YOU KNOW WHATS GOOD FOR YOU!**"!

The rest of us were looking on, open-mouthed and speechless with amazement. But as Dan shouted, "Forward – MARCH!" and the children began to move towards the south-western edge of the stone circle, Pat darted forward, crying in an agonised wail, "*No*! No, you *can't* . . . "

The little squad halted. Kirstie broke ranks, and went over and took her mother's hand. "Mummy," she said firmly, "we *have* to! And you can *help* us – *please* help us – we *need* your help! We have to *believe* to work the Magic, and it will be much easier for us if *you* believe too! Trust us, Mummy – *believe* in us! *All* of you – *believe* – *please* believe!" And she fell back into line, leaving a stricken Pat with her hands over her mouth and tears streaming down her face! Then, without a backward glance, the six of them marched away – Dan on one side, Derek on the other, and the four children in the middle.

Just inside the boundary of the stone-circle Dan yelled, "Troop – *halt*! Prepare for battle! Stand firm, and *BELIEVE*!" And now the loathsome spider-like creature was approaching the brow of the hill, its ghastly glowing aura already visible. It slowed a little as it came to the edge of the plateau where we stood – its head moving from side to side as if scanning and weighing up the opposition. *Opposition*?! What was I *thinking*? How could that pathetic line of strangely-garbed *children*, armed with *toys,* stand again this terrifying monster? It was *enormous* – fifteen feet high, at least! – a foul stench oozed out of it and swirled like smoke around it, and pure Evil radiated from it in waves! But Kirstie's voice was still ringing in my head: "*Believe – please* believe!" So I drew a deep breath and tried my best to do as she had asked. But, if I am honest, I don't think I ever actually achieved any very spectacular success! I had never in my whole life truly managed to believe *one* impossible thing, at *any* time of day, never mind six before breakfast – and even *that* would have been child's play compared to what we were being asked to do now!

I'm not sure whether it was the tangible Power radiating from the stone circle that made the great beast pause, but it did stop briefly at the brow of the hill. It hesitated only a moment, then began to creep slowly and cautiously towards us. I was almost retching on the nauseous odour that preceded it, and I was sure that my last moment was nearly upon me. I could now see the creature's fangs – maybe a foot long, curved and gleaming like sabres in the light, and dripping poison. Its many multi-faceted eyes were a deep, glowing crimson, with crimson rays darting from them, and I felt transfixed by the hate-filled gaze that promised death and worse than death. At that moment, I believed I knew how a mouse must feel when confronted by the hypnotic stare of a snake. Then, incredibly in the midst of this overwhelming horror, Dan gave a signal and the little group began to *chant*! It reminded me of the simple rhymes that little girls used to turn their skipping-ropes to, in the playgrounds of my long-gone youth:

> *"Here comes Dan*
> *Of the Spider-Killing Brigade!*
> *The Spider tries to frighten him,*
> *But Dan's not afraid!"*

And as they chanted, Dan actually started to walk towards the Spider! He was now carrying the oil-can that Derek had handed to him, and just as I was sure that he was within range of the Spider's grasp, he made a sweeping motion with the oil-can, as if he were throwing water from a pail to wash down a yard! And all the while, Derek and the children were chanting:

> *"Dan has glue –*
> *It's awful sticky truck!*
> *Dan pours the goo,*
> *And the Spider is STUCK!"*

And – impossibly! – out of that perfectly empty container flew a glutinous amber substance that swirled around the Spider's legs! And – posing grave danger to my few remaining shreds of sanity and reason – the damn' Spider *WAS* stuck! The minute it touched that purely imaginary substance, it was trapped! It struggled desperately to drag one foot after another out of the sticky mess, but to no avail. And the Troop carried on chanting:

257

"See it wriggle, and see it buck!
The more it squiggles, the more it's STUCK!"

Dan actually turned his back on it as he returned to his place in line! Then my poor, stressed heart gave *another* lurch, as Kyle's tiny figure stepped forward! The thrashing, heaving monster, hissing in anger and frustration, loomed above him, but it was hopelessly snared, and couldn't quite reach him.

"Here comes Captain Kyle
Of the Spider-Killing Brigade!
The Spider tries to frighten him,
But Kyle's not afraid!"

The chant went on, as the little boy raised his plastic weapon and aimed it at the Spider!

"Kyle has a ray-gun –
Die, Spider, Die!
ZAP! ZAP! POW! POW!
Kyle shoots it in the eye!"

And – impossibility upon impossibility! – from that inert pink-and-green plastic toy, hurtled a streak of pure energy! It was like a beautiful but deadly ribbon of power, a *rainbow* of energy – pinker than Athaney's hair, more golden than sunbeams, more sweetly green than newly-burst leaves, bluer than forget-me-nots! Even *Kyle* was so surprised that he nearly dropped the gun, but he quickly recovered and aimed the laser-like beam right into one of the Spider's eyes. The eye exploded, in a spray of foul-smelling matter, and the glowing orb became a dark empty crater! Kyle, struggling to hold the bucking weapon steady in both his chubby little hands, directed it from one eye to another. One by one, the eyes of the frantically-thrashing Spider grew dark, and the hissing had changed to a horrible screeching whine! But the remorseless taunting went on:

> *"Ha-ha-ha! and hee-hee-hee!*
> *Poor old Spider, you can't see me!"*

Kyle fell back into line, and little Elizabeth stepped forward:

> *"Here's Princess Elizabeth*
> *Of the Spider-Killing Brigade!*
> *The Spider tries to frighten her,*
> *But she's not afraid!"*

Well, Elizabeth *may* not have been, but her Grandpa certainly was! She approached the writhing insect so closely that my breath was trapped in my chest, and my heart was pounding like a buffalo-stampede!

> *"Elizabeth has a sword,*
> *It goes SLASH! SLASH! SLASH!*
> *She chops the Spider's legs off,*
> *It falls with a CRASH!"*

She suited the actions to the words, slashing mercilessly with a harmless, plastic sword – and the Spider collapsed in a helpless, legless heap upon the ground!

> *"Wiggle-wiggle-wiggle! and squirm-squirm-squirm!*
> *A poor legless Spider is more like a worm!"*

taunted the troop, as Elizabeth, waving her sword above her head in triumph, made her way back to her place. I was finally *beginning* to dare to *believe*, and I suffered slightly-less-intense agonies as Kirstie made *her* way forward – as long as she didn't get *too* close, the Spider was now so mutilated that it posed no great danger. Or so I *hoped*!

> *"Here's Fairy Kirstie*
> *Of the Spider-Killing Brigade!*
> *The Spider tries to frighten her,*
> *But she's not afraid!*

Kirstie has a can
Of Bug-Killing Spray,
She goes SHHHH! SHHHH! SHHHH!
And the Spider melts away!

The spray's so strong, and it smells so pooey -
Hard old spider is now all gooey!"

As before, the pretend-actions produced the intended result! As Kirstie pushed and pulled at the plunger of a totally empty spray, huge jets of bright green liquid fountained out, drenching the spider, and it did, indeed, appear to lose the rigidity of its shape, and sag in upon itself. Its screaming had now died to a moaning whimper, as Kirstie retired, and Kurt took her place:

"Here comes Kurt
Of the Spider-Killing Brigade!
The Spider tries to frighten him,
But Kurt's not afraid!
Kurt has a flame-thrower –
Flames can roast!
WHOOSH! WHOOSH! WHOOSH!
And the Spider is TOAST!"

It seems that the brain can reach a sort of 'amazement threshold', beyond which the most astounding things actually cease to surprise. I was, by this time, almost **expecting** the bloom of bright flame from the vacuum-cleaner nozzle! The roar of it, as it flung its fiery arms hungrily towards the mangled creature, almost drowned the last awful, wailing scream as Kurt kept the flame trained on the Spider until its body became a seething mass of fire, and was finally consumed. The children's chant went on implacably:

"Die, Spider, die! Your bones will crack!
Burn, Spider, burn! Now you can't come back!"

Kurt stood watching the awful conflagration until the last of the Spider's carapace crumbled into ashes and flew up in sparks. Then he gave a grim nod, and returned to his place in line. Lastly, Derek stepped forward, looking ridiculous in his outlandish outfit. The children chanted:

> *"Here comes Derek,*
> *He looks like a slob,*
> *But someone has to clear up*
> *And finish off the job!*
> *The Spider's burned up,*
> *But to make the job complete,*
> *Derek stamps on the ashes*
> *With his great big feet!"*

Vigorously, Derek set to work, with both his feet ***and*** the broom he was carrying, and ashes flew everywhere!

> *"Ashes fly to the sky!*
> *Blow, wind, blow! There they go!*
> *We are the Troops*
> *Of the Spider-Killing Brigade,*
> *The Spider tried to frighten us,*
> *But WE WEREN'T AFRAID!"*

As their jubilant voices ceased, the night was suddenly filled with a vast, enormous silence. It was over – the Spider was ***gone***! Strangely – or maybe not, considering the magical nature of the encounter! – not a sign of the battle remained! There was not a hint of glue on the grass, there was not a scorch-mark from that flaming pyre, there was not a flake of ash to be seen anywhere. And once again the night felt ***clean***!

"Good job, Troops!" cried Dan, a huge grin splitting his face. "Squad – fall out . . . ***dis – miss***!"

As soon as the order was given, Kyle spun round, his round face glowing and his eyes seeming as big as saucers. "Mummy! Mummy!" he squealed, scampering at full speed across the grass to his mother's waiting arms, "Did you see my ray?! I zapped it, I zapped it!"

Jenny had already run over to sweep Elizabeth into a big hug, tears of relief streaming down her face, and Derek had gathered Kurt and Kirstie into his arms, where they all clung together, trembling with reaction. Practical Dan began to pick up the discarded sword, broom and greenfly spray, putting them all inside his oil-drum.

"Went pretty good, huh, Doc?" he said wryly, cocking an eyebrow at me!

"Was *that* what you were planning all day?" I demanded, trying desperately to control my legs, which felt more like jelly than muscle and bone! "If I had had any *inkling* . . . ! Thank God I didn't *know!*"

"That's why we didn't *tell* you, Doc!" he said. "Come on – let's go see if anybody's got the strength to rustle up a cup of cawfee – I could purely use one! Let's find you a chair, Millie – you look done in!"

He put an arm around each of us and shepherded us over to the far side of the circle, where Mabel and Orilla had somehow managed to pull themselves together and had already got the kettle on. Before I could sit down, I went in search of Mary, and we simply held each other close for a few precious minutes. We didn't say much. Somehow, there didn't seem to be much to say.

A cup of strong coffee did help to pull us together, and as I sat holding Mary's hand for comfort, I looked around and saw that at the eastern horizon, the sky was showing a hint – maybe just a promise – of brightness: this incredible night was actually drawing to an end. But – was that *it?* Now that the *Spider* was gone, did that mean that we were in the clear and could go back home to bed? Apparently not.

Wearily, Lira stood up and clapped her hands to get everyone's attention. "Finally – after many centuries," she said, "the Ancient Evil is gone. When my ancestor, Athaney, performed this ritual before, she and her daughters were able to destroy the Web, but they did not have the strength to actually destroy the *Spinner* of the Web. They wounded it, and they drove it off, and for many years it has been lurking in the deep, dark places under the Roddenhill, nursing its malice and rebuilding its strength – and eventually, respinning its Web. But my Foremother was not blessed with a powerful Magician to aid *her*, as Dan has helped and supported *me*! And they did not think to use the Power of *Children*! The courage and determination of these brave little people has rid the world for ever of that particular menace – although I am afraid there are many more to take its place! Well done, all of you – you can be very proud of the way you conducted this night's work! But we are not yet finished. The Spinner is gone, but the Web is still in place. The trapped souls cannot yet escape. With the Power you have all generated and put at our disposal, I believe that my daughters and I can destroy the Web, and leave the way free for those souls to resume their delayed journeys. Come! I know you are all exhausted, but will you call upon your last reserves of strength? In the east, the new day will soon be breaking. Come and help us to release them into the dawn!"

Once again, remotivated, we made our weary way back to our places in the circle. "Oh, Mother Urtha!" cried Lira, "We thank thee with all our hearts for the strength thou hast granted us. The Spinner is gone, but we must now undo the spinning! Grant thy humble handmaidens, representing the three sacred aspects of Womanhood – the Maid (even if she is pregnant!), the Matron and the Crone – the Power to break the evil strands that bar the way, and to release all the souls trapped in this valley to fly at last to the Unknown Regions beyond this Earth!"

She raised her staff high into the air, and Orilla and Athaney raised theirs to touch it at the tips. Once again their ancient cry rang out into the hushed air, damp with the dews of daybreak:

"URTHA SAHANTHA! SARAN SAHANTHA!"

This time the beam that poured forth was a deep gold, almost red, and it flowed straight up into a sky that was now more violet than black. High, high in the air, almost at the edge of my sight, the ray seemed to spread out, and as its brightness travelled, the vast strands of what looked like an enormous cobweb gradually became visible, stretching from horizon to horizon! We all stood, with upturned faces, gazing in awe and wonder at the Soul Trap revealed!

"Help us!" panted Lira, and I realised with a jolt the tremendous strain that the three women were under, trying to maintain the incredible flow of Power, which seemed to be dimming slightly. We *could* not fail at the last! "URTHA SAHANTHA!" I cried, at the top of my lungs, "SARAN SAHANTHA!"

And suddenly, we were *all* shouting, willing, with every last ounce of our strength, for the Power of the ray to increase! The three women were now immersed in a halo of light, as the energy that we had stored through the long night was drawn from the sacred springs on the hilltops, down the streams, through the sacred pool, and seemingly, through the very ground on which we stood, to pass through those frail human bodies, into the magic staffs, and concentrate into the furious beam that jetted into the sky!

"URTHA SAHANTHA!" we chanted desperately, over and over, "SARAN SAHANTHA!" Just as I began to feel that I simply could not shout any more, I noticed a jagged tear begin to separate the strands of the Web, and suddenly, the whole fabric of it began to disintegrate! It tore into scraps, and tatters, and began to fall in flaming strands from the sky! I put up my hands to shield my head, but just before they touched us, the fiery cinders dissipated, and were gone.

And, suddenly, at that very moment, I heard my noble cockerel down on Thompson's farm, announce the daybreak with his triumphal cry! And every bird in the whole world was suddenly in full song! The first ray of sunshine broke free of the hills to the east, and the dawn, the wonderful dawn, had come! Above the clamour of the birds, I caught a sound that I could not immediately identify: then I saw a host of golden lights that were not sunbeams, but halos, rainbow-globes, iridescent bubbles, hastening upwards into the spreading arch of blue – and I realised that the sound was a sigh of joy from released souls, finally allowed to continue their mysterious journey! And my own soul almost burst with the glory of it!

The three brave Wardwells sank panting to their knees in exhaustion, utterly spent. We hurried over to them, and Mabel cried, "Mary – let's get that kettle on, quick! They'll need something to revive them after that!" I think we *all* did!

Orilla and Athaney recovered fairly quickly, but Lira was too weak to even lift her head. "Dan!" she whispered urgently, "Quickly – carry me – over to the Spring! I want to watch the sun rise for the last time, over by the well!"

Her lips were blue, and her eyes already far away. "Never mind that," said Dad, in his no-nonsense voice, "You'd better get her to a hospital, quickly. Get her into Chris's jeep, Dan, and . . . "

"With respect, Sir," said Dan, gently lifting the frail old body in his arms, "I think the lady's earned whatever she chooses to ask for – don't you?" And he carried her carefully over to the brink of the pool below the spring, and laid her softly on the grass, with her head cradled in his arm and her face towards the rising sun.

"It's my birthday!" she said, her old face aglow with pride. "I'm 93 years old today! And now – I can go. I can go gladly, with pride, knowing I have fulfilled my duty. Oh! I see them! I see them! My daughter Annis, my mother, my grandmother – *all* my Foremothers, so many, many, many, all waiting to welcome me! Oh, Mum! Oh, Gran! Oh, my dearest daughter! I'm coming! I'm coming! Orilla . . . Athaney . . . little Linna . . . they're waiting for me, just as I shall wait for you! Be happy for me! And guard the sacred Well!"

Her words faded into less than a whisper, and her old eyes clouded over, the light in them now only the reflected sunlight. And I think all of us, clustered around her, had tears rolling down our faces. But they were not really tears of grief. How could we *grieve*, when she went so joyfully, so happily, into the Light?

"Goodbye, Gran," said Orilla softly, kissing the wrinkled cheek, and closing the sightless eyes. "I'll come when you call, but meanwhile, I *will* guard the Well!"

"Goodbye, Grams!" whispered Athaney, nearly choking on her tears, and gently lifting one of the old hands and pressing it to her stomach. "I wish Linna could have known you, but I'll tell her all about you! And she *will* meet you one day! Because of *you*, there is no Web to bar the way for any of us!"

It was a wonderful thought! I'm not sure just how long we stood there, gazing down at the peaceful old face, but suddenly Kurt tugged at Derek's sleeve, saying urgently, "Dad . . . look!" We all turned in the direction he was indicating, and up the hill was striding the unmistakable form of Thomas Hillyer, his axe grasped firmly in both hands. The evil grin on his face sent shudders down my spine! He looked very *solid*, and that axe looked *very* sharp! We were all in total disarray, bereft of Lira, our leader, and we were too far from the stone circle to be able to reach any protection it might have been able to offer. We all sprang to our feet – we needed to think fast. The apparition, if apparition he was, was striding purposefully towards us, the rising sunbeams glinting on the blade of his axe – and we were trapped in the little hollow under the upturned roots of the mighty wychelm.

Suddenly – before any of us could think of stopping her, Millicent Campbell raced towards him. "You killed my sister, you beast!" she raged, "I hate you, I always hated you, I'll . . . " but the moment her grasping fingers touched his neck, she fell in a boneless heap at his feet! He paused briefly, sneered evilly down at her for a moment, then walked right through her inert body! *Now* what?! He stopped in front of Derek, who had stepped forward with the hopeless intention of trying to protect his wife and children, and raised his axe threateningly above his head . . .

But Lira, Dan and the children had prepared for even this eventuality! As Hillyer raised his axe, all of us except Derek automatically took an involuntary step backwards, but the four children bunched into a group, and stepped *forward*. Again, I was transported back in memory to the schoolyard, as a 'Nair-nair-ne-nair-nair!" type of chant rang out, ridiculing the malevolent old man!

> *"Your axe is made of rubber,*
> *You silly old lubber!*
> *You couldn't cut blubber,*
> *Your axe is made of rubber!"*

And – of course! – suddenly it *was*! Instantly, the axe-head changed from lethal, shining steel into harmless, soft grey rubber, and even that was too heavy for the rubber handle, which bent under the weight, and flopped uselessly! Thomas Hillyer was obviously not prepared for *this* turn of events, and stood stock-still in open-mouthed bewilderment! At that, Derek took Pat by the hand, and they walked a few steps forward until they were only a couple of feet away from the evil old man.

"Thomas Hillyer," said Derek, in a voice I have never heard him use before. "You once worked for Mr. Jeffries, and as his employee you were allowed to live upon this land. All that has changed. Now, the Title Deeds to this property are in the joint names of my wife and myself. You were never employed by *us*, and *we* never invited you on to our land. You are no longer welcome here – you are *dead*, *and* you are trespassing on private property. While you were alive, you murdered your own family. Since your death, you have tormented them, and – in front of all of us – you have just attacked your sister-in-law. You are responsible for the deaths of my children's pet cats, and are guilty of causing Malicious Damage to our property. You escaped earthly justice, but your crimes are now exposed – I leave your punishment to whatever Power may usually deal with these things. Meanwhile, as the legal owners of this land, we demand that you depart immediately, and never return. **Go**!"

As he said that last word, the expression on Hillyer's face changed to a look of horrified surprise – it almost seemed as if his arms were grabbed by invisible entities, and he was forcibly hauled out of our dimension! Whatever actually happened – he disappeared completely, and the air rushed into the space he had been occupying with an audible 'pop'!

I realised that Dan was on his knees beside poor Millie, desperately feeling for a pulse. "One of you doctors – quick!" he pleaded, and we all rushed over to him, Jenny arriving first.

"She's very cold, but she's still breathing!" she reassured him. "I think it's the same sort of effect he had on Judy, when *she* touched him that day in the meadow! We'd better . . . "

"What we'd **better** do," said Orilla, gently interrupting, "is get her over to the spring! If her soul is still in her body, Urtha will heal her, never fear!"

Dan quickly scooped the limp body into his arms, and carried her to the edge of the water. Orilla drew a deep breath, dipped her finger in the spring, and traced the shape of a five-pointed star on Millie's forehead. Then she scooped water up in her cupped palm, and poured it gently over Millie's face, muttering softly in the same ancient tongue that her grandmother had used earlier. Gradually, the ashen skin began to regain a pink flush, Millie's breathing normalised, and a long moment later, she opened her eyes. They instantly filled with panic, and she struggled to sit up, but Orilla gently restrained her. "Don't be afraid," she said comfortingly, "it's over now – all over. Tom Hillyer has been sent to his judgement and his just reward, and what that will be is out of our hands, praise be! Just rest, dear – rest and grow strong!"

Dan was kneeling beside Millie, clasping her hand, but he suddenly looked round in surprise, and said, "Millie, dear – I think there's somebody else here to see you . . . "

We all looked to see what he meant, and – behind the grouped members of our party, I could see a glow that was not the sun, but a pale golden aura, something over five feet high. It was faint in the daylight, and no real features could be distinguished, but we never really questioned what – or rather who! – it could be! We all drew back – even Dan – and Millie raised herself to a sitting position, with her arms outstetched, and a look of joyful wonder on her face! The glow floated silently forward, until she was completely enveloped in it, and for several long minutes, it seemed that she clasped it to her. Then gradually, the shining orb drew away from her, and began to rise slowly, silently, into the air. Up, up it floated, until its faint brightness was lost in the brightness of the dawn sky, and we could follow it no more.

"Goodbye, Arthur!" whispered little Kirstie, waving as it disappeared. "Goodbye, Annie! Goodbye, Mrs. Hillyer!"

"'bye, Arthur!" joined in Kurt quietly, and little Kyle, waving like billy-ho, yelled at the top of his voice, "Bye-bye, Arthur! Take care of Ripper for me!" At which, I didn't know whether to laugh or cry!

Millie was struggling to get up off the ground, and Dan and Orilla helped her back to her feet. The tears were pouring down her face unnoticed, as she cried, "They came! They came to say goodbye to me! They hugged me and kissed me, and – oh, they're really *free* now!"

It was a wonderful moment. It seemed the job was really done, the task completed. We had achieved what we had set out to do, and the Valley of the Star lay fresh and clean around us in the sunshine. But then Reality began to worm its way back into my consciousness, pushing aside the euphoria – here we were, stuck up on a hilltop, with the wreckage of an all-night picnic, and a dead body on our hands! A body, what is more, of a woman whom *I* had signed out of hospital against her doctor's orders! I think Mary must have deduced what I was thinking by the dismay on my face, and she put her hand on my arm and said reassuringly, "Don't worry, George – we'll think of something! Orilla, dear – don't you think it would be a good idea if your grandmother were found dead in bed this morning? I don't suppose anyone would be too surprised if she had died peacefully in her sleep – after all, she *is* 93 years old, and with all the trouble she's had recently . . . ?"

At that, it seemed to be 'All Systems Go'! Everyone snapped out of their exalted mood, and came back down to earth with a vengeance. Dan climbed into the jeep, with Lira's body in his arms, and Chris drove them, along with

Orilla, Mary and Millie, back to Manor Farm House. Derek went too, to open up the house and check on the dogs.

Mavis, Pauline and Jenny began to help Helen clear away the crockery and pack up the remaining food. Roger and Albert collected up the soggy torches and folded up the chairs, with a little help from yours truly! Athaney, Paula, Pat and the children decided to walk home down the hill to save Chris a journey, although I think Kyle, Kirstie and Elizabeth had to be carried most of the way. Old Harry, Mum and Dad and the Rogers trio waited anxiously, trying not to get in the way of the bustle – and I must say, Dad has no room to talk about *me* 'chuntering'! It was still early, but the sooner we could get things back to normal the better! Farmer Thompson, at least, would be up and milking by now, and he just *might* notice all the coming-and-going, and wonder what on earth was going on – *if* he had somehow managed to miss the mayhem during the night, that is!

It didn't seem *too* long before I saw Chris driving back up the hill, and he quickly packed me, Mum, Dad, Kathleen, Dennis and Flora into the vehicle, and drove us off down the hill. He reported that they had put Lira's body into the bed she has been occupying in the buttery, and the women had taken off her clothes and dressed her in her nightie. He said she looked so peaceful and comfortable, that he doubted if anyone would even suspect that she had died anywhere else! I just hoped he was right! If there had to be a post-mortem, and there was any sign of brain trauma, George would be for the chop!

Chris dropped our Oldsters off for long enough for them to fortify themselves with a cup of tea, while he made one more journey up the hill. He came back with Old Harry, Millie, Helen, Albert and Mabel – Pauline and Roger had said they would walk. Chris dropped Harry, Albert and Mabel home first, then came back and collected Mum and Dad, Kathleen, Dennis and Flora, and had departed with them by six o-clock. Dan led Millie out to his van, and took her home to Warwick. As soon as the door had closed behind them, Mary took me by the arm and said, "Bed, George – no arguments! There's nothing you can usefully do, and you look dead on your feet!" I was simply too tired to argue, and almost before my head hit the pillow, I was out for the count!

When I finally awoke, the daylight told me it was well past noon, and when I groped for the clock, my bleary eyes confirmed that it was half-past three! Desperate to know what had happened in my absence, I grabbed my dressing-gown and hurried to the kitchen. Nobody was there, but I could hear voices on the patio, so I changed direction, and went out through the french-doors. Derek and Pat, Jenny, Mary, Orilla and the four children were relaxing on hammocks and loungers, drinking lemonade – although, when I looked closer, I saw that Kyle was actually fast asleep, cuddled up beside Pat. The dogs, to my great relief, were lying by Derek's feet, their pink tongues lolling, and looking none the worse for their night alone!

"What happened?" I demanded. Mary patted the hammock beside her, and said, "Come and sit down, George – everything's all right! The Oldsters rang to say they all got home safe, and were heading for bed to sleep it off. Your Dad said to tell you it was *not* a disappointment! Athaney has gone with Pauline and Roger – she's going to spend a few days with Paula – they seem to have struck up a promising friendship! Mabel rang about half-an-hour ago to report that *they* are all fine, and to ask how *we* are. Dan rang just a few minutes ago, to say Millie has just woken up after sleeping all day, and she seems tired but otherwise all right. And . . . "

"But what about the . . . what about *Lira*?!" I cried, almost bursting with agonised impatience!

"I'm just coming to that!" said Mary placidly. "Pat rang that nice lady doctor down in the village – Dr. Beckett, is it, Pat, dear? – at about 8.30, to tell her we couldn't wake Lira up. We had taken in an early-morning cup of tea for Lira, just before Pat rang, so that everything would look authentic, and it would be at just the right heat when the doctor arrived! I think it was quite a convincing touch, don't you? Anyway, Dr. Beckett kindly came straight up here, and immediately agreed that the poor old soul had passed away peacefully in her sleep. From the temperature of the body, and that sort of thing, she estimated that death took place some time in the early hours, and most likely Lira's heart simply gave out. She was quite happy to sign a Death Certificate stating the cause of death as heart-failure due to old age, and the undertakers came, about 11 o'clock, and took the body away. We are hoping the funeral will be on Wednesday or Thursday, but we haven't got final details yet. And Jolly Olly called, as soon as his service was over, to offer Orilla his deepest condolences. So – you can stop worrying yourself into a decline, George, and have some lemonade!"

So I did.

PHEW!!

Thursday, 4th July

In the event, that account took me the last three days to complete, but it seemed a shame to spoil the flow of the narrative by stopping to record the dates when I actually wrote it. During those days, I have done little except write and nap – oh, and *eat*, of course! But the prostrating exhaustion is gradually easing, and I am beginning to feel that I should be pretty much back to normal by the end of the week.

In the intervening days, a few things have happened which, I think, are worthy of note. Chris rang on Tuesday and, after we had exchanged a few comments about the Ritual, he said, "You'll be glad to hear, George, that things are much better down here in the village – the atmosphere has changed again completely! That feeling of brooding aggression has completely gone, and people are back to their normal, friendly selves! Oh – by the way – how are the children? What rotten luck to come down with chickenpox after all they went through!"

"I beg your pardon?" I cried. "Whatever gave you the idea they had chickenpox? They're absolutely fine – still a little tired, maybe, but not a spot in sight!"

"Really?!" he exclaimed. "Well, how very strange! I wonder what made her . . . you see, George, Helen and I met Vera Blakemore in the street at lunch-time, and she seemed to want to stop and talk. I was feeling a little shirty, if I'm honest, about the way she treated Pat and Jenny and the kids, but – well, there's no point in keeping these things going, is there? So I tried to be civil, and she suddenly said, 'Isn't it a shame about the Hanson children and that little cousin of theirs? She seemed a sweet little girl, and was going to join us, you know, until the end of term. But Mr. Hanson phoned, and said they were all down with the chickenpox – so I'm afraid they'll miss Sports Day and all the fun we have at the end of term! Still – with a little luck, they should be better in time to enjoy the summer holidays! Lovely family – wish we had a few more like them!' So – what d'you make of *that*, George?"

"Well, it's certainly a bit of turn-round!" I said, amazed. "The only thing I can think of, Chris, is that your 'cloud' – or whatever was causing it! – was really starting to affect people! Even somebody who is normally nice and responsible, like Mrs. Blakemore! I wonder whether the cloud has actually gone now? Have you been up to have a look, Chris?"

"No," he said, "but I'd put money on it that it *has* gone! We'll take a run up there and check, if you like, as soon as you feel up to it!"

So we have arranged to go tomorrow morning, as long as the weather is clear enough to give us a good view across the valley. I'm sure he's right, but it will be satisfying to confirm the point! Still – if the effects it was having on people have disappeared, that *has* to be the most important thing. It is difficult to imagine the decent, normal, friendly people who congregated at that Village Fete just a few short weeks ago turning into the sort of violent mob who burned down Lira's bungalow! There had to be *some* pretty strong force to account for it! I did just wonder whether maybe Derek had pleaded 'chickenpox' when he phoned Mrs. Blakemore that day to say the children wouldn't be coming to school but, when I asked him about it later, he said, "What kind of a creep do you take me for, Dad? *I* didn't make any wimpy excuses about chickenpox or anything else – I just told the woman exactly what I thought about her!" So *something* very strange occurred – she seems to have remembered the whole incident completely differently from the way it actually happened! Anyway – thank goodness things seem to be back to normal! And the children should be able to go back to school as usual next term.

Orilla and Ben Bowman have definitely decided on a divorce. At the moment she is still staying here, but she is such a pleasant, hard-working woman that we are all enjoying her company. She and Athaney are Lira's only close surviving family. Evidently, there are several more Wardwell off-shoots in the surrounding area but they preferred to cut those ties many years ago. They violently disclaim any connection to the Old Ways, and especially to 'Crazy Lira'! So Orilla and Athany are the sole beneficiaries named in her Will.

They are planning to combine their resources, and to open a bakery shop of their own in one of the local villages. Although Lira had little in the way of actual money, the insurance company is covering the damage to the bungalow, so Orilla is hoping that she may be able to use that as surety for a loan to get them started. She knows of a property up for lease in Roddenhill, with a shop on the ground floor, and living accommodation above, which sounds as if it would be ideal. It is situated on the main street, facing Chris's museum across the village-green – and I can personally vouch for the quality of Orilla's baking! I am confident the venture will be a huge success.

Athaney is still staying with Paula, but they are all coming down here just after lunch to join the rest of us for Lira's funeral. She had left instructions that her body was to be cremated, and her ashes scattered from the top of the hill by the stone circle, if Derek would permit it. Well, he would never have objected in any case, but after the events of the weekend, the conclusion is guaranteed. And all the participants in the Ritual are determined to attend, so it is going to be another complicated exercise in logistics! Nobody minds that, though – we owe her far more than we shall ever be able to repay. It will obviously be an emotional experience, although *not* – I hope! – *quite* so exciting as our last trip up to that hilltop!

Millicent Campbell also got in touch, to let us know that the remains of Emily Hillyer and the children have now been released, and she can arrange their funeral. She and Orilla have decided to have a joint service in the Crematorium Chapel, and Ollie has agreed to the ashes being interred in the churchyard of St. Mary's, which was the church that Emily attended during her lifetime, where she and Tom Hillyer began their ill-fated marriage, and where the children were christened and went to Sunday School.

Later:

I only have a few minutes, but I am all set to go to the funeral, and I'm waiting for the rest of them to get ready. As I finished that last paragraph, Dan turned up, looking excited. "Is Orilla here?" he asked, and looked disappointed when I told him that she had popped off with Mary to do some last minute preparations for the reception after the funeral.

"Can *I* help at all?" I asked, wondering what was going on now.

"Well – not *help*, exactly," he said, "but – if you'd care for a little trip up the hill in my van, I've got something I want to show to *somebody*!"

I wasn't 100% sure if that van would actually make it up the hill, but Dan assured me he had just gone up and come down again with no trouble, so I allowed my curiosity to override my better judgement, and climbed in! Actually, apart from one slightly steep bit, we sailed up with no difficulty, and I heaved a sigh of relief as I climbed out at the top of the hill.

It was clear and breezy up there, and the events of the other night seemed more like a fevered dream than reality. The stone circle still stood, as it had stood for so many centuries, looking completely dead and inert – just some old stones standing in the grass. The streams on the far hills were visible only as occasional flashes of silver when the sun caught them – the glowing gold was now only a memory. I noticed that the roots of the old wychelm had gone – Dan had evidently been busy with his chain-saw, and the remaining pieces had been neatly stacked below the lip of the hollow, a little way from the pool.

"Look!" said Dan, in an awed whisper, as he led me over to the place where the mighty tree had once stood. "I was just clearing the roots away, and – look what I found!"

He stooped down, and I looked where he was pointing – and there, right in the middle of the spot where the old tree had stood, I saw a tiny sapling, hardly more than a shoot, with just a couple of leaves beginning to unfurl at the top.

"It's a new wychelm!" said Dan, hoarse with emotion. "Don't ask me how it got there – I want to say it *can't* be there, but – heck! There it is! Damn, what would I give if Lira could only see this! It's another miracle, Doc, that's what it is! Urtha's Magic – what you reckon, Doc?"

"What I reckon," I said, "is that at least it would seem to be *good* magic, whether you call it Urtha's magic, or whether you want to call it simply the magic of Old Mother Nature. At least I prefer it to the sort of magic that made its forebear fall *up*hill instead of down! I don't think I will *ever* get my head round that! By the way – did I ever thank you for hauling me out of there?"

"Only about fifty times!" he grinned. "But, heck – lay it on *thick*, if it like to make you *feel* better – *I* fit stand it! Come on, Doc – we best get back before they all commence to wondering where you got lost to!"

So off we bounced down the hill, with the van's suspension complaining as much as my bones! By this time, Orilla and Mary had returned, and Dan was able to tell Orilla his news. She literally *wept* with joy! "I know what I'd *like* to do!" she said when she got herself under control. "I'd like to bury

Gran's ashes at its roots! Do you think Derek and Pat would allow it?"

We went and asked Pat immediately, just to reassure Orilla – although the answer was never in doubt. And Derek, who had the afternoon off to attend the funeral, confirmed it as soon as he came in.

Now everybody seems to be ready, so I shall have to pack up for the moment, and go to pay my respects and say my goodbyes to a very fine and unusual old lady. ***And*** to a little family who I never met while they were alive, but who, for the last few weeks, have been very much a part of life at Manor Farm!

Friday, 5th July

Well, the funeral went as well as such an occasion can possibly go. It must have cost Orilla a bit, hiring those two big funeral cars, as well as the hearse, for that sort of distance; but she absolutely insisted, and it did solve the problem of getting everyone there and back.

Mary and I went in the first car with Orilla and Athaney, plus Dan and Millie, who had arrived in the trusty old van. Pat and Jenny and the four children travelled in the second car, and Chris and Helen provided transport for Harry, Mavis and Albert. Derek went to fetch Kathleen, Flora and Dennis; and Pauline, Roger and Paula went on to bring Mum and Dad to the Crematorium after they dropped Athaney off at Manor Farm.

A surprising number of people from the village attended the simple service in the Crematorium Chapel, which was tastefully conducted by good old Jolly Olly. The four coffins stood together at the front, each bearing a beautiful wreath of white lilies. We sang 'Lead Kindly Light' and 'Abide with Me', which – Orilla said – would satisfy local opinion, and avoid too much adverse comment. As Lira herself had maintained, a little 'blending in' is always desirable, and hurts nobody! And Millicent, of course, has attended church regularly throughout her life, as had her sister.

Everybody certainly did seem to be back to their usual kindly selves, offering what seemed like very genuine condolences to Orilla and Athaney as well as Millicent. (There were even commiserations upon the fate of Lira's home! ***That*** seems to be remembered now as having been caused by faulty wiring! Mob violence seems to have been completely forgotten!) Of course, many of these people had known old Lira all their lives – she had been part of the village since long before most of them were born. It was only the older people who really remembered the Hillyers, although the whole village had been brought up on the story of their supposed death during the Blitz! The floral tributes were many, and very beautiful, and I found the occasion very moving.

Afterwards, we all congregated at the Church Hall, where Helen and the rest of the women had somehow managed to lay out a very welcome cold collation. During this reception, I managed to have a few words with Albert and Old Harry – I was interested to hear their reaction to what had gone on during our Ritual. Albert's comment was brief – "That were a rum do, right enough! Aaaaah!" And Harry's was even briefer – "Aaaaah! That it were. Aaaaah!" The pair of them seem to be very well matched in-laws, and very much in charity with one another! Eventually, the conventions suitably adhered to, we were all able to go home.

Dan has offered to collect Lira's ashes this morning, as well as those of Millies's family, and bring them over when he and Millie come, so that saves anybody else an extra journey. And Chris should be here any minute to take me over to the Thorn Well, to see what – if anything! – we can see.

Later:

It would appear that the affair of the Soul Trap is finally over, after – what? – about seven centuries? Something like that. Chris and I went back up to the field, where the potatoes seem to be doing very nicely, and made our way down to the flat spot where we had an open view across the whole valley. It was a clear, bright morning, and Chris had brought his binoculars as before, but however hard we looked we could see no trace of that murky vapour in the air over the village or over Manor Farm. "Looks like we *did* it, Good Buddy!" Chris pronounced at last, in a satisfied tone. "It's gone. I can still hardly believe it! I mean – was that whole thing weird, or was it WEIRD! Especially that bit with the damn' Spider! I am still having severe credibility problems!"

Join the club, Chris – you're in good company!

He also had another piece of good news to impart – Gary Pike and his cronies have decided to shake the dust of this 'dead and alive hole' off their boots, and have departed, heading for the bright lights of London. Chris and Helen are sure that almost everyone in the whole village feels that London is very welcome to them! They had already pulled up all the flowers that Lira and Dan had planted around the Holy Well, but Helen, who is a keen gardener, says she has some plants with which she can replace them. ***This*** time, with Pike & Co. out of the village, they may have a chance to survive! In the meantime, Dan and Chris laid out Lira's wreaths around the Pool, as there was no grave-plot to accommodate them, and any bunches of flowers were sent to the hospital. Instead of a memorial stone, Orilla is planning to have a couple of benches with memorial plaques placed beside the Pool, so that people can come and sit beside the water and enjoy the tranquillity. Thanks to Dan's hard work, the village has a new opportunity to take a pride in its Holy Well and – hopefully! – may take better care of it in future.

Dan and Millie have just arrived, bearing four caskets of ashes, so I had better pack up now and rejoin all my colleagues in the 'Curse Removing Brigade' for what ***should*** be the final episode in the Soul Trap Saga!

Later:

There was quite a congregation in the little cemetery of St. Mary's, including quite a few members of the press, some of them with cameras, following up the conclusion of the Hillyers' dramatic story. As we had the ceremony yesterday, Ollie said only a few simple, though beautiful, words as Dan carefully lowered the three little caskets into the plot. We left the Hillyers, surrounded by a surprising number of flowers – ***we*** had all sent wreaths, of course, and many of the village families, too, but there were also wreaths from total strangers, who only knew of what had happened via the television! Our children had sent a beautiful little heart-shaped wreath of pink rosebuds, with a card saying, "To Arthur, Annie and their Mummy. Goodbye, sleep tight, from your friends, Kurt, Kirstie, Elizabeth and Kyle."

It was very satisfying to know that after all the trauma, the tormented family were resting at last in the peace of the churchyard where they belonged, with the silent remains of so many people they knew in life. There were tears in Millie's eyes as she looked around her at the marble memorials, old and new, the neatly-clipped grass, and the ancient yew-trees, but the peace and relief upon her old face were beautiful to behold. The rest of the village dispersed to their everyday affairs, the reporters and cameramen went off to cover another story, and *we* headed back to the source of the Wiccabrook, to say our farewells to Lira.

This time, there were only 26 of us to congregate on the hilltop beside the Wiccawell. And this time, it was a fresh, breezy afternoon, with the sun blazing confidently down from an almost-cloudless sky. The grass had grown quite considerably since Dan cut it a week ago, and the bees *were* 'feasting on clover' as if their lives depended on it – which, I suppose, they actually *do*! (I do come out with some daft remarks at times!)

We were a solemn party – I think death is always sobering, even one as triumphant as Lira's. And with Flora at 93 herself, and another six of the party over 80, I think we all felt the shadow of Old Father Time and his scythe looming very close to us. The children were all subdued and big-eyed, but bravely bearing out Lira's assertion about the strength and resilience of the very young.

When everyone was finally assembled, we gathered at the brow of the hill beside the spring. Orilla was carrying the plain wooden casket containing her mother's ashes. She opened the lid, and carefully poured the contents of the casket into a hole which Dan had dug beneath the roots of the new wychelm sapling.

"This new tree," she said quietly, "I take as a sign that Urtha has blessed our work, and set it as her seal upon the ultimate success of my grandmother in her role as Guardian of the Holy Well. May it grow in strength and beauty here for many years, may it glory in sunshine and rain, and – when its allotted span is ended – may it produce a strong new successor in its turn, keeping the Circle of Life revolving. Goodbye, dearest Lira – my grandmother, my teacher and my friend. May Urtha bless and protect you. May Urtha bless and protect us all."

As she finished, Dan picked up his guitar, and sang a final prayer, to the same melody as the 'Awakening' hymn he sang to begin the Ritual:

'Urtha, receive me
Into thy presence;
Catch me and hold me
Close to thy breast.
Life with its duties
Now is behind me –
In thine arms fold me,
There let me rest.
Urtha, thou knowest
Long was the struggle,
Weary the journey
Lonely and far;
Now I haste homeward,
Longing to meet thee,
Guided to safety
By the light of thy star'

With that, the simple little ceremony was concluded, and Dan put down his guitar, picked up a trowel, and filled in the hole with earth. "Goodbye, spunky little lady!" he said softly, then turned away and helped Orilla and Millie to climb over the brow of the hollow back up to the hilltop.

When we were all back on the crown of the hill, Derek said, "While we're all here together, there's something I want to ask you. This land belongs to Pat and me but, when we bought it, we had no idea that it was the site of an ancient monument like this stone circle. I tend to assume that it's one that the archaeologist have somehow missed, and as far as I know, *we* are the only people who are aware of its existence. I'd like some advice on what we should do about it. I mean – in a way, it has to belong to the nation, doesn't it? But I can't say I'm exactly *keen* on having Anybody and Everybody trooping up here to look at it! I'd have to start putting railings round that little tree to stop people from wrecking it, and we'd probably have spray-paint graffiti all over the stones before we could turn round! After what happened here the other night, the thought of that sort of sacrilege really upsets me. So – what do you all think we should do – go public, or keep our big mouths shut?"

For a moment, everyone considered the matter in grave silence. Finally,

Chris spoke up. "You're right in what you say about it really belonging to everyone," he said. "But you're also right that a great many people wouldn't really appreciate it. Up until last week, no-one but the Wardwells knew of its existence – as far as the rest of the world was concerned, it was just a mass of brambles on top of a hill. My advice would be to keep it that way. If you're not careful, you'll be overrun by neo-pagans and sun-worshippers and left-over hippies, not to mention the out-and-out vandals you mentioned. And not one of the scientific community would believe the supernatural aspect of it, anyway. They've got plenty of other sites to excavate and argue over – they can live without one more. We seem to have been breaking rules right, left and centre, anyway – we might as well cover the board! Did you just cut the brambles back, Dan, or did you pull out the roots?"

"Cut 'em back, merely;" Dan assured him. "all I had time for! Heck – if you look close, you fit see 'em shooting up already! You fit have a whole new briar patch here before the cat fit flick its ear! If we're voting – me, I say 'let 'em grow'!"

And, with no dissenting voices, so said all of us!

"One more thing, while we're on the subject," put in Dad. "What about the healing properties of this water? What are you planning to do about *that*?"

"Orilla?" asked Derek, shrugging helplessly.

"I've been thinking about it a lot," said Orilla slowly. "And it's rather tempting to think that we could ease a lot of the suffering in the world. But I can't help feeling that it's not really meant to *be* that way – not these days, whatever may have actually happened in the past, and we can't really be *sure* about that, can we? I think that the other night was a special occasion, and special concessions applied because of it. Neither Helen nor Millie would have been hurt if they hadn't been fighting bravely to rid us all of the Evil, and Urtha was willing to heal them. But – can you imagine the chaos if people got to hear about it? We'd have another Lourdes on our hands! My foremothers got into quite enough trouble with the Church about that sort of thing in days gone by – I'm not sure I could face the religious and legal turmoil it would cause! I think it would be better and safer to rely on the N.H.S. – after all, medical science has progressed a lot since the Dark Ages! I think we should leave Urtha in peace – her day is long gone, and the world has changed. Unless there is another real emergency, like this one, I think we should keep it secret among ourselves, and resist the temptation to use it. What do the rest of you think?"

"Sensible woman!" grunted Dad, "I was hoping you'd see it that way. Tempting, yes – but not really practicable."

"It was interesting, indulging in a spot of Magic!" agreed Dennis, "Never would have believed it, if I hadn't helped to make it happen! But I don't think it's quite the thing for this day and age! Let it be."

There were murmurs of assent from the rest of the party. Then little Elizabeth piped up, "I don't think people would believe us anyway!" she decided, which was somehow such a convincing argument that it seemed to clinch the matter! So we gave the soul-searching a rest, and got back to the logistics of ferrying all those people back down the hill and getting them home.

Did we make the right decisions? I *think* so. But – right or wrong – they were unanimous, and I don't think any of us are likely to change our minds. So pithy old Lira can rest in peace and isolation on her hilltop, with the music of the trickling water and the sound of the wind in the leaves of the new wychelm for company. Orilla says she feels that Dan was right, and that the Guardianship of the Well could do with a little updating! She thinks the Old Wisdom could survive without the Old Words and the Old Ways, so she will try to uphold the *spirit* of the thing, in keeping with modern thinking and modern customs. I'm sure that is wise. Now that the Ancient Curse has been dispelled, there is no more need for such close links with the Past. Time has moved on, and we all have to try to move on with it.

At least Tomorrow should be safer for all the children in these parts, especially our own. I am still amazed at how well they coped with all that, and how quickly they seem to have recovered and got right back to normal. You would never *guess* the trauma they went through, only a week ago! Kirstie did come and sit on my knee for a while this afternoon, a little pensive and subdued. "Grampy," she said quietly, "I didn't *like* having to hurt that poor Spider. But we *did* have to kill it, didn't we? Or poor Arthur and all the other people could *never* escape. So I *had* to spray it – but it was horrible when it went all *oogly* because of what *I* did!"

She always was a soft-hearted little soul! "Never mind, sweetheart!" I said, cuddling her tight. "Sometimes we *do* have to do things we would much rather not – sometimes there simply is no other way. So try not to think about it too much. And if you do, try to tell yourself that the Spider was Evil, not a real spider – and that a lot of people have benefited from what you did. It took a *lot* of courage to do that, Kirstie – you were *very* brave, all of you! *And* very clever! And you nearly frightened your poor old Grampy to death!"

She clung tightly around my neck for some minutes, then she kissed me and whispered, "I do love you, Grampy!" Then she climbed down off my knee and went back to play!

God, but I am one lucky man!

Saturday, 6th July

I have done a few trial runs up and down the stairs here now, and I can manage if I take it steady, so Mary has decreed that I am well enough to go home tomorrow! "I think it's about time," she said, "that we let Pat and Derek get back to a normal family life, without all these bodies cluttering the place up!"

She is quite right, of course, although they will still have Orilla for a little while, until she can pin down her own arrangements. But she seems hopeful that there will be no problems with her plans for the shop in Roddenhill and, as the premises are standing empty, it shouldn't be too long before she and Athaney can move in.

Jenny and Mary made a quick trip home today, to do some dusting and get Elizabeth's school clothes ready for the last few days of term – *and* to stock up on groceries. Pat swears she hasn't minded at all, but I can't help feeling it will be a relief when she can *stop* 'feeding the five thousand'!

I must admit, I was wrong in my initial expectations of my stay here – I find it difficult to believe I was actually dreading *boredom*! Somehow, that has been the least of my worries! As for 'rest' and 'taking it easy' and 'peace and quiet' . . . ! I think this must be a whole new definition of 'convalescence'! In fact, after all this excitement, it's probably going to feel awfully slow at home! And I am really going to miss being so close to Chris and Helen. Still – we have promised to stay in touch by telephone, and it's not a prohibitively long journey – we shall be able to arrange plenty of visits either way.

Derek is planning to contact a demolition firm on Monday, and make arrangements to get rid of the remains of that dratted cottage just as soon as possible. He and Pat have decided that they will take down the fences around the cottage gardens, and throw the whole thing into the surrounding field – of which, I would imagine, it was originally a part. Then they are planning to use the ground as grazing for the horses they intend to buy – one for each of them, and ponies for the children. They are also hoping to be able to get the old barn repaired, so that the children can play out there on wet days.

It is strange, but the whole atmosphere around Manor Farm seems to have changed. The air seems somehow sweeter and cleaner, and breathing it is more pleasant. The vague feeling of threat which, right up until these last couple of weeks, was so subtle that one was not consciously aware of it, has completely dissipated, and everyone seems more relaxed. Now it *is* exactly what it always seemed on the surface – just a mellow, ancient manor house, rich with years, and surrounded by beautiful countryside. I never thought I would say this, but – I am almost reluctant to go home! And I am *not* looking forward to seeing what sort of state my own poor garden is in! I have nasty feeling Mary is *not* going to allow me to get stuck in to the kind of work which is going to be needed to put it back to rights after my long absence!

Later:

Dan came round this afternoon, with a strange young man in tow. He had come to tell Derek and Pat that he is back off to America – Millie is evidently longing to go and visit her sister and the rest of the family. She wants to tell them all about the incredible events at Manor Farm face to face, although I think the trans-Atlantic phone lines have been kept pretty busy! She has never done any long-distance travelling, so will be glad of Dan to escort her, but he didn't want to leave his regular customers in the lurch. The young man, whose name is Ted Bedloe, is evidently the son of the farmer who owns Thornwell Farm – the owner of that flourishing crop of potatoes! Ted works for his father, but is trying to branch out on his own a little, by contracting out to do hedge-cutting, ploughing, etc. He has managed to borrow the money to buy his own tractor and attachments, but will be glad of any other work he can get, to help with the repayments on the loan. He seems a cheerful, steady young chap, and Dan obviously feels he is honest and reliable. So, while Derek and Pat – **and** the rest of us! – will be sorry to see Dan go, they are happy with the new arrangement. At least the grass will get cut! Dan says he **will** be back, but he's not exactly sure how long Millie will want to stay – she hasn't seen her sister in more than fifty years, so they have a lot of catching-up to do! Well, she's a nice old soul, with a surprising amount of what Dan would call 'spunk' – I hope she enjoys her trip, and that the family reunion will be all she could wish!

Sunday, 7th July

Well, I'll be blowed! I was sitting in the family-room yesterday evening, while Pat and Derek were putting the children to bed. Mary and Jenny had been washing-up, and I was idly looking out of the window, reflecting on the strange events of the last few weeks. Suddenly, I saw two figures walking slowly towards the gate into the meadow, and for a moment I couldn't make out who they could be. Then I realised it was Jenny – with Dan! For a while, they leaned on the gate, with their heads awfully close together. Next thing I knew, the darned chap was holding her hand!

"Mary!" I cried indignantly, "Mary – come and look at this!"

"What is it, dear?" she asked, drying her hands as she came into the room. "Ah! Yes. Isn't that lovely!"

"Lovely?!" I exploded. "But . . . he's holding her hand! Now he's putting his arm round her! And she's **letting** him!"

"About time too!" she said, calmly sitting down and taking out her knitting. "Do calm down, George, and give them a bit of privacy!"

"He's opened the gate, and they're off down the meadow!" I yelled. "It should be 'private' enough down there! Mary – what on earth are we going to *do*?!"

"*Do*, George?" she enquired, in a rather exasperated tone. "What we are going to do is to wish them all the best, and hope he doesn't have to be away too long! How many times have you said you wished she could find the right man, pray?"

"Yes, but this is *Dan*!" I argued. "And she hardly knows the fella – she only met him a few weeks ago, and they've hardly exchanged more than a couple of words!"

"Jenny met Dan several weeks before you did, remember?" countered Mary. "*She* met him while you were still in hospital."

"But . . . but . . . he's a . . . an *odd-job man*!" I burst out. "*And* an American! What if he were to take her off to *America*?"

"George, do calm down and talk sense, dear!" she pleaded. "Aren't *you* the man who has always maintained that one should never use 'labels', but judge an individual on his merits? That young man is not *just* an 'odd-job man', now is he? He's a very brave, intelligent, hard-working, considerate, *kind* young man – and we owe him quite a lot, if you remember! And he is very fond of *Elizabeth*, and she is very fond of him, which is a major consideration! So what if he *did* 'take them off to America' as you put it? Jenny is 35 years old, George! She is *more* than capable of making her own decisions and living her own life; and while – yes, of course I would *miss* them! – I would be only too glad to see her happily settled with a man like that! Unfortunately – or maybe fortunately to your way of thinking! – I doubt if she will be *able* to go to America. *I* can't see David allowing her to take Elizabeth out of the country, can you?"

"Well – no . . . " I said, a little mollified. "But – it's just so sudden!"

"George – are you completely *blind?*" asked my wife incredulously. "*I* noticed how attracted they were, the minute they laid eyes on each other! And there they've been, smelling of April and May ever since! Your parents saw it – and so did mine – *and* Aunt Flora! I don't know how you could miss something so *obvious*!"

Well – it may have been obvious to everybody else. But not to *me*! And I *know* Mary is quite right about all of Dan's worthy attributes. *But!*

"George," she said gently, after a few minutes. "I *know* how you have always felt about Jenny – but when you get over the shock, you'll realise she *needs* a partner, George – somebody all her own, like I've been lucky enough to have *you* all these years! Now – get out of that caveman suit of yours again, and be nice when they come in, or you'll only feel guilty afterwards! Remember Lord Ullin!"

That brought me up with a start! That poem by T. Campbell about a father who forbade his daughter to marry a Highland chief, only to cause her death by drowning when she fled from him with her lover, has always upset me quite badly, and Mary often uses it against me when she feels I am showing what she calls my 'patriarchal tendencies'!

> *'"Come back! Come back!" he cried in grief,*
> *"Across this stormy water:*
> *And I'll forgive your Highland chief,*
> *My daugher! Oh, my daughter!"*
>
> *'twas vain; the loud waves lash'd the shore,*
> *Return or aid preventing:*
> *The waters wild closed o'er his child,*
> *And he was left lamenting.'*

God, poor fella! No doubt, as her father, he **thought** he had her welfare at heart. But **how** did he ever get through the rest of his life, after **that**? So I resolved to behave myself, and remember that **I** am not **always** right, and that Dan does have a lot of redeeming features.

"Don't worry, Mary," I assured her, "I wasn't thinking of 'pistols at dawn' – or even claymores, come to that!"

"Which is a **very** good thing, dear," she said placidly. "I can't help feeling you wouldn't stand much chance with **either** against **that** young man!" Well, that puts **me** in my place!

When Derek and Pat came down and asked where Jenny was, Pat seemed thrilled to hear she was off down the meadow with Dan, and Derek seemed to think it a great joke! (Well, **he** would!)

"About time she tried a **real** man for a change," he cried, "not like those **creeps** she usually goes out with! Old Dan's OK – maybe she's getting a bit of sense at last! **Dan**'ll be able to manage her!"

Luckily, Mary managed to calm him down before I had to leave the room – I simply wasn't in the mood for it!

It was about 9.30, and getting dark, before the two love-birds straggled back in. Jenny was looking radiant, and Dan looked a little sheepish. Mary and Pat went to make us all coffee, and I decided I had better try to be civil to the chap – **and**, maybe, to find out a little more **about** him!

It seems his family are living in Florida, at the moment – at a place called Clearwater on the Gulf Coast. When I remarked that his accent and dialect didn't sound much like Florida to me, he admitted that he was 'born and raised' in an isolated valley in the backwoods of the Grand Smoky Mountains of Tennessee, but had moved around a lot since then, so maybe he did 'talk some pe-culiar'! Well – that's putting it mildly! When I asked what he normally does for a living, he was a little evasive, saying he did 'a little of this, a little of that – farming mostly, some ranching, rodeo riding, such!' Good grief! I wasn't quite sure **what** to say to that, so I changed the subject and asked him where he learned to sing so well. He got quite embarrassed, and muttered, 'Didn't never **learn**, exactly, didn't never take me no lessons, such – I do just **like** to sing!" Well, with a voice like that, I would imagine he does! Derek asked why he didn't take it up professionally, and he sounded almost guilty as he admitted, "Done **that** one time, also. But I didn't cotton to the life-style so good – all that travelling 'round, yeah? Working nights and sleeping days, never getting me no fresh air and daylight. I'd kinda like to settle down some."

It was Mary who asked what kind of job he has in mind for the future, and it seems he has set his sights on buying an old forge, just this side of Saltrap! The property consists of several acres of land, with an old dilapidated cottage and quite a few outbuildings, as well as the forge, which evidently went out of use some years ago. But he is hoping that he may still be able to get Planning Permission, as it stands pretty much on its own, just outside the village, so the fire-hazard shouldn't be **too** great. He wants to set up as a black-smith/farrier, and maybe do some leatherwork on the side! He assures us he **is** qualified in the trade, and Derek and Pat agree that there is a great shortage of good farriers in the neighbourhood. They have promised to be his first customers! And if he does take the place, none of us have any fears that it will stay dilapidated for very long! We have ample evidence of what short work Dan makes of clearing a place up!

Mary dragged me away to bed shortly after that, and Pat and Derek diplomatically left the pair of them to say their farewells in private. I **think** I'm becoming reconciled to the idea – maybe Dan **is** exactly what Jenny and Elizabeth need, as everyone else seems to think. Although I'm not sure that David Morris is going to make it totally plain sailing for them!

About half-an-hour ago, Jenny came out and sat beside me on the lawn. She kicked off her sandals, and wiggled her toes in the grass, stretching luxuriously. "Isn't it great to be able to watch the children playing safely in the sunshine again?" she said. "I don't think I dared to let myself admit just how *terrified* I was until it was all over!"

"I know how you must have felt," I sympathised. "It was so fantastic – and yet, somehow, it was awfully *real* at the same time! How are *you* coping, trying to assimilate all that into your world-view?"

"Well, it's certainly opened my eyes and made me look at everything from a whole new perspective!" she admitted. "I feel I've been awfully blinkered and short-sighted, up to now. I honestly didn't believe there was a whole invisible dimension so close to ours, and able to interact with us! And I *still* wouldn't believe it, if I hadn't experienced it for myself. If anybody had tried to convince *me* of all that, I would have thought they were suffering from terrible delusions, or that they were the most awful liars! But we've all learned a lot, haven't we? And didn't the children cope well, Dad? I mean – they were absolutely terrified at the thought of that beastly 'Spider' thing – and yet, when the time came, they all faced it with such incredible courage, I still have a job to believe they really did it! And as for the 'Magic' angle – I'm *still* floundering! Dan says that Lira told him there was a possibility that if they managed to damage the thing, it might be able to simply re-arrange itself – like, growing new legs, or rejoining the old ones! It wasn't flesh and blood, so it didn't have to obey physical laws. But he and the children just hurled one thing after another at it, so fast that it simply had no time to put one thing to rights before something else happened."

"Was that whole thing *his* idea?" I asked.

"No," she said. "he says the whole idea came from the children. Well – *you* heard them, that first night we discussed actually fighting it! *Kyle,* of all people, was the one who started it, wasn't he, and the others followed it up. Dan says he and Lira just helped to *organise* things, and gave a bit of assistance with the rhymes, but left it up to the children as much as they could. I don't know how he *dared* to do that with that '*glue*', though! He said he wasn't 100% *certain* if it would work, but he had to try, because he didn't dare let the kids face that thing unless it was immobilised. But I would never have *dreamed* that could actually *work,* would you? All that 'glue' out of a totally empty can?! And that 'ray' of Kyle's – I've never seen anything quite so spectacular! I shall obviously have to rethink all my ideas about what Reality actually is! But I have never been so frightened in my life! Dad – to change the subject – Dan is awfully afraid that you don't like him much, and he's sure you will think he's 'not good enough' for me. I told him I've never known you to be less than *fair*, and that I know you will be only too happy to accept anyone who can make Elizabeth and me happy. I am *right*, aren't I, Dad?"

"Of course you are, sweetheart!" I said heartily. "I can't help worrying just a *little* – after all, none of us knows much about him . . . "

"We were sure we knew all about David," she said quietly. "But – *try* not to worry – we're not planning to rush into anything! I've got Elizabeth to consider, and she has to come first, whatever else may happen. Dan agrees that we've got a lot of what he calls 'getting to know you' to do before we can begin to make any sort of decisions or commitments. I mean, our backgrounds and our lifestyles are so totally different, and we've got an awful lot to learn about each other! He's promised to phone me and write to me – even though he swears he 'ain't no great hand to write'! He tells me folks say his writing looks like a drunken chicken crawled out the inkpot and staggered across the page, and he hopes I fit not bust my britches laughing, because his spelling is powerful bad! So I can't say I haven't been warned! But he also promises he *will* come back – he'll be escorting Millie home, anyway – and we'll see how it goes after that. In one way, I wish he didn't have to go, but at the same time I'm glad he does take his family commitments so seriously, even though they 'ain't blood kin' as he would put it! It's nice to come across someone who is so fond of his *step*mother! So – try not to worry, Dad – we've got a long way to go yet! And *I'd* better go and give Pat a hand with the lunch! Love you, Dad – thanks for being you!"

She kissed my cheek, and disappeared into the kitchen, leaving me feeling vastly reassured. I'm glad we can *talk* about it! That, in itself, is a great comfort. But – once Jenny makes up her mind, *I've* never known her to change it! She fought with all she'd got to make a go of it with David Morris once she'd married him. But it does take two, and she couldn't solve *that* problem on her own. So I have a funny feeling that I am going to be 'Doc', not 'Dad' to *one* of my sons-in-law before any of us are too much older!

Pat has just called to tell me that lunch is ready, so I will finish what should be my last entry at Manor Farm – Mary, Jenny and Elizabeth are leaving after lunch and, this time, *I* am going with them! It's been quite an experience, but I think, after all, that I shan't be sorry to get home!

HYMN TO URTHA

Ur-tha a - wa - ken Gently from slum - ber!

Pi - ty thy chil - dren, Rise from the deep,

Thou who hast helped us, Times with out num - ber,

Once more we ne-ed thee, Rouse from thy sleep!

2.	3.
Sweet, tender Mother,	Urtha, awaken!
Kind and forgiving,	Darkness is falling,
Since from thy wisdom	Strong is the Evil
We wandered afar,	That shadows our way!
All are in peril,	Bring us thy blessing!
The dead and the living,	Answer our calling!
Send to protect us	Lead us in safety
The power of thy Star!	To the new day!

HYMN TO URTHA 2

Urtha, receive me
Into thy presence;
Catch me and hold me
Close to thy breast.
Life with its duties
Now is behind me
In thine arms fold me,
There let me rest.

Urtha, thou knowest
Long was the struggle,
Weary the journey,
Lonely and far;
Now I haste homeward,
Longing to meet thee,
Guided to safety
By the light of thy star.

PITTER-PITTER-PATTER

Pit - ter pit - ter   pat - ter, Feel the raindrops splat-ter,

But there's no need to fear now, Dark clouds soon will clear now!

Winds may rush and tear now, Tossing clothes and hair now,

But stormy winds are   dying,   To breezes gently   sighing!

2.

Rumble-bumble-bumble!
Hear the thunder grumble!
But never mind the roaring -
It's just an old man snoring!
Sudden flash of lightning
Can be kind-of frightening,
But, honey, don't be frightened -
Skies will soon be brightened!

3.

Shining through the raindrops,
Moonbeams paint the cloud-tops -
Rainbow's archway bending,
Rainbow-colours blending!
What the storm is doing
Is but Life renewing,
Cleaning dusty air, now,
Will make the world more fair, now.

4.

Racing down each hill, now,
Foams many a sparkling rill, now -
Dried-up streams will spring, now,
With regained voices sing, now!
Sleeping seeds will wake, now,
Buds will flush and break, now,
Down reach thirsty roots, now,
Up spring tender shoots, now!

5.

Sweet new grass will grow, now,
Flowers will bloom and glow, now;
And at each puddle's brink, now,
Critters fit come drink, now!
Water in the ditches
All the land enriches,
So when the storm is over,
Bees may feast on clover!